Ghosts of her broken family and relinquished ambitions haunt stoic dreamer Rhea Sioui. A twist of fate finds her in Scotland, ghostwriting for reclusive action film star Niall Shaw. She could finally attain her goal of writing professionally, a dream lost forever if she fails.

Shadows of the past also torment Niall Shaw. Hiding from the limelight at his cottage, White Heather, he finds temporary peace. Now he must make a comeback to fund his dreams of revitalizing an ancient castle, providing work skills to the street kids at his shelter, but an old nemesis is complicating things.

Niall must cohabitate with the attractive, sensitive, young woman he had previously offended. Overcoming their initial misgivings, as they share their secrets, their attraction becomes palpable, electric. Both feel love is perilous, yet each finds a kindred spirit in the other.

On the journey, a true phantom sidetracks their progress. Rhea has an otherworldly connection with a lost soul inhabiting Niall's grounds, and they must help her reunite with her lost love. In doing so, Niall and Rhea may escape their demons and gain their heart's desire.

Hindered by responsibilities in separate countries and lingering fears of intimacy, parting is inevitable. However, if a spirit can cross time and space for her true love, maybe she can teach Rhea and Niall to fight for theirs.

The Ghost of White Heather
Copyright © 2022 Aurela Lee
ISBN: 978-1-4874-3331-4
Cover art by Martine Jardin

Published by eXtasy Books Inc

Look for us online at:
www.eXtasybooks.com

THE GHOST OF WHITE HEATHER

BY

AURELA LEE

DEDICATION

To all those who had faith in me, my friends, love is what I got for you.

Thank you, L for the beauty, E for the laughter, and KK for the immeasurable joy in my life.

My crazy, extraordinary family, through our losses and gains, one thing has always been our fiercest strength . . . we love with all our might, and we always will.

Thank you to the staff of Extasy: my editor Larriane, Proofreader Brigit, EIC Jay, and CEO Tina

Pretty Things

CHAPTER ONE: LAMENTING ITS DEEPEST DESIRE

I am their ghost.

A gust of warm September air blew a tress of Rhea's hair across her face as she slammed down the hood of the car. Adjusting her messy bun, she looked over the raw, lonely grandeur of the Scottish Highlands. She came around to the driver's side of the taxicab, telling the driver, Trace, "I think it's your starter."

Trace stuck his phone in his breast pocket. "No luck getting a signal. I guess we wait until someone comes by. Sorry about this."

"Don't worry about it," Rhea gave his shoulder a little shake. "I've got time, and I can't think of a more splendid place to be stranded."

Deciduous trees had just started turning yellow, red, and orange along the road, and the sky was heavy and overcast. Large grey and blue clouds loomed to the north over a nearby hill gently sloping up from the road. On top was a large boulder, a semi-circle of trees behind it. The massive rock was grey and streaked with pale scarlet, looking almost entirely pink at a distance.

Trace leaned against the driver's-side door and folded his thick arms across his chest, his blue eyes scanning Rhea's face. "What kind of books do you write?"

"Horror. I'm writing something set in Scotland, and I've

come to research old superstitions and beliefs."

Ghost-writing for retired action star Niall Shaw's biography was her long-awaited break, and while she did write horror and was interested in Scottish myths, it was a cover story. She needed to protect her client's privacy, and if she did well, she'd be able to write full-time and give up translating.

Trace had followed her line of vision, "There's a legend about that very stone."

"I'd love to hear it."

"A young man named Thomas fell in love with the chieftain's daughter, Islean, from a neighboring rival clan, and their meeting spot was that boulder. On the night they were to elope, her father and his men found them and killed Thomas. Islaen ran to her lover, who was bleeding out on the boulder. Gripping the dirk hidden in her cloak that Thomas had given her, she held it to her throat, cursing her father and her clan. A strange fog crept upon the lovers, hiding the boulder, and the clansmen were too terrified to walk into the unnatural fog. That night, the blood of the innocent couple stained the rock, and it's been pink ever since."

Rhea inhaled deeply with her khaki-colored eyes glued to Trace's face. "How awful."

Trace looked into the distance, "My wife loves one part of the story. They say if true lovers are near the boulder, they hear a woman crying, sobbing and heartbroken, but only true lovers hear her, those meant to be together."

"I like that part, too." Rhea smiled, a little sigh escaping her lips.

Trace chuckled gently. "The sigh of a true romantic. When you sigh like that, your soul's lamenting its deepest desire."

"Not I." Rhea leaned against the car. "I'm not exactly the romantic type. My soul's lamenting a ham sandwich."

Trace lit a cigarette. "I guess you must have a dark side when writing horror."

"History is filled with horror. Romance is a waste of time." Admiring the beauty around her, she couldn't shake an unsettling feeling. Everything, the smell, the air, the energy, reminded her of her island home. Since her sister and father's deaths and her mother's disappearance, she had barely returned home. Maybe her ghosts had followed her to Scotland. "It's strange, but this place reminds me of home. My mother's people have a lot of old stories about the land, too."

"Your mother's family?"

"My mother was from an island in the Maritimes, and my father was born in Québec. They were both First Nations with some European thrown in."

Trace looked at Rhea's profile with curiosity. "Native American. That would account for your look."

Rhea turned to him, a grin splitting her lips. "My look?"

People often told her she looked like a cat, as the nasal bridge between her eyebrows was a little wider than average, giving her a lioness-like face that was a little flat in profile. Adding to the feline look were tapered, curving eyebrows over almond-shaped eyes of dark green with orange and yellow flecks and an iris rimmed with navy blue, *Sunflower eyes*, according to her father. *Baby-shit green*, according to her brothers.

Trace chuckled. "No offense. You're lovely, but you've got an unusual face for around here. I thought all American Indians had dark skin and straight black hair."

"The characteristics vary a lot."

Unlike her mother and siblings, her coloring was more like her father's family, dark mahogany hair and skin a lighter shade of tawny bronze with a splattering of freckles along her nose and chiseled cheekbones. Her forehead was high and slightly curved, with a dainty chin and a mouth with a larger bottom lip and cupid's bow top.

Rhea admired the creek that ran along the side of the road

and opened up to a small loch with islands scattered intermittently throughout. The mist gathered at the base of the mountains, and it stirred her blood. The ghosts of hills and the spirits of water grow in the mist.

The place, the space, begged to be explored.

Telling Trace she was going to look at the boulder, she climbed the hill. Near the top, she slipped and steadied herself by putting her hands into the wet grass. Immediately, it was as if her hands were magnets, and an unseen force pulled her toward the ground. Her breathing became erratic, and her heart pounded as something invisible crawled from the earth, creeping along her arms until her entire body tingled. A euphoria followed as she had never experienced before, alertness and a sense of power. Energy coursed from the earth into her body, heightening her senses. Submitting to the strength of the pull, Rhea pressed her face into the wet grass, tasting the sweet moisture, smelling the musky freshness of the living soil beneath the grass.

The force suddenly released her. Panting, Rhea leaped to her feet, scrambling up to the boulder. Just as she reached it, Trace gave a little yelp and pointed at another hill in the distance. A vehicle was making its way down toward them.

Disappointed at being unable to explore the area more, she glanced back at the rock and noticed a glint of metal at the very edge where it met soil. Bending and digging, she managed to unearth a circular metal object crusted with compacted dirt. She stuffed it into her jean pocket and hurried down the hill, where a black jeep pulled up to Trace.

The driver's side window rolled down, and a deep voice spoke. "Trace Dickson. Broken down?"

"Aye, Roarke." Trace gestured to Rhea. "I collected my client at The Crossroads, and we were on our way to the inn when we broke down."

Trace did a double take at Rhea, smiling but pulling his

eyebrows together in confusion.

"What?" She put her hand to her face, still panting a little.

"Nothing," Trace commented. "You just look full of . . . vitality. Radiant."

The driver spoke again. "Are you two coming or not? Flirt on your own time."

Annoyed with the man's rudeness, yet knowing they had no other option, Rhea hopped in the back after chucking in her backpack and suitcase. With Trace in the front, the jeep rolled away from the car.

"Where's your truck?" Trace asked the driver, whose bulky frame took up a great deal of space, especially since he wore an oversized, black, slick jacket.

"In for repairs again." The large man squirmed in his seat. "The boss lent me the jeep so I could pick up Brian for tonight."

"Oh, that's right!" Trace turned halfway around in the seat to look at Rhea. "The inn's having a show tonight. This is Roarke. He's in the band. Roarke, this is Rhea Sioui, visiting from Canada."

"Your family name is Seaweed?" Roarke looked at her in the rear-view mirror, but his cap was very low on his forehead. All she could make out was a strong jawline covered in dark scruff, deep-brown curls spilling out from under the cap.

"That's what it sounds like it, but it's a native name pronounced Sea-wee" She smiled into the mirror, but the firm mouth didn't smile back.

Lacking Trace's easy charm, this man had a very stern, nononsense tone to his voice, bordering on unfriendly. "Touring the area?" "For the most part," Trace chimed in. "I just told Rhea the story of Islean's boulder. Such a romantic tale."

Roarke snorted in derision. "I could never understand the female fascination with romance. Women all love romance until real life gets in the way."

Unintimidated, she countered. "Yes, many women are romantic. There's nothing wrong with that."

"Not you, at any rate." Trace turned to the driver. "She told me romance was a waste of time after trying to fix my car. I don't think she's all that girly."

"Hey!" Rhea reached up to jab him in the shoulder as he laughed. "You can be girly and still fix cars."

Looking at her in the mirror again, Roarke mumbled, "You fix cars?"

"Yeah, I know my way around cars."

Jerking his thumb back in the direction of Trace's taxi, he added, "Couldn't fix that one."

Rhea was just about to say something snappy when Trace cleared his throat. "Um, so Roarke, how's Pearl?"

The driver's tone changed. "Oh, she's well. Come up some time and see the changes made to the house."

Rhea didn't care for the driver's attitude and was happy when the men conversed with each other. She became engrossed in the scenery.

The trees thinned as they headed toward the rugged mountains in the distance, and the ground became flatter with fewer twists and turns in the road. The mountains were huge, blue-black, grey, and green. The grass swayed in the wind.

The window was open a little, letting in the air, which danced across her skin. She was a jumble of emotions, elated yet apprehensive, as she didn't know what type of situation she was entering. Her publishing house had sent her to Scotland to interview, research, and ghostwrite the biography for a retired movie star, Niall Shaw. Everyone knew him as a famous action hero, with films grossing millions. However, he had taken an early retirement about ten years ago and disappeared from the limelight. Deciding to make a comeback, he was returning to begin another series of action films. Mr. Shaw's management team believed a biography of his life would garner much publicity for the movies and renew interest in him.

When her friend Lisa, who originally had the assignment, had fallen ill, she'd put in a good word for Rhea, who though not the most experienced writer could write about him with a fresh perspective. Knowing nothing about action films nor Niall Shaw, Rhea was chosen. Her agent told her not to research or even look at an image of Niall Shaw's face. Instead, she had to describe him based on first impressions alone and learn about the details of his life from him firsthand.

Rhea now had a chance to make an impression that would lead to other opportunities. After her sister, Poppy, had died, she'd returned from Asia to raise her sister's son, Liam, and establish a secure, comfortable life with him and her ex-partner Patrice. While she had published a few things, she'd had to put her writing on the back burner and devote herself to her job of translating documents from English to French and vice-versa.

Having to prove her worth was something she had always struggled with, fear of failure often rendering her into a ball of nerves that lead to debilitating panic attacks. Here she was with one night to herself before heading off to spend three weeks trapped in a cottage with a middle-aged hermit. She'd had many misgivings about it in the beginning, and Liam and Patrice had almost forbidden her to go. However, all parties involved assured her she would be perfectly safe. Just in case, she had still taken a few extra Kung Fu sessions, something she had studied in China.

"Young lady?" the driver addressed her, and Rhea realized he had asked her a question.

"Yes?" She blinked a few times and shook her head. "Sorry. I was somewhere else."

"Trace says you're a writer. What do you write about?"

"In the horror genre, but I don't want to tell people that. I don't want to be the tourist cliché researching banshees and ghosts, scarfing down haggis, and asking what you wear under your kilts."

"Are you going to have Scottish characters? For the love of God, please don't write the Scottish accent."

"I would never." Rhea chuckled. "My French father hated it when writers tried to capture the French accent when writing in English. He once threw a book in the river because of it. *Je ne sonne pas comme ça! I don't sound like that!*"

Both men laughed, the driver's shoulders moving up and down.

"I've a few projects I'm working on," she told them.

The driver tilted his hat back a little, exposing deep brown eyes under angular eyebrows. "Horror certainly is different from romance."

"In my experience, romance is horror." Rhea looked out the side window and bounced in the back seat as the jeep hit a pothole.

Trace glanced back at Rhea and then the driver. "Pretty cynical. She's just about as stony as you, Roarke."

"I'm not stony," he replied. "I just have realistic concepts when it comes to love."

"As do I." Rhea leaned forward a little further in her seat. "Love is the most destructive force on this planet."

"How can you say that?" Trace leaned on the back of the seat and looked at her in shock. "I didn't come to life until I met my wife, Tamara. Before her, I was waiting for the better part of myself, my second self."

The jeep turned left at a fork in the road. "Something in your chemistry matches something in hers, and dumb luck that a woman like Tam even looked sideways at the likes of you," Roarke told him.

"Oi!" Trace punched his shoulder.

"I agree with your friend. Roarke, is it?" Once again, Rhea

found herself under the scrutiny of the deep eyes in the mirror, and she looked back with a two-fingered salute. "Chemistry. Those butterflies in your stomach eventually die, and all you have is butterfly carcasses and-and—"

"Butterfly shit?" the driver added, grinning into the mirror, full lips revealing a row of white teeth.

"Exactly!" Rhea laughed, the mood in the jeep becoming more comfortable.

"You two are crazy!" Trace shook his head. "There's nothing like being in love."

"Speaking of feelings." Rhea turned around to watch the hill with the boulder get smaller and smaller. "I got some sort of strange, energy rush up on that hill. Strangest feeling."

"Really?" Trace's head spun around to look at her face. "My wife says that boulder is on a ley line."

"Lay line?" the driver asked. "Like in sailing?"

"No," Rhea answered. "Ley lines are supposed invisible lines connecting sacred areas, and that makes them power spots of earth energy."

"Tam says Scotland itself forms a sacred pentagram."

"That would account for the surge of energy I felt."

The driver shook his head. "If I knew I stood on a pentagram, I'd run like hell."

Rhea laughed. "Pentagrams aren't bad things. There's nothing evil about them. It's just geometry, angles, and lines that connect certain points of power."

"How do you know so much about it?"

"I studied that kind of thing a little in college, nature and the supernatural. The earth is a fountain of energy flowing through a circuit of soil, plants, and animals. The earth, the soil, is a living thing."

"You sound like a bit of a crack-pot hippie?" He grinned at her in the mirror again.

"Look at that, Rhea." Trace pointed to the driver's side

window.

Half-surrounded by a loch, a glorious pale castle loomed on a hilltop. A large rectangular wing jutted out to the left of its massive tower, and several small turrets rose from the top of the rectangular area. The castle looked as if it belonged to the land itself, sublime and majestic, yet gloomy.

"Alloway Castle." Trace half-whispered.

Roarke glanced at it as he drove, and Rhea saw he was younger than his voice and gruff attitude betrayed. She still couldn't see much of his face, but his profile beneath the brim of his cap showed a Roman nose and strong jaw.

"Isn't the castle beautiful?"

The castle drew her eyes again, and all she could do was nod.

Trace looked over his shoulder at Rhea. "Built in the seventeenth century, it was the stronghold of a famous clan in the area. Some friends of ours own it, but they can't keep it up. They don't want to sell it, but they might not have much choice. Someone wants to turn it into a golf resort."

Trace rolled his eyes, and the driver returned his look and curled his lip, saying, "Let's not talk about that ball sack."

The jeep slowed as they came to a small herd of shaggy, reddish cattle resting near the road on the grass.

"What are those two birds?" Two grey birds of prey flew across the road close enough that she could see their hooked beaks, sharp eyes, and massive talons.

The driver picked up speed and turned toward a conical mountain. "Osprey. You usually see two together because they mate for life. How romantic is that?"

"Wow. Scotland's so romantic even the birds get married." Rhea smiled at the eyes in the rear-view mirror.

Going deeper into the Highlands, the scenery was breathtaking. They were heading toward a batch of hills in the distance, and as they traveled north, the land rose gradually from small knolls to large, looming mountains. The sky was darker, making the hills blend into one far-off form, resembling a woman lying on her side, her back turned to them. The small knolls made up her heel and the slight rise of the calf to the knee. One mountain made up the gentle rise and fall of a generous hip, only to rise again up to a shoulder. Another small mountain created the shape of a woman's head. For some reason, Rhea thought of Islaen and Thomas.

Eventually, they drove to a two-story stone building perfectly centered in front of a large, rocky hill. There was an intense, eerie allure to the tall imposing building with two small attachments and arched entryways.

Trace turned again to Rhea, "The inn was originally for drovers, who drove cattle or sheep to market, and travelers passing through the area. That's why there's nothing else around. I always thought this place felt lonely. Great place to eat and drink, and there's often live music. My wife and I come up here often, but you wouldn't catch Tam sleeping here."

"Really. Why not?"

"She says the place is riddled with ghosts."

Chapter Two: Selkies

The beautiful Selkie male weaves a mystical, magical spell over any mortal woman that crosses his path.

"Ghosts?"

The driver chuckled. "Don't worry. They won't bother you if you don't bother them."

Stopping in front of the main doors, Trace hopped out, and Rhea backed out of her seat, pulling her backpack and a small suitcase. The minute the back door closed, the jeep sped off, the driver waving his hand out the window by way of good-bye.

Rhea clicked her tongue. "I didn't get a chance to thank him."

Reaching the front door, Trace held it open for her. "Probably in a rush. He had to pick up a friend. I'm sure he knows we're grateful."

As she walked inside, the scent of pine-cleaner hit her first, accompanied by the savoury scent of food. She was in a dark-walled but bright entrance that extended to the back of the building. To her left was a parlor of sorts, with paisley wall-paper, several wooden tables, tartan-patterned couches, and easy chairs. Ahead of her, a dark mahogany staircase with an elaborate railing led up to the second floor. She could hear the sounds of what she assumed to be the dining area or pub to her right.

Trace refused to discuss any payment. They said their goodbyes, and he left for a quick bite in the pub.

Under the stairs was a little office space where a young girl with a blond ponytail perched high atop her head sat at a computer screen. She looked up when she saw Rhea and gave her a cheery smile that crinkled the corners of her eyes. "Oh, hello! How are you today?"

A few minutes later, Rhea headed up the long flight of stairs with Rebecca. She dragged Rhea's wheeled suitcase, and by the time they got to her room, they were laughing about how much noise they had made. "Enough to wake the dead."

"Rebecca, "Rhea tried to sound nonchalant. "Is it true that this place is haunted?"

The young woman turned the key in the lock and said with as much indifference as if they were discussing the weather, "'Course it is."

They stepped into a small bright peach-colored room with twin beds, a small dresser with a television, a chest of drawers, and a small desk. Rebecca left, and Rhea fell onto the bed, smiling contently. At home, sometimes she felt as if she had stepped into another person's life, and the responsibilities were making her feel more and more suffocated as the years had passed. Here, however, it felt like the first morning waking up in Asia. Finally, she felt like herself and had time to get to know Rhea again

After sending off a quick message to Liam and Patrice, she grabbed her bag and headed downstairs.

Walking into the pub was a feast for the eyes. The bar covered the length of one wall, and every inch of wall space had shelves stocked with innumerable bottles of every shape and size. Behind the bar were nozzles and handles of various shapes and sizes, surrounded by green and red tartan bar stools. Each of the polished, wooden tables had a candle set in a wine bottle and dark oak chairs with red leather cushions.

The walls were stone, mottled brown and grey and covered

in paintings and pictures. Dispersed throughout the pub were various objects, such as a sword, a bow and arrow quiver, a full suit of armor, a coat of arms, and different stuffed birds and animals. The style was old, rustic, and comfortable, as if nothing had changed in a hundred years.

Rebecca scurried around the pub, and a stout black-haired woman poured beer behind the bar in front of a handsome salt-and-pepper-haired man wearing a grey Guernsey. Trace was still there, finishing off a sandwich and sitting with a dapper-looking older man.

When she walked in, he waved her over to the table. "Rhea, I'd like you to meet my friend Ian. Ian, Rhea's a writer curious about Scottish legends."

"Is that so?" Ian leaned forward on the table and rested on his elbows, his black eyes seeming strangely familiar to Rhea. "What kind of legends? William Wallace or banshees?"

"Please don't talk about banshees," she said with a shudder. "Just the thought gives me the willies."

They both chuckled. "Here, take a seat with us." Trace halfstood and pulled at the back of the chair next to him. "You must be starving."

"Sure you don't mind?"

"Not at all," Ian replied.

The woman from the bar came over with a menu, smiling at Rhea and topping up Trace's coffee as he introduced them. "Thanks, Ellie. Meet Rhea. She'll be staying with you for the night."

"Nice to meet you, Rhea," said the attractive full-figured woman with eyes of the same black as Ian's.

Ellie handed her the menu. "You'll be with us for the night, yeah?" she asked with an air of friendly authority.

"Yes." She leaned back in her chair as she looked at Ellie over the menu. "Trace tells me the inn is haunted and the food is fantastic."

Ellie chuckled. "Now, don't go believing everything Trace says, but both are true. Can I get you something to drink?" She tossed her heavy bangs off her forehead.

"Guinness, please." She turned to the men. "Can I get you gentlemen a drink?"

"Not me. I'm on the coffee. I'm driving."

"I'm considering another, but not just now," said Ian with a slight wink. "I'll let you know."

"Right." Ellie had already started walking away. "I'll get your beer, and you take a look at the menu."

"Ellie," said Trace as he got out of his chair. "I'm going to square up with you. Enjoy the ghosts, Rhea." He grinned at her and left the table.

"Ian, if you'd rather be alone, I can go sit at the bar."

"Don't be silly. If I wanted to be alone, I'd have stayed home."

"I'm hungry enough to eat the hind leg off a mule. What should I get?"

"I'm partial to the cheese and onion chutney toasty, and the Scotch broth is amazing."

Ellie returned with her beer, and Rhea ordered both. After a short conversation about the pub and the menu, she asked, "If you don't mind me saying, you have the most unusual eyes. Are they black or just very dark brown?"

"Black as far as I know. My father had black eyes, too, and his before him." He took a drink of his beer and looked over his glass at Rhea. "They say we've got a splash of Selkie blood."

"Selkies? The seals that take on human form at night?"

"Aye." He took another sip on his beer and put down his glass. Leaning forward, he rested his elbows on the table. "My mother's people came from the islands around here, and we've a lot of stories concerning Selkies. In our family, a story got passed down to explain our black eyes. I think we might have some blood from Africa or something from the slave trade. My mother used to say we have the blood of Princess Scota herself."

"Not everyone in your family has those black eyes, though?"

"Strangely, the vast majority of us do. The story goes that a great-great-grandmother of mine named Ellen was married to a merchant-laird who left for extended periods, leaving his young wife alone in a secluded area of one of the islands. When he was home, he didn't treat her very well. They'd been married for ten years and had no children, leading to further abuse from her husband.

"One night, she walked to the beach and wept into the sea. Finally, she looked up to see a dark-haired, handsome man walking toward her. She jumped up and ran to her house, startled to see he followed her.

"The old people say if you cry seven tears or shed seven drops of blood into the ocean, that's a summons for your Selkie. Unable to resist his musical voice and deep black eyes that held all the mysteries of the sea, she let him ease her pain. From then on, she pleased her husband by giving him a child every year. They were blessed with seven, fine children with lively black eyes."

"The Selkie had given Ellen her heart's desire." Rhea was entranced, her chin resting on her knuckles.

Ellie bustled over with their food. "Uncle Ian, you're not boring that girl with that old Selkie story, are you?"

Ian pressed his back on the chair. "It makes for good conversation."

After thanking Ellie, Rhea asked, "I'm curious about Scottish traditions and cooking, and Ian told me the recipes you use are inspired by his mother's cookbook."

Ellie stuck out her chest and squared her shoulders. "Our family's recipes. My brother Paul's head cook, trained at the

Edinburgh New Town Cookery School. He took our Granny's recipes and tweaked a few of them, but they're straight from our family's cookbook."

As Rhea dug into her food, her phone sounded, and she saw a message from Patrice saying they would call her later. Putting her phone away, she lifted her glass. "Ian, why are there horseshoes in the garden outside?"

"Keeps the fairies away. That's why there's a rowan tree and ivy. My niece is a wee bit superstitious."

"I guess if I owned a haunted inn, I'd be superstitious, too."

"With my niece and a few of the women around here, it's more than a wee bit." He winked at her. "You know, not all Scottish people are as superstitious as us around here, but we have our reasons."

Ian's kind, gentle nature reminded her of her father, and she found herself charmed by him. Thoughts of her father came freely, and for once, she didn't try to suppress them. Instead, she asked Ian if he knew any ghost stories about the inn.

Ian had just started another story when they heard yelling from outside. Everyone in the bar quieted when the outside door opened with a crash, and heavy footsteps could be heard. Rounding the corner, two enormous men burst into the pub, both towering and broad with serious faces. Rain dripped off their jackets as they hid their right hands, appearing to grasp at concealed guns.

The larger of the two bellowed, "All right, no one moves, and no one gets hurt!"

Everyone froze and stared in the direction of the door, and all noise, except the traditional music playing in the background, stopped.

However, Rhea glanced at Ian, who grinned from ear to ear and shook his head.

Ellie ran out from behind the bar and whipped at the two

huge men with a wet tea towel, punctuating every word with a swipe at one of them. "How many times have I told you two not to do that?"

They took their hands out of their jackets, revealing that they had no weapons, laughing and trying to defend themselves from Ellie's onslaught.

After a few seconds, she stormed off into the kitchen, pausing once to look back at them. "Idiots!"

The older man was shorter and older, over six feet tall, with short, reddish hair and a long, thick beard. His beige shirt and jean jacket stuck to him with rain.

The other man was at least six-foot-four or six-foot-five and very wide across the shoulders, with a narrow waist and strong legs. One of his hands rested on the other man's shoulder, while the other was in his jean pocket, pulling his plaid jacket away from the white t-shirt stretched across his muscular chest. A ball cap rested low on his head and dark brown curls hung below it.

Both men scanned the room, their eyes settling on Ian at the same time. "Ian!" they exclaimed and walked toward him.

Ian smiled broadly, still shaking his head. "Here comes trouble."

The taller led the way, and as he walked, he pulled the cap from his head and shook out his hair. He had an elegant brow, a widow's peak at the center of his forehead. His brown eyes were wide-set and heavy-lidded under dark angular eyebrows. A small scar split his left eyebrow, giving him a dangerous look. Nevertheless, the overall effect of his face was striking and magnanimously attractive.

Shifting his gaze from Ian's face to Rhea's, he smiled. She felt an eerie familiarity. Along with an intense rush of adrenaline, her stomach tightened as something inside her fought to fly out. Fearing one of her panic attacks, she inhaled and fidgeted with her necklace.

The red-haired man put both of his hands down on the table. "Ian, how the hell are you?" He glanced at Rhea and gave her a warm, charming smile that crinkled up the corners of his dark blue eyes.

Folding his arms across his chest, the other man cocked his head to one side, frowning at her. "What? Too stuck up to say hello? I saved you from being stuck in the country with Trace?"

Sucking in her breath, she stammered, "Y-you? I'm so sorry. I couldn't see your face very well." *I guess that explains the familiarity.*

Full, sun-damaged lips split into a brilliant smile that lit his eyes and caused a dimple to pop out on his cheek.

The redhead nodded his head at Rhea. "Is this the young lady you were telling me about?"

Still looking at Rhea, he mumbled to his friend without moving his lips. "The very one."

Something in the intensity of his gaze made Rhea uncomfortable. She broke eye contact just as Ian said, "Go get a beer and join us, fellas."

At the bar, Jack, Ellie's tall, rugged-looking husband, poured their beer. Roarke leaned toward him. "What's the story with the girl at Ian's table?"

Ellie popped up from behind the bar, where she had been stocking, causing the big man to jump back. "McCallum! You leave that young woman alone. She not your type at all."

"Ellie, I was merely asking a question. Regardless, I don't think she likes me much."

"Then she's even smarter than I thought." Ellie wagged her finger in his face. "Listen, You. She's staying here, and if you so much as look at her the wrong way, I'll—"

"Okay, I follow your meaning." Roarke chuckled as Ellie

stuck out her chin to him. "That woman's too uppity, anyway."

"Don't be stupid. Rhea's not uppity at all. Look at the way she is with Ian. She makes him feel great."

Ian was smiling and talking about something, and Rhea had her head resting on her knuckles, listening intently to what he was saying.

"I thought you didn't want me near her? You're not doing very much to dissuade me," Roarke teased.

"I know you, Roarke McCallum." She grinned at him. "You like your women with two feet and a heartbeat. Now, leave her be."

Roarke grinned back at her. "Fine." He looked at Jack. "I can't win. Women." He threw his hands over his head in a gesture of resignation.

Joining them at the table, Roarke leaned forward in his chair. "Proper introductions. I'm Roarke, this is my friend Doug, and you're Rhea, isn't it?"

Feeling shy and shocked by her body's intrinsic reaction to the large man before her, Rhea nodded.

"Pretty name." He grabbed one of Ian's chicken fingers and bit into it. "Does it mean anything?"

"It's the Greek goddess of the mountains. My full name's Heather Rhea, but my French grandfather couldn't say Heather. He elected Rhea to be the name we used."

"You're Greek?"

"No, but my parents were . . . children of nature. My sister and I were given names of goddesses and flowers. She was Poppy Athena, and my brothers are named for fish and birds.

"What are their names?"

"I can't tell you. You'd laugh. Everyone does."

"I won't laugh," Roarke said after a long drink of his beer.

"Promise?"

"Promise." Roarke grabbed a potato wedge, and Doug and Ian mumbled the same promise.

Rhea looked down at the table to hide her smile. "My younger brother is Raven Pike. Not so bad, but my older brother was not so lucky. He goes by Sal and not his full name."

"Which is?" Ian was laughing already.

Looking into her pint, she grinned. "Salmon Cardinal."

Ian and Doug did their best to fight the urge to laugh, but Roarke could not contain himself. He laughed so hard he almost fell off his chair.

"Look, my parents wanted names from nature. The laughter subsided to a light chuckle as Rhea continued. "I'll have you know that salmon represent determination and prosperity."

"Salmon have always been respected here by the old fishermen," Ian said as he rubbed at his eyes and continued to chuckle.

"You all promised not to laugh." She sat up further in her chair and pointed at Roarke in admonishment. "There now, you've broken the first promise you ever made to me."

"Sorry. Couldn't be helped." Roarke picked up his glass again and looked at the entrance where two young women had walked in.

"Anyway." Rhea cleared her throat. "I wanted to thank you for today. Unfortunately, you left too fast for me to do so."

Roarke turned back to her with a crooked grin. "I'm sorry if I was stupid in the jeep. I was starving and tired. I'm gruff when I'm hungry."

"Aren't we all?"

Roarke tapped Doug on the chest with the back of his hand. "Don't let me forget to bring up those trout I have for the movie star when we come tonight."

The words movie star caught Rhea's attention immediately. "Movie star? There's a movie star here?"

Could Niall Shaw be here, in this area? Will I have to meet him for the first time in this pub?

Roarke laughed lightly. "No, not really." He looked at his hands, and Doug gave him a sidelong glance. "That's just a nickname for the chef, Paul. He's a bit of a pretty boy, so we all tease him about looking like a movie star."

"Speak of the Devil," Doug said. Everyone at the table followed his gaze to a man walking out from the small corridor from the kitchen.

"Sweet Jesus," Rhea muttered the words under her breath, but the men heard them anyway, causing all of them to snicker. *Movie star indeed! Is he moving in slow motion?*

The man was tall with a swimmer's body. His dirty blond hair was shaved at the back and sides, long in front but swept to one side, and he had aristocratic features. Elegant eyebrows arched over curved, bright baby-blue eyes. Light stubble covered his strong jawline, and well-shaped lips split in a smile, revealing perfect white teeth.

Doug looked at Rhea in amusement. "Um, *that's* why we call him the movie star."

Staring at him as if hypnotized, she nodded her understanding.

"Lads," Paul greeted the table in a musical yet quiet voice. "Nice to see you all, safe and sound. I wish I could sit for a bit, but we're training the new guy in the kitchen."

Roarke addressed him. "No worries. I'll bring some nice fat trout when I come up tonight. Bit of a thank you for getting me out of that tight spot a few weeks back."

"You needn't do that. I was glad to help."

"All the same." Roarke looked across the table at Rhea. "Oh, this is our new friend, Rhea."

Paul glanced at Rhea from under his lashes. "The writer?"

"Yes," she replied, a little surprised that he knew she was a writer.

"Ellie said you're interested in Scottish traditions and superstitions, so I thought you might like to look at a few books I have on the subject. My cousin's on his way down. I'll have him bring them."

The swinging door to the kitchen opened, and a dark-haired young man bellowed, "Paul, we need you!"

"Coming!" He looked back at the table. "Gotta run."

"Will we see you at the show tonight?" Doug asked him.

"Come on." Paul cocked his head to one side, running his hand through the front of his hair. "You know I don't like crowds."

"One day we'll get you out." Roarke smiled at him.

"Doubt it. Nice to meet you." He pointed in Rhea's direction before turning and disappearing down the corridor.

Rhea watched him the entire way, and when he turned into the kitchen, she shook her head and looked back at the table to find Roarke gazing at her with an amused expression.

She returned his gaze. "Seriously, what's in the water around here?"

He looked at her in a confused manner. "What do you mean?"

She looked from the kitchen door that elegant, dashing Paul had just disappeared behind to Roarke's rugged, handsome face. "Oh, nothing at all."

A little while later, they were listening to a story Doug told about the sailing trip he had just returned from, and Rhea was enjoying herself.

Out of nowhere, Jack turned up the volume of the TV hanging over the bar. "Hey, Roarke. It's your old buddy."

On the screen, a young man holding a microphone interviewed a dark exotic-looking well-dressed man at what seemed to be an exquisite affair. "Here we have our favorite philanthropist, Mr. David Cojocaru. Congratulations on your latest award. How do you feel?"

"Excellent."

He flashed a beaming smile at the camera, his thick, black hair combed off his forehead, and the flashing lights highlighted his flawless, olive complexion. Other stylish smiling people in the frame held their champagne flutes and hung on his every word.

"It just feels good to give back."

Doug and Ian snorted sarcastically, but Roarke kept glaring at the man on the screen as if he wanted to kill him.

The interviewer leaned in a little closer. "You grew up in this neighborhood, did you not?"

"Yes, I did." Mr. Cojocaru looked right into the camera. "I was raised in one of the toughest neighborhoods in this city, but with education and hard work, I made something of myself. My goal is to make things easier for kids growing up as I did."

"The scholarship fund will be in your mother's name. How does she feel about that?"

The young man stumbled a little toward Mr. Cojocaru as someone bumped into him, and a small flash of annoyance crossed the man's handsome face.

"She's tickled with it." Smiling again, he turned back to the camera. "It just feels good to be able to do something for the neighborhood that did so much for me."

Roarke stood up and marched to the bar with his empty pint in his hand. "Jack, for pity sakes, turn that off. I can't stand to look at his smug face."

Jack changed to the weather network and poured him another pint.

Rhea turned to Ian. "Who was that man on the news?"

"Oh, just a restauranteur who made a fortune selling artifacts." Ian jerked his chin in Roarke's direction. "He and Roarke grew up in the same area, and they can't stand each other."

Doug stroked his blond beard. "A piece of shit is always a piece of shit, even if it's in a fancy suit."

"You can say that again." Roarke returned to the table with a fresh pint for everyone and put them down with a smile. "Anyway, let's change the subject."

Ian dabbed at his nose with a handkerchief and turned his attention to Rhea. "Say, you said your first name is Heather?"

Rhea nodded.

"Did you know that heather, particularly white heather, is good luck?" Roarke chimed in. "So lovely when the hills and glens are full. What are you writing about Scotland?"

"I'm writing something about Scotland, but I can't write about a place if I've never been there, so here I am. Plus, there is a huge market for novels set in Scotland, especially the Highlands. I'd love to understand why."

Doug put a hand on his heart, fluttering his eyelashes. "Because there's nowhere more romantic."

"What makes it so romantic? Why is it that half of the romance novels I've ever seen show a shirtless man in a kilt?"

Ian laughed and coughed into his glass. "You don't find the kilt sexy then, do you, girl?"

Roarke answered for her. "I happen to know she's not the romantic type. She's a realist like myself."

Rhea grinned and blushed under Roarke's gaze as Ian looked from one to the other. "Aye," he muttered. "You're both made of stone."

"Professional writer then?"

"I'm trying to be. I'm a translator, really." Rhea brushed her hair out of her eye and tried to change the subject. "What do you fine gentlemen do?"

"Our Ian here is a farmer, and I'm a retired mechanic. Sold the shop and hit the open sea." Doug raised his glass as he spoke, and Roarke half-raised his own.

Roarke folded his arms across his chest. "As for myself, I do a variety of things."

Rhea cocked her head to one side. "Can I see your hands and try to guess?"

"They're kinda dirty."

"A man's hands should be dirty." Rhea looked him straight in the eye, and he stared back, smiling.

Roarke placed a massive hand on top of hers. His hands were square with a very thick wrist and long, thick, elegant fingers, topped by fingernails cut very short with a small dirt line under the thin tips. Turning them over, she found callouses on the pads below the fingers and the left-hand fingertips. "A musician's hand."

Roarke looked at her thoughtfully. "How can you tell I'm a musician?"

"Knew it. You play guitar." Rhea dropped his hand and sat back in her chair. "I've dated a few musicians. Besides, Trace told me you were a musician in the jeep today, remember?"

"Ah, yes." He slid his hand back across the table and gripped his beer. "Pretty slick, but I wouldn't call myself a musician. I spend most of my time working outside, usually with Ian."

"Hence, the calluses?" Rhea leaned her elbows on the table.

"Hence the calluses." Roarke leaned forward in his chair and peered at her. The rain had stopped, and a ray of light broke through the clouds, landing where Rhea sat. Sitting back with a strange smile, Roarke flicked his eyes toward the window. "Rain stopped."

Doug slapped his hands on his thighs. "We should take advantage of it and get our gear out of the jeep. We're playing here tonight, Rhea. You should come and hear a few songs."

Rhea turned to him and smiled. "I might just do that."

"You'll see us for sure," Doug remarked as he stood.

"I expect a dance from you on my break," Roarke added.

"I don't know, smooth-talker." Rhea narrowed her eyes suspiciously. "I've met too many men like you."

Though he smiled, his face took on a more brutal look as he whispered in his raspy voice. "I can guarantee you've never met a man like me."

As she looked into his chocolate-brown eyes, something about them reminded her of a wolf. A shiver started low on her back and made her quiver as it shot up to her shoulders.

Rhea and Roarke continued to gaze at each other until Doug coughed to get Roarke's attention.

As they got to the door, Roarke turned back. "See you later, Rhea." He winked and shot her a grin before bounding out after Doug.

Once inside her room, with the books delivered from Paul's library, she settled down at the desk. Propping open her notebook, she started going through the three books, the Folklore of the Scottish Highlands, Scottish Object Superstitions, and Scottish Ghost Stories.

Though she tried to pay attention to what she was reading, her thoughts kept returning to her handsome new friend Roarke. It seemed as if someone had taped his smile to the edge of her brain, and she couldn't shake him from her thoughts. She had just met him, yet her brain was processing him as if she were remembering things about him, rather than learning.

Pragmatically deciding that such thoughts were useless, she fell into the books, turning her mind from all else.

One frightening tale was about a castle and the woman starved to death by her husband when he fell in love with a young girl. On the night he brought his new bride into their bed, the first wife returned and carved her name, upside down, on the windowsill outside their bedroom.

Rhea looked out the window, at the vast expanse of Scottish landscape, her mind swimming with ideas for a potential book, when a loud thump behind her caused her heart to jump to her throat and she bolted straight out of the chair.

CHAPTER THREE: NOTHING BUT PRETTY

Her first night in Scotland ended in the strangest of ways, with a heart full of fear, excitement, and fascination, such as she had never before experienced.

Her phone fell from the bed to the floor with a clatter. The vibrating phone lay there on the floor. It must have been on the edge of the bed, and the vibration had caused it to fall, to startle her. She answered when she saw Patrice's name.

"Hey . . . How's my buddy?

Liam answered on the other end. "Great, Mom. We just arrived at Aunt Sophie's."

Liam chatted about his journey non-stop until Rhea heard a woman's voice yell out to him.

"Mom, Aunt Sophie has lunch ready. Can I call you back later? I'm starving."

"Sure, but remember I'm five hours ahead of you, so pay attention to the time."

"I will. I miss you."

"I miss you too, buddy. Every second. Can I speak to your dad for a minute?"

"He's right here. I love you."

"I love you, too."

Patrice's quiet, calm voice sounded tired. "You made it. How's Scotland?"

"Awesome, but it is weird not to be with you guys."

"We're great. Sophie's taking Li to the amusement park tomorrow. The day after, I'm taking him to his father's family in Orlando. His grandmother's been calling me three times a day."

"They haven't seen him much since they moved to Florida."

"Yeah, I know, but I'm always afraid they're going to try and get him to stay with them."

"He loves us, Pat. He's always been happy with us. Don't worry."

"It's just always in the back of my head, especially after we told them we live separately now."

"They're fine with it." Rhea sighed. "Did you have any trouble at the airport?"

"No, but they did ask to see his birth certificate and the consent form from you. You know, it'd be a lot easier if we had the same name, or if I were his legal guardian, too."

"I don't want to get into that now."

"I'm the one who always travels with him. I should be legal. You always put off having this conversation."

"We'll discuss it when I get back."

"Sure, but I won't hold my breath."

There were a few long seconds of silence until Patrice spoke again, the edge out of his voice, "I'm glad you arrived safely."

"Me, too." Rhea was happy about the change of subject. "Have you decided what you're going to do all by yourself for a week?"

"Yeah, Sophie and I are going hiking and then spend a few days at the beach. We'll be off the grid for a while."

A few minutes later, she hung up and walked over to the window, relieved Li and Pat had arrived in Florida safely and happy with the excitement she heard in Liam's voice.

Rhea spent another hour or so at her books before grabbing a quick shower. As she put on a deep green shirt and a pair of jeans, Roarke flashed into her mind, and she applied extra make-up to emphasize the almond shape of her eyes. There was no harm in dressing up a little.

The pub was filling up when she walked in and heard someone yell her name. Turning, she saw Trace waving at her. She smiled at him, got a pint at the bar, and made her way to the table.

"Hey, Rhea, how ya been?" asked Trace with his patented, warm smile.

"Bit tired, but all right."

"Rhea." He motioned toward the attractive redhead beside him. "This is my wife, Tamara."

"Pleased to meet you." Tamara was tall and slender, with freckles sprinkled all over her dainty face and chest. The sapphire blue shirt she wore was the same shade as her large eyes.

"Please join us." Trace motioned toward an empty chair.

"Sure you don't mind?"

"Not a bit." Tamara shifted her chair a little closer to Rhea's. "Trace says you write horror stories."

They chatted amicably while eating dinner together, and Rhea met twins, Agnes and Senga, who sat with them. Dark and attractive, their soft grey eyes were nearly luminescent.

"Their family home owns a famous castle around here," Tamara said proudly.

"Castle?" Rhea repeated.

"Yeah, well. We've always lived in the house next to it, but we own the castle also."

"Not that huge, old castle south of here? Alloway Castle?" Rhea's mouth dropped open.

"The very one," Agnes laughed. "It's been in our family for centuries, but I don't think Senga and I'll be able to care for it."

Senga smoothed down a lock of her hair. "Aye, it'll soon be

time to move on." She turned to speak to Rhea. "My husband's in the military, and we'll have to move to Edinburgh."

"My husband only comes home on the weekends now," Agnes added.

"How's the shop coming?" Tam asked her.

"Great!" Agnes grinned. "Everyone's eating up the designs and loves that he went back to the old ways of softening the tartans by brushing them with rows of thistles."

"Are you definitely going to sell the castle?" Trace asked with a furrowed brow.

"Don't have much choice."

"We've gone to the government to see if we could get some financial help with it, but it's the same bureaucratic bullshit. There's just not enough money to give to its maintenance."

"Aye, and our lives are taking us away from it." Senga looked wistful. "Wish we could figure something out."

"It'll come to you." Tam patted Senga's hand.

Trace turned to look at Agnes with a perplexed look on his face. "Hey Ag, didn't David Cojocaru put in a bid on the castle if you don't mind me asking?"

"Aye, but he's going to turn it into a golf resort." Agnes looked over to the bandstand. "I wish Roarke could get the money. He's got great plans for it."

Rhea followed Agnes' gaze to the bandstand, where Roarke and Doug were just putting down guitar cases. Roarke scanned the room, and when he saw her, he smiled and gave a two-finger salute. She returned his smile, wondering why and by what means a part-time musician would want to buy a castle.

Later that evening, the bar was packed, patrons were chatting and laughing, and music poured from the corner of the room where Roarke played guitar and Doug alternated playing flute, Bodhran, and guitar.

After a toe-tapping jig, Roarke announced that they were taking a short break. They put down their instruments and headed toward the bar. An attractive blond woman in tight, stylish clothing followed Roarke and grabbed his arm, boxing him into the small corridor leading to the kitchen. The woman leaned toward him, but he backed away from her, smiling and shaking his head. She went toward him again, and he grabbed both of her wrists, his face taking on a severe expression.

During their short exchange, her expression changed from flirtatious to almost pleading. Finally, he nudged her out of his way and strode out of the corridor. She put her hands on her hips, looking upset, and then half-ran to the lady's room.

Witnessing this exchange upset Rhea, reminding her of how her friend, Lisa, would run after an encounter with her abusive ex-boyfriend. As attractive as Roarke was, she had seen enough from him to know that he was a flirt, jaded toward romance, and was not someone she should take up with, even briefly.

Thinking that maybe it was time she went upstairs, she half-rose from her seat. Since she was notorious for spilling food on herself, Rhea turned to Agnes and asked, "Do I have anything on my face?"

"Nothing but pretty," a deep voice answered behind her.

She turned to find Roarke half-crouched behind her chair. "You've got pretty all over your face."

Not knowing what to say or do, Rhea only smiled. It was strange that someone would make her feel flustered and inarticulate, and it confused her. If not astute, people who knew her would say she was a bit of a control freak and impassive.

Still grinning at her, Roarke stood and greeted the table at large. He was sweating slightly, and a few unruly curls hung at each temple. He nodded his head toward Rhea. "You've not got this one drunk yet?"

"We've been threatening her with whisky, but we're not

sure she's ready." Trace laughed.

"So." Roarke leaned on the back of Tam's chair, looking at Rhea. "Would you like to come on stage and join us in a song?"

"Oh, no, I couldn't," she confessed, waving her hands in front of her. "I get terrible stage fright. I tried in the past to sing with my brother, but I just can't do it. I freeze, turn bright red, can't make a sound." The truth was she suffered from debilitating panic attacks, and some days even had to call in sick when an attack got the better of her.

Doug whistled at Roarke and jacked his thumb in the direction of the bandstand.

Roarke nodded to him and turned back to Rhea. "Gotta run, but I'll be watching to see if you're singing."

"I'll be singing from my chair." They grinned at each other, and he walked away, chugging his beer at the same time. She watched him, back straight as a whip, shoulders swaying as his long legs propelled him forward.

Rhea didn't notice Trace and Tam watching her until Tam's laughter broke her from her thoughts.

She turned to look at them. "What?"

Tamara shook her head from side to side. "You'd be better off having nothing to do with him."

"I have no intention of doing anything with him." She cocked her head in Roarke's direction. "I think he's funny. That's all."

"Yeah, a lot of women think he's funny." Tam glanced over her shoulder at a group of women watching him. "Until they're bawling their eyes out."

Rhea shook her head. "Tamara, you've got the wrong idea. I didn't come here for a fling. I'm here to see the country and do some work. That's all."

"Still," added Agnes. "He glances at the table a bit too much for my liking."

"Okay, girls." Rhea put her drink on the table and leaned forward. "Let's be serious. Look at me and look at him." *Plus, didn't Trace ask him something about a woman named Pearl?*

"You sell yourself short, Rhea," admonished Tam. "You're lovely."

"Don't forget, you're new around here," added Agnes. "Only here for a short time. That's perfect for —"

"Girls," interrupted Rhea. "Trust me. Nothing's going to happen." *Still, it doesn't hurt to look at him.*

Doug and Roarke played a merry song, followed by another, and soon everyone in the bar was singing, dancing, and clapping their hands. Jack grabbed Ellie and pulled her into the middle of the floor while everyone clapped their encouragement.

Happy and content in such a vibrant, joyful atmosphere, Rhea recognized some songs. When each song ended, everyone cheered the musicians, and Roarke stepped to the mike and raised his hands to quiet the crowd. "All right, are you all having a good time?"

Everyone cheered, and in the far corner, a young man fell off his stool, causing everyone to roar with laughter.

Roarke raised his hands again. "We'd like to slow things down with a traditional ballad, and we've got a friend visiting who would love to sing with us."

Rhea didn't react for a moment until what he said hit her. Her head spun around to the stage. *Son of a bitch.* Shock turned to anger, and she whipped back around to Tam. "He can't be serious."

Tam screwed up her face in a sympathetic expression. "Oh, I'm afraid so."

Rhea looked back at Roarke, shaking her head from side to side, mouthing, "No."

He laughed and motioned her to the stage. When she still didn't move, he gave her an obsequious bow. *Bastard!* She remembered how rude he had been in the jeep and realized he was not playful. He was trying to humiliate her.

"Come on, Rhea. We'll help with the words." He turned to address the crowd. "Everyone put your hands together for her."

Roarke led the clapping, and everyone in the bar turned toward her, encouraging her with applause.

Rhea continued to shake her head, getting angrier but not wanting it to show. To her horror, her heart raced. Becoming short of breath, she knew a panic attack was coming. *I have to get out of here.* Intense fear hit just as she stood up, and her chair fell to the floor, to the shock of her tablemates.

Mumbling a vague "Sorry," she spun around, almost tripped on a chair leg, and dashed to the staircase. As she ran up the stairs, struggling for breath, she was vaguely aware of someone running after her and numerous people saying her name.

Once in her room, she slid down the back of the door, telling herself she was safe, and doing the counting technique her therapist had taught her, Four-two-six. Inhale for four, hold for two, and exhale for six.

A few minutes later, she was sitting on her bed and feeling better when her phone rang. Unfortunately, she had forgotten that she had given Tamara her number. After explaining her departure and that all was fine, she fell back on the bed, exhausted.

A few moments later, she roused herself to change into her knee-length white cotton shift, as her mother called it, and sent off a quick message to Liam.

After she had turned off her phone, she had the feeling that the light in the room was a little brighter than it had been a moment before. The air was thick and charged with energy, denser, with a sweet, pleasant scent. It almost felt as if she was in an invisible fog. The rustle of fabric, as if someone leaned on the outside of her door, froze her with terror. The promise of touch lurked in the heavy air, as if an unseen hand crept closer and closer to her shoulder.

A light knock on her bedroom door caused her to gasp and leap to the door, shaking with panic and fear. She was afraid to open the door and fearful of what might be inside the room with her. Her palms pressed on the door as she contemplated opening it, too afraid to look over her shoulder. Finally, three more raps rattled the door, and she mustered up enough courage to say, "Hello?"

Receiving no reply, she took a deep breath and opened the door a crack, peering out into the dim corridor. Her pulse quickened as a dark shadow came toward her. A scream rose in her throat as she tried to shut her door, but a strong force kept it open.

"Rhea, it's me."

The dark shadow was Roarke McCallum. "Son of a bitch! You scared the shit out of me!" she hissed through the crack in the door.

"Did you think it was a ghost?" He tapped his finger on the door. "Two-eleven, that's one of the haunted rooms."

Still trying to get the door closed, she strained against it as she spoke. "You didn't answer when I said hello."

"Didn't think you'd open it for me."

"You thought correctly." She pushed at the door. "Why can't I close this thing?"

"Rhea?"

"Yes?"

Pointing down at the floor, she followed his finger to see the toe of his boot wedged between door and doorframe.

"Move your foot." She had stopped trying to force at the door and rested a hand on the edge of it.

"Can I speak to you for a moment?"

"Go ahead."

"Can I come in?"

She opened the door a little wider. "No. Now, what do you have to say?"

Stepping back, he leaned back against the opposite wall of the narrow hallway and stuffed his hands in his jean pockets. His t-shirt fit him like skin, showing the ridges and ripples of his torso, and he smelled a little musky, yet clean, mossy, and oddly familiar.

"You ran off before I could apologize for putting you on the spot tonight."

"Apologize? Panic attacks are no joke, and you almost put me in a situation that could have been humiliating."

"I didn't know." He put his hands in the air and slapped them down on his thighs. "It was meant to be a joke."

Stepping a little further out into the hallway, shaking from the strain of trying to keep her voice in check. "You tried to make a joke of me."

Propping one foot against the wall behind him, he gazed at her a little too intently. "It was a terrible thing to do, and I'm truly sorry. Doug's sister gets panic attacks. I've seen it, and I know they're serious. I don't know what got into me."

"Fair enough." She sighed, her voice losing its edge.

They stood in silence for a few seconds before he asked again, "Can I come in?"

"Why?"

"For a nightcap." He shrugged his shoulders and cleared his throat.

"I don't have anything to drink."

"Just to talk then." He used his foot to push himself off the wall and step toward her, their faces being very close.

"I'm afraid not." She moved to close the door.

"Why not?" His voice had dropped to a half-whisper.

She tried to keep her voice level, but his proximity made

her head swim. "First, I'm not that type of woman, and second, you're not the kind of man I tend to associate with."

"Not the kind of man . . ." He had stepped back again and scowled at her angrily. "What the hell does that mean?"

Rhea held up her hand. "I'm tired. Anything else?"

Roarke's expression turned stern and aggressive. "It was stupid of me to think that an uppity—" Stopping mid-sentence, he turned on his heel and headed down the corridor.

Rhea stepped back into her room and closed the door. Lying in bed, staring up at the ceiling, she tried to shake the image of him leaning against the wall in the hallway from her mind. Instead, she found herself replaying every interaction they'd had that evening and thinking about what she should have said. Keeping her awake, despite her exhaustion, was her traitorous brain, which kept playing out scenarios of what might have happened had she let him in.

After a few hours of sleep, dressed in blue jeans and a white t-shirt, she headed downstairs. Sitting at the same table she had shared with Ian and Roarke, she ordered a full Scottish breakfast.

After breakfast, her waiter delivered an invitation to the kitchen from Paul. He thought she would like to watch as he prepared a few traditional dishes. She checked the clock above the bar first. Mr. Shaw expected her at noon.

When Rhea entered the kitchen, two young men were chopping vegetables, and Paul was stirring a pot with one hand, scribbling on a clipboard with the other. She gently cleared her throat to make her presence known.

Paul half-turned. "Rhea! Nice to see you again."

Wearing a white chef's jacket, edged in blue, the same shade as his luminescent eyes, he was just as handsome as she remembered. The bright sunlight picked up the golden strands in his hair, and his flawless skin had a flush high on his cheeks from the heat of the stove.

"It smells amazing in here."

"Oh." He smiled. "That might be the Scotch broth."

"I know you're busy. I don't want to be in your way."

"Oh, you won't be."

She was introduced to his sous-chefs and shown around the small kitchen. Paul had her taste the food and gave details about the dishes. Rhea found him insightful, intelligent, and very proud of his work.

"Would you like to see something extraordinary?" he whispered.

"Always."

Paul went to an old wooden desk and pulled a key ring from his pocket. He unlocked a drawer and took out an old leather-bound tired-looking book. "My Granny's cookbook. The recipes are centuries old."

Together they perused the recipes and family stories written in neat, rounded cursive on the fragile pages decorated with images of plants, animals, and symbols.

"You're right." She poured over the pages, marked by the spills and stains of kitchen life. "This is extraordinary."

"She was a howdie as well, so she knew all of the old superstitions."

"What's a howdie?"

"Like a midwife. She looked after the mothers and told them how to keep their babies safe. The majority of the women in our family were howdies, medicine women, witchy. Legend has it they had a sacred meeting place and performed ceremonies over the grave of an ancestor of ours."

"Do you know a lot of the old beliefs?" Rhea looked up from taking notes. "The main reason for superstitions was to keep people safe from the unknown."

"Exactly." He hung his jacket up on a coat rack and threw on a shirt. "This wasn't the easiest place to live. People had to be tough and depended on each other. The community would have shared beliefs about things that might not exist."

"The superstitions led to daily rituals as a form of self-protection."

Bending to pick up the book gingerly, he returned it to its drawer. "We cherish and protect this book, and Ellie is convinced Granny hid secrets in here."

"What kind of secrets?"

"Witchy stuff I know nothing about." He grinned at her. "Ellie, Agnes, Senga, and some other women in the area still practice, but you didn't hear that from me."

"My lips are sealed."

"Would you like to see the herb garden?" He motioned for her to step outside.

At the side of the barn, they turned the corner to find a small sectioned garden. Paul pointed out rhubarb, carrots, onion, leek, and potatoes as well as fragrant herbs.

Rhea walked around in the garden while Paul bent and gathered herbs, giving her a little bouquet. "Oh, thank you," she said as she raised it to her nose.

She looked up into his deep blue eyes. "May I ask you a question?"

"Certainly." He smiled down at her.

"Why don't you have the same black eyes as Ian and Ellie?"

"I do, actually." His smile faltered a little. "I wear contact lenses."

"But that black shade is so special and unique."

"Yes, but I'm blond and pale. The black eyes make me look like a demon."

Rhea chuckled.

"It is too bad you aren't staying longer. It's nice to have someone around who's interested in our history. A lot of people take it for granted." He nudged at an embedded rock with the toe of his shoe and cleared his throat.

"I'll be in Scotland for awhile and not too far from here."

"We can see each other from time to time?"

Rhea returned his smile, flattered that he would like to see her again. *Paul's the right kind of man.*

Someone yelled Paul's name from the other side of the barn.

Paul rolled his eyes and turned in the direction of the inn. "Yeah?"

Rhea, standing on a rock, started when Paul yelled. She wobbled and would have fallen, but Paul steadied her with his hands on her waist. Face-to-face, they smiled at one another.

The intimate moment was interrupted by heavy footsteps on the gravel in the direction of the corner of the barn. "Hey, Paul!" A deep, raspy voice called. "The lads said I could find you here. Last night, I forgot to give . . ." Roarke McCallum rounded the corner, his sentence trailing off when he saw Rhea, her arms around Paul's shoulders and his hands on her waist.

"I'm sorry, didn't know you were entertaining." He grinned at Rhea and winked.

Paul let go of her waist as Rhea stepped from the rock "Just showing Rhea the garden."

"Bet you were." He raised an eyebrow. "Anyway, I left some fish in the kitchen for you."

"Thanks," Paul said as he stepped toward him. "Got time for a coffee?"

"Not now." He jerked his thumb in the direction of the parking lot. "Gotta get going. Been gone too long as it is."

Paul snapped his fingers as if remembering something. "Will you be seeing Uncle Ian?"

"Sure. I need to go pick up Pearl."

"Can you just wait a few minutes?" Paul started jogging

toward the inn. "I've something for him. Rhea, I'll be right back."

"Actually, Paul. I need to get going myself." She stepped toward Roarke and swerved around him without a glance. "I'm expected elsewhere, but thanks for showing me around."

"No problem at all. I hope to see you again soon."

Rhea headed for the main door. Roarke caught up to her and whispered, "Not so prissy after all."

Spinning around, she almost collided with him. "What's that supposed to mean?"

"I thought I'd lost my touch with the fairer sex, but it turns out you've a thing for the movie star."

"I don't have a thing for anyone."

"Hey, I don't blame you. Paul's an attractive man if you like the docile type," he said the last under his breath.

She stalked toward the inn, arms swinging like an angry child. "Is it so hard for you to believe that a woman could just not be interested in you?" she half-yelled. "You're arrogant, conceited, and mean-natured."

"Let's set the record straight." He passed her and stood in her way on the small path, glaring down at her. "I had too much to drink last night and would have hit on anyone, even someone like you."

The words stung as if she'd been slapped in the face. *Even someone like you* rang in her ears. She knew she wasn't the greatest-looking woman in the world, but the comment made her feel very small. Tears stung her eyes. She dodged him on the path. "Get out of my way, jack-ass."

Though she heard him say something behind her, she ran in the inn and stormed up the stairs to her room.

Once packed and feeling calmer, she assumed enough time had passed to go downstairs without running into Roarke.

Even though it was a little early, she called for a cab to take her up to Niall Shaw's cottage. *The sooner I get there, the better.*

Seeing Ellie in the pub, she went to say her goodbyes, and Ellie put her hands on Rhea's shoulders. "Give us a call when you get where you are going. It speaks for bad weather."

Rhea promised she would, feeling touched by the other woman's concern. Ellie squeezed her and ran her hand down the length of Rhea's straight, reddish-brown ponytail. "My, your hair smells nice."

Leaning against the doorframe and waiting for her cab, Rhea touched her hair. Ellie's inadvertent caress had reminded her of her mother, Margot, and remembering the braid-train she used to make with her mother and sister. Her mother would braid Rhea's hair, and Rhea would braid Poppy's. Afterward, Rhea would tend to her mother's hair, rubbing Margot's long, straight, black hair with the mixture of stinging nettle, yarrow, and wild mint oils she always used.

Once, Margot had leaned back contentedly regarding her daughter upside-down. "Oh, Rhea. Isn't it nice to be touched? How we women loved to be touched." Taking her daughter's hand, she rubbed it against her soft cheek.

Thinking of her mother, Rhea was glad she had rubbed her hair with the herb mixture that morning. *With all the wonderful people around here, I can't let Roarke McCallum ruin my time.*

A minute later, she sat in the back of a taxi, heading toward her next adventure.

The road went up into the hills, through valleys and glens, and across a small river before the driver, a stocky, bearded man of about fifty, turned onto the small dirt road that led to Niall Shaw's cottage.

The cottage and farm nestled between two hillocks near a small, forested area and a loch. To the south were cliffs and vast steep hills that dropped down into the turquoise waters of the West Coast, surrounded by white, sandy beaches and rocky bays dotted with rock pools.

The driver, James, came from the nearby village. "This area has everything, fertile farmland, a forest, lochs, and rivers. It's on the coastline but full of fields and wildlife."

"It appears to have it all."

"Here we are."

Cresting a large hill, they took a right turn. The cottage came into view, set in rolling farmland with a sheltering backdrop of woodland to the north, jagged cliffs and the seaside to the east.

The cottage was cozy and quaint, a small two-story white dwelling with a grey roof, gabled ends of stone blocks, and a porch spanning the entire structure. A low-lying brick wall with a large wooden gate surrounded the farm. To the left was a wooded area, to the right, a steep hill with another small thatch of woods at the top. An enclosure for animals sat between two large barns on a ridge behind the house.

Driving through the wooden gate, James stopped next to an old, orange truck. "He's at home. That's his truck."

I guess he does adhere to a simple lifestyle. Not the type of truck a movie star would drive.

James left her on the small path leading to the front door, already thinking of how she would describe the quaint cottage in the book.

Looking up at one of the second-floor windows, she noticed one of the curtains moving as if someone had just touched them, and she had the chilled feeling someone was watching her.

Walking toward the steps before the large door, she stopped to read a white wooden sign on the side of the door, *Fraoch Geal.* Country music came from the back of the house. Making her way in that direction, Rhea froze when she heard a deep bark. A second later, a massive, black Newfoundland dog came bounding toward her.

Rhea didn't move, and the dog stopped in front of her but

continued to bark.

The sound of heavy footsteps on gravel came around the side of the house, and a deep voice yelled out, "Be right there. Pearl, shut it!"

Pearl?

The dog stopped barking, so Rhea extended her hand, and the beast took a step toward her. After smelling her hand, it began to wag its tail.

Talking as he walked, a large man stepped around the corner of the house, looking down and wiping his hands on a rag. "Sorry, "I didn't hear the car pull up. Neither did the dog."

Rhea head snapped up. She knew the voice.

"I was out back, and the music was . . ." His voice petered out as he looked up from wiping his hands.

Rhea found herself face to face; or rather face to chest, with Roarke McCallum.

Roarke gave her a baffled face, his eyebrows pulling together. "What the hell are you doing up here?" He slung the rag over his shoulder.

"I . . . I'm expected." The air had been ripped from Rhea's body. "I have an interview with Mr. Shaw."

"That's funny." His expression hardened. "He told me he was waiting for a writer who was coming up to stay with him for a few weeks."

"Yes." She tossed her long braid over her shoulder. "That would be me. Do you work for him?"

"Sometimes." He took the rag off his shoulder and gave the palm of his hand a rub. "He was expecting a man."

"Yes, well. I'd rather speak to Mr. Shaw about it."

"I don't understand this," he scowled at her. "You told me you were a writer visiting Scotland for a personal project. You didn't say anything about Niall Shaw."

"Look, I don't want to be rude, especially since you and I

don't get along very well the best of times, but what I am doing here is none of your business." She was beginning to feel uncomfortable. "Where is Mr. Shaw? Can I find him somewhere on the property?"

"No, you cannot." His voice had taken on an aggressive tone. "It's interesting to me that you show up at the inn and lied to everyone."

"I don't care how it seems to you." Her voice had risen, and fists clenched at her sides. "I'm here to see Mr. Niall Shaw, and I am done talking to you."

"If you'd like to speak to Mr. Niall Shaw, then you are not done talking to me."

Stepping toward her, she stumbled a little as she backed away from him. "Why? Are you his bodyguard or something?" *What other kind of job would this dumbass have?*

"No, I'm not his bodyguard." Anger flashed into his eyes and sent a shiver up her spine, just as a deep rumble of thunder sounded nearby. "I don't work for Niall Shaw."

Rhea shook her head in confusion. "Then what —"

"You're nowhere near as smart as you think you are." He shook his head and leaned toward her to say through gritted teeth, "I am Niall Shaw!"

Chapter Four: I'm Your Ghost

After I died, everything had new meaning, and I realized how naïve and vulnerable the living are. They are the dead.

R hea took another step back, and her hand flew to her mouth. "You . . . you can't be."

"Really? Because I am."

"Your name's Roarke McCallum."

"My real name's Roarke McCallum. My stage name is Niall Shaw." He put his hands on either side of his head. "You're the writer from Portenders Publishing?"

"Yeah. I'm your ghost."

"Ghost?"

"Your ghost-writer."

"They were sending a man named K.K. Sullivan."

"I'm K.K. Sullivan. I write under that name."

"I see we both work under pseudonyms. You never mentioned interviewing me when we were at the pub."

"Wait! You really are Niall Shaw?" When he nodded his head, she exhaled and swept her hair off her face. "I didn't say anything because I didn't know you were you. I was respecting my client's privacy. I was told that Mr. Shaw, er, you were a very private person."

"You're my ghost-writer?"

"I'm here to write your biography, and I'm researching for a personal project as well."

"Right, I'm going to ask you some questions, and you will give me the answers." He took a few steps to one side. "Or

I'm going to throw you and your bags over the fence. Got it?"

"Don't talk to me like that." Her lip curled slightly. "I'll answer your question."

"How did you not recognize me? It's been a few years, but I'm recognized wherever I go."

"I didn't do any research about you, and I've never seen your films."

The thunder boomed again in the distance, and drops hit her arm and cheek.

"With everything that's out there today, you didn't research anything or even see a picture?" His voice was thick with disbelief.

"My editor was very clear that I was to write from an unbiased point of view. Therefore, anything written should be only what you tell me or what I perceived myself."

"You've never seen any of my films?"

"The years you were the most active, I was living in a very secluded place. The years I've been back, you've been off the grid. I couldn't put a face on half of the celebrities whose names I might recognize."

"You don't watch television or anything?"

"No, except for some kid's shows with my son."

"Whatever." He rubbed at his forehead. "I think you knew exactly who I was, and you didn't tell me who you were so I would let my guard down. It worked, too. I do not enjoy being lied to, especially by someone I have invited into my home!"

He was yelling his words by the time he finished, and Pearl sat at his feet. The air was becoming very chilly, and rain had begun. Roarke seemed oblivious to the weather, though Rhea stood shivering in her light sweater.

"Not . . . not true." She stammered her words as she shook. "I didn't know who you were."

Pearl looked up at him and barked as the rain came down harder while Rhea glared at him, turned on her heel, and by the time she reached the porch, had her phone in her hand.

Glaring at her, he barked, "What are you doing?"

"Calling for a cab." The rain started pelting down, but Roarke seemed nonplussed about the icy rain trailing down his handsome, furious face.

"You're not going to get a signal up here in this weather."

"Surely you have a landline I can use."

"I do." He folded his arms in front of his chest and looked at her smugly. "However, since Trace isn't working today, James is the only taxi in the area. You'll only be able to reach him when he gets back to town."

James had mentioned he had another two fares after me. "I'll walk back to town," Rhea stuffed her cell in her pocket and started down the steps.

"In this?" He gestured to the sky just as a strong wind hit the house.

Rhea was soaking wet, and she bounded back up the stairs to shiver under the porch.

"I know you're cold, but you need to answer a few more questions if I'm going to let you in my house."

"I don't want to get in your house!" she bellowed at him. "This was a huge mistake!"

"Why wouldn't they tell me you were a woman?" He stormed up onto the porch. "I never would've agreed to this!"

"Maybe your agent didn't know!" She raised her hands into the air. "Or, shit, maybe you're such a misogynist they thought you wouldn't trust a woman with the job!"

"A misogynist?"

"You haven't shown me much else!" Happy to be able to yell at him, she continued. "Oh, and you're an arrogant womanizer as well!"

Glaring at her and grinding his teeth, he stepped toward the door. "To hell with this! I'm calling my agent!"

"Please get this straightened out! I don't want to stay here another minute! Job or no job!"

As he stormed into the house and slammed the door, she felt a little wave of warm air that made her desperate to be inside the house. Throwing off her sweater, fishing her rain jacket out of her backpack and putting it on she felt a little warmer, but she was still wet.

A few minutes later, and Roarke reappeared at the door. "My agent had no idea, and I'm not comfortable sharing my home with a woman." He poked his finger at her face. "This is your agency's fault."

"I don't care whose fault it is, and get your finger out of my face." She slapped at his hand with the back of hers, causing him to step back a little, a shocked look on his face.

Roarke looked up at the roof of the porch. "Show me your ID and credentials."

Rummaging in her bag, she found her passport and identification card from her agency, both of which she shoved toward him.

He looked them over and passed them back to her wordlessly.

"What do you want me to say? If your problem is that I'm a woman, I can't change that. I'm here because my agency thought I was the best person for the job." She kicked at her suitcase. "I'll leave as soon as possible if I make you that uncomfortable. However, if your anger is because of yesterday, then I think that is highly unfair, as you were behaving like a jackass!"

"You—" He began angrily, taking a step toward her.

"You, nothing!" She screamed at him, waving a hand around her head. "I didn't say anything about the book because that's what I was told to do, and I didn't know who you were. Either you believe me, or you don't. End of story!"

His anger started to dissipate a little as he looked down on her. "I'm just perplexed. I need you to explain."

Rhea's hands went to her hips. "I have. Now what?"

"I need a little more than that."

"That's all I have for you right now." Turning from him, she faced the hill. He seemed a little calmer, but Rhea was getting angrier.

In a softer voice, he said, "Look, what are we doing out here? Get inside." He stepped up to the door and turned the knob.

"No." She rested her hands on the railing of the white porch.

"No?"

"Did I stutter?" she groused, glaring at him over her shoulder.

"I know you're cold. Go inside."

"No." She spun around and rested her behind against the railing. "You don't want me here, and I don't stay where I'm not wanted. Besides, if I'm not going to be working for you, then you don't get to tell me what to do."

In a sort of stalemate, arms folded and legs spread, each glared at the other.

His eyes shot daggers at her as he spoke. "I can tell you one thing. You're not going anywhere tonight. This weather is only going to get worse, so get inside and at least get warm."

"I wasn't properly invited." She glared back at him, unblinking. "You haven't asked me politely."

"Politely?"

Tilting her head to one side, she smirked a little. "Yes, politely. You ordered me inside. You didn't ask me inside."

"So smug." He screwed up his face into a look of sheer malice. "I'm not the one who's stuck here. I am offering you to come into my home, and you just give this bitchy attitude."

"Politely," she repeated, making sure not to break eye contact. *No man has ever ordered me around, and it will not happen now.*

"I'm not going to argue." He put his hand on the doorknob.

"Stay here and freeze."

"I've been in worse situations," she shot back.

Roarke strode inside and slammed the door so hard the cottage shook.

Rhea looked around, proud of herself, but she realized what kind of situation she was in as she looked out at the vast countryside. *Shit! What am I going to do now?*

Roarke stood with palms pressed against the door. *I let my temper get the better of me.* He raised his head and slapped both hands hard on the green oak. *No, to hell with that. If she's stuck outside, it's her own fault.*

Pearl sat on the mat next to the door as Roarke organized dinner and tried not to think about the woman shivering on his porch. *Ask her politely indeed! Persnickety wee twit.*

After putting a chicken in the oven, he peeled potatoes and a turnip and dropped them in copper pots. *Of course, her explanation was somewhat plausible.*

Roarke chopped vegetables for a salad. *I need to get this book done. It'll bring in money for the projects.*

He took a tomato and fresh basil to the chopping board. *Finding her a tad attractive is a problem. We can't have any complications if she does stay here to work for me.*

Lifting the tomato to his nose, he breathed in the grassy scent. *I can be around an attractive woman with nothing happening.*

Bang!

Behind him, a cupboard door he had left open slammed shut, causing him to jump and his hair to stand on end. *Shit, not this again!*

As had happened a few times in the past few months, a still, uncomfortable silence filled the small cottage. Roarke was suddenly very eager to have someone else in the kitchen, especially when Pearl whimpered and stared down the hall-way before running into the mudroom.

Roarke crossed the kitchen to the door, swinging it open. "Will you please get inside, you daft..." His words trailed off as he saw that though her bags were still there, she was not.

Grabbing his raincoat, he headed out, followed by Pearl, who ambled toward the large hill where he saw a small, yellow figure. Relief was followed by anger. *Idiot! What the hell is she doing?*

With his long strides, it didn't take long for him to get close to her, though the sound of the pouring rain drowned out his cries, and Rhea kept climbing the hill.

Pearl caught up to Rhea and nudged her knee with her head. Turning in Pearl's direction, Rhea stopped walking and watched Roarke climb the hill.

In a few short steps, with clenched fists, he stopped a few feet away from her, and since she was a little higher on the hill, they were almost the same height. Pearl jumped at his side and placed her paws on his thigh.

"What the hell are you doing?" he roared at her.

"Talking a walk," she said with her nose in the air.

"Talking a walk?"

She wiped a drop of water from off the tip of her nose. "Yes. In this fine Scottish weather."

"That's it!" he hollered.

Bending at the waist, he threw her over his shoulder as if she were a sack of potatoes. Turning, he stalked down the hill to the cottage.

Rhea screamed at him the entire way, "Roarke! Put me down! You idiot! You're going to slip! I'll kill myself from this height! Roarke!"

Her complaints were ignored, yet he never lost his footing on the slippery grass. He stomped up the three steps to the porch and deposited her, none too gently, in front of the door.

Giving an obsequious little bow, he said in a saccharine voice, "Rhea, would you do me the bloody honor of coming inside my humble abode?" He opened the door and stood back, gesturing for her to enter. "If it's not too much bloody trouble."

Rhea squared her shoulders, smiled slightly, and stepped inside. Behind her back, with a sarcastic smirk, Roarke McCallum gave her the middle finger.

After hanging up her rain clothes in the small mudroom to the left of the doorway, Rhea treaded into the kitchen in her stocking feet. The air smelled of roast chicken and herbs, the lighting layered and soft. The kitchen was spacious and white with a grey countertop, sundry black appliances, and a large island with a stovetop taking up a great deal of space.

The bathroom was to her left around the corner from the mudroom and ran along the same wall as an open pantry full of root vegetables, dried and canned foods, preserves, and spices.

To her right was a small, cozy sitting room with a fireplace in the middle of the wall, a leather couch, and two old, brown, easy chairs. Between both chambers, a dark corridor ran the length of the house. Her gaze fixed on the small window at the end of the hall, where white lace curtains were moving slightly.

Roarke came around the island from where he'd been checking his pots. "Nothing burning."

Outside, a blast of wind hit the house, and he stepped out to bring in her luggage.

"You came prepared for the weather. Good rain gear kept you dry." A smile flitted across Roarke's face.

"Roarke, I . . . ," she began. Now she was inside, her anger had subsided, and she wanted to clear the air, but he motioned with his hands to silence her.

"No, not yet. Go and get settled away. You must be . . ." Roarke furrowed his brow because other than the front of her hair, Rhea was bone dry. "Why aren't you wet? You got soaking wet."

"I didn't know how long I'd be out there, so I changed on the porch."

"You changed outside."

"Yes."

"On the porch?"

"Behind my towel, yes."

"Wasn't that cold?"

"I was already cold. As people say in China, the dead pig doesn't feel the boiling water."

"What?" His face split in a smile.

"I'll explain later." She smiled back and looked down at her socks. "Anyway, I was warm once I changed."

"What if I had come back out?"

"Then you might have gotten an eyeful." She laughed as his eyebrows flew up. "No, I watched you through the window storming around the kitchen as I changed."

"Right." Picking up her suitcase, he slung her backpack over his shoulder.

Bang!

Rhea jumped and spun around to face the door when a heavy weight hit it and long nails started scratching. "What the . . .?"

Roarke chuckled. "It's just Pearl back from snooping around. Let her in, will you?"

He started down the hallway as she let Pearl in. "Hey, Pearl, what have you — ?"

Her question turned into a squeal as Pearl shook the water out of her long, thick fur. Rhea was splattered with water, soaking her t-shirt and dripping down her face.

Roarke turned just in time to see Pearl shake and then wobble off into the kitchen to drink from her silver bowl. Rhea felt ridiculous, her mouth gaping open in shock, and Roarke let out a loud guffaw, laughing as his shoulders shook.

Rhea laughed, tossing her hair around her head. "So much for staying dry."

"Sorry." He rubbed his eye with the back of his hand. "Too funny. Here's your room. It's small, but I hope you'll be comfortable."

There were two doors on the right. Roarke opened the first, flicked on the light, and stepped back to let her enter. Painted a pale green, it had a chest of drawers, a writing desk and chair facing a long, low window, and a large featherbed, covered with a thick forest-green duvet. A painting of a castle in the middle of a peaceful loch hung above the bed.

"You're right." She smiled up at him. "Very comfortable. I love the color."

"Ah, yes." He placed her bags on the floor. "Mystic Cove."

"Huh?"

"That's the name of the color," he explained. "To be honest, the name's the reason I took the color. Wouldn't you want to sleep in a Mystic Cove?"

"I would indeed."

"Please, don't be mad at Pearl."

"I would never. I love dogs. My mother's people say dogs are spiritual gifts to humans." She cleared her throat. "Besides, I'd never cross the mistress of the house."

He glanced at the ceiling and then back at her almost shyly. "I'll leave you to it. Dinner will be ready shortly."

"Okay, thank you."

He was about to close the door when Rhea noticed a door across from her own, sealed with duct tape. "An unused room?"

"It leads to the stairway for the second floor. After a few

months in the house, I realized I didn't need the second floor for now, so I installed the door and sealed it off. This place can get quite drafty, especially in certain winds. Sealing it up keeps the heat down here."

"No one's up there?"

He looked at her with a strange expression. "Why do you ask?"

"When I arrived, it seemed to me that the curtain moved as if someone had just stepped away from it." She didn't mention the feeling of being watched.

"Probably just a draft." He turned to leave. "Excuse me."

When the door closed behind Roarke, the first thing she did was to fall back onto the featherbed. She realized how exhausted she was and could have fallen asleep, but a gentle rap on the door roused her.

Roarke held a glass of red wine. He looked over her shoulder at the dent in the fluffy duvet. "Tired?"

"I couldn't resist." She laughed gently. "I had a feather bed growing up."

He held out the wine to her. "Here you go. A peace offering. Might do to chase off the rest of the chill."

Taking it from him, she accidentally ran her fingers on his. *Damn.* "Thank you." She looked down into the glass. "It's a funny thing."

"What?" He leaned against the doorframe.

"We said terrible things out there, and yet as soon as we get inside, our attitude changed. At least, I know mine did. I'm sorry if I was a jackass. I was just surprised at everything."

"As was I." He picked at a spot on the door. "I'm hotheaded. I thought I was doing better with it, but I guess I still have a ways to go."

"I'm short-tempered, too, so I won't be casting any stones your way when it comes to making self-improvements."

"Maybe the rain washed away our sins, so to speak."

"I'm glad it did." She shook her head, an exasperated, little smile playing on her lips. "You were right. I can be such a priss."

"No, I should be the one to apologize. I was horrible last night and today. I don't know what got into me."

Glancing at him from under her lashes, she mumbled, "Truce?"

"Truce." He pushed himself off the doorframe. "From now on, I'll be a gentleman."

"I'll be a perfect guest, that is, if you'd like me to stay."

"I'd like you to stay." He shoved his hands into his pockets. "Can I ask you a question?"

"Sure." She sniffed the warm, floral wine in her hands.

"How do you feel in this house? I mean is, what kind of energy did you get on the first impression."

Answering honestly, she said, "There's definitely a, ah, creepy energy despite its quaintness. Outside, I felt agitated and jittery. Now, I feel good, all anger gone, and I feel calm."

"Really?" He drew his lips tight around his teeth and looked at the ceiling. "I've always been at odds with the house. When I first moved in, it felt like a place where children had laughed and played, but a while ago, it changed. Weird things would happen, and there came a low, almost angry energy. Something I couldn't place, but I could identify with." Stepped back into the hall, he smiled. "Since you walked in, that feeling seems to have dissipated. It's like you brought a lightness to the house that had been absent."

A flush crept over her cheeks. "What a nice thing to say."

Backing out of the room, he pointed to her glass. "Enjoy your wine."

"Don't worry. I will." She held up her hand to still him. "Roarke, what does the sign say next to the door?"

"It's the name of the cottage." He turned and walked down the hall, talking over his shoulder. "*Fraoch Geal*, it means

White Heather."

Sitting on the bed and sipping her wine, she tried to wrap her head around everything. Her experiences with Roarke in the past few days had been a bit of a roller coaster. First, in the jeep, he'd been rude and then playful. At the inn, flirtatious, then callus and brazen. This morning, incredibly insulting. An hour ago, aggressive, angry, and suspicious. Now, he was warm and welcoming.

Rhea knew enough to be wary of men with changeable characters, yet she had to understand him to go ahead with the book. He certainly had an allure, a mysterious appeal, and it was her job to communicate everything to his fans.

Deciding she had to adapt to her situation, she carried her wine and walked down the corridor toward the sound of chopping.

Roarke had his back turned in the well-lit kitchen. Wearing relaxed blue jeans and a short-sleeved black button-up shirt, open at the neck, he chopped herbs. He scooped up the herbs and deposited them in a small saucepan, stirring the contents with a wooden spoon that seemed very small in his massive hand. Stirred the pot, the long muscles of his forearm stretched and strained, as did those of his strong shoulders.

As she entered the kitchen, she was surprised to hear him humming. "That's nice." Her voice sounded much louder than she had intended in the quiet of the kitchen.

Roarke spun around so quickly some hot liquid splashed onto his wrist. "Shit." He brought his wrist up to his mouth and sucked on it.

How can someone have sexy wrists?

"I'm so sorry." Her hand flew to her mouth, partially to cover her grin.

He took his wrist away from his lips with a gentle thwack. "My mind was somewhere else. I didn't hear you come in."

"I should have made my presence known. My father always said I walk like a cat. Did you burn yourself?"

"Naw, it's fine." Roarke picked the wooden spoon off the floor and put it in the sink. "What's nice?"

"Beg pardon?"

"When you snuck up behind me like an alley cat, you said that's nice."

"You were humming." She put her wine glass on the counter. "What was it?"

"Some old diddle." He took the small pot to the stovetop. "Did you settle in?"

"Yes, I did, but could I place a short call on your landline, as I can't get any service on my cellphone?"

"Oh, go ahead. The phone's next to the bar in the sitting room. Just dial the country code with the number."

"Thanks, I need to check in with my son."

"How old?"

"Eight," she answered as she reached the phone. "He's traveling with his father in Florida."

"You're divorced?"

"Never married. I haven't found my soul mate yet." She punched buttons. "You? Ever married?"

"Nope. Thanks be to God."

"You've got soulmate issues, too, eh?"

"Where would another person fit in my boat when there's barely enough room for me?" He waved his knife in the air as he spoke. "Besides, I couldn't give up my freedom, and asking a woman to understand that wouldn't be fair."

"I think it's very understandable and fair. I was never boy-crazy like my friends, yet my mother used to tell me that one day I'd want a man to look at me the way Daddy looked at her."

"How did he look at her?" Putting down his knife, he watched her as she waited with the phone to her ear, forehead puckered.

"Like she was the only woman in the world."

"Have you ever wanted a man to look at you like that?"

"Who says they haven't, Roarke?" She smiled.

Receiving no answer, she left a message and went back to the kitchen.

"No answer. Pat warned me he'd be off the grid for awhile and there's no answer with Liam's grandparents. I'll try again tomorrow." She stepped toward the bathroom. "I'll just be a sec."

"Take your time."

As soon as she had closed the door, the bathroom felt small and claustrophobic. On the back of the door was an old beige robe, which made Rhea understand the intimacy of their situation. She ran her hand down the nubby old cotton of the robe, then turned away, facing a window behind burgundy curtains. The toilet was underneath it, and to the right, an old, wooden chest of drawers sat next to a white pedestal sink, with an old-fashioned oval mirror above it. Picking up Roarke's aftershave, she breathed in its crisp, musky fragrance.

The feeling of being watched returned, as if someone stood behind her, yet the mirror showed no one. A Chinese ghost story popped into her mind about a man who had murdered his wife. When he questioned his small son about why he never asked where his mother had gone, the boy said, "Because she's still here, but I have been wondering why you've been carrying her on your back for the past few weeks."

Shivering slightly, she freshened up and went back out to find Roarke setting the table.

Chapter Five: Night Bird

The fear of the unknown is the oldest and most powerful human fear, which perhaps explains the trepidation and dread that stirs the soul when hearing the mournful cries of the night bird.

"Did you find everything you needed?" Roarke asked as Rhea returned and sat at the island.

"Yes, thank you."

Roarke watched her tilt her head back to drain the last of her wine, wiping at her bottom lip with her index finger. The little fringe around her face was wet at the ends, and her Cupid's bow lips had a burgundy tint from the wine. Clearing her throat, she asked, "Can I help you with anything?"

Heat crept across his neck and cheeks. "Sorry?"

"Do you need help?"

"Um, yes." He handed her an empty whisky glass. "Refill this for me? On the small bar. The stout, square decanter."

"What is it?"

"Whisky."

"Sorry, I don't know spirits very well."

"Hey, have you had any whisky since you've been here?"

"No."

"We'll have to remedy that situation."

Sniffing at the glass, she screwed up her face a little. "Maybe after I eat."

Chuckling, he refilled her wine and watched her walk the width of the house to the bar. It was true that she made no sound when she walked. With quick steps, her feet barely left the floor. Well-shaped legs led to a callipygian bottom and a small waist. She was, as Doug had whispered to him, "well-put-together."

"You don't walk like a cat. You move like a ghost." He picked up the tomato and basil and carried them over to the sink to wash. "My ghost, right?"

"Your ghost. If you still want me to do the job."

"Do you still want the job?" he asked, rubbing the tomato on a dry rag.

"It's a great opportunity for me."

"I need to get this book done." He sighed and rested his hands on the island. "Let's try to make a fresh start."

"Then we needn't discuss it again, and I can get to work." She grinned as she looked around. "Your home is very tidy, very cozy."

"I don't watch television or anything." He looked over his chicken. "I like to work. I like to be busy."

"If I'm going to stay, you need to let me help you with your work around the house and the farm. I can't just follow you around and watch you. That'd get creepy fast."

"Sure would." He took a drink. "Tomorrow, I'll give you a tour of the farm. Show you what to do and not do."

"Great!" She picked up her refilled glass and lifted it toward him. "Would it be cheesy to toast to new beginnings?"

"A bit." He shook his head in disappointment. "Here I thought you were creative." Then, raising his glass, he glanced down as Pearl settled at his feet. "How about to ghosts?"

"To ghosts."

When she lowered her glass, she gestured her chin at Pearl. "I guess she'll be having her pups soon."

"Yeah. You can tell?"

"She's huge! My parents raised huskies. I grew up around dogs."

"Aye, I could tell you were comfortable with dogs." Roarke bent down to ruffle her fur. "Any day now. It's her first brood, so I'll be bringing her up to Ian's tomorrow. When it's their first, they sometimes have trouble, and I've never done it before."

She brightened. "Ian lives near here?"

"Aye. Just over the hill. He takes care of the farm and Pearl when I go out of town, travel, or go to sea, and you know the guy from the TV that's making an offer on the castle? David? He owns the plot of land on the other side. He's been buying up a lot of land in the area as of late. If he gets the castle, he'll be the king of the castle around here."

Rhea carried the dishes of food over to the table as Roarke carved the beautiful roast chicken.

"What part of the chicken do you like?" he asked as he poised his knife over a breast.

"Thigh, please. The greasier, the better."

"Rhea, I have to ask, what were you doing on that hill in the rain?"

Setting down the bowls of *neeps and tatties*, mashed turnips and potatoes, she went back for the salad. "I don't intend on wasting a minute in Scotland. I'm going to see everything I can, rain or shine. Besides, I've got great rain gear. I'm ready for Scotland."

"Aye." Setting down the plates on the table, he gave her an impish grin. "But is Scotland ready for you?"

Rhea put down her knife and fork and cradled her wine glass in both hands. "Wonderful chicken. I need to slow down. I'm eating too fast."

"The herbs came from Paul's garden." He smirked at her, and she narrowed her eyes at him. "No, that was not a dig at you. I was an arse this morning. If I had to explain myself, I might say that—"

"I don't need an explanation."

"Aye, you do." He put down his knife and fork and folded his fingers. "Look, I've stopped dating the women around here because it always gets me into trouble. When you showed up, I kind of thought you might be worth having a bit of fun with."

Rhea's jaw dropped in indignation, but Roarke kept talking. "When I went to your room to apologize, I never meant to insinuate anything. Then the next morning, to see you cozying up with Paul—"

"I was not cozying."

"I know, but it hit my ego." He leaned forward a little and dropped his voice. "I've not understood it myself, but I seem to have a way with the fairer sex."

"Egomaniac." She shook her head and smirked.

"Either way." He leaned back and grinned. "For you to be all chummy with one of my close buddies, it annoyed me. I made a pass at you because you are an attractive woman, but rest assured, as long as you're under my roof, I'll be a complete gentleman. This is work, and I take care of business."

While she appreciated his words, a jolt of disappointment followed with them. "Perfect."

"How is this supposed to work, exactly? I mean, what happens now?"

"I follow you around for a few weeks, watching what you do, finding out how you tick, and your opinions on things."

"I live a quiet life. That's why I live here."

"Why did you retire, anyway?"

"I hope you don't have a list of questions. Chat me up as we did yesterday. It was nice."

"I'm not sure I can do that. Yesterday, you were just some guy in a pub. Now, you're my job."

Roarke put his hands in front of him on the table. "I'll not be interviewed. If you want to get information, you need to give me some. We're going to chat, eat, drink, work, explore, but I won't live with a stranger. I won't be comfortable."

Shrugging her shoulders, she played with her fork. "Yeah, I'll answer your questions."

"Shit, that was easier than expected. You know, I've always had doubts about doing this, and I still can't imagine you studying me."

Knowing she had to find a way to make him comfortable, an idea crossed her mind. "What if we don't make this about you? What if we make this about me?"

One side of his mouth twitched. "What do you mean?"

Excited by her idea, she leaned forward and placed her elbows on either side of her plate. "When I arrived, I told everyone I was researching a new gothic novel I'm writing. What if we imagine that to be true?"

"Imagine what?"

"Come on. You're an actor! You're just a kind gentleman I met at the inn who's letting me stay with him while I research Scottish myths and legends. Very nice of you, really." She nodded her head at him. "If I get to know you in the process, all the better."

Roarke laughed and dabbed at the corners of his mouth with his napkin. "Not the worst idea."

"I want to research myths and legends and see if there's a correlation with any stories from my area. The Europeans who settled and married my mother's people were mainly from Scotland and England."

"To be honest, it might help with my attitude around the whole thing." He snapped his fingers. "It would explain why you're staying with me. We don't want to say we're dating, and we don't want the few people I'm around to be uncomfortable thinking that you are just picking them for information about me."

"Very true."

"All right." He picked up his glass and angled it toward her. "Let's proceed as if I'm just letting you stay here to study and work."

"Sure, but may I ask about something?"

As Roarke chewed a forkful of salad, he nodded.

"Why is it that no one at the inn let slip who you are? Why didn't Ian or Doug tell me you were a retired actor?"

"I guess they figured you didn't know, and I'd not like you to know, so they didn't say. When I came back here, I wanted to put Niall Shaw behind me and start fresh here at home. Maybe lead the life I could have led, had I not—"

"Gone to Hollywood?" she finished for him.

"Around here, I'm just Roarke. The way I like it." He leaned his elbows on the table and interlaced his fingers. "My new friend, you should know that I've put everything on hold for the next few weeks. The only thing I'll be doing is working on my farm, going for a sail, and relaxing. We're on a stay-cation. I may have a thing or two, but nothing pressing."

Grinning at him, happy he enjoyed her little idea, she gave him a quick head nod. "A vacation of sorts, it is."

They continued eating for a few minutes until her knife and fork clattered on her plate. "Okay, I'm a hypocrite."

"Hey." Roarke put up his hands. "Don't take it out on my flatware."

"I think my ego got hurt, too."

"How so?"

"I liked the attention you were giving me. Then, I saw a blond woman talking to you, and it made me feel strange."

"Who? Janice?" He laughed. "I haven't laid a finger or anything else on Janice since we were teenagers. She enjoys the company of men, is all. Paul's thinking about getting a restraining order."

Another silence fell between them before Rhea spoke

again, her eyes on her plate. "I was flattered to think you were hitting on me, but I was a little uncomfortable with the attention. Women like me aren't used to it."

"What does that mean?" He picked up his water glass and downed what remained in it.

"*Someone like me.* This morning, you said you were so drunk last night that you would've hit on anyone, even someone like me." She looked into his eyes to try to gauge his reaction.

It was his turn to drop his knife and fork. "Oh, my God, I didn't mean because of the way you look. I meant because of your holier-than-thou attitude. I think you're lovely, and you have a nice trim physique."

"It's okay, Roarke." She waved her hands in front of him. "You needn't wet your pants. I get it."

Roarke sighed and put down his cutlery. "If you don't mind my asking, what's your ethnicity? Your face is just so unique."

"My father's from Québec. His father was Native American, Huron-Wendat First Nations, and his mother was white, French-Canadian. My mother was from an island in the Maritimes, where I grew up, Miqm'aq with a splash of British."

"So, you're . . ."

"A mix."

Looking at the curves and angles of her face, he smiled softly. "Whatever's in the mix, I hope no one ever forgets the recipe."

Roarke and Rhea sat in front of the fire, sipping wine and munching shortbread cookies twenty minutes later. Rhea jotted down details about the house and complimented him on being a good cook.

"Yeah, I guess I do all right."

"Who taught you to cook?" She leaned back and rubbed

her stomach contentedly.

"Lots of trial and error. My mother worked a lot, so I had to cook for my brother and baby sister."

"Where was your father?"

"Gone. Story for another time." He glanced at the hand on her stomach. "You enjoyed your meal?"

"Mr. McCallum, if I were a cat, I'd be purring."

"I'm glad to hear it." Staring into the fire, he asked, "If you want to learn about Scotland while you're here, what do you want to know?"

"Everything I can. I want to write about Scotland. It reminds me of my home, and it would be interesting to compare the two, especially regarding superstitions and beliefs."

"Our beliefs stem from wanting some control over our world. Nature is not necessarily kind here, and we fought a lot in the past. Had to defend and protect what was ours."

"It's kind of the same for any group of people from an unforgiving landscape with temperamental climate. Food and supplies are sometimes hard to come by. People have to be tough and resilient and share."

"Shared beliefs unite a society. Society grows and evolves around those beliefs. In small, isolated areas, people are close, making them similar in many aspects of their lives and personalities."

"Yeah." Rhea smiled. "Did you know that many supernatural experts say that Scottish people are ethnically predisposed to ESP?"

"Extra Sensory Perception?"

"Think about it. Humans look around at the natural world and make connections. We use the natural world and past events to try to predict the future. People who are in tune with the world around them will detect subtle changes."

"You got me there."

The fire crackled and spat as they spoke, and the wind hit

the side of the house as a faint whistling sound came from the bottom of the window above Roarke's head.

"Where there's a gap in our understanding of the world around us, we need something to fill the gap. That leads to . . ."

"Heavy drinking?" He offered with a flourish of his whisky glass.

"Philosophical thinking." She shook her head and reached for another cookie. "Roarke?"

"Aye."

"Are you happy?" She stopped jotting notes and looked over at him. "If you don't mind me asking."

After a few seconds, he spoke, "Aye. I believe I'm as happy now as I've ever been in my life. The farm and the shelter give me purpose, and I feel like I am doing something that makes a difference."

"The shelter?" she questioned. "I recall hearing something about that."

"I've set up a shelter for at-risk kids in the city, and my team manages a small farm outside the city. For kids who want to learn a trade, we have a small certified school where they can get credit to graduate high school, and then we set them up at a trade school. Still, a lot of them need to get out of the city, so the farm gets them grounded and away from bad influences."

"Wow. That's impressive and admirable."

"To be honest, I got around with a rough crew when I was young. Luckily, I had someone who came along and helped me out. Kids just need someone to see their potential."

Eyes on the ceiling, she took a sip of wine and tried to look nonchalant as she struggled to keep from asking more questions.

"Anyway, that's the main reason for my grand comeback. We get funding from public donations, but it's no longer enough. The shelter, the farm for the kids, and White Heather have eaten the vast majority of my savings."

"You're going back to a world you hate to make money to help troubled youths?" Her voice had taken on a softer tone.

"That's the main reason, aye."

He seemed to be avoiding making eye contact, and his head had lowered a little shyly.

"I love that." She slid the pendants around on her silver chain on her neck.

Roarke sat forward and pointed at Rhea's necklace. "What's on your chain?"

Rhea's fingers brushed the silver cross, silver cuff link with a cut black stone, and a piece of polished dark green stone with engravings.

"Little gifts. My cross is from my grandparents. The Alaskan Black Diamond cufflink was my father's. I wear one, and Liam wears the other. This charm is Labradorite. My mother carved it for me."

Roarke leaned very close her and held the stone. Rhea breath hitched at his proximity.

"Are those arrows?"

The engraving was of a circle surrounding two arrows. The points faced each other, pointing to another small circle in the center.

"Yes." She smiled. "This is a symbol of protection. The outside circle means family, and the arrows are weapons, defense against evil spirits. The inside circle is for air, life."

"Evil spirits, eh?" He looked at the stone very closely.

"I don't think evil is the right term. My mother always said spirits aren't evil, but their actions can be. That's why she used Labradorite. It raises your level of consciousness, so you always know what's around you, but it also acts as a barrier to negative forces."

Letting go of the stone, he settled back in his chair. "Do you think that stuff works?"

"I don't know for certain, but I have a bit of a sixth sense about certain things. As for the negative forces, better safe than sorry."

Roarke didn't respond and stared at her again. "I've never seen anyone who looks like you."

"I didn't like it much growing up. The kids teased me that I looked like a cat."

"You do look like a cat, and to be honest, your face is strange and *insanely* beautiful."

Aware of the blush exploding all over her visage, she cleared her throat and sipped more wine.

"If you don't mind me saying so." He cleared his throat and looked from her face to the fire. "I guess I shouldn't say things like that to you if we're going to be staying together."

"Probably not."

"I'll find other ways to make you blush." He grinned, and she narrowed her eyes at him, stifling a yawn.

Roarke stood. "That's it! I'm going to do a quick check of the animals, and you're going to bed."

He stopped her protest with a wave of his hand. "Not another word. You're exhausted." Getting to his feet, he started toward the door, but he turned as he placed his hand on his jacket.

"Fine," Rhea mumbled before she slumped her shoulders and started shuffling down the hallway.

As Roarke opened the front door, a cacophony of noise filled the small cottage, and Rhea spun around. "Whoa! What a racket!" Rhea rushed to stand behind him.

Above the slight droning of insects were trills, strange whistles, and shrieks. At the same time, they both sat on the front step and watched as night birds flitted across the deep blue, darkening sky before them. Roarke tried his best to explain the noises to her.

"Up here, we usually have wind, but when the winds die down, sounds are carried from far away. That jarring, chirring sound is a nightjar, the cracking noise is a corncrake, and of course, those beautiful melodies are from the robins. Their songs become very melancholy as autumn sets in."

"The *twit-twoo* is an owl," Rhea added.

"Aye. If the wind stays low, you'll hear the belching of rutting red stags, followed by the crash of antlers. Their fights echo through the hills."

A sudden ethereal shriek filled the air from somewhere in the treetops of the nearby woods. It ended in a high trill that silenced the other birds, caused most of them to fly into the air and away from the sound. Something about it chilled Rhea to the very core. "What was that?"

A strange look fell over his face as he looked up at the crescent moon. "I don't know. I've never heard that night bird before."

With a shiver, Rhea decided it was time to turn in.

The following day, after a solid sleep, Rhea eased open her bedroom door. The smell of coffee and bacon hit her immediately.

As she entered the kitchen, Roarke looked up and smiled. "Good morning. Sleep well?"

"I did indeed." She stretched a little. "Have you been up for long?"

"Oh, aye." He grinned. "Actually, I was up very early. Pearl was walking around the house all night, and she vomited. I took her up to Ian's. Oh, and despite what we discussed last night, I told Ian why you're really here. He's the keeper of all my secrets anyway."

The toast popped out of the toaster, and he flipped something in a sizzling pan as he talked. "Before I left, Pearl had already settled into the birthing bed."

"Won't she miss you?" He turned toward the sink, and her eyes roamed down the back of his body, the t-shirt and jeans accentuating his broad shoulders, narrow waist, and long, muscular thighs. *I'd miss you.*

"Aye, I guess, but I'll be seeing her, and besides, Ian's place is her second home." He gave a pan a gentle shake. "Breakfast's almost ready."

She hurried to the bathroom. "Okay. I need a few to freshen up."

After breakfast, Roarke went into the bathroom and came out holding a facecloth. The piece of metal Rhea had found at the boulder the day before rested on it. "What's this?"

"I found that yesterday up by the pink boulder. I cleaned it this morning and left it to dry."

Roarke put it on the counter, and together they looked down at the corroded, silver brooch, in the shape of an M with a crown on top.

Rhea stepped closer to Roarke. "It must be someone's initial. An M.

"Very pretty." Roarke reached out to touch it but jumped back with a yelp. "Shit! I cut myself."

A few minutes later, with his finger bandaged, Roarke returned to the kitchen to find Rhea still gazing at the brooch. "Don't touch it, Rhea. It's bloody sharp."

"Roarke, the edges aren't even sharp." She lifted the brooch and cradled it in her palm. "I don't know how you cut yourself."

"Hurts like hell." He shook his hand. "And my finger's cold. It's weird."

"What should I do with it?" Rhea held it up to her eyes.

"You could keep it." Roarke leaned on the counter. "Or we can bring it to The Treasure Trove Unit."

At that moment, a heavy bang from the second floor shook the small cottage, causing both to jump.

"What the hell was that?" Rhea put down the brooch and took a step toward the corridor. "I thought there was nothing up there?"

"I keep a few old artifacts up there for safe-keeping." Roarke stepped behind Rhea, and she smirked at the look of fear on his face.

"Are you afraid, big man?"

Frozen where he was, he said, "I told you sometimes strange things happen here."

"We need to go up there." She inched toward the door leading to the second landing.

"Why?" Roarke still hadn't moved but stood with his arms folded across his chest.

"Because I'm living here, too, and I won't be able to rest not knowing what made a bang so loud and heavy that the cottage shook."

"You're right, but you stay here until I check it out." He stepped toward the door as Rhea stepped back.

"You sure?" She grinned at him again. "I can go if you're scared."

Narrowing his eyes at her, he pulled off the tape surrounding the plastic on the door. After opening it, he ran up the stairs and called down a few minutes later. "Rhea, it's okay."

Looking up the stairs, into the dark landing a few feet above her, Rhea felt the strangest of sensations. First, a lightness floated around her, like being on the surface of the water or swinging in a hammock. A vibration resonated in the air, the same feeling as touching a speaker. Tiny sparkles twinkled at the top of the stairs around the light in the middle of the ceiling.

On one side was a small sitting room, and on the other, two small bedrooms. The only furniture was a wooden table in the largest room and a wooden chest underneath the window. The emptiness gave her a sense of foreboding.

The table held books, old jewelry, various weapons, a bronze cauldron that Roarke said was from the fourteenth century, and various other treasures. In the trunk was an old set of bagpipes from the eighteenth century and a length of ancient tartan. On the floor was a large sword.

"This sword must have fallen somehow. It was on the table." When Roarke pulled the sword out of its sheath, the air seemed to vibrate with energy. Handing it over to Rhea by its handle, she marveled at its beauty. Tiny jewels ran down the length and clustered in the center of the hilt, and the blade had a curved, single edge with a flaring tip. It had a cross-shaped guard, and a curving handle that ended with a downward turned pommel.

Rhea nodded and reluctantly handed over the sword. "That would account for the sound, for certain."

Roarke replaced in its sheath and put it in the wooden chest, shuddering slightly. He looked at her almost expectantly.

"What?" Rhea asked in confusion.

"Just wondering if you felt anything weird when you held the sword." Rhea shook her head, and Roarke smiled and started down the stairs. "There's plenty weird around here."

Caching a draft in the still, empty room, Rhea followed tight after him.

Chapter Six: Entre Chien et Loup

Neither could have known the impact of the coming storm, nor how it would change them forever.

Walking up to the barns, Roarke explained his usual morning. "Ian works for me, but we share the farm duties quite a bit. If I'm gone, he does it all. He only has a few animals himself."

The next little while was a flurry of activity. Rhea jotted notes and followed Roarke. Finally, he took her to where he kept the feed in large metal trash bins and explained everything.

Roarke filled the duck and chicken water dishes and feeders, checking the oyster shell containers. He opened the small wire gate, let them out of the coops into the larger enclosure and scattered corn meal worms around the area. In the coops, he put down fresh sawdust and collected the eggs.

Rhea opened the small door of the barn to release the pigs into the pen between the two barns, fed and watered them. Finally, the small flock of sheep and trip of goats were watered and given their pellets, corn, and hay before given access to the rest of the land, where they could spread out and graze.

"They all graze together?"

Roarke petted a goat who wanted his attention. He caressed her ears and patted her head before answering. "Aye, Ian and I share our land to give them more space."

Back at the house, Roarke washed up and drank almost a

liter of water as Rhea added details to her notes. Being engrossed, she didn't notice when he left the kitchen until he stood at the door rubbing his hands together and changed into sweats. "Time to hit the gym."

"The gym?"

He gestured to the open door. "Follow me, my dear."

Walking toward the barn, they took a little path that led to a clearing in the woods, where, to her shock and delight, was an outdoor gym.

In the center was a large, plywood platform, which was two feet off the ground and covered by a peaked wooden roof, open on all sides. To the left was an obstacle course, with monkey bars, parallel bars, a pulley weighed down with concrete blocks, a long wooden bench, a chin-up bar, an old, beat-up punching bag, and a series of knotted ropes. To the right was a cart full of wood, tires, rocks, and rope. Outside the structure was a pile of wood, a chopping block, and a small woodpile.

"Wow!" She beamed as she gestured around her. Walking straight to the punching bag, she assaulted it with various kicks and punches.

"Hey! You've got some power in those strikes!" Roarke walked over to her. "Have you studied any martial arts?"

Rhea stopped and began walking around the area. "I started some Kung Fu training in China but only for a few months. My instructor was a stickler for obedience, and I've always hated being told what to do. One day, I took off my sweater because I was hot, and he told me to put it back on. I didn't see the point, so I kept it off. He kicked me out, telling the co-teacher I'd never be any good because I didn't understand the importance of following without questioning."

"Probably had something to do with your body temperature and your *qi*."

"Yes, I know. One of many things in my past that I wish I

could change." Rhea poked at the speed bag hanging above her head. "You made this place?"

"Aye." He grinned as he put on a pair of black fingerless gloves. "Built it myself."

"What do you do in the winter?"

"Same thing, only in snow."

Rhea didn't ask anything further. He had already begun with his exercises. Instead, she took the chopped wood, packed it into the wheelbarrow, and then caught up on her notes while watching him from under her lashes.

Eventually, Roarke stopped to drink, wiping his face as he watched her walk around the gym picking at various things. "Your son's eight?"

"He's really my nephew. My sister's son. She was young when she had him."

Sitting on the log, he gestured for her to sit with him. "You're raising him?"

"When Poppy died, everyone wanted him, but I'm his god-mother. That's why I returned home from Asia. I had gone there to get a fresh start and some cultural information, since those countries have such a long history and wealth of super-stitions and beliefs."

"You met, um, Patrice in Québec?"

"No, we met in Asia and bonded over our Québec connection. Patrice and I had been dating for a year and when I set out to return home, Pat came, too. He's from Québec, like my sister's husband, Pierre-Luc. At first, everyone was skeptical about us having Liam, but who better to raise him?"

"Why would they question you having him?"

Rhea arranged herself cross-legged on the log and turned to face him. "I hadn't lived home for years, and I didn't visit often. Pat was the same. He'd been living in Asia for five years."

"He was tired of being there?"

"Aren't you supposed to be exercising?"

"I need a break, and you're here to talk. Let's talk."

"Technically, I'm here to listen."

"Rhea, I don't trust many people, and I'm giving you a shot. Talk."

"Fine." She picked at a piece of bark. "I wanted to keep Liam in Québec City. He had a nice life there, and Pat always raved about the place. Liam's bilingual, as is Pat. There were many jobs for translators. We thought we could make a go of it."

"Let me get this straight, you'd only been dating for a year, and Patrice returned home to help you raise a child?"

"I told him he didn't have to make any promises, and we had no idea how to care for a child who'd had his little world destroyed. There was school, hockey practice, lunches, the whole shebang. We got jobs, an apartment, but we struggled, and it put a heavy strain on our relationship."

"You're still together?"

"No, we're not. We live in the same condominium complex, on the same floor. It's easy like that. We have the rule to keep our private lives private. I don't date, anyway."

He raised his eyebrows and looked at her. "Why not? You're a young woman."

"I don't want to. I want to focus on the things I'm doing. I barely have time to write, let alone date. It just complicates things, and Liam's had enough upheavals in his young life. I know Pat dates, but he feels the same way about Liam's life. He'll find someone, but I know he'll wait until Liam is older."

"That's impressive." Roarke stood up. "It's not even his son, and he's built his world around him."

"I guess we were both ready to stop dicking around and have a more grounded life. Pat and Liam fell in love with each other from day one."

"He never regretted it?"

"Not as far as I know. Patrice's childhood was precarious. He only saw his father a handful of times, but he knows how important it is for a boy to have a male role model. He's Liam's biggest cheerleader. Liam remembers his parents and misses them. He calls them Mommy and Daddy, and we're his Mom and Dad."

Roarke moved over to the punching bag and jabbed at it, startling her a little with the force of his punches.

"Patrice sounds like a good man."

"He is."

"My father left us when I was twelve." He cleared his throat.

"Really?"

"Yeah. Left my mother with three kids. Trevor was nine, and Tessa, my sister, was four."

"Must have been hard on your mother?"

"Aye, and I'm afraid for a while, I didn't make it easy on her."

"How so?"

Roarke was quiet for several, long seconds, staring down at his feet. "I blamed her for his leaving. They argued all the time, he never seemed to bring home enough money, and toward the end, my mother had stopped speaking to him altogether. She just regarded him with disdain. Nothing he did was good enough, and I suppose over time, he was sick of it."

"He left her alone with three kids."

"Oh, don't get me wrong, I'm not excusing what he did, I waited and waited for him to come home, or at least check on us. He never did. Eventually, I forgave my mother for what I felt were her mistakes. She always gave us unconditional love. It's just too bad she couldn't give that kind of love to him." He picked up his gloves, giving her a fleeting smile. "Water under the bridge."

"Is it?"

Turning, he bowed his head and put his hands on his hips. "In my experience, forgive me, but women give up on men too easily, expecting us to fulfill some idealistic fantasy of the dream guy and then blame us for disappointing them."

Rhea shook her head. "That's bullshit."

Choking on the mouthful of water he had just taken, Roarke coughed and looked down at her. "What? How's that bullshit? That's how I feel."

"I'm sorry you feel that way, but in my experience, men will find a way to blame women for anything, even their own faults and weaknesses. You all prefer to mold us into what you want and then scold us when you think we've failed. You want us intelligent, but not so intelligent as to upstage you. Beautiful, but then you mistrust us because other men look in our direction. Why are you all so desperate for a woman to need you? Men never know what they want from women."

"You don't seem to put men in high regard."

"Some men are spectacular, but they're few and far between. I'm single for a reason."

"As am I. Other than my mother and sister, every woman I've ever known has let me down."

"At least you're honest enough to admit that you keep women at a distance because you're afraid of being hurt again."

"I didn't say that." He furrowed his brow at her.

Taken a step closer to him, she looked him in the eye. "Yes, you did."

The silence stretched out between them until Roarke dropped his eyes and grinned at the ground. "Aye. I guess I did. Look, I've had a few serious relationships, but none ended well."

"Don't worry." Rhea threw him the towel he had left on the log. "I can write it in a way that makes you look like a man of stone with a scarred, bloodied heart."

He rolled his eyes and wiped his mouth with the towel. "Oh, excellent."

Picking up her notebook, she looked at the sky. "Your mother had to raise you alone."

"Aye. Ma worked two jobs, and I did what I could. That's why I'm such a top-notch cook. My shitty father didn't send us a cent, so while Ma worked, I cooked and cleaned."

"You were just a kid."

"I was always a serious kid, thirty when I was twelve. Some nights, Mother wouldn't get in until we were in bed. She'd tip-toe into our rooms and slide Mars bars under our pillows."

"That's so sweet."

Smiling, he wiped his forehead. "Aye, but one night, she tanned Trevor's hide because he'd gone under our pillows and stolen our Mars bars."

"Oh, no!" She smiled and covered her mouth with her hands.

"Oh, yes, but Trev never stole anything again."

"Did you ever hear from your father?"

"He tried to get in contact when we were older, especially when I got a little something to line my pockets. To hell with him. To hell with Patrice's father, too, for leaving him." He raised his water bottle. "To Patrice and all fathers like him."

She didn't have anything in her hand, so she just grinned and saluted. "To Patrice."

Roarke showered and changed. After a late lunch of salad and leftover chicken, they headed out so Rhea could see the land. White and black cows dotted the hills, grazing and lowing from time to time. Roarke had been telling her that his land ended at cliffs overlooking the sea in the other direction.

Looking up at the grey sky, he squinted. "The radio spoke

of a storm tonight."

A breeze stirred Rhea's hair, and she tucked the edges behind her ears. "Always a breeze here, eh?"

"Most of the time, which is a good thing, as the midges can't get around in the wind. They're busier at dusk and dawn."

"Crepuscular?"

"Aye, love that word." He stopped to watch a few goats scamper in a thicket of tall grass.

"Crepuscular animals. In Québec, there's an expression for the twilight time of day. *Entre chien et loup.*"

"What does that mean?" He had picked up a long stick and whipped the air. "Terribly sexy when you speak French, by the way." He poked her in the ribs with his elbow.

Ignoring the last comment, she jerked away from his elbow. "It means *"between dog and wolf."* Because of the dim, shadowy lighting of dusk, if you saw a creature in the distance, you'd be hard-pressed to say whether it was a dog or a wolf."

"Nice." He threw the stick, which flew end over end for a long distance.

"My friend Lisa told me the expression also has a deeper meaning. During the day, a dog is man's best friend, obedient to us, but as day turns to night, the blood of their wolf ancestors kicks in, and their true nature takes over. It's at twilight that they're *entre chien et loup.*

"Some nights, when wolves howl in the mountains, Pearl howls back. They're talking. The best music I've ever heard."

"Do you think she imagines herself running free?"

"Pearl's free to come and go as she pleases."

"You think so? Some ties that bind us aren't visible. She's bound to you as if she had actual ropes around her."

"Some people are bound, too, I guess." He smiled lightly. "We all feel the call of the wild sometimes."

"What's that?" she pointed to a dark form on the hill in front of them.

"Probably just Midas. He's Ian's Newfoundland dog and Pearl's mate."

"Are you sure it's him?"

"Yeah, it's him. Just sniffing out a rabbit or something."

The huge Newfoundland dog bounded down the hill toward them as Roarke continued. "Speaking of wolves, the ancient Romans believed if you wanted your love to last forever, you should consummate your relationship to the sound of wolves howling."

He glanced at Rhea to find her blushing and chuckled, "Sorry."

Roarke touched Rhea's arm to still her as the dog came running toward them. Neither of them noticed at first, but Roarke's hand dropped and for the slightest length of time, they were walking forward, holding hands.

After he realized it, he blushed and pulled his hand away. "Sorry, again." He mumbled before Midas collided with him, pushing him down onto the ground and planting his front paws on his chest. Then, lowering his nuzzle, he covered Roarke's face with licks as Roarke laughed and tried to push the heavy dog off.

The touch had been brief, but it had been enough to addle her thoughts and make her heart beat erratically.

Roarke hung up the phone and ran into the kitchen. Rhea almost dropped the pot she'd been drying.

"I have to go! Pearl's whelping."

Rhea grabbed her coat and ran through the door Roarke hadn't bothered to close. Scrambling into the passenger's seat, she hadn't even closed the door when Roarke pulled out of the drive.

"Shit, Roarke! You almost ripped the door off on the gatepost!"

"Then you should have closed it faster." He drove up the hill at a rate that scared her. "She's already had some. Ian didn't want to leave her, and he couldn't reach me. Times like these I do regret not having a mobile."

"Why don't you just get one?" Rhea braced herself from being thrown into the windshield every time they hit a pothole that sent them jostling all over the cab of the truck.

"I always misplace them. I even dropped one in a urinal. Besides, I hate that anyone can reach me at any time. I'd rather be unavailable until I want to be available. The exception being my family as they always know how to reach me. People are slaves to the bloody mobiles."

"I feel the same way." Rhea banged the back of her head on the window when they hit a pothole. "But, with a child, you need to have one."

Roarke glanced at her. "Maybe she should've had the pups at my house." He bit his bottom lip.

"Roarke, your dog's fine." She tried to reassure him. "Shouldn't you keep Midas away from the pups at first?" She remembered her parents had always separated the bitch and her puppies from the males when the pups were tiny.

"If the dogs are raised together, it shouldn't be a problem, and Midas has a gentle character. If either of them reacts badly, we'll take Midas with us."

When they pulled into the driveway of Ian's small, grey stone home, Ian met them at the door and ushered them into the back room where Pearl lay, looking exhausted, with her puppies. "She's finished."

"How many?" Roarke smiled down at Pearl and rubbed her gently.

"Six, well, seven really." He picked up a small lump in the corner. "This last wee one didn't make it."

In his hands was a small black pup, his eyes closed, and his little white-pink tongue stuck out. The tiny body was stiff as a board, little legs sticking out rigidly.

"How long ago was he born?" Rhea asked Ian, reaching for the puppy.

Ian handed it to her apprehensively. "Not that long, though it's hard to say. I thought she was finished, so I left for a few minutes. When I returned, I found this guy. Pearl had gotten him out of his sack, but it was too late."

"It might not be. Do you have another hand towel?"

Ian handed her a clean towel, and Rhea vigorously rubbed the pup's back and sides.

"What're you doing?" Roarke looked as if he thought what she was doing was obscene.

"I saw my mother do this a few times when one of our huskies had a stillborn. Sometimes you can revive them."

She continued to rub the pup as she spoke, turning him over to do his chest and stomach. Cupping the pup in her hands, his face toward her fingers, she raised her hands over her head and brought them down hard in the air. "The force might loosen what's in his chest." She repeated the motion as the men sat on stools and watched her, casting each other wary glances.

Rhea placed her mouth over the small snout, breathing into his tiny lungs before returning to her rubbing, and then used two fingers to press under the little rib cage. Altering between rubbing, pressing, and breathing, she worked on the small pup until Roarke grabbed Ian by the wrist.

"Look, he's not as stiff!"

The tiny black lump began to lull its head around, its little legs flopping with Rhea's movements.

"His head's moving!" exclaimed Ian.

Rhea paused to press her ear to the tiny chest. "I can hear fluid on his lungs, but that's a good thing. He's breathing."

Rhea never stopped until the pup mulled and protested his treatment. The entire time, Pearl watched. About fifteen minutes after she started, Rhea placed the wiggling, black lump close to his mother's face so Pearl could clean him.

Ian hopped out of his stool. "I'll go get a bottle. That deserves a toast." He headed out of the room and into the hallway.

"That was incredible." Roarke looked at Rhea with an unveiled look of awe. "Don't let me ever call you prissy again."

"He should be okay. He's strong. I think his size is why he didn't get enough air. He was just so big, and Pearl so exhausted." She shook out her ponytail and ran her fingers through the ends.

Roarke pulled a straw of hay out of her hair while running strands of her hair through his fingers.

The sound of glass clinking announced Ian's arrival, and they pulled their heads away from each other just as Ian rounded the corner, a bottle in one hand and a stack of three glasses in the other. His black eyes were alight with humor. "I've got the perfect name for the wee tyke."

Roarke took a glass for himself and Rhea. "What's that?"

Ian grinned at them. "I'd have thought it obvious."

Roarke and Rhea gave him withering looks.

Ian sat down and lit a cigarette, letting out a stream of smoke before answering, "Lazarus, of course."

Back at White Heather, Roarke handed Rhea a glass of wine.

A glow had come over his entire countenance, his dark, handsome face split with a huge grin that made her feel as if her legs had turned to butter, and her hand shook as she reached for her wine.

Raising his glass. "To the pups and wee Lazarus."

"The pups and wee Laz."

"How do you like your steaks?" He picked up a set of tongs.

"Medium-rare." She looked at the dark red meat with fine marbling. "Aberdeen Angus Beef."

"Scotch fillet," he corrected, glancing at her from under his eyelashes as he took out a device that reminded Rhea of a cat, with a square face and suction cups for feet.

"What the Devil is that?"

"A French fry cutter. Weston." Pulling back the tail of the cat — the lever — he placed a potato in the middle, pushed it forward, and perfect French fries emerged from the other side.

"Fun."

She reached for a potato. Roarke stepped behind her and slid his index finger down the neck of her t-shirt, pressing against the soft skin of her back.

Goosebumps spread over her body, and she spun around. "Hey!" She found herself very close to him, and though she pressed against the island, he didn't step back.

"Your tag was up." He looked down at her and pulled another straw of hay out of her hair. "You're a mess." Then, smoothing down some errant hairs on the top of her head, his hand slid down the length of her ponytail. "Your hair is very fine."

Struggled to breathe, Rhea froze on the spot until he stepped back and turned his attention to the steak, rolling up his sleeves to reveal muscular forearms lined with veins.

Roarke didn't see her blush as she sat on the stool and watched him work. "Roarke, would you call yourself a farmer?"

"The farmers here would laugh if I called myself a farmer or a crofter."

"What's a crofter?"

"A small-scale agricultural practice." He turned back to the sink. "Farming here is difficult because of the weather. You have to farm as the weather allows, learning from those who worked and shaped the land before you. When you're stockmen, it gets tricky with the summer rains. With the number of animals they have, a lot of damage gets done to the wet earth."

A few minutes later, they were sitting at the island, each with a plate of succulent steak, chips, and peas. Rhea refilled their wine glasses. "Getting money for the shelter is the main reason you're returning to films, or is it for the farm?"

Picking up his steak knife and fork and smiling mysteriously, he cut into his steak.

"You're going to leave me hanging?" With the first piece of steak in her mouth, her eyes closed in pleasure, as it was rich, buttery, and meaty.

"The castle."

"Da cas-el?" she exclaimed through a large mouthful of beef, covering her mouth with her hand. "Wha cas-el?"

Roarke chuckled. "Alloway Castle." He speared several chips with his fork. "I want to buy it and restore it. The kids can help, and it has a lot of potential."

"What would you do with it?"

"Attract tourists, train, and give jobs to the kids and people in the area. Make an inn out of it, and I could set up my artifacts on display, but first, I've got to buy it from the twins."

"Agnes and Senga?"

"Oh, aye, I'd forgotten you met them. The castle's right up your alley. Apparently, full to the brim with ghosts."

She managed to tear her eyes away from her plate to look up at him in interest.

"Tell you what. I'll get the keys in the morning and take you."

"To the castle."

"Aye."

"Really?"

"Yes." He chuckled. "Would you enjoy that?"

"Very much."

"You want to do some research while you're here. Spirits and banshees?"

"Myths and beliefs evolve in society as a form of protection. In a society governed by ritual, a community connected by shared beliefs, our myths and legends evolve as we evolve. Our ability to predict the future is part of what makes human beings intelligent."

"What does predicting the future have to do with it?"

"We have superstitions to be able to foretell what's coming and try to change what we don't like. We look for correlations between the natural world and future events.

"Very interesting."

"Scotland's a kind of mysterious place, isn't it? The waves make eerie sounds as they crash against the shore. The glens are full of mist, and the lochs are deep and murky. Who knows what lurks in their depths? Now that I'm here, I can feel it. It's like the land itself is alive and breathing."

A short time later, Roarke gathered their dishes, placing them next to the sink. He took out a bowl of strawberries and a container of heavy cream and brought them to the table.

Rhea got up and went to the small bar to get the whisky decanter and a glass.

Laughing, he asked, "Am I so predictable? Grab a glass for yourself. You need to learn to appreciate whisky."

"Okay, just a little glass."

"Concerning what we were talking about," Roarke began. "I've always thought the Highlands, in particular, to be kind of sublime. The way the wind blows over the hills, how powerless you feel in a strong gale, how small you feel on top of a mountain."

Rhea stuck out the tip of her tongue, catching a drop of cream on her bottom lip. "I was once discussing the sublime with a friend of mine. He told me he hates the seashore because when he looks at the ocean, it reminds him of his sins."

Roarke looked up as a sad expression passed across his face, and he exhaled deeply. Feeling the need to change the subject, Rhea took a sip of her drink and winced. "This whisky is very nice."

"Your face is very descriptive, you know."

"It's just strong, and I'm not used to it."

"Take your fruit and glass, go in by the fire, and I'll be right behind you."

Rhea watched the flames and listened to the wind howl outside until Roarke returned with a glass of water and a straw. He sat on the small coffee table in front of her and asked for her whisky. Taking the straw into his mouth, he sucked up some water and blocked the end with the tip of his finger. Holding it over her glass, he put four or five drops into it. In the glow of the firelight, his eyes burned a rich amber, almost the exact shade of the whisky.

After giving the whisky a little stir, he handed it back to Rhea. "Now, give it a sip."

Glancing at Roarke over the rim, she took a pull of whisky. Something had changed in the flavor, and she raised her eyebrows at him, thinking that some of the water might have been in his mouth. "It tastes different. Earthy and fruity, and my mouth feels a little dry."

"It's a dry whisky." He stretched out his legs in front of the fire. "From Aberdeen. There're five major Scotch regions in Scotland, but I prefer those distilled in the Highlands. You can taste the heather."

"Is that the earthy taste? It might sound strange, but the whisky tastes as you smell."

"Jesus. I better get my drinking sorted out if I'm starting to sweat whisky."

She laughed. "No, I mean you smell woodsy and mossy. Like, I guess, heather."

He gave a non-committal shrug of his shoulder and popped out his bottom lip a little. "I guess there are worse things to smell of."

"Strange how water can change everything." She drank a little deeper the second time.

"It's chemistry. The chains of amino acids in the whisky are tightly wound, and the water relaxes them. Brings out the flavor. Opens it up."

Rhea lifted her glass to study the whisky's color in the light of the fire, and the neck of her t-shirt fell toward one side, exposing her shoulder and prominent clavicle. When she glanced at Roarke, she saw that he was smiling slightly and staring where her shirt had fallen.

"Yup," he muttered, lightly licking his bottom lip. "You can't fight chemistry."

Chapter Seven: Mysteries of the Night

I was desperate for the sun and the wind in my hair. I was kept in that horrid castle for weeks because I advised my maid about her sick child. What good Christian man would want me if I clung to old pagan beliefs? That is how he justified my punishment.

What did my father know about being a good Christian? Mother says the Lord puts the plants and animals here for us and puts knowledge in our heads. Father punishes us for practicing the ancient ways.

My mind had turned very dark, and I needed to feel the earth, wind, and water. At the river, I thought of how the rocks I would put in my pockets would sink me, and I could walk along the bottom, my hair and skirts flowing behind me in the current.

Hearing the twig snap, I turned to find him there, watching me, the quiet boy from the village with strange blue eyes.

"Go and leave me in peace."

"I will if you smile. Just once."

'You are wasting your breath. I am immune to the words of men."

"Are you immune to the bites of clegs? Two of them just landed on either side of your head."

I jumped to my feet and started swatting at my head like a madwoman, only to find him bent over with laughter. I picked up some pebbles, pelting him. A few minutes later, we were sitting in the grass on the edge of the burn, holding our sides with laughter and trying to catch our breath.

"Your laugh is just as lovely as your smile."

His fingers reached up to twirl a tendril of my hair around his finger, and I let him.

R hea was tired, but Roarke was so open and speaking without reservation that she didn't want to waste the moment. "How did you get into acting?"

"At eighteen, I ran into my old drama teacher, and she convinced me to try out for a part in a local play. I met a few people after that, got a manager, and worked for a few years. Finally, a film was looking for a tall guy to play a thug. I got the part, and that started everything."

"When did you change your name?"

"When I got that first part in the local play. I didn't want to use my real name because I still had some ties to old friends."

"When did you go to The States?"

"At the end of my twenty-first year, I moved to LA. A studio was looking for a tall, European man to lead their latest action film. I got the part, and the movie was a hit. Before I knew it, I was making movies one after the other."

"Those must have been exhilarating times."

"They were. If I wasn't filming, I was training. I loved it. I studied martial arts, boxing, sword-fighting, guns, everything, but the luster soon wore off. In a short time, I found I was losing sight of who I was. I was becoming someone I didn't recognize."

"Living a lie?"

"Absolutely. I started to feel worthless, even if I had all of this money." Roarke leaned forward a little. "I looked around me, and all I saw were desperate people spending money on things they didn't want. I'd practically gone into hiding and spent my downtime camping and hiking."

"But you stayed?"

"I stayed, but the movies eventually became monotonous. Of course, people still wanted to see them, but for me, it was the same thing over again with the same people."

"Did you try doing different types of films?"

He rolled his eyes at her. "Of course, I tried, but Niall had become so much of an icon that I had become typecast. No one could see me as anything else."

Rhea got up to refill her glass, stretching as she did so, and settled back into her chair. "When did you leave?"

"Ten years was enough. I had invested wisely when the time was right. I came home."

"Never regretted it?"

"Not for a millisecond." His hand beat a light tattoo on his knee. "Being homesick and lonely are terrible feelings. Have you ever felt that way?"

Rhea felt very comfortable, as if she could talk about anything. The crackling and popping of the fire in the otherwise quiet room held power to make anyone pensive. Looking down at her hands and then back up at him, she admitted, "From time to time."

Draining his glass, Roarke stood up, stretching. "Okay, you, off to bed, and I'm going to check on everything before it gets too dark. Bad weather's coming."

"Can I come?" She brightened.

"I'd rather you stayed here. The weather might be getting nasty."

"Don't be silly."

He chuckled. "Sure. Grab your sweater."

Despite the hour, the sky was not completely dark, and the soft light of twilight had come over the land. A slight ridge of pink sunset outlined the horizon.

As they walked toward the barn, a fine mist spread along the edge of the forest in spite of the wind that had picked up. Roarke came back to where she stood.

"Wondering what's in there?" He stood watching her with his hands stuck in the pockets of his jeans.

Nodding, she never took her focus off the forest's edge, her imagination alive with a sense of foreboding, curiosity, fear, and something else. A mad urge to run. To run deep into the forest as fast as she could, feeling the chill of the mist on her skin and tree limbs pulling at her hair.

Roarke stood directly behind her, looking down at the top of her hair.

"Banshees." Roarke's whispered word echoed inside her skull, his deep, husky voice vibrated her eardrum, and a cold shiver passed through her entire body. His warm breath passed along the back of her neck, stirring the tiny hairs at the base of her hairline.

"I felt you shiver, Ghost. Someone just walked over your grave," he whispered as he turned to walk away. "Could be the *Bean Nighe.*"

"The what?" Rhea still hadn't moved.

Roarke stopped and turned around. "She's much the same as a banshee."

"Tell me." She turned from the woods and stepped toward him.

"The Old Washer-Woman. She washes clothes covered in blood near creeks and streams. The clothes she's washing are those of one of your family members who's going to die. Some say they're the spirits of women who have died in childbirth, locked in their pain and grief for all time."

"I don't know why those old female creatures scare me so much."

"I know. Living, breathing women scare me enough, let alone the ones in spirit form."

"Funny, Roarke," she scoffed. "Seriously, is there anything that scares you? Some irrational fear you have?"

"Well." He looked down at his feet as he walked. "I will admit I'm not too fond of rodents, mice, rats, that kind of creature."

"Really?" She grinned. "Any reason for that?"

"Let's just say I had a few run-ins with some rats that I care not to talk nor even think about."

Something about the strained tremor in his voice kept her from asking anything further.

They made their way around the farm as Roarke checked the animals and shut everything tight for the evening.

Rhea walked again toward the small wood, watching the mist dance at the edges. Soon she was aware of heavy footsteps behind her and Roarke softly humming a song. She felt uncomfortable walking ahead of him, so she started to whistle.

"Shouldn't whistle into the wind. You'll bring the storm." A strong gust of wind rustled the grass and hit them, causing Rhea to stumble to the side of the path.

"Careful now." Roarke steadied her by holding her elbow. "You're slight, and the wind could carry you off."

As he stood with his eyes closed, hands on his hips, breathing deeply, Roarke's handsome face was almost horizontal with the heavens. "Aye, a storm's coming." He righted his head and looked at her with a wide grin, pointing his finger accusingly. "You're what caused it."

"My father used to say, "A woman that whistles and a hen that crows bring bad luck wherever she goes." Grinning, she turned and whistled as she walked back to the house.

"Stop whistling, Rhea!"

They walked toward the dying light of the sun playing on the hills.

"You have red in your hair, it almost turns burgundy in certain light," he commented as he closed in the space between them. "It smells so nice, powdery and flowery."

Unaware that he was so close behind, Rhea lost her footing again as the ground descended slightly. Strong arms shot around her waist and upper arm to prevent her from falling.

"You all right?"

The chill evening air made her very aware of the heat coming off his long frame. Every place where his body touched hers, she tingled.

"Watch your step. The grass is quite slippery."

Roarke released her and took the last few steps to the cottage, but she could still feel the places where his hands had touched her body.

Later, as Roarke undressed for bed, the sky opened up, and heavy rain pounded on the roof and windowpanes. Settling his long frame in the feather bed and pulling up the heavy white duvet against his chest, he laced his fingers behind his head and lay there listening to the rain and wind. Trying to sleep, he chastised himself on how his hand had lingered on the curve of her waist and he had begun having many warm thoughts about the young woman asleep in the next room. Then, turning onto his side, he forced himself to concentrate on the sounds of the storm, and eventually he fell into a deep sleep.

The loud crash of broken glass roused him from a nightmare, and a blood-curling scream rend the air.

The sound of a woman crying had lured Rhea into the dark woods. She couldn't see a hand in front of her face through the mist which clung to every tree branch. Even though the sound came from very nearby, she could not locate the woman.

Over her shoulder, she felt, rather than heard, someone behind her. As she felt warm breath on her neck, the air around her was suddenly sweet, fresh, and scented. Then she heard a woman whisper, "Wake up. Wake up."

Rhea didn't move, as the sweet air around her was so soothing, but the next time the woman spoke, it was much louder, "Wake up, now!"

Jerking herself awake, she was startled to hear scratching and thumping on the glass of her window. Thoughts of the *Bean Nighe* sprang to her mind, and in her fright, she rolled off her bed. She alit on her feet just as a large branch came crashing through the window, showered glass everywhere and landed on her pillow, exactly where her head had been.

When Roarke burst into the room, she was still screaming. He rounded the bed to stand in front of her, grasped her shoulders, and pulled her toward him. "Rhea, what happened?"

When he bent his knees to look at her face, she was as stiff as a board. He let go of one of her shoulders and cupped her chin, forcing her to look up at him. "Rhea, snap out of it! Answer me!"

Shaking her lightly, she blinked a few times. He grabbed a blanket and wrapped it around her shoulders.

"Panic attack," she gasped, clutching the blanket tightly.

"Rhea, a tree branch fell through your window. You're in shock, not a panic attack."

"Same . . . feeling." Her breathing was still ragged but was starting to regulate.

"Did you get any glass on you?"

"I'm fine. I was already out of bed when the branch came through the window."

She screamed again as a gust of wind broke another piece from the windowpane, showering more glass on the floor. Rain poured in, forming a puddle.

Pressing herself against him, she crossed her arms over her chest, clutching the blanket to her. When his arms went around her, she flattened her face against his chest and let go of the blanket, her hands running up his back, pushing her body closer.

Cradling her against him, Roarke buried one hand in her hair. The other hand rubbed her back, tracing a path from her shoulder blades to the gentle swell of her bottom. All the while he whispered reassuring words into her ear. "You're all right. Everything's fine."

Roarke continued to hold her until her body relaxed. Then he whispered, "I'm going to let you go. I need to board up that window." He pulled back from her just enough to cup her chin again and bring her gaze up to his. "Will that be okay?"

Rhea was suddenly aware that he wasn't wearing a shirt, and she could feel the muscles of his chest under his light chest hair. When Roarke ran his hand down the length of her back, she stiffened, pulling away from him, and he let her go.

Picking the discarded blanket off the floor, she wrapped it back around her shoulders. "I'm fine. You can go."

"Okay." He quickly scanned her face again. "If you're sure you're all right, I'll be right back."

"I'm okay." She hoped she sounded more confident than she felt.

"You should go out into the sitting room. I'll take care of things here."

"Can I help?"

Turning toward her, he smiled. "Thank you for offering, but please go to the sitting room."

Making her way out into the hallway, she turned back to look at him, the muscles of his arms and back tightening as he maneuvered to push the branch out. His loose pajama pants rode low on his hips, accentuating his slender waist and the curves of his muscular bottom.

A short time later, Rhea was drinking water in the kitchen when Roarke walked from the hallway toward the door. "I need to board up that window. You stay here."

"No, I'll come and help you." She made a move to follow him.

He spun around. "No," he practically growled. "Stay here. I mean it."

Wellingtons and rain jacket on, he headed out the front door. She watched him from the kitchen window as he ran up to the shed and then came back down with a large piece of plywood under one arm and a toolbox in the other, rain pelting down on him.

Back into the room, Rhea listened to Roarke hammering the plywood in place and swearing as she gathered each corner of the sheet and pulled the blankets off the bed. She had just finished cleaning up the glass and water, when Roarke burst through the kitchen door, slamming it shut behind him.

Leaning his back against the door, he closed his eyes, panting to catch his breath. A second later, his eyes opened, and he turned his head to glare at her. "I told you not to whistle into the wind!"

"Hell! We haven't had a storm like this in years." Roarke struggled to get out of his rain jacket and stormed down the hallway to change his clothes.

Returning, he was pleased to find that Rhea had built a fire, filling the small area with warm heat. Seating himself in his favorite brown chair, he gladly accepted a tumbler of whisky Rhea handed him.

"Thank you." He placed a hand on each armrest as Rhea laid the blanket, knitted by his mother, across his long legs, then turned toward the sofa. The lamp behind her silhouetted her figure, and he caught the subtle curves of her body as she arranged herself on the couch, her feet tucked under her.

"What? You're looking at me funny."

"Am I?" He turned to look at the fire, hoping the orange glow would hide his blush.

"I've cleaned up the mess as best I could. I'll finish the rest in the morning."

"I like what you have on." He gave her a mischievous, lop-sided grin. Her long white nightgown's drawstring neck was open around her shoulders, displaying a beautiful clavicle, prominent and defined.

"Don't start flirting with me, Roarke McCallum." She squirmed into a more comfortable position and looked him in the eye. "If you remember, I'm immune to your Scottish charm."

"Oh, I remember." He smiled, not taking his focus off her.

Rhea pulled her knees up under her gown. "Mother always called it a shift. Nothing more comfortable."

"It makes you look like a lady from a storybook." Roarke turned his attention to the fire. "Why were you out of bed?"

"What do you mean?"

"You said you were already out of bed when the branch fell. Why had you gotten up?"

"I had a dream." She picked her wine glass off the end table. "I'll tell you about it, but you have to promise not to scoff at me."

"Of course."

"I was in the forest, and a woman was crying. I couldn't find her, but then I heard a woman telling me to wake up. I jumped out of bed just before the branch came through the window."

"You heard a woman?" He dipped his finger into his whisky, then circled the edge of his glass, making an eerie singing that echoed in the quiet of the cottage. "Sometimes I hear a woman's voice when I am half asleep, and I've had two lady friends tell me they've seen a woman in the house."

"Lady friends?" She stammered over her words. "Di-did she scare them?"

"She appeared behind one in the bathroom mirror and the other at the end of the hallway." He enjoyed the fact that Rhea looked a little startled.

"What did she look like?" she asked, her eyes dancing with interest.

"A young woman in a long, loose dress, with hair that hung below her waist. She had an angry look."

"Roarke, you're saying this to frighten me."

"You don't feel afraid here?"

"No. I have a variety of feelings here, but fear isn't one of them."

"Maybe my ghost likes you." He got up to refill his glass. "Who wouldn't?"

"I have to tell you, I've been sensing panic attacks coming on since I've been here. Small indications of panic. Shortness of breath, pounding heart. I want you to know just in case I have one."

"If you do, what can I do?"

"Not much. Just wait it out. Maybe just hold my hand and remind me that it'll be over soon. Attacks usually last from five to ten minutes, and I might feel drained when it's over."

"Doug's sister, Cheryl, gets them. When she was young, she thought her panic attacks were her body reacting to a supernatural presence—kind of a fight-or-flight reaction. Like if a dog attacked you, you would react with similar symptoms. The body senses danger even if none is present. She knows better now, but she's still interested in the supernatural."

"Yes, I've often found that the attack comes with a sense of unreality. Detachment from the world. Most people who have attacks have a sensitive temperament."

"Do you know why you get them?"

Rhea swallowed hard but dropped her gaze and shook her head.

"When Cheryl was young, in her teens, she was with a young man who was abusive to her. Her therapist says that may be why she has the attacks. The body can sense danger, and in her case, she was sensing real danger day and night."

"I have no idea why it happens to me," she snapped. "I just wanted you to know because it's embarrassing when it happens."

"I'm glad I know."

"Not meaning to change the subject, but since you brought up lady friends, if you ever wanted to have a date or anything, I could make myself scarce."

Chuckling, he raised his eyebrows. "I don't like to have women at my house. Social calls are few and far between."

"Why's that?"

"Most women are either high maintenance or crazy. Meaning no offense."

"None taken."

Rhea looked about to ask him another question when he remembered the event he had to attend and leaned forward, slapping his thigh. "Bugger! I completely forgot about that!"

"What?"

"Just remembered something I have to do." He shook his head. "I'll tell you about it in the morning."

Roarke stood up from the chair. "Go sleep in my bed. I'll sleep here."

Rhea laughed. "No way can you sleep here. You wouldn't even fit one of your legs on the couch."

"Don't be daft. I can't let you sleep out here." Roarke screwed up his face.

"I'm *so* comfortable. I can sleep anywhere. I once fell asleep standing up on a crowded train in Japan." Pulling up the blanket, she rested her head on the pillow she had taken from her room. "Roarke, I know you think it ungentlemanly to have me sleep here, but it isn't."

He put up his hands in submission. "Okay. I'll get your window fixed tomorrow."

"I have no doubt." She smiled up at him with such a calm,

sweet expression that it was all he could do not to touch her. Instead, he reached down and adjusted the blanket around her foot. "Right then. My Lady Whisky and I are off to bed. Sleep well and try not to think of the *Bean Nighe*." *It wouldn't be the worst thing in the world if she got too scared to sleep alone.*

The sound of the storm still raged outside, but he was sure he heard her mutter *bastard* as he entered the hallway.

The following day, Roarke walked a few paces to the hallway. "Rhea?"

"Yes?" She stuck her head out the door, hair still a little messy from sleep.

"Could you make up a quick breakfast and fill a thermos while I do my chores and tell Ian we'll be up at the castle today?"

"No problem, but what about the window?"

"It can keep for a day. You know, last night when I was outside your window, I could smell that strange odor that passes around here from time to time, but this morning, it's gone again."

"Dead animal?"

"No." He tipped up his hat to scratch his forehead. "I've smelled it before, just can't figure out where it comes from. Did you smell anything?"

"I could smell something, but it was great like fruit pastries, but I did feel a chill or something. Almost like a cold breeze lifting my hair."

Bacon sandwiches in hand, they drove east around the bends in the hard-packed gravel road, toward the castle.

Roarke enjoyed the peaceful drive, chuckling to himself every few moments as Rhea's head bobbed around tiredly.

"Rhea, rest your head. You're exhausted."

"No. I need to stay awake. I might miss something."

"Miss Nosey!" He laughed.

Jutting out her chin, she grinned. "I'll sleep when I'm home."

A few minutes later, she was sound asleep, head lolling to the side on the soft leather of the seat. Roarke turned into the narrow stretch of land facing a lovely loch and turned off the truck. He knew Rhea would want to see it but did not wake her. Taking off the heavy plaid shirt he wore over his t-shirt, he lifted her head and slid the makeshift pillow under it, and she didn't budge.

Looking out over the loch and the small, rust-colored cliffs to one side, surrounded by original Caledonian pine, he rolled down the window and breathed in the fresh air. No place on Earth fed his soul like his native land. His mother had played along the shore of this loch with her father and brothers. Roarke reminded himself every day of how blessed he was.

Resting his head, he looked over the land until sleep overtook him, and his eyes closed.

When Rhea awoke, she saw two things she had never seen before — the fascinating colors surrounding the loch, and Roarke sleeping. In the crook formed between the headrest and the window, his face was turned toward her, his fingers interlaced across his chest, and his strong face mellow and tender. The tiny lines around his eyes and mouth were relaxed, and his lips parted. In addition to the scar splitting his right eyebrow, she could see numerous others.

The rain pitter-pattering on the roof of the truck intensified, and realizing Roarke's window was open, she reached across him to roll up it up as quietly as possible. He didn't wake, and she was so close to him that she could smell his clean masculine scent. It made her think of his body wash called forest dew. *Fitting.*

Leaning over his mouth, she thought how easy it would be

to press her lips against his or nestle her nose in the deep groove beneath his Adam's apple. Without warning, his hand grasped the curve of her hip, and his brown eyes opened, gazing at her with an intensity that made her insides turn to butter.

His other hand came to rest on the side of her face, and he whispered, "What're you doing?"

Embarrassed, she mumbled that his window had been down and hopped back into the passenger seat.

Roarke laughed. "Thanks for closing it, but for a moment there, I'd thought you had finally succumbed to my charms."

"Don't be an idiot, Roarke," she blurted out before she could stop herself, and then clapped her hand over her mouth.

Laughing, he leaned toward her. "It's okay, Rhea. I *am* an idiot." He leaned back into his seat, rubbing his wet shoulder. "Just having a bit of fun with you."

"You seem to enjoy doing that." She scowled at him as she reached behind her and pulled out his plaid shirt. "Yours?"

"Aye. Your head was at an awkward angle."

The keys jingled as he moved, and she turned to him. "Why did you stop here?"

"I knew you wouldn't want to miss this. I swam here as a child, as my mother grew up near here."

"You pulled over so I wouldn't miss it?"

"I know how nosey you are." He turned the key in the ignition.

"Thank you." She looked over her shoulder at the loch again. "You're kind to me."

"Please don't write about how kind I am." He rolled his eyes. "I've a reputation as an arsehole to keep up. You write that I'm kind and soft, and the next thing interviewers will start asking me who my favorite poets are."

"Contemporary poets like Kathleen Jamie and Robin Robertson."

"How the hell do you know that?" His shocked yell filled the small cab, causing her to start in her seat.

"Those were the books open on your coffee table when I arrived," she explained in a loud voice. "And your bookshelf was one of the first things I investigated."

He chortled and shook his head.

"Can I keep your shirt for a while? My sweater's in the back, and I'm a little chilly."

Still grinning, he nodded.

"Thank you."

"Pleasure."

Rhea curled under his plaid shirt, her nose beneath its collar. It occurred to her that they had become comfortable with each other, sharing an easy intimacy. It both elated and terrified her.

CHAPTER EIGHT: DAGGERS

They will be arriving soon, and I will be ready.

Once on the road, Roarke informed Rhea that they were driving across an extinct volcano. Their progress was hindered on the twisty, single-track road, and they sometimes had to pull over and yield the right of way to other vehicles.

Eventually, Roarke pulled the truck into a small carport near a trail leading down to the sea. "The castle is still a ways away, but I thought you might like to see this beach. I come here quite a bit to collect my thoughts."

Vast patches of long blue-green beach grasses, which Roarke said were marram and sea Lyme, were interspersed among cresting dunes down a long stretch of coastline. Spread out in a crescent of gleaming, golden-white shell sand, it stretched along the margin of the turquoise bay. Cliffs edged one end, supporting a small picturesque town. A spattering of large rocks sat into the sand amid numerous rock pools and sea sculptures, creating a dramatic seascape.

Two men stood beside a small fire close to three small tents staked on the edge of grass, and their laughter reached Rhea and Roarke on top of the hill.

Rhea turned to Roarke to tell him how lovely the beach was but paused at his expression. He stood with his hands on his hips. As he stared down on the men, a look of intense anger marred his handsome features, giving him a perilous, savage look.

Before she could react, he stormed off down the sandy hill

toward the men, arms swinging to maintain his balance on the sandy slope.

Their laughter died away as they saw the large man coming down the hill. One casually folded his arms across his chest, while the other stood with legs spread, both heads tilted back, looking as if they meant business.

Roarke halted about five feet before them, and Rhea, who had scrambled to keep up, stopped when Roarke did. His voice was deep and ominous when he spoke. "What're you hooligans doing here?"

The tall, thin man with a handlebar mustache on his angular, aggressive face replied, "Minding our own business, which is what you should be doing."

"You're not allowed to have an open fire on this beach."

"We'll cover it in and pick up the litter before we leave, if it's any of your concern." The older, square-shouldered, bearded man took a step closer to Roarke.

"What if the wind picks up and flankers hit the grass?"

"It just stopped raining, you daft idiot! Nothing is going to catch fire."

"Daft idiot, is it? Just for that, I'm going to call the authorities.

"It's going to be hard if you've got a hand full of broken fingers."

"Who's going to break them? You?"

"Aye. It'll be me."

Rhea stood in shock behind Roarke, watching open-mouthed. *What the hell does he think he's doing?* She barely had time to form the thought when their angry looks changed into broad grins.

Roarke's shoulders were shaking with laugher, and he stepped forward to clasp the hand of the muscular man, "Ah, Mike, I had you scared for a minute."

"As if I'd ever be scared of the likes of you."

"Why didn't you tell me you fellas were going camping?"

"I spoke to Ian the other day, and he told me you were going to be out of commission for a few weeks. Someone coming to write a book about you?" the tall man replied.

"Why anyone would want to read that, I don't know," said the other with a laugh.

"Oh, right. Shit! Sorry, Rhea." He motioned for her to come forward.

She did, though apprehensively.

"Fellas, this is Rhea. She's a writer staying with me for a few weeks. Rhea, this is Mike." He pointed to the older man, who regarded her thoughtfully, almost suspiciously.

"I'm Ken." The tall, thin young man grinned at her, dimples popping out all over his face.

"I'd know that voice anywhere." An ample backside popped out the door of the nearest tent, and Rhea and Roarke both grinned when Doug turned around.

"Rhea." Roarke came to stand behind her, one hand resting on her shoulder. "These are my old, dear friends. We camp together, but they seem to have left me out of this trip."

"What are you complaining about? You'd rather look at Mike's old, wrinkled face than this young lady's?"

"No, I'm not complaining. Just hate to miss a good meal."

"You haven't missed anything yet. We just got back from a walk on the high rocks.

"Aye, there's plenty, if you'd both like to stay." Doug tipped his hat at Rhea. "The lighthouse keeper brought us down a nice piece of venison to repay Mike for helping him with his car. Ken went up to the store and got everything he needs to make his famous venison stew."

"I'm going to have enough to feed twenty." Ken was speaking to Roarke but still looking at Rhea. "And the wife fitted me out with a huge bag of buns."

"I'm making my famous sandwiches," Doug added.

"Wouldn't want to impose, and we don't have anything to share."

Rhea touched him on the elbow. "Actually, I picked up some cookies and pastries when we stopped for gas."

"You did?"

"I figured I'd grab us some snacks. If I've learned anything in the past few days, it's that I don't want to be stuck anywhere with you if you have no food."

"See there, no problem." Doug took Rhea by the arm. "We were missing dessert. So nice to see you again, Rhea. Come over and sit by the fire."

Looking over her shoulder at him as Doug led her to the fire, Roarke put his hands in the air. "I guess we're staying."

Soon everyone was chatting amicably, except for Mike, who Rhea thought was a little standoffish. When the subject of politics came up, she politely excused herself, saying she wanted to explore the high rocks and build her appetite.

Rhea skipped over the rocks, as she had grown up on a rocky beach. She had seated herself on the edge of a large rock looking out over the sea when Roarke came up behind her.

"Are you not supposed to stay with me at all times?"

"I grew up on a beach like this." Rhea muttered. "I don't think Mike likes me much. He's barely spoken to me."

"Oh, don't mind him. He's an old grump. I've always suspected he's a bit afraid of women."

Roarke walked over to a large patch of tall seagrass, the wind tossing it back and forth.

Rhea stood and joined him. "My mother would say the wind is making love to the grass."

"She sounds like an interesting woman."

"Oh, yeah." She laughed. "She would've had your ticket from day one."

"What do you mean?"

"She was dark and beautiful. Sexy without trying. Men loved her, and she would've had you wrapped around her finger in no time."

"Without a doubt. Her daughter certainly did."

Rhea grinned and rolled her eyes at him. "Not in the same way."

"That's what you think," Roark muttered before pointing to a dark area in the cliff face. "See that hole?"

Rhea nodded.

"In the seventeenth century, a man and his wife settled in that cave. It goes back about two hundred yards. The lowest kind of characters, evil and depraved. They had a load of children, numerous grandkids, and great grandkids, most being born of incest. They resorted to robbing people and eating their flesh, becoming cannibals. They emerged at night to find victims. Eventually, they were sentenced to die for their crimes, and every family member was killed, except for one daughter who had married a boy from a village not far away."

"What an awful story!"

"Aye. The guys are brave to stay here. People say after her husband died of mysterious circumstances, the daughter returned to the cave with her two daughters, and when they can catch a victim, they drag them back to the cave for a feast."

She poked him gently. "Stop trying to scare me."

"I'll not be sleeping here." He stood and held out his hand to her. "But I'm looking forward to that stew. Ken's the best cook around, but don't tell Paul that."

Doug walked to meet them going into the camp. "Ah, just in time for my famous canned meat burgers."

Ken looked up from his pot. "Ach, how can you eat that shite, Doug? Don't eat it, Rhea. Save your appetite for my stew."

"Actually, I'd love one. I grew up eating that type of thing."

Doug handed Rhea a large bread rolled stuffed with two fried slices of processed meat, giving Ken the middle finger.

The fire-toasted bread was warm and buttery even though the sandwich was fatty and salty. The taste reminded her of her childhood. She smiled as she chewed and gave Doug a thumbs up.

After everyone had praised Ken for his mouth-watering stew, Doug and Ken started cleaning, and Mike sat in his chair, eyes closed for a nap.

Roarke and Rhea sat on a piece of wood facing the fire. "You loved the burger, did you?"

"Yes, very much."

"Ah, you're sweet. I've had one of those burgers. *One.*"

"Roarke, seriously. I really enjoyed it."

"Come on." He looked at her in shock.

"Okay, Mr. McCallum." She turned to face him. "Did that man share his food with me?"

Roarke nodded.

"Was he proud of what he prepared? Did he take pleasure in seeing me enjoy it? Did he give it to me with a heart and a half?"

Roarke had been nodding along to every question. "Yes, I imagine so."

"Then believe me when I say it was one of the best things I've ever eaten."

Regarding her with his head tilted to one side, he broke into laughter, shaking his head. When she glanced down at the contents of her mug, he affectionately ruffled her hair, then jumped up and headed over to Doug and Ken.

Rhea had always hated having the top of her head touched, but Roarke's gesture made her beam. She placed her hand where his had been and looked over at the kind-hearted man as he tucked a lock of his hair behind his ear.

As she shifted her focus back to the fire, she was mortified to find Mike staring at her with an amused smile on his lips and humor dancing in his eyes. His look told her he'd seen everything, including her reaction to Roarke's gesture. She knew Mike had seen the emotions she had begun feeling toward Roarke on her face.

They gazed at each other for a second or two, and then with resignation, Rhea gave a slight shrug of her shoulders and pinched up one side of her face in a look that asked Mike *What're ya gonna do?*

To her surprise, Mike lifted a hand to his mouth, sealed it with an imaginary zipper, and closed his eyes again, the slight smile still playing on his lips.

Rhea watched little birds flying out of small holes in the compacted sand of the dunes, and Mike joined her. "Sand martins." Walking along the shore, Mike identified the local flora and fauna. Pointing to a small patch of periwinkle flowers. "Those are harebells."

"At home, we call them bluebells. When I was a child, I would pick five and place them upside down on each of my fingertips."

Watching a sea eagle fly off with a wriggling fish in its talons, he commented, "That must be something new for the salmon. Not every fish gets to fly."

"Yup." She smiled. "If I were a fish, that'd be an interesting way to go."

After returning to the campsite, the other men suggested having a pint at the inn.

"Maybe you gentlemen would like an hour alone. I don't mind staying here."

"Rhea, it would be a pleasure to have you with us." Mike took her hand and dropped a bunch of harebells into it. "For your fingertips."

Holding out his elbow to her, she linked her arm under his, and as they took their first steps, Rhea looked over her shoulder and winked at Roarke.

"Might want to break out your benny hats tonight, fellas," Roarke said to the other men as they watched their grumpy friend walk up the beach, arm in arm with Rhea. "Cuz I'm pretty sure Hell just froze over."

Ken did a scan of their track with the metal detector he had brought along as they walked up the beach. He explained his newfound hobby and distinguished the beeps for low and high-quality valuables, describing even the sound a buried coin makes.

Halfway up the beach, they encountered a tall ginger-haired young man in his early teens with his metal detector, scanning the beach grass up closer toward the forest.

"Chris!" Ken yelled to him, "Finding anything today?"

"Not a thing!" He smiled and waved back.

"Chris is our local metal detecting expert," Ken explained to Rhea. "He finds stuff everywhere. He started doing it when he was about twelve."

"Aye," Roarke added. "He spends more time at the river near my cottage than I do."

"Roarke." Mike tapped a beat on Rhea's wrist as they walk arm in arm. "You're the one who gave him permission to go there and to be able to keep anything he finds."

"What's he going to find on my farmland?"

"This is Scotland," Mike admonished. "There's treasure everywhere, and there was a village on your land a long time ago."

"If he digs up any old pieces of pottery and some such, he's welcome to it."

"If he finds something like The Galloway Hoard?"

Roarke grinned at the older man. "The finder of the artifacts had to split the reward money with the landowner. He finds anything worth a fair amount, and he has to split it with me. Let him look all he wants."

"What's The Galloway Hoard?" Rhea asked.

"A young man found a large amount of tenth century Viking artifacts on another man's land. They split two million."

"Whew!" she exclaimed, "that's some treasure!"

"Aye." Mike smiled. "That'd be something if a find was here. Before long, there'd be more detectorists than midges."

In the long white building, under the watchful eye of Miriam, the pub owner, Rhea explored. Her son, Chris, the same young man from the beach, had found the majority of the artifacts in the museum attached to the pub. She learned about kitchen and fishing tools, weaponry, clothing, fossils, and bagpipes. Some things were exceptional, such as a Quaich from the eighteenth century, an old prayer book, the psalms in Gaelic, a small dirk, and several old nails and pennies that Miriam told her came from an old pile of rocks near Roarke's cottage.

Back in the rustic pub, Doug, Mike, and Ken were arguing about politics. Rhea sat beside Roarke and chatted about the treasures in the next room.

"Aye, yes, the pennies." Roarke looked up at Miriam as she brought over a pint for Rhea. "Have you had those pennies sent to The Treasure Trove, Miriam?"

"Don't be daft," the thin, salt-and-pepper-haired woman replied. "They're not worth that much, if anything. Chris is so proud just to display his treasures — don't you be taking them from him, Roarke McCallum. You're too lazy to search yourself."

"Ack, Miriam." Roarke laughed. "You know I wouldn't begrudge the boy anything."

A few minutes later, Miriam returned with steaming cups of butternut squash and bacon soup, as Doug told his friends how his young son had been waking lately from bad dreams.

"Bad dreams, eh?" Miriam placed a bowl with tabs of butter in the middle of the table. "Might be that his blood sugar drops when he sleeps. Give him a boiled egg or small piece of meat before bed. Should cure him right up."

"Think so?"

"I know so." Miriam winked at Doug and walked away.

"Dreams." Rhea had a flash of something from the night before.

"What?" Roarke eyed her curiously.

"Funny that you're talking about dreams." Rhea flicked her hair over her shoulder, aware of him staring at the birthmark on her neck as if he had never noticed it before. "Last night, I had a very vivid dream. I was walking with a young blond girl that I'd never met."

At that moment, three young men came into the pub, laughing and pushing at each other, silencing each man at the table as they all watched them and sat back in their chairs.

Two of the youths looked very similar to each other with the same pale blond features. The taller more muscular one had a wild mop of dark brown curls and a handsome face with hard eyes hidden beneath a bored expression. Walking toward a table, the tall youth smiled and raised a finger to his forehead in a salute directed at Roarke, whose face took on a dangerous scowl. He started to get to his feet, only to be pushed back into his chair by Mike.

Miriam came over and sat down two plates of bacon-wrapped scallops and sausage-stuffed rolls. "Shit, I didn't want them in here today."

"Where they go, trouble follows," Mike muttered.

The table's mood had changed. The air trembled with nervous energy, and Roarke had moved his chair to enable him to see the entire bar.

Rhea's curiosity got the better of her. "Who are those young men?"

"Arseholes. Ball sacks." Roarke took a long drink from his pint.

Ken leaned over toward her. "Those wee shits sell drugs around here."

"Police can't even arrest them," Mike chimed in. "They're well protected. The tall one's David Cojocaru's son."

"Let's not talk about it."

Roarke's eyes held a shadow Rhea had never seen before. She could tell there were things Roarke didn't want her to know. "If you gentlemen will excuse me, I have to go to the lady's room."

Getting up, she had to pass by the young men's table. As she made her way, the tall youth reached out and ran his hand down her thigh.

Indignant, Rhea grabbed his glass and, without thinking, dumped the contents over his head with a splash.

"Bitch," he snarled, grabbing for her, but she dodged his attempt, just Roarke and Ken stepped in front of her.

"Touch her again, and I'll skin you alive." Roarke stood with fists clenched as the two blondes held the young man back, beer dripping from his hair and face onto the floor.

The burly bartender emerged from behind the bar and stood with his hands on his hips. "Come on, Willem. You guys have to go."

"I didn't do anything."

"Get out before Miriam gets back, or she'll report you again."

"All I did was stand up." Willem spoke to the bartender but looked at Roarke.

"You put your hands on the young lady. Now out you go."

"Gobshite," Mike muttered as he turned and led Rhea back to their seats.

"Come on, Willem." One of the blondes edged Willem toward the door.

When they were a few feet away, Willem turned to Roarke. "I'll tell Father I ran into you, Roarke. I'll let him know you've got a new trinket."

Roarke lunged after the young man, and it took the other three to hold him back. He watched the young men walk out, leering and laughing. Finally, he wrenched free of his friend's grasp and stormed into the bathroom.

Rhea addressed the bartender. "Sorry about the trouble."

"Don't be sorry," said the bartender. "If they'd stuck around, they'd be harassing the girls and passing drugs in the bathroom. You did me a favor."

"I still feel bad about making a mess."

"Don't be. I can't tell you how glad it made me to see that mouthy gobshite covered in beer."

Rhea glanced at the floor to see the bluebells Mike had given her scattered and crushed.

After thanking the men, Roarke and Rhea continued on their way to the castle. Roarke stopped the truck as they passed the ruins of another small castle on an arm of land in the middle of a loch. "A mermaid haunts that castle."

"A mermaid?"

"Aye, in the fifteenth century, the family who owned the land were having trouble building the castle, so they made a deal with Clootie—"

"Who?" she interrupted.

"Oh, sorry. That's the name for the Devil around here."

"Oh." She shivered.

"Anyway, the father said Clootie could make a bride of his beautiful daughter if he helped build a strong castle, but once the castle was built, the daughter refused to marry and jumped from the tower into the water. She didn't die. Instead, she made her home in the caves below the loch, and there she remains to this day. People see her from time to time." Roarke shifted his gaze from the castle to Rhea. "The water spirits took pity on her and changed her into a mermaid. Another sad story about this region, I'm afraid."

"Sad?" she questioned. "I don't think it's sad. I'd love to be a mermaid! Be strong and beautiful forever, swimming around in the bright water and dark caves."

"You wouldn't miss your life on land?" Roarke kidded.

"I'd miss Liam and Patrice. That's about it."

Glanced at her sideways. "Why don't you talk about them more?"

Suppressing the urge to tell him to mind his own business, she answered him honestly. "That's my personal life and has nothing to do with why I'm here. I know they're safe and happy. While I'm here, I want to be *here*."

They were silent for a moment until Roarke attempted to change the subject. "Fishermen report seeing the mermaid the most, swimming amongst the rocks of the small harbour."

"Harbour." She looked out at the castle, "Funny, but I always thought if I had a little girl, I'd call her Harbour, a safe place."

"Would you like to have a child of your own?"

"Liam is my own. I couldn't love a child of my own more than I love him. I don't think there's room in my heart for another."

"My mother says a woman's heart gets bigger each time she has a child to make room for more love."

"Forgive me if it's too personal, Roarke, but do you think of having children?"

"It wouldn't do me any good to think of it."

"What do you mean?"

"I can't have children." He turned and gave her a half-hearted smile. "I had mumps when I was a teenager, and it resulted in infertility. It's rare, but it happens to some men."

"You've been tested?"

"Aye."

Putting her hand on his arm very tenderly, she spoke gently. "Roarke, there's no . . ."

Raising his hand and sighing, he tightened his lips and looked at her. "Off the record?"

She nodded slowly.

"That boy in the pub, Willem. I used to date his mother, Isabel. She was Ellie and Paul's sister, Ian's niece. My mother is from here, and Isabel and I would be together every chance we could. Each other's first love. She followed me to the city one summer and met David through me."

"And?"

"I hadn't told her I was infertile because I was sensitive about it. Then, one day, she came to me and said she was pregnant as if it was mine. I knew it wasn't."

Her jaw slackened, but she said nothing.

"She had already begun sleeping with David Cojocaru because I had grown distant with her, but she wanted to stay with me. Eventually, she admitted the truth and went to David. Unfortunately, she had their son, Willem, and died of cancer the following year."

"I'm so sorry."

"David raised Willem alone until he married Meredith."

"You really are the tragic jaded swain. I hope you're not a woman-hater."

"Of course not." He looked at her angrily. "Women have just disillusioned me."

"Poor darling," she said sarcastically. "Men never lie to

women. Trust me. Men have tried to do a lot worse to me than just breaking my heart."

Looking at her with a mix of concern and confusion, he moved to touch her arm but retracted his hand. "What do you . . ."

"Roarke, honey, forget it." She reached out to touch his hand. "I'm just sorry you can't have children."

He patted the back of her hand. "Doesn't bother me, Rhea. I wouldn't be a good father. I didn't exactly have the best role model."

"If you don't mind me saying, it's a bit of a shame."

"Explain." He furrowed his brow.

"Look at you." She pointed a finger from the top of his head to his feet. "You're extraordinary. Why would you have all this if you weren't meant to pass it on?"

"You think I'm extraordinary?" He puffed out his chest and cocked an eyebrow.

She laughed. "Calm down. Most times, I just think you're *extra ordinary*."

Ego deflated, he let the air out of his chest.

"I'm sorry that happened to you. In all my years of mistrusting men, I've never stopped to think of how women can be assholes, too."

"Oh, they can indeed. One of the marks on my — what was it — scarred and bloodied heart?"

"You remembered that?"

"I think I'm going to remember everything you say."

"That's sweet."

"Anyway. We'd best get going to my castle." Roarke turned the key in the ignition, and the truck sprang to life. "And if you ever get your wee Harbour, I hope she has your eyes."

"Agnes and Senga are both out of town for the week. They left the keys with Ian," Roarke explained as the truck bumped and jostled on the rough road.

Driving along the margin of the bay, the open windows letting in the clean, crisp sea air, Rhea watched two otters playing around the rocks near the shore. When she turned, ahead of her was Alloway Castle.

The splendid ancient building on a hillside overlooking the bay was an L-plan tower house with an additional projecting stair tower to the northeast. Four stories high with small windows on each floor, it had fallen into disrepair.

As they mounted the slight incline ridged with small shrubs, Roarke pointed in the direction of the manor, where Rhea could only see the roof. "That's where the family lives, just off the main road, near the gatehouse. Agnes, Senga, and their family started renovations after Historic Scotland gave them a substantial grant. You can see where the renovations started and stopped. A large chimney had caused the south side to sag, but when they took it down a large crack on the sidewall caused the wall to collapse. The cost to repair it was too high, and the money from the grant was gone. They couldn't afford to continue."

Turning into the long driveway in front of the tall building, he continued. "Plus, Agnes and Senga's spouses have jobs in the city, and they need to focus on their own lives."

Stopping the truck in front of the castle, Roarke came around to her side and pointed to the tower. "Renovations started on the stair tower, as it's a bit younger than the main tower. They used pink sandstone to fill in the openings."

The walls of the stair tower were of the palest pink, yet from a distance, they had seemed white. The building was so impressive Rhea was at a loss for words.

"See these two buildings?" He pointed to the two small white structures separated from the main castle by a small path. "We could convert them into dormitories for the kids, even add a few more small houses or add onto the castle. Kids could learn about electricity, carpentry, construction, as the castle will always need repairs. Build a museum, a restaurant and the kids could give tours and study the history of the area with hotel and restaurant management courses. Hiking, boating, and adventure guides. Farming and livestock care, the possibilities are endless."

"That is indeed a grand scheme." She took out the old hand-held recorder she had brought along after being warned about potential issues in phone service in the hills and forests. Earlier that day Rhea had recorded segments of their conversations, and Roarke had mentioned that he liked the recorder better than when she whipped out her notebook.

"Just the beginning." They reached the heavy wooden door to the stair tower, and looking down at the keys, he exclaimed. "Oh, shit!"

Rhea thought she saw a shadow move across the windowpane in the top window of the stair tower. *A trick of the light.* "What?" she asked in distraction.

"I only have keys to the tower and the old, attached part. The newer, semi-renovated part we have no access to."

With her attention back to him, Rhea pointed at the heavy grey clouds over their heads. "Looks like rain's coming."

"Aye, and the wind's picking up."

The rain began to fall in heavy droplets. Opening the heavy wooden door required force, and Roarke heaved against the door with his shoulder until it opened to a rectangular room. The space was bare except for a pile of old furniture pushed into one corner and covered in a tarp. A large, woven tapestry of a coat of arms against a black background hung on the front wall and to the left the spiral staircase reached upward.

The corner of the room to the left of the stairwell pulled at Rhea's attention. There was nothing there, but her eyes were fixed on the space anyway. "That stairwell's interesting. I wonder if—"

"Shit, I left the windows down in the truck," Roarke exclaimed, bounding out.

The corner that caught her attention seemed to be throbbing with energy and reminded her of her mother's belief that evil spirits resided in corners, spying on the living. Rhea had grown up in a dome-shaped home her father had spent two years designing and building for her mother.

She jumped as Roarke returned and pushed the door closed.

He shook his hair free of rain. "The inside of the truck is soaking wet, and the bloody thing won't start. I tried to move it closer so you wouldn't get too wet when we leave."

"How will we get out of here?"

"I might be able to fix it if the weather clears, and if I can't, I can walk to the village to get a tow. I guess we'll hunker down in here for a while."

Rhea didn't tell Roarke, but she had an uneasy feeling and wanted nothing more than to get out of the castle. It might have been another trick of the light, but she could have sworn a shadow had passed across the room, even though there was no other person there who could have cast it.

CHAPTER NINE: CONFESSIONS

I am so happy running up the hill and into the glen beside the burn. I am soaking wet, and my hem catches on thistles. My Thomas says we can run soon. He has some money and a relative who will help us get to England. We just need to wait for a good time.

I enter the stone courtyard when a sudden blow to my abdomen knocks the wind out of me, and I fall into the mud trying to breathe. A hand pulls at my hair, and I am looking into my father's furious face.

Roarke had settled himself in a chair, and Rhea sat on an old settee.

"Didn't Trace tell you the story of Thomas and Islean?"

"Yes, they died on that big rock near the inn, and their blood stained it pink. So many stories around here."

"Aye, and this castle has seen it all. It was even requisitioned for children evacuated from Glasgow during World War Two."

"Amazing."

"Their story involves this castle. Did you know that?"

Shaking her head, she settled into the crook of the settee.

"In the early sixteenth century, Scotland was undergoing a Protestant reformation, and people were choosing sides, as were the Kings and Queens. Mary, Queen of Scots, had decided to persecute the Protestant sect that had taken root in Scotland, and many of its most well-known leaders had to go into hiding. One such leader went into hiding here because the family was Protestant and feuded with the clan a few miles away, who was Catholic. The leader of that clan was a very determined papal churchman, and the different religious views led to serious clashes.

"The Protestant's daughter was Islean, who had fallen in love with Thomas, the nephew of the Catholic churchman. Islean's father suspected she had a lover, so he had a young man named Steaphan follow his daughter. Now, Steaphan had discovered the affair, but he loved Islean and didn't wish her to suffer the wrath of her violent father. Instead, Steaphan met with Thomas to ask him to end the affair with Islean, something he couldn't do. Thomas's uncle didn't know about the affair, and one night he informed Thomas that he and some others were going to the castle because the chieftain was harboring the Reform leader. They had plans to arrest everyone for crimes against the church.

"Fearing for his love, Thomas fled to the castle where he found Steaphan and told him of his uncle's plans. The family had just enough time to orchestrate the escape of the reform leader, who was on his way out of the country by the time the churchman arrived. They searched the castle but found nothing and left them in peace. Finding his daughter missing, they went to look for her.

"Steaphan tried to pacify Islean's father by telling him it had been Thomas who had warned him. However, after seeing his only daughter with the nephew of his nemesis, he ran Thomas through where he stood. Islean cursed her clan and killed herself."

"She cursed the men of her clan."

"Aye, that's right. More's the pity."

"Why do you say that?"

"My mother's from her clan. I'm a part of Islean's clan."

Rhea was silent with shock for a moment.

"Rhea." Roarke looked at her with exaggerated exasperation. "It's an old wives' tale." He was pensive for a moment before glancing at the window. "Doesn't matter anyway."

"It would matter to me."

"The ironic thing is my cottage is in the area where Thomas's old village used to be."

"Really?"

"The very spot. Actually, the pink rock is directly between this castle and my cottage."

They fell silent as Rhea wrote down some of the past few days' events while Roarke stretched out and was soon fast asleep. A creak on the floor caused her hand to fly to her throat. The staircase was out of sight, and Rhea caught a glimpse of something white near the bottom. She blinked, and it was gone.

Rhea was too scared to move for a few seconds, and her gaze flitted over to where Roarke lay, breathing peacefully. Listening carefully for a few moments, Rhea heard nothing. Finally, tiptoeing over to the stairwell, she looked up. Nothing was there. She began her tentative ascent to the second floor.

The top of the staircase ended with a small, circular room hosting a window overlooking the garden and a large, barred door. Sighing, Rhea went to the window. The rain had lifted, and the well-kept garden was a vivid green with colorful flowers and herbs in tidy swirls and rows. Her eyes followed the trail leading from the gate to a small path in the wood. There, at the break in the trees, something metallic glinted as clouds passed across the sun.

Hearing another creak, Rhea froze—she had the distinct impression someone stood behind her, but a glance proved no one was there. Yet again she experienced the sensation that someone was about to touch her, and she bolted down the stairs to find Roarke still asleep. She tiptoed to the door and crept outside, not closing it behind her.

Rhea's rubber boots squeaked in the wet grass as she

headed through the path in the woods toward the beach. Looking back, the castle, which earlier had seemed gothic and mysterious, seemed formidable and eerie in its grey solitude amongst the vivid green of the hills and forest.

Heading toward the path, she froze on the spot. Directly inside the ridge of trees, a woman with long hair stared in her direction. Though she could distinguish no distinct features, she could feel the lady's stare. As she looked back, Rhea could hear the sound of rushing wind, yet nothing moved but a small patch of harebells, at her feet. She remembered how her mother would shake the flowers to call in the fairies. When she looked back, the woman took a step backward into the forest and vanished.

Roarke awoke to an empty room. Getting up, he yelled Rhea's name. Feeling uneasy when he didn't get a reply, he went to the open door and peered outside, only to freeze in fright.

A man was staring at him. Dressed in old-fashioned garb, the long kilt of centuries before, he stood in the tall grass next to the path to the beach.

Roarke broke out in a cold sweat, and shivers ran down his spine, yet he raised his hand in a hesitant salute.

The young man continued to stare at Roarke before turning and walking down the path leading to the beach.

Was he being led somewhere? Cold fingers of fear crept up his back as he took the first halting steps to follow the strange young man.

Rhea was sitting on a rock by the sea when Roarke stepped onto the beach. Sitting down, Roarke elbowed her. "What are you doing?"

"You wouldn't believe me if I told you."

Leaning his body to the side and bumping her hip, he whispered, "Try me."

Rhea sighed and recounted what had happened in the castle. "I think I was led here."

"By whom?"

"Roarke." She turned to look him in the face and placed her hands on one of his. "I know you're going to think I'm crazy, but I think something is trying to communicate with us."

His expression didn't change.

"You don't appear shocked?"

"Why would I be?" He sucked on his bottom lip. "I'm fairly certain I followed a ghost down here."

They exchanged stories. Roarke's ended with the young man disappearing in the path, and Rhea's ended with finding nothing metallic.

Rhea watched two seagulls dip and dive above her head. "Show-offs! They know they can fly, and we can't. They just show off because they know they're beautiful."

"Might be some truth to that."

Standing and then walking up the beach, Rhea turned to Roarke. "Why do you spend so much time alone?"

It took him a while to answer. "It equates to freedom. When you're alone, you get to know yourself, and you're free to think your thoughts, feel your feelings, find out what you want and don't want out of life."

"What do you want?"

"To be in nature. To be able to hike, sail, and live off the earth. To always have a full belly. I guess to help people."

After searching the beach for wood, they sat in front of a small cave next to a jagged cliff.

"Rhea." Roarke threw her a lighter and started walking down the beach. "Dig a shallow hole between these two rocks and start a fire. I'll be back soon."

Rhea dug a hole, after which she started the fire and sat

feeding it as she waited for Roarke. A stiff wind picked up, and sand blew into her eyes. Rubbing them and looking down, she saw something sticking out from beneath a large rock.

After digging until she had almost freed it, she heard a light rustle of footsteps on the small beach rocks, and a shiver ran through her as she felt the weight of a gentle hand on her shoulder. "Roarke, there's something stuck under this rock. Could you lift it for me so I can get it out?"

Receiving no reply, she turned around. "Roarke? Could you lift the—"

Rhea sucked in her breath when Roarke approached her but from at least twenty feet away. The weight on her shoulder was gone, and it couldn't have been him.

Roarke jogged the remaining feet between them. "Rhea, what's wrong? You're white as a sheet." He crouched on his haunches and ran a hand across her forehead.

"Nothing's wrong." Smiling and shaking slightly, she moved his hand away. "I just . . . I thought I heard footsteps, but it was my imagination."

"You sure?" He still looked worried.

Rhea nodded. "I think I've found something. Could you lift this rock for me? There's something stuck underneath."

Roarke lifted the stone as Rhea loosened a long, thin piece of metal from the compacted soil and sand.

"A nail." Roarke took it from her and held it to the light sky. "A really old nail."

"Look! There's another." Rhea pulled the other out of the sand and dusted it with her shirttail. "Why would nails be here?"

"Got me," Roarke mumbled. "Wrought iron. They were used for buildings and bridges. See here?" He pointed to the nail's edges. "Four sharp edges on the shank, to cut deep into timber and swell when damp, making solid fixing."

"What should we do with them?"

"Keep them." He brushed a few grains of sand off her cheek.

"No." She shook her head. "I'll donate them to the McCallum Castle Museum. When you look at them, you'll remember me."

"My friend, I doubt I'll need any knickknacks to remember you."

Walking back to the castle, Roarke took a few minutes to pick a few handfuls of gooseberries, which he stuffed into his breast pockets. Upon returning to the castle, he found Rhea banging at things beneath the hood of the truck with the heel of her hiking boot.

"Hey!" Roarke jogged up to her, frowning. "Don't just go banging things around in there! It's a vehicle, not a vending machine!"

"Trust me, Roarke." Rhea jerked her chin at the cab. "Try to start her."

Hesitantly, Roarke got into the cab, and the truck started with little resistance. Rhea slammed down the hood and hopped inside, grinning at him. "The battery's weak. I wasn't just banging around. I used the heel of my boot to tap on the terminals on the battery. It gets them loose, and you get better contact on the posts."

Blushing lightly, Roarke cleared his throat. "I knew that. It's exactly what I was going to do."

"Oh, really?"

"Yes, really."

"*La fragilité de l'ego masculin,*" Rhea muttered.

"What?" Roarke turned to her and grinned.

"I said men have fragile egos." She jutted her chin at him. "I told you I knew a thing or two about vehicles."

He started to say that he had not suspected otherwise but figured it would insult her further. Instead, he smiled and nodded. "My dear, I'll never doubt you nor your abilities again."

Back on the farm that evening, Roarke took down a small crystal cognac snifter and placed the two nails in it. "I'll show them to Ian the next time he comes. He loves stuff like that."

After eating thick, roast beef sandwiches, they both turned in early. After sleeping deeply for several hours, Rhea woke and stumbled to the kitchen for water. Before returning to bed, she walked over to the window. Clouds flitted across a midnight blue sky, the winding path on the purple hill in front of her was snakelike, and for some reason, she thought of her mother.

A light in the condemned building on the other hill caught her eye as she turned away from the window. Roarke had told her it used to be a bothy, an old simple dwelling left unlocked to provide shelter for outdoor enthusiasts which was now locked up.

If it's locked up and condemned, why is there a light on inside? Moving from room to room, a yellow glow spilled out from the large cracks between the boards over the windows. Like in an ancient castle in an old horror movie, the light seemed to move with a will of its own, and after a few seconds, it disappeared.

The tapping began.

A light tapping sound came from under the window. Rhea thought maybe it was from a low branch on the tree outside, but when the sound moved along the bottom of the windowsill and up the side toward the top, she knew it couldn't be. The tapping moved along the top of the windowpane in a constant rhythm. Rhea stood paralyzed, as the sound seemed to have a consciousness that terrified her to the core.

Rhea remembered a story she had read of a ghost writing her name upside down on the windowsill. Then, perhaps more frightening than the tapping itself, the tapping stopped. A deep silence filled the small cottage and an expectation hung in the air — of what, she didn't know.

Spinning around on the spot, Rhea ran, as quietly as possible, to her bedroom.

The following morning, Roarke left the house. Ian and Midas met him at the barn door. After Roarke told them about the events of the day before, Ian's eyes clouded over, "You kind of fancy Rhea, don't you?"

"Oh, no, Ian. Our arrangement is strictly professional."

"Then why did you look at your feet when you said strictly professional?"

"Because you're glaring at me with those black seal eyes of yours."

"She has a boy at home?"

"Aye."

"Listen." Ian took a step to close the gap between them and pointed his finger up into Roarke's face. "You can't play around with her."

"I know that."

"You bloody well better make sure you do nothing to hurt that young lady. She's to go home to her family."

"I know." Roarke turned with his hands on his hips.

Ian's voice softened. "Roarke, I've known you most of your life, and I know the majority of your secrets. Cojocaru and his son know that she's here."

"He won't do anything. We've got an understanding."

"Son," Ian said as he saw Rhea's silhouette pass in front of the kitchen window. "Just make sure that nice girl doesn't get hurt."

"My hand to God, she won't get hurt."

As the two men worked around the farm together, Roarke thought about how he couldn't let Rhea get involved in his crazy world. He had to maintain some distance between them and stay focused on why Rhea was here. She had a job to do, and then she would be leaving.

Smiling to herself, Rhea prepared breakfast while watching Ian and Roarke, fascinated by how Roarke moved, hoisting large bags of grain onto his shoulder yet gently carrying a runaway lamb back to its mother. At one point, both men burst into laughter. Roarke had his head thrown back, and Ian was clapping him on the back in merriment.

The smile dissolved when she realized her feelings for Roarke were deepening day by day. *How do I distance myself from a man I need to stay with at all times?*

When Ian and Roarke entered the house, she had bacon, eggs, and toast ready. Turning from the stove, she came around the island to give Ian a big hug. Then, over his shoulder, she made eye contact with Roarke and dropped her gaze.

"Um, Ian's going to help me repair the window."

"Great! Come and sit. I've made breakfast."

After breakfast, Roarke said he and Ian had to take a short trip into town to get supplies. "We shouldn't be gone too long, but I'm expecting a delivery. Rhea, I hope you wouldn't mind staying and signing for it."

"I don't mind, but am I not supposed to stay with you?"

"Won't be long. Midas will stay with you."

Roarke was at the door when he turned to look back. "Rhea?"

"Yes?" She rubbed Midas's thick brown-black fur.

"Is your father still alive?" He looked down at her kindly.

Taken aback by his question, she stood and furrowed her

brow. "Why do you ask?"

"It's just the way you are with Ian." He picked up his jacket from the chair.

Clearing her throat, she tilted her head back as she looked at his chin. "I was very close to my father. Unfortunately, he died almost a year to the day of when Poppy did."

"How did he die?"

She drew a deep breath. "He drowned."

"I'm so sorry."

"He always knew he would drown. He used to tell us one day he'd be called home."

Roarke stood digesting her words until Ian honked the horn from the truck.

Rhea took a step closer to Roarke and reached up, adjusting the collar of his shirt. "Enough sad stories, Roarke. Bring me back a treat. The sooner you leave, the sooner you'll be back."

Rhea waved at them from the porch and pacified Midas with small pieces of leftover bacon as Roarke put the key in the ignition. Turning to his friend, he smiled, remembering how Rhea avoided making eye contact with him and the way she doted on Ian, fetching jam for him, refilling coffee, and laughing at everything he said.

"If I want to keep her at arm's length, I just need to have you around. She doesn't even notice me when she's doting on you."

Ian smiled and winked at the younger man. "Robertsons have a way with the ladies. It's all about the eyes."

"Those eyes?" Grinned Roarke. "You're full of evil. That's why your eyes are black."

Ian squinted at Roarke. "Now I understand why your eyes are brown."

"Why's that?" Roarke asked as he pulled out of the gravel

driveway.

"Cuz you're so full of shit."

After a walk with Midas in the clean, fresh air, Rhea went to work on her notes. She was just closing her laptop when Midas let out a booming bark and bolted for the front door.

"Midas! It's just the guys!" She yelled after the dog.

However, after peeking out the window, it wasn't Roarke's old truck parked in front but rather a sleek black sports car. *It must be the delivery.*

Pulling Midas back from the door by his collar, giving herself enough space to squeeze through, she stepped onto the porch. The dog barked and growled behind the door.

Two young men were facing her at the bottom of the stairs, tall, thin, and blond. It had just dawned on her who they were when another young man stepped around the corner of the house and stopped short when he saw her.

"What are you doing here?" She narrowed her eyes suspiciously.

Willem put his hands on his narrow hips. "Look who it is."

"I thought you were a delivery." She felt stupid as she realized that deliverymen don't usually deliver goods to a farm in a sports car.

Willem laughed. "No. We're not with a delivery. Just checking on something." Willem's smirk grew. "You're living out here now?"

Ignoring the question, she straightened herself to her full height. "What can I do for you?"

He leered at her salaciously. "Where's Roarke?"

"At the barn."

"Where's his truck?"

"Someone borrowed it."

"Who would borrow that piece of shit?"

"Ian."

"What a cool liar you are." He stepped toward her. "We were parked a few miles back and saw him and the old man leaving."

"Why are you here if you know he's not?"

One of the blond brothers answered. "Just looking around is all. What a fine piece of land this is."

Willem spoke to him without turning around, keeping his focus on Rhea. "Aye, Malcolm. It seems Roarke has an eye for lovely things."

He had casually taken a few steps toward her as he spook, and she took a few steps back, her hand going to the doorknob.

Willem's hand came to rest on the handrail of the steps, his foot on the bottom step. "I was hoping to see you again. You've no drink to throw today, have you?"

"No, but if I open this door, you will be set upon by an irate dog." Midas still was still barking and scratching at the door, and she knew Willem could hear him.

The sound of gravel crunching under tires made them all turn. Rhea dropped her hand from the doorknob when Roarke's truck reached the path to the door. It had not even completely stopped when Roarke burst out of the cab, his face more furious than Rhea had ever seen it.

Pushing the blondes aside, in five steps, he had closed the distance between himself and Willem, grabbing the younger man by the front of the shirt and pushing him back against the cottage with a massive thud. "What the hell are you doing here?"

Roarke had roared with a face so full of rage Rhea was confused by Willem's calm reaction—he seemed almost on the verge of laughter.

"Just having a look around." He glanced sideways at Rhea. "And look what I found."

Roarke pulled him off the wall, only to slam him against it

again with even more force.

That time, Willem winced in pain and tried to push Roarke off him, to no avail.

"I'm going to ask you one more time what you're doing here, or I'll drive your teeth down your throat." Then, without looking at her, he said, "Rhea, get inside."

With a worried glance at Roarke and then Ian, she pushed her way into the house, using her leg to keep Midas inside the house. Standing at the door, she heard Willem.

"David wanted us to come and ask if you had considered his new offer."

Roarke's voice lowered a little. "Why would he do that when he has a telephone?"

Rhea peeked out the sitting room window. Willem glared at Roarke, and the confident smirk was gone. Ian held an ax at the bottom of the steps and faced the other two young men, who hadn't moved.

Roarke continued. "He doesn't know you're here, does he?"

When Willem still didn't answer, Roarke let go of his collar, and he fell against the railing of the porch, breathing deeply, his face crimson with anger. "Just doing what I was told."

With surprising speed and agility, Roarke spun around and flung Willem off the porch. The boy hit the ground on his backside, then sat in the dirt glaring at Roarke until one of the others went to help him up. He jerked away from the other boy's hand and got up, dusting off his clothes, head down and shoulders hunched like a dog ready to strike.

Roarke took a step off the porch. "If I see you anywhere near here again, I'll shoot first and ask questions later."

"That's my land just over the ridge there, don't forget." Willem jerked his head in the direction of the old bothy on the hill.

"What would the likes of you be doing over there? Planting

potatoes? Piss off."

The young men got into their sleek black vehicle. From the passenger side, Willem's eyes flickered to one of the windows on the second story. His eyebrows pulled together, and his head jutted a little forward, looking at something and squinting slightly. Rhea caught a look of fear on his face just as they drove away.

Rhea flung open the door just as Roarke turned toward it. Placing a hand on either side of her face, he grabbed her so hard she almost fell. "Are you all right?"

Putting her hands on his hands, she muttered, "I'm fine. They didn't even get near me. I was just about to let Midas out when you arrived."

"What did he say to you? Did he threaten you?"

"No. Not really"

"What did they want?" He still had her face between his hands.

"I got the feeling they were looking for something." She then summarized their short conversation.

Roarke pulled her toward him without commenting and enveloped her in an enormous bear hug, her face pressed against his chest.

"Roarke," she gasped. "I can't breathe."

Letting her go, he gave her a quick once-over. "Sure you're okay?"

She nodded, trying to recover her breath as Roarke went to the open front door, where Ian stood. "Ian, do me a favor and take Rhea up to your house, and she can bring down the tools I need."

"I can bring down . . ."

Roarke cut him off and took a step toward him. "Please, Ian, I need a moment to myself."

Rhea went to see Pearl and the puppies, happy to find them all strong and healthy, and little Laz was thriving.

As she was leaving to return to White Heather, Ian called out to her, "Rhea! Check the truck when you get down there. We brought you something, but Roarke might have forgotten."

She blew him a kiss. "You're so sweet!"

He smiled at her and looked down at his hands. "Rhea, try not to ask Roarke questions you know he doesn't want to answer. He'll just shut down and get in his head."

"He has a lot of secrets, doesn't he?"

"Don't we all?" He looked up at her. "My grandmother used to say everyone has a book that's the story of their lives, and in each there are a few pages we don't read out loud."

After arriving back at White Heather, she checked the truck's front seat, finding a plastic bag with a box of various small pies. She put them inside and found Roarke at the back of the house, chopping wood. His back was to her, and he swung the ax aggressively. He cast a glance at her over his shoulder, and then turned back to his work.

"I brought down the tools." She set them next to the house.

"Thanks," he muttered as he swung the ax.

"Did you eat lunch? I could make you something."

He spoke without turning, and she could hear a strain in his voice. "No, thanks. I'm fine."

"Roarke?"

He stopped what he was doing and placed the ax head on the ground, one hand on his hip. "I'm not in any fit state for talking at the moment."

"I just . . ."

His voice had an edge. "Please leave me be for a while."

She said nothing but turned and walked away. Going down the slight incline from the house, she walked east until she reached the river and sat on a large rock at the edge of its widest expanse.

Rhea knew there was more to the incident than she knew, but it was also none of her business. She would never write about it. The logical thing was to forget about what had happened.

Lying back on the flat surface of the rock, she watched the sky and let her mind go blank. The sun was trying to break out of the heavy cloud cover, and the air was warm and thick. Two birds raced above her, passing each other in the sky.

Rolling over onto her belly and looking down at the water, she relaxed to the sound of lapping waves and small pebbles clicking against each other. Closing her eyes, she was almost asleep until her body suddenly broke out in goosebumps. She instinctively felt she was being watched.

Pushing herself up, she saw nothing amongst the trees on the hill nor in the grass. However, just as she settled on the rock again, she glimpsed what appeared to be the top of a pale head sink soundlessly into the water, without making even the slightest ripple on the surface.

Rhea's brow furrowed as she tried to think of what it was, being earless and too large to be an otter, and she knew seals would not be in the area. When it didn't reappear, she thought maybe her sleepy brain had imagined it, until her fanciful mind shifted through many Scottish creatures known to be fond of rivers and settled on the Kelpie, a water horse said to lure humans to a watery grave.

Rather than being afraid, the mystic in her thrilled at the thought. After checking in every direction, she pulled off her shorts and t-shirt and waded into the cool, clear, pale amber water of the river until it reached her waist, and then dove below the surface.

Underwater, she saw nothing but algae-covered rock as she swam and walked along the bottom on her hands. Breaking the surface to feel the warm sun on her cold skin, she dipped her head back into the water, her hair floating around her in a soft cloud, imagining herself a nymph waiting for the kelpie to remerge.

CHAPTER TEN: WHISPERS

I had managed to sneak away again. Now that father was off, the household is more at ease. I can meet my Thomas. The days I do not see him are the longest of my life, and I pray that each second with Thomas could become a long, winter's night.

I can finally see the world for the beautiful place it truly is. All my life, I only saw the misery of it.

The other day, I walked on one side of the burn, and he walked on the other. We dipped our hands into the water and walked across the small bridge, joining our wet hands when we reached the middle. My Thomas said it meant that we are betrothed and as good as married.

Roarke sat on his chopping block, exhausted from his frantic physical exertion. He was happy he had gotten out some of his aggression, as his call to David had left him frustrated but relieved that David was not coming after him or Rhea. Not yet, anyway.

Inside the house, he changed his clothes, grabbed a bun, and went to find Rhea. He checked all the places she could be, even Ian's, but could see neither hide nor hair of her.

He was in a complete panic by the time he left Ian's. *Where could she have gone?* Ian had suggested checking the river, and as a last resort, he took the small path that led in that direction. *What if those shits came back and did something to her? So help me, I'll gut them.*

Approaching the river, he saw clothes on the flat rock and two shapely legs sticking out of the water. Relief flooded through him as he continued down the path, watching her play in the water. By the time he reached the edge of the grass, which petered off into pebbles, Rhea was doing flips.

Eventually, she burst to the surface, gasping, "Seventeen."

"Seventeen what?"

Rhea struggled to get her hair out of her face, squinting from the water in her eyes. "Jesus!" she cried, still wiping her face. "You scared the life out of me!"

"You left without telling me where you were going!" He took a step toward her, and his voice was angry. "You can't just go wandering off! You don't know the countryside!"

Standing in the water, shivering, she tried to control her voice. "You made it clear that you wanted me to bugger off, so I did!"

"You could have left a note!"

"Why? I hadn't left the country!"

"You don't know how dangerous this place can be!"

"Oh, yes! Just look around!" She flailed her arms about her head. "The little birdies are coming to get me!"

"That's not—"

"Oh, throw me my shirt so I can get out, and you can yell at me on dry land."

Picking up her t-shirt, he held it out as she walked toward him.

"Avert your eyes and don't say anything witty or snarky, I'm warning you.

Roarke turned as Rhea struggled to shore, shaking and stepping carefully on the rocks.

"Why are you in such a tither? I'm the one who should be angry."

Grabbing her shirt, she pulled it over her head and reached for her shorts, struggling to get them on over her wet skin.

"Typical male!"

"What was that?"

He made to turn, and she yelled, "Don't turn around!" Continuing her struggle to into her clothes, she added, "I said you're a typical male!"

"Meaning?"

"You all get cranky or moody at something and take it out on everyone around you. The only exception being my son, and that's just because he was raised better."

"Hey, now!" He turned around to find her fully clothed and standing on the rock, putting them at about the same height. "There's no need to insult my upbringing."

"I barely *know* anything about your upbringing."

His face took on an angry expression, and he pointed his finger at her. "I'll have you know my mother is a saint of a woman, and . . ."

"I'd thank you for telling me about her." Rhea took a step toward the edge of the rock, angry at his attitude. "Because you haven't exactly been an open book. You tell me what you want me to know, and that's it." She took another step toward him, neglecting to look down. "And that won't be enough to make this book sell. I need to know . . ."

Her toes hit empty air with the next step, and she fell forward. He grabbed her shoulders, took a step closer, and one hand closed around the side of her neck. He squeezed her windpipe as she caught a look of something dangerous in his eyes.

"I'm not sure what you're thinking right now, but let me tell you that if you ever hurt me or try to scare me, you'd better make certain you're successful. I'm evil enough to pay you back, creatively, and clever enough to get away with it."

Eye to eye, she watched as the dangerous look left, replaced by surprise, then amusement, then something she couldn't quite identify. With his other hand on the opposite side of her head, he pulled her forward, placing the lightest, gentlest of kisses on her forehead.

"That's what I was thinking of." He stepped back. "You're right." The wolfishness replaced with a look of serenity. "I'm a typical male, but I'm evolving. Slowly but surely."

Righting herself, she shivered as clouds passed over the sun, and the sky turned grey.

"You're shivering. It seems like you're always shivering." Grabbing his shirt by the neck, Roarke pulled it over his head. "Put this on. The day's warm, but with the sun has gone. There'll be a chill."

She shook her head. "No, I'm fine."

"Please, put it on. Yours is soaking wet."

"No, really. The air's warm, and I find it hard to talk to you with your shirt off."

Dropping the hand that held the t-shirt, he laughed. "Why?"

"Not used to it." She sat on the rock. "Hand me my shoes there on the heather."

Reaching for her sneakers, he then handed them to her. "Does no one call you Heather?"

"No one."

"Why would your mother give you a name if she didn't want you called by it?"

"Why would my mother give me a name half of my family couldn't pronounce?"

He smiled and shrugged his shoulders.

"My father's from Québec, and Poppy and I went to university there. My grandpapa just started calling me Rhea. Heather, when said with a French accent, sounds like edder."

"Heather came from . . ."

"My mother read a novel set in Scotland, and the first image of the heroine was of her laying on purple heather, with long red hair and a green dress."

"It's a lovely image. Did your mother write?"

"No." She played with a few small stones on the rock. "She did have a way with words."

"Your parents had a good marriage?"

"My parents had an amazing marriage. They loved each other very much. Too much, if anything, but why would you ask me about my parent's marriage?"

"Typical male," he answered. "It's not the first time you've said something that made me think you have a problem with men. I was just wondering about the household you grew up in."

"I had an amazing, loving father and two wonderful brothers." Deciding to be as honest with him, she added, "I've had other experiences which were not so great."

Swallowing hard, his face a mask of concern, he looked her up and down as if checking to see if she were injured. "Oh, Rhea, were you . . ."

Realization dawning on her, she touched his hand. "No, well, I had a cousin who was a little too friendly, and it made me very uncomfortable around boys. Then, in high school, a guy I'd known my entire life came over to be tutored. My parents were out, and nothing happened, but the next day, he told everyone at school that we, well . . ."

"Bastard."

"Yup." She sighed loudly, blowing out her cheeks. "Some girls were thrilled, because they considered me stuck up, and after that, they called me a slut. God, I wanted to get out of that place. I was always careful never to be alone with any guy, because after what Mike said, they all tried to get handsy with me."

"Ball sacks."

"They were the same kind of guys as Willem, that little shit today. When I was alone with them, it brought back many old feelings. I mistrust most men."

They were silent for a while, both lost in their thoughts.

"Rhea." Roarke played with a blade of grass and sighed loudly. "I think you should go."

Just as her head spun around and her mouth opened to protest, he held up his hand. "Wait. Let me explain."

She waited for him to continue, but inside, her head spun.

"Those boys today are dangerous men, and they work for an even more dangerous man. Seeing them here scared the shit out of me, and it reminded me that you could be in danger being around me. I don't think they'd hurt you, but I'd rather not take the chance."

"But?"

"I'm sorry, but I feel you should go."

They sat in silence again until Rhea put her hand over his. "Roarke, did you choose your profession, or did it choose you?"

"I guess I got lucky, and I chose my profession."

"I never wanted to be a translator. I want to be a writer. I'm a translator because I needed a steady job for my family. If I do well writing this book, it'll lead to other opportunities. I'll be able to write full-time. The ideas cluttering my head will finally have an outlet."

He listened and curled the blade of grass around his index finger.

"I'll go if it gives you peace of mind, but you need to understand what I'll be giving up. You will get another ghost-writer, and your book will be published. I'll go home and have no prospects for creative writing."

Standing up, he took a step away from the rock, his back to her. She got up and moved to stand in front of him, her hand around his thick wrist.

"I need this. I'm not going to beg you to stay. I'm asking you to forget the reasons you want me to leave. I'm here to do a job. I won't lose this opportunity because you're afraid of things that may never happen."

"What if you get hurt? What if you're in the wrong place at the wrong time?"

"Slim chance of that happening."

"A slim chance is still a chance."

"Life is chance. You could send me home and I get hit by a bus in the airport parking lot."

"It's not the same thing."

"It is the same thing."

"What about Liam? What would happen to him if something happened to you?"

Pointing her finger up at him, a look of fury marred her features. "Do not do that. That is so unfair. When you become a mother, you can't do this, and you can't do that. People don't say the same things to men. Patrice isn't chastised for rock climbing, even though he could break his neck."

Roarke tried to turn away from her, but she held his wrist and continued. "How can I tell Liam that he can do and be whatever he wants, to chase his dreams and be brave, if I can't do the same? If I don't fight for my dreams, for the things I want?"

He kicked at a stone, not looking at her.

"Look at me." She stepped closer to him. "I said look at me, you son of a bitch."

His gaze flew to her face in shock and a touch of humor.

"You can fire me, tell me to go, and I'll have no choice but to do it, but I won't go freely. I won't permit you to piss on my dreams. I've made my choice. I choose to stay and do my job. Now, you choose, and I don't care if you let me stay because I made you feel guilty."

He laughed and held up his hands in resignation. "Okay, I surrender."

"All right then." Her shoulders relaxed, and she stepped away from him. "And Roarke, just one more thing."

"Yes?" He looked at her kindly.

She put her hands on her hips. "I do not want to have this discussion again." Walking back to the house, Rhea resisted the urge to pull her wet underwear out of her butt.

As they crested the hill, Roarke paused. "There's violence in me, Rhea. I fight it every day, but it's always there."

"Where does it come from?"

Sitting in the grass at the top of the hill, he pulled her down beside him. "Off the record?"

"Certainly."

"I told you I worked for David Cojocaru, but he's not completely out of my life."

Roarke heard the quiet zip, zip as Rhea ran her pendants across their silver chain. Sighing, he lay back in the grass, his hands behind his head, and Rhea followed suit.

"I managed to get away from Davey with my step-father's help, and he let me go because he had no other choice. I need to keep as many kids off the streets as I can. They're prime targets for assholes that would use them up and throw them away. Davey sees these kids as disposable, and they are not." He turned to look at her. "Every kid on the street has people who love them and want to help them."

"We all make our choices." She squeezed his hand. "The only person who can ever know the secrets of someone's soul is that person and that person alone."

He glanced over at her and gave her the smallest, briefest of smiles.

"Do you find that working with the kids at your shelter helps?" she asked, brushing a stray strand of hair off his forehead.

"Works wonders."

"Do they come from troubled homes?"

"Not all. Some come from loving homes, but with each of

them, there's something they're looking for, some peace they can never quite attain. They have a hole inside them no one can fill until they decide to fill it themselves. The hole that lives in these kids has to be filled with something concrete. Self-worth and confidence. If I could get my hands on the castle, it could open up new doors for all of us."

Opening her eyes and looking over at him, she nodded. "I'm a big fan of opening new doors."

Roarke chuckled and turned toward her, their faces being only a few inches apart. Rhea's heart stopped when he looked into her eyes, and his hand reached out to caress her cheek.

"Your eyes are the same color as the grass."

Rhea shrugged, and her eyelids began to droop closed as Roarke leaned even closer toward her, his jaw dropping a little as he licked his bottom lip.

Then, quicker than she thought possible of such a large man, he tapped the tip of her nose with his index finger and hopped to his feet, reaching down to pull her up with him. "Come. Enough secrets for one day. Let's eat and get a good night's sleep."

Roarke's haste was due in part to him needing to put some physical distance between them. He was learning to trust her, and he didn't want to do anything to jeopardize the bond that was forming, but he'd just been dangerously close to kissing her. *Those damn cat eyes are going to be my undoing.*

As they crossed the small stream next to the barn, Rhea asked, "Roarke, are there any seals in the river?"

"No, why?"

"Nothing. I just saw a head in the water when I was swimming." Then she headed toward to door of the house before his open mouth could form a question.

Roarke prepared a meal of *stovies,* a stew of leftover meat and vegetables, and listened to the radio. Rhea sat in the small sitting room listening to the snippets of conversation she had recorded over the past few days. Taking notes as she went along, she had the recorder close to her ear, to hear over the music.

Rhea was jotting down the details Roarke had been giving her about the castle when she heard a strange hissing sound in the background. She initially thought it was an insect, but there was a peculiar inflection to the sound. She rewound and listened until realization dawned on her, and fear crept up her spine.

Going into the kitchen, she stood next to Roarke. "Turn the radio off."

Switching off the radio, he turned back to her, "Are you okay? You have the strangest look on your face."

"Listen to what the recorder picked up at the castle the other day."

"What is it?"

"Listen for yourself. I don't want you to be influenced by me."

Rhea increased the volume and played the section with the strange hiss. "Listen to what you hear in the background."

After listening carefully, he said, "I hear insects only."

"Listen again."

This time his jaw dropped, his brow furrowing, "A woman's voice, haunting and lonely."

"Can you hear what she said?"

"A single word, drawn out and distant — and eerie."

"That's what I hear too."

He looked down at her, confusion and fear in his eyes. "She was asking for Thomas."

The next morning, laying in bed in the early light, Roarke realized that despite some weird things happening in general, the creepy atmosphere inside the cottage had all but disappeared. Maybe his tranquil disposition was due to being introspective, thanks to the funny girl who walked like a ghost.

Heading out in the fresh mist, neither spoke as Roarke led the way to the gym. Rhea was bursting with energy and excitement after a good night's rest. The clean air felt green in her lungs, and the cool mist on her face made her feel deliciously alive.

Catching up with Roarke, Rhea asked, "Ready to talk about the recording now?"

The night before, after hearing the voice on the recording from the castle, Roarke had told Rhea he was tired, needed sleep, and they would discuss it in the morning. Rhea suspected the voice scared him a little.

Stopping with his hands on his hips, he sighed. "Not really, that could have been anything, an animal, an insect, and echo carried over the hills."

"You don't believe that. I saw your face. You thought the same as I did."

"What? A ghost-lady was around us calling out to her long-lost lover?"

"Yeah. Exactly."

"Listen, Rhea, I know this is a mythical, mystic place, especially the Highlands. The truth is Scotland is not riddled with ghosts. It's made-up nonsense."

"Said everyone in a book or movie about Scotland or Ireland just before the ghost appears." She chuckled.

Smiling down at her, he laid a hand on her shoulder. "My

dear, your imaginative, creative mind, and these ancient surroundings are getting the better of you. Don't you think maybe you *want* to find a ghost to write about?"

"Come on, Roarke!" She stepped a little closer to him. "We wanted this to be about both of us, remember? Your book and my research. Something is trying to communicate with both of us. I think we need to listen."

"All right." He sighed. "But before we start ghost-hunting, could I get to my workout? I've got very little time left to get myself in top shape."

Turning from her, Rhea watched his long legs propel him into the woods, a moving wall of corded, roiling muscles and broad shoulders. *I need to ask him to define top shape.*

Roarke sat down on the plank and motioned for her to join him. "Rhea. I knew this book thing was going to be a difficult job for both of us, because there are many things about my past no one knows about, pertaining to my youth."

He glanced up at her from under his eyelashes, but she said nothing.

"I need to tell you some things which may make you understand who I am. First, you must swear you'll never write about them nor tell a soul. I've come to trust you, and maybe you can use the information to understand me better. Does that make sense?"

She nodded.

"And you can promise me those things?"

She nodded again.

"When I was young after my father left, I started doing odd jobs and errands for David. At first, it was innocent enough, and eventually, I was heavily under his influence. Before long, I was selling drugs.

"Davey told me those people made their own choices, and we might as well profit from it. I sold drugs for several years, feeling guilty the whole time, but the money I brought in made a huge difference to my family. I told my mother I was working at a corner store in another neighborhood, and she never questioned me."

"One day, a few of Davey's guys asked me to go on an errand. We drove to a fancy hotel and parked in the back. Two guys came out with a very scared-looking man between them, and we ended up in an industrial park. Davey was there and furious that they'd brought me along. He told me to find my way home. I later saw that scared-looking man on the television. He was a politician, and Davey told me later that he had to be taught a lesson because his views were at odds with those of some important people."

"They beat him?" Rhea stared at Roarke in shock.

It took a few minutes before Roarke spoke again. "He died in hospital a few days later."

"Oh, my God." She placed her hand on her heart.

Roarke spilled out the rest of the words in a rush. "I told Davey I wanted to stop working for him, and he told me it was impossible because I knew too much. If he went down, I went down with him. I had no way out."

"Jesus."

"Eventually, I had help getting out from Martin, who would become my step-father."

"Roarke, that's a crazy story." She looked down at the deep brown dirt at her feet.

"It's not a story. It's my life." He took a drink from his water bottle. "I don't like getting close to people because I feel I'm putting them in danger."

"If Davey's out of your life, then why?"

"He isn't out of my life." He took a deep breath before he continued, "Long story short, he's been blackmailing me for years. I give him a substantial amount every year, provided he never releases information about my past, our past. Now that I'm going back in the public eye, he wants to renegotiate the terms of our arrangement."

"Roark, you can't."

"I didn't tell you these things to get your opinion of them. I'm serious now." Roarke gave her a serious look and resisted an urge to tuck a loose lock of her hair behind her ear. "I've told you so you can truly understand who I am."

"I do. I just don't think you should beat yourself up." Blowing an insect off her arm, she chuckled as it hit Roarke's face before flying off. "Things worked out for you. You're a bona fide celebrity."

Roarke smiled just before his brow furrowed, and he slapped his thigh with his hand. "Damn it to Hell!"

"What?"

"I forgot about this event I have to go to tonight in the city. It is a celebration of Scottish actors, and my agent says I have to do some press for the movie."

"You don't want to go?"

"Hell no! I'd rather be shot in the foot, but I am afraid I have to."

He chewed on his lip for a moment until a grin spread across his face.

"What?" She looked at him suspiciously.

"My agent was pushing me to bring a date. Kind of food for gossip, as it were. Since you need to stay with me, at my side, it would only make sense that—"

"Me? Go to a fancy party? No way!"

"It's a small thing. A few photos, dinner, and a few awards."

Swallowing hard, she shook her head. "Oh, Roarke, I'm not good with that kind of thing, and fancy people make me nervous."

Grabbed both of her hands in his, he leaned toward her. "We can both be socially awkward together. Come on. I'll have the prettiest date there."

Pulling her hands away from his, she frowned. "Don't try and charm me. You know it doesn't work."

"Then I'll appeal to your rational side. You have to stay with me anyway."

"But—but I don't have anything to wear."

"Once we reach the city, you can go shopping."

"I detest shopping."

"You can go in your nightgown for all I care."

"Okay, if I have to go shopping to attend your shindig, you have to go shopping with me."

"Oh, no."

"Fair's fair." She folded her arms in front of her chest.

"All right, but we have to leave right away. Pack a small bag. I'll go and see Ian. Be back soon."

His long strides took him out of the woods and up the hill. He was glad she would be going with him and glad he had managed to avoid discussing the voice on the recording. It had turned his insides into jelly. He didn't need to hear it again to know that it was otherworldly, as it had a tremor, a cadence, that hit the ear strangely.

Rhea studied her reflection in the mirror. *What can I do with my hair?* She took down her ponytail and shook out her red-brown tresses, piling them into a bun on the top of her head. *God, no. That just makes me look like my Aunt Mildred.*

She removed her white tank top and sports bra, to see her face, shoulders, neck, and chest were tanned differently. *How am I going to be able to get away with any dress?*

Hearing Roarke come back into the house, she pulled on her tank top, grabbed her bag and sweater, and walked down the hall into the kitchen.

Roarke passed her in the hallway. "I just need to throw some things into a bag. You ready?"

"Yup," she yelled up to him as he entered his bedroom.

"As ready as I'll ever be."

A short time later, showered and changed, he dropped his bag next to the door, as Rhea was putting her reading glasses and a fresh notebook into her bag. He glanced up at her and then looked down at the floor. "You're ready, then?"

She furrowed her brow at him. "Yes, I was ready the first time you asked me."

Roarke scratched his forehead and a few curls spilled forward over his hand. "I hate to draw attention to this, but are you sure you want to go out in public like that?" He glanced at her chest. "I mean, I have no problem with it, but it'll be rather distracting."

Not sure of what he was talking about, she glanced down at her chest, to her complete horror. When she'd heard Roarke enter the house, she threw on her tank top, forgetting to put on her sports bar.

Being a little top-heavy, the sports bras she wore kept her breasts smashed against her body. Without the sports bra and wearing just a thin tank top, she was practically shirtless.

Covering her chest with her arms, she headed for the bathroom, pulled a bra out of her bag, and changed.

A light breeze stirred her hair, and she went to close the window, but it wasn't open. A shiver ran through her when from nearby, she could hear a woman's laughter, a light tinkling giggle like wind chimes on a tree. She spun around and ran out of the bathroom.

Roarke stood with one hand on the doorknob and the other on his hips, trying to hide his smile.

Pointing her finger at him, she issued a warning. "Not a word, McCallum."

Chapter Eleven: Butterflies

She picked the most terrible time to get sick.

R oarke stepped back, opened the front door, and followed her out.

Rhea stormed down the steps to the truck. Appraising her as she moved, he noticed once again that she had the type of body he adored, which would be warm and sweet when pressed against him. *Cuddly.*

She was off-limits, regardless of how much he wanted to grab her and kiss her until she was breathless.

As they entered the city, a light rain had started, and Roarke pointed out various landmarks, cathedrals, museums, cemeteries, and renowned streets as they headed toward the shopping district.

A friendly-looking blond girl with a pixie cut greeted them as they entered a small, neat dress shop.

Rhea walked up to her. "Hi. I'm going to a function tonight and need a cocktail dress. Green or blue, nothing too fancy, and as I detest shopping, if you could make this as painless as possible for me, I'd appreciate it."

The girl laughed. "Okay. Let's see what we can do."

A few minutes later, Rhea emerged from the changing room in a beautifully tailored, dark green silk dress, ending just above the knee. Tight and sleeveless, it bared her toned arms and shapely shoulders while hiding her irregular tan lines. The material dipped low in the back, and two thin silver chains connected both sides, meeting in the middle and falling midway down her back.

Roarke took a step toward her, shoving his hands into his jean pockets. "Wow, that . . . that dress looks lovely on you."

After about ten minutes in a shoe shop, Rhea walked out with a pair of high-heeled strappy silver sandals.

Back in the car, Roarke didn't start it right away. Instead, he exhaled, resting his forehead on the steering wheel. "Ah, Rhea. There is something I should have mentioned earlier."

"What is it?"

"Ah, I can't be here without visiting my mother. She'd never forgive me."

"Oh, that's wonderful!" she exclaimed, excited at the prospect of meeting his mother. "Can I come?"

"Of course," he stammered, looking up at the sky from beneath the windshield. "Chances are some of my extended family will be there, and they're a bit, well, unfiltered."

"Just tell me if there's something you don't want me to write about."

"All right, but don't say I didn't warn you about the unfiltered part." A smile split his handsome face. "I didn't tell anyone I was coming. Going to surprise my mother."

"What if she's not there?"

"They'll be there. My stepfather's not in the best of health these days. They don't go far." He started the truck and pulled away from the curb, "Besides, she's always after me to bring home a nice girl. She'll be over the moon when she sees you."

Her jaw dropped. "You're going to tell her I'm working for you, right?"

"Sure, and you're escorting me to a soiree."

"What about the people at the event tonight? I'm your date?"

Looking over at her mischievously. "Friends with benefits?"

"Not hardly!" After a few seconds, she added shyly, looking at her fingers. "You won't ditch me, will you?"

"No, ma'am. I'll stay by your side all evening being a perfect gentleman."

"Even though I've seen some strange antics from you, I assumed you'd be a gentleman. You always are."

"Don't exactly know what to say to that." He winked at her. "Thank you, Rhea."

Roarke pointed out more sights until they reached an area of block apartments and corner shops. Outside a row of attached houses, Roarke pointed over Rhea's shoulder. "That's ours."

After hopping out of the truck, he ran around to hold the door for Rhea after she had put her pen and notebook back in her bag.

"I hope she didn't hear the truck pull up. Noisy, shitty thing."

"Does it get you from Point A to Point B?" She threw her bag over her shoulder, and they walked down the small concrete walkway to the front door.

"Aye."

"Then it's not so shitty."

He chuckled. "Ms. Sioui, you do have a way with words. So no, I guess it's not so shitty."

The quaint Victorian three-story apartment building looked old but well maintained. Flowers bloomed in boxes on every windowsill.

"We own the building, mother lives on the ground floor, and we rent the two upper apartments. This is where I grew up, but we didn't own it then. First thing I bought when I had a bit of money."

"I love her flowers."

"Red, blue, and yellow. The colors of her tartan."

Roarke opened the door, facing two long flights of stairs. Everything was spotless with an old painting of a foxhunt halfway up the first staircase. The small entryway smelled of food and the old, mildew scent that old buildings always seemed to carry regardless of renovations.

Stepping to the large navy door, Roarke knocked a short tattoo. From inside, Rhea heard slippered footsteps hurrying to the door and a melodic woman's voice saying, "Roarke! It's Roarke!"

The door swung open, and a friendly-faced stocky woman stood on the other side.

"Roarke." She reached for his head with her hands, and he bent toward his mother and hugged her as she peppered his face with kisses. She pulled away from him to batter his arms and chests with light punches.

"Why didn't you tell me you were coming?"

He laughed as he dodged her fists. "Ouch! I wanted to surprise you."

"You succeeded! You're nothing but trouble to me, but I wouldn't change you a bit!" Reaching up, she gave him another kiss, and then clearly realized Rhea was there. She turned to look at her son with amused brown eyes, tilting her head to one side. "And who is this?"

Roarke cleared his throat. "Ma, this is my friend Rhea. She's writing a biography on me to come out before the new film. She'll be following me around for the next two weeks.

His mother said nothing but continued to gaze at Rhea, who held out her hand.

"How do you do, Ms. McCallum?"

Her face split into a large, beautiful smile, and she gripped Rhea's hand. "Pretty eyes"

Rhea blushed slightly. "Thank you, Ms. McCallum. I've

been looking forward to meeting you. Roarke's told me wonderful things."

"Yes, he'd better, and it's Mrs. Coffey, I've remarried."

She had her hand on the small of Rhea's back and shoved
her toward the kitchen. When she stood in the kitchen doorframe, the sound of cutlery on plates and happy chatter died
out as a table full of people turned to look at her with surprised expressions.

Mrs. Coffey broke the silence, "Didn't any of you lot hear
me when I yelled that it was Roarke at the door? Too busy
stuffing your faces?"

Roarke stepped up behind Rhea. "Everyone, this is Rhea."

Rhea lifted a hand and uttered a squeaky *Hi.*

The room erupted in noise as everyone got out of their
chairs and headed in their direction, hugging Roarke and
shaking Rhea's hand.

"Roarke! You Devil! Why didn't you say you were coming
when I spoke to you?"

"Forgot about it till today."

"Roarke, you look tired."

"Hello, Rhea. Have you eaten? We're just sitting down."

"Big game on tonight, Roarke."

"We're having one of your favorites for lunch."

Mrs. Coffey yelled for everyone to take their seats, and the
chatter continued as chairs, plates, and cutlery appeared to
accommodate Roarke and Rhea. As they sat across from each
other, Mrs. Coffey presented them with heaping plates of
bangers and mash, covered in thick gravy.

Roarke's mother sat at the head of the table, and at the
other end was a broad heavy-set silver-haired man, Roarke's
stepfather, Martin. To his left sat a small, wiry man of about
the same age with sharp features and eyes dancing with mischief, Mrs. Coffey's brother Angus. Next to him was a tall,
pretty woman with wavy chestnut brown hair and deep

brown eyes, Roarke's sister Tessa, who had eyes for no one but her big brother, and Roarke held her hand as they chatted. Tessa's husband, Yans, originally from Norway, sat to the right of Martin. Between Yans and Rhea was Tessa's young daughter Maren, who appeared to be around six or seven.

Maren turned to Rhea and asked, "Are you Uncle Roarke's girlfriend?"

Rhea coughed in surprise, and Tessa elbowed Roarke, both of them stifling grins behind their hands.

"Gosh, No. We're just friends."

"Do you want to be his girlfriend?"

Tessa admonished her daughter. "Maren, stop asking personal questions."

"No, it's all right." Rhea shook her hand at Tessa before turning again to Maren. "No, really, we're just friends."

"Why don't you want to be his girlfriend?" Maren shot back.

Everyone at the table chuckled, including Rhea, and Yans took that opportunity to engage his daughter in conversation, saving Rhea from further questions.

Rhea caught his eye over Maren's shoulder and mouthed a silent, "Thank you," to which he grinned and gave her a friendly wink.

Tessa turned to her brother. "I hope you can stay a few days at least. That young violinist out of Ayrshire is giving a concert, and I know we can round up another ticket." She glanced at Rhea and smiled. "Or two."

"No time, Sis," he explained. "Only in for the night, and we'll be off in the morning."

"I'll be sure to get you up for a nice big breakfast," Mrs. Coffey said as she pushed aside her plate and picked up her teacup.

"We'll just stay at the hotel. No trouble for you."

"Have you lost your mind?" Martin looked down the table

at his wife's horrified face. "Do you want your mother to lose her mind? It's me who'll have to hear about it if you stay at a hotel."

Roarke's mother still hadn't said anything, yet she regarded her son with an icy look that spoke volumes. When she did speak, it was to Rhea and not Roarke. "Would you rather stay in a stuffy hotel room, laying on sheets where God knows who has done God knows what, or stay in a nice, clean room in a tidy house where you get home cooking?"

"I really shouldn't have a say in it, but if it were up to me, I'd rather stay where I could get meals like this."

Both women turned their eyes gradually over to gaze at Roarke's face, who threw up his hands and laughed. "I'd rather stay here, too. I just didn't want you put to any trouble, Mother."

"As if my son were ever any trouble." She looked at him so lovingly that Rhea's heart ached for Liam.

Rhea looked at Tessa, whose brown eyes were exactly like her brother's. "Speaking of the party, I'm not very good at styling my hair, is there a hair salon around that might squeeze me in?"

Tessa laughed. "A hair salon? Didn't Roarke tell you I'm a hairstylist?"

"No, he didn't."

Tessa's face lit up with excitement. "Oh, that'll be fun! Mother needs to get ready for her dart party tonight. I say we kick the men over to our house, and we have a girl's day over here."

"Wonderful idea, and we can help Maren with her bake sale for her Taekwondo class."

Rhea looked down at Maren. "My mother was famous for her Tulip cookies. I could make them for you if you'd like."

"Okay." The little girl beamed up at her. "If you can bake

well, you'd be a good girlfriend for my uncle. He loves cookies."

Everyone chuckled, but Roarke and Rhea just smiled before looking down at their plates.

Mrs. Coffey turned to her granddaughter, and muttered,
"Might be a good girlfriend indeed."

A half-hour later, the men were heading out the door.
Roarke was the last to leave, and as Rhea walked him to the
door, he whispered, "You don't mind being left alone here?"

"Not if you don't," Rhea answered honestly. "I won't be
wasting my time. I fully intend to wrestle every story I can get
out of your mother and sister."

"Just do me a favor. If my mother tries to show you any
photos of me in the bathtub, avert your eyes."

"Will do."

Turning to walk out, Rhea had half-closed the door before
Roarke turned back around. "First time in a few days that
we've been apart."

"I know." She sighed in exaggerated relief. "Enjoy your
freedom."

That afternoon, Rhea chatted with Tessa and Mrs. Coffey
about Roarke, making madeleines, whipping up the butter-
cream, finally arranging the cookies in a large Tupperware
bin.

"Oh, they are nice," said Tessa as she helped herself to another fluffy, buttery cookie from a plate on the table.

Her mother tapped her wrist. "Don't eat them all, or Maren
won't have any to sell."

"Don't worry, Ma." Tess laughed at her. "Rhea's already
put Maren's away. These are extra."

Rhea washed the pans and bowls. "I wanted to save a few
for Roarke."

The two women exchanged long, knowing looks at each other, smiling and tapping their fingers on their noses. For some reason, the look between the women embarrassed Rhea.

Mrs. Coffey went to prepare a casserole, and Tessa and Rhea moved into Mrs. Coffey's bedroom to get ready.

By the time the men noisily burst in the door and headed into the kitchen, Tess had just finished Rhea's hair as Yans came into the bedroom with Tessa's make-up case.

"My God, Tessa." Rhea laughed. "The suitcase I brought here isn't as big as that!"

"It's my job to make women feel beautiful."

Tessa had styled Rhea's hair in a side part so that one side was pulled tight and pinned with glittery clips, and the other side fell in tousled waves down the side of her face and over her shoulder.

Twenty minutes later, Rhea looked at her reflection in absolute wonder. Her skin was highlighted, bronzed, and flawless. Her lips looked fuller and glossed a color with a hint of orange, and a smoky eye exaggerated the unusual shape and brought out the orange and yellow dots. Her green dress and silver shoes completed the look.

"Oh my God, Tessa." She spun around. "You're a miracle worker. I've never looked better in my life."

"What jewelry are you wearing?" Mrs. Coffey asked.

"Just my diamond studs," she replied as she played with her silver chain. "I thought that would be enough."

"Are you going to take off your chain? It's a tad casual for this evening," Tessa remarked.

Rhea's fingers closed protectively over her pendants. "I never take this off."

"You need a little something," Mrs. Coffey shook her head, "I've just the thing."

Going over to her jewelry case, she pulled out a set of gorgeous earrings, emerald studs with a link of silver chain from which small, emerald teardrop-shaped stones dangled. "Put these on."

"They're exquisite." She reached for them but then retracted her hand. "I can't wear them. I might lose them."

"Don't be silly." Mrs. Coffey took another step toward her and laid them in her open palm. "You won't lose them. Roarke gave them to me a few years ago."

When the women decided she was ready, they opened the door just as Roarke yelled, "Rhea!"

"I'm coming!" she yelled back from the hall with Tessa. "The girls have been playing dress-up with me."

Rhea was pinning the back of an earring as she rounded the corner to the kitchen to find Roarke sitting at the table with Angus and Martin. Lifting his glass of whisky to his lips, he saw her and his hand froze, a blank expression on his face.

Her hand flew to her hair. "What's wrong? Do I look all right?"

"No, you don't look all right." His smile made her insides turn to jelly. "You look smashing! Out of this world!"

Rhea blushed and looked down, pretending to brush something off her dress, but really, she found it hard to look at Roarke.

His hair was sleek and secured behind his head, and his cleanly-shaven face defined his distinct cheekbones and angular jaw. He wore a black tuxedo-style jacket, a matching vest with silver buttons, a white shirt, and a black bowtie, his height and broad shoulders making him seem massive at the table.

Roarke cleared his throat as he tried to think of something to say. She looked exquisite, and her haunted cat eyes were mesmerizing. Exaggerated in black, they glittered and shone with an otherworldly quality, but the only thing he could think to say was, "I guess we'd better get going."

Without breaking eye contact with Rhea, he put his hands on the table in front of him and slowly rose to his feet.

As he stepped from around the table, Rhea saw that he wore a kilt and was traditionally dressed with hose, flashes, black, a sporran, and *sgian-dubh*, a small dagger. Her breath caught in her throat as her heart pounded in her chest, hands at her cheeks as she realized she was blushing furiously.

Taken aback by her reaction, she felt her knees buckle, and she would have fallen if she hadn't steadied herself with the doorframe.

Mrs. Coffey had just come around the corner and grabbed her arm to make sure she didn't fall. "Rhea, are you all right?"

"Yes . . . yes. I just stumbled in the shoes. I-I'm not used to high heels."

Mrs. Coffey looked from Rhea to her son, and Tessa, Angus, and Martin chuckled together. The corners of Roarke's mouth twitched, and Rhea allowed a small smile to spread across her face.

Tessa looked at her with a broad grin. "Your shoes?"

"My shoes."

"You stumbled?"

"I stumbled." Smoothing down the front of her dress. She glanced at Roarke, who stepped toward her and held out his hand.

Mrs. Coffey kissed her on the cheek. "Have a wonderful time, dear."

Touching his mother's arm, Rhea smiled at Tessa. "Thank you both. I couldn't have gotten ready on my own."

As the door was closing behind them, Rhea could hear the conversation in the kitchen.

"She fell."

"Aye."

"It was her shoes."

"Clara, do your knees buckle when I'm in Scottish tartan?" Martin asked.

"No, but they buckle when I see you loading the dishwasher." Mrs. Coffey chuckled, "Nothing sexier than that."

Outside the grand hotel, the door to the limo opened, and Roarke swung his legs out of the car. Pulling himself to his full height, he straightened his jacket before holding out his hand for Rhea.

At his touch, a jolt of energy jumped between them, and she feared she would vomit all over the red carpet. The next second, he lifted her hand to his lips and pressed a gentle kiss on her knuckles, smiling down at her. "I promised I'd be a perfect gentleman, didn't I?"

In her periphery, she saw flashing lights and a crowd of well-dressed people. Roarke flashed a beaming smile to all around, raising his hand in salute. People jostled to look at him, his usual relaxed posture replaced by a calm, elegant demeanor, and he seemed to have grown another two feet. Regardless of how he felt about being in the public eye, he knew how to handle it, and the funny man Rhea had been growing closer to was replaced by a movie star.

The press wanted photos, and he stood for one photographer after another, one hand behind his back and the other gripping Rhea's. She angled her body and did as he did, naturally smiling and turning to each photographer, until Roarke turned to the main door and guided her to the entrance.

They walked into the elegant room, and Roarke beamed at

her. "You did great! I swear you've done this before."

"It wasn't as bad as I thought it would be."

"I could use a drink."

"I'll take two," Rhea grinned, "One for each hand."

As the first part of the evening progressed, Roarke circulated the room with Rhea in tow. People were constantly stopping to speak to him, and he never seemed able to finish a conversation because he was continually interrupted.

Looking around while Roarke was speaking to a group of men, she was conscious of how much attention he was commanding. Even if they didn't talk to him, people always noticed and followed him with their eyes, especially women. Eventually, to her horror, she realized she was jealous.

Some women smiled at her, others practically glared, but what disturbed Rhea were those who looked at her with unbridled confusion, looking her up and down. Having such beautiful, elegant women looking at her made her feel uncomfortable and aware that she didn't belong.

"Rhea?" His forehead furrowed in worry. "Is something wrong?"

Before she had time to answer, they both turned at the sound of his name. A tall leggy blond with striking features smiled at Roarke. Letting go of Rhea's hand, he gave the blond an enormous hug.

"Alicia!" He pulled his head back just as a photographer arrived and started taking pictures of the two embracing. Alicia even tilted her head to rest on Roarke's shoulder, and Rhea moved to the side, more uncomfortable than ever.

The photographer left, and Roarke turned to Alicia, giving her a weathering look, "Why do you always seem to know where every photographer is?" He then turned to Rhea. "Oh, Rhea, Alicia. Alicia, Rhea."

Both women smiled at the other, and Alicia did a clean sweep of Rhea.

"Well," she smirked, "Give me a jingle the next time you're here, or if you need some stimulating company for a screening."

"I certainly will."

Kissing Roarke on the cheek and smiling at Rhea, Alicia walked a few feet and tapped another man on the shoulder before the crowd blocked her from view.

Roarke walked forward with his hand on Rhea's side. "We used to work together." He made no further comment, and she didn't ask.

Shortly there afterward, a man on the stage with a microphone asked everyone to sit. Roarke and Rhea made their way to their seats, escorted by a young waiter. The young man lingered by Roarke's chair after they had seated themselves, and Roarke glanced up at him.

"Yes?"

"You don't recognize me, do you?" A smile spread across the young man's handsome face, and his brown eyes twinkled with mischief.

Suddenly, Roarke grinned back. "Owen Jarvis?"

The young man nodded, and Roarke jumped up to embrace him warmly, the smaller man wincing slightly in the massive bear hug. "Um, could you let go? We're not supposed to mingle with the guests."

Roarke released him from the hug and whacked him on the back. "Tell them to speak to me if they have a problem. How've you been?"

"Grand. I'm in university now."

"What're you studying?"

"Mechanical Engineering. I want to go into robotics."

"That's impressive, young man."

The man on stage asked everyone to sit again, and Owen said he had to continue working.

"Call if you need anything."

"Will do," said Owen, but after two steps, he turned back. "Thanks for everything. The shelter saved my life."

Roarke just nodded at the boy, and Owen turned and walked away.

Taking a swig of his whisky, he answered Rhea's question before she asked. "He started coming to the shelter when he was about fifteen. His father had kicked him out for being gay."

"Poor kid."

"Aye, but if they're serious, they can change and keep a job. We cover tuition if the kid stays in school."

"That's wonderful."

"That's why I need to get all dressed up and strut about like a peacock." He grinned and puffed out his chest. "Money doesn't grow on trees."

Later, as Roarke nodded goodbye to another well-wisher, Rhea began eating her Caprese salad.

"Are you enjoying the food? Roarke asked.

"It's delicious." She licked some balsamic glaze off the tongs of her fork.

"I hope I can eat something before I have to chat again."

As artists received awards for film, television, games, and children's television, they dined on crab salad with pickled radish, soft quail egg, and tomato gazpacho. The main course was seared duck breast with butternut squash purée, potato foam, sweet roasted onion, and red wine jus. Lemon and ginger cake, verbena sorbet, and citrus salad completed the meal.

As everyone enjoyed coffee and brandy, a young woman came over to remind Roarke that he had an interview scheduled in another room.

"My apologies, Rhea."

"No worries. I'll sit here and enjoy my whisky. You know, I think I'm developing a taste for it."

He smiled at her and promised to return as soon as possible.

Rhea took out her phone and made a few notes. A few minutes later, a large man sat in the seat beside her. She turned. "That didn't take long."

Roarke wasn't sitting there. Instead, it was another tall, shockingly handsome man with smooth black hair, angular eyebrows set over deep brown eyes, and a flawless, toothy smile.

"Expecting someone else?" His voice was silky with inflections quite like Roarke's. "I know I'm disappointing when you're expecting the great Niall Shaw."

"He's doing an interview."

"Yes. Everyone wants a piece of Niall now he's back on the scene."

"All evening, people have wanted his attention."

"I imagine they don't have to look far to find him, but I mean, it's terribly hard to miss a tree wearing a kilt."

That would have made her chuckle, but for the humorless way he said it.

"I've brought you another whisky." He handed her a small glass half full of amber liquid. "Try it. It's better than the one Roarke selected, I'm sure."

He used Roarke and not Niall, so he knew him well but did not hold him in much regard. Then she realized she had seen him before, on television in the pub the first day she arrived. He was the man Roarke despised. David Cojocaru, Isabel's lover, and Willem's father.

Deciding to be cordial, she took a sip and laid the glass on the table in front of her. "Roarke should be back soon."

"Oh, I'm not interested in him at all. Unlike so many others, I don't find him particularly interesting. I'm more interested in you." He reached to take her hand. "Are you American?"

"Canadian."

"Potato, Pot-*ah*-to." Releasing her hand, he sipped his drink. "You're the flavor of the month."

"Are you a friend of his?"

"I wouldn't say friend." He angled his head. "We're not too friendly, but we used to be quite good friends. Ask him about it someday."

"I don't know your name, so I can't ask him anything."

"I don't know yours either." He sized her up and down in a manner that made her squirm.

Rhea sighed, getting annoyed and uncomfortable with him. "Will Roarke be happy to find you sitting here?"

"Probably not. I do have the habit of getting under his skin."

"You're here simply to annoy him?"

"He's amusing when he is annoyed."

"Others might say he's dangerous when he is annoyed."

"Yes, like most bears," He leaned toward her again, looking straight into her eyes. "But I still don't know who you are."

"I guess you'll have to walk away disappointed." She began to turn away from him until his strong hand squeezed her wrist.

"There is no need to be rude." His handsome face changed as he leaned toward her. "Be careful in Roarke's company."

"David!"

Rhea started as she heard Roarke's angry voice behind her chair. "You have two seconds to let her go before your expensive teeth wind up on the ground."

He released her hand and leaned back in his chair, feigning surprise. "Roarke, how good to see you!"

"What do you want, Davey?" They were both smiling at each other, but it was apparent their smiles were fake.

David glanced over at Rhea. "Just keeping your little lady

company, but you really shouldn't leave her alone. Any number of lascivious individuals might take advantage of your absence."

"Yes," Roarke said, his smile dropping a little. "I can see that. Why don't you leave before we make a scene? Neither of us needs that."

"Indeed." David stood up and straightened his jacket. "If you do need to step away again, no worries, I'll be keeping a watchful eye over your wee lassie."

"Come near her again, and the only thing you'll need to watch is my fist smashing into your face." Roarke closed the distance between them in one stride, anger and danger dancing in both pairs of brown eyes.

Rhea stood and placed her hand on Roarke's arm, tilting her head to smile coyly up at David. "I'm sorry you have to be going, but thank you for the whisky. It has a very complex presence."

David pulled his eyes away from Roarke's and cocked an eyebrow at Rhea. "Indeed."

Bowing his head by way of salutation, he ignored Roarke and sauntered off to chat with a group of young women, who reacted with delight as he approached.

Roarke thumped into his chair and leaned toward Rhea. "What'd he say to you?"

"Just passive-aggressive remarks about your character." She didn't want to upset him further. "That was the man you worked for, who sold drugs."

"That, my dear, is David Cojocaru. Local restauranteur, art dealer, philanthropist. That's how he would like to be known, at least. He wasn't so high and mighty when I knew him."

Roarke informed Rhea that he had fulfilled his obligations and was ready to leave. As they stood, Rhea turned to Roarke. "Would you say he knows you well? How long have you known each other?"

Roarke cleared his throat and stared at David's back. "He once told me that he knew me before we had bones."

By the time they reached Ms. Coffey's home, Rhea was laughing so hard her cheeks hurt. They were both still giggling as the driver left them on the sidewalk.

The front door opened with a creak as Rhea gingerly stepped through and held it open for Roarke.

He swayed slightly in the small entranceway. "Don't worry about noise. My mother and Martin sleep like the dead."

"I'd rather not wake anyone."

"Everyone's had some drink tonight. You wouldn't wake them with a chainsaw."

The living room was dark, but a soft, yellow light spilled into the hall from the kitchen. Without saying a word, they both headed toward the warm glow.

Roarke removed his jacket, placing it on the back of a chair. He had removed his tie and opened his collar as soon as they got into the car. His watch came off next and landed on the spotless table with a slight clink. Finally, he took down his hair and shook out his brown curls.

Rhea sat opposite him and removed her shoes, placing them side by side under the table. She noticed a small, folded piece of paper. "I think your mother left you a note."

Roarke reached across the table and picked it up. "It's for you."

"Me?" She took the note from him, her hand lightly brushing his, and a blush crept up her neck. Unfolding the small piece of light green paper, she admired the neat, delicate handwriting before reading it aloud,

Rhea,

The spare room is ready for you. Roarke knows which one. I left plates in the oven for you both. If you're still interested in going to

church in the morning, leave me a wee note, and I'll get you up in time for breakfast. Any chance my son might accompany us?

I hope you had fun,
Clara

Rhea refolded the note and placed it on the table. She looked up to find him regarding her warmly.

"Clara? Made a bit of an impression on my mother, I think."

"*Elle est si gentile.* She's a very kind lady." Rhea smiled down on the note, as she hadn't had a message from a mom in many years, and it made her feel cherished. "I'm going to pop in and change."

"I'll get the plates from the oven."

Picking up her shoes, Rhea headed from the kitchen, but then tiptoed back and slid the little note from the table.

Roarke was putting the plates down when Rhea entered soundlessly, wearing grey yoga pants and a green t-shirt.

"That smells amazing, and I could use it. I'm a little wobbly from the drink."

Roarke picked up her discarded glass by the sink. He filled it with water and placed it in front of Rhea. "You always take water with your meals."

They ate in silence for a few minutes before Roarke commented, "You look more like yourself now." She had piled her hair into a loose bun and removed most of the make-up. "I can see your freckles again."

"Stop with the freckles," she grumbled.

"My mother's beef casserole. It's got red wine in it, so you'll like it," he teased.

"Funny, Roarke." She noticed a tumbler of whisky next to her water glass. "Sorry, but I don't think I can drink that. I've had wine, champagne, whisky, beer."

"I probably don't need it either. I've had more than

enough, but there's an air of ceremony." Roarke raised his glass to Rhea slightly. "Anyway, it'll give my Uncle Angus something to complain about, someone being into his best whisky."

The wind stirred the chimes outside the kitchen window, filling the otherwise silent room with soft tinkling.

"It was nice seeing you all dressed up. I saw a different side of you."

"Seeing Owen was my favorite part."

"I could tell." Rhea used a piece of bread to soak up the gravy on her plate. "You're proud."

"Aye, and proud of what my team does," he admitted honestly. "I'm there as often as I can be, but I'm a figurehead. I don't have any education or training. I do what I can, but my staff is amazing. I wish I could do what they do, know what they know."

"Why don't you go back to school?"

"School?" he scoffed, "Ach, no, I'll leave the tough stuff to the tough people."

"How did you get to know Owen if you're barely there?"

"My senior director, Jesse, told me sometimes we can't help clicking with a kid. They sometimes remind us of ourselves. With myself and Owen, both of us have Daddy issues."

"You don't talk about your father much."

"Nope." He finished his drink and stood. "I'm not talking about him now." He spoke the last few words over his shoulder as he walked into the sitting room, returning with a full drink. When he sat, he thudded rather heavily onto his chair. "What did you like about tonight?"

"The lights, the photographers, everyone looking. Such fun."

"You're beautiful." He leaned forward in his chair. "People look at you."

"Alicia's opinion of me was understood." The moment she

said it, she wished she hadn't. She sounded like a jealous teenager.

Roarke shook his head, "She just wanted to see your reactions. She's a decent person under the tan and jewelry."

"She was rude to me."

"Look, she's used to competing with other women for everything. It's tough in the industry, despite how glamorous it looks, and after a certain age, it gets even worse."

Rhea was too emotional to let Roarke's words sink in. "She was trying to make me jealous."

He swirled the whisky in his glass. "Did it work?"

Finding herself under the full force of his gaze, she was unable to look away. "Did you date her?"

"Briefly," he answered honestly. "But Alicia wanted more than I could give."

"She loved you?"

"She was in love with the idea of us. I could never give her enough, whether it was attention, time, money. She always wanted more than I could give. Eventually, she moved on."

"I don't think she's over it." She wanted to kick herself for sounding like a pouty child.

"I know she is," he sounded confident. "She's just protective of me."

Not wanting to press the issue, Rhea stood, pushed in her chair, and put her plate in the dishwasher. "I think I'll hit the hay. I have to get up early tomorrow."

"Rhea?"

As she turned to leave, Roarke closed his hand around her wrist. Stopping, she didn't turn around, as her heart was pounding so hard she felt sure he must be able to feel her pulse beneath his fingertips or at least hear it. Her blood rushed to her head, and she felt faint. Something in his touch and the way he said her name made her nervous, excited, and terrified all at the same time. Butterflies in her stomach fluttered their way up toward her throat.

"Rhea, look at me."

Knowing her face was crimson, she slowly turned to him. Although she knew he was tipsy, his eyes were clear as they regarded her.

"I get a distinct impression that I make you uncomfortable."

"You don't."

"I do."

"You dooonnn'tttt." She dragged out the last word in a playful manner.

"I dooooooo." He mimicked her, smiling.

"Fine." She sighed. "You're just a little . . . intimidating sometimes."

"Is it my size?"

"A little." She lied.

"Is that all?" He narrowed his eyes.

"Yes." She lied again. "That's all."

His chocolate brown eyes were full of warmth and glowed with unspoken emotions, almost as if he were thinking about something painful. Then he tilted his head, and his gaze dropped from hers to her mouth. His jaw slackened a little, drawing her focus to his mouth as well.

Past his smooth lower lip, she could see the line of his bottom teeth as he worked his jaw to one side and seemed to bite the tip of his tongue. Once again, he reminded her of a dangerous animal, an irresistible, unbelievably beautiful, yet dangerous animal. His gaze flicked back to hers, and she found herself unable to move. The only thing she could do was close her eyes and hope that when she opened her eyes again, he was looking somewhere else.

Rhea felt hot and dizzy—something in her stomach was doing cartwheels. She placed her open palm on her abdomen to try to calm it as Roarke slowly dragged his knuckles across her jawline.

The air around them was thick, and she tried to talk to change the energy in the room. Finally, she opened her eyes but looked down. "You were the movie star tonight?"

He inclined his head once as a reply.

"Who are you now?" she whispered.

"The person I usually am when I am with you."

"Who's that?"

"Myself." He blushed slightly, a warm glow lighting his cheekbones. "But a different version of me. More nervous, but calmer, more excited but reflective, happy and sad, myself and someone else."

Both confused and gladdened by his words, she still sought to escape the uncomfortable energy of this new brush with intimacy between them. "That sounds confusing."

"Ever since that day at the pub, whenever you're around, all I see is you. My eyes find you everywhere."

Roarke pulled her hand, effortlessly gravitating her toward him. With a slight tug at her wrist, she was in front of him, her head only slightly above his. He spread his knees apart, and with one arm wrapped around her waist, he pulled her closer and dropped her wrist, reaching up to caress the side of her face. His hand traveled down the side of her neck, turning as he ran his fingertips along the clavicle. Then up to cup the curve of her shoulder, running under the sleeve of her t-shirt. "Your skin feels like rose petals."

Having no idea where he was going to touch her next, she looked up to tell him to stop, but his hands came to rest on either side of her hips, finding the points of each hipbone and rubbing them. The sensation caused her to tremble.

One hand inched up her spine to cradle the back of her head, tangling itself in her hair. She was powerless to move as he drew her closer and pressed the cold tip of his nose at the tiny dip at her throat, and then his warm cheek rested on her chest, just above the swell of her breasts.

The creatures in her stomach lurched upwards, getting closer and closer to her throat.

Roarke inhaled, and his lips burned a path of tender kisses along the base of her throat. Time froze when she felt his breath on her cheek, his breath hot on the corner of her mouth, and she turned toward it, wanting to take his breath, his smell, his essence, into her mouth, into her.

There he stopped, breathing into her open mouth. "Is this all right?"

Her body betraying every command given by her rational brain, she nodded, and his lips brushed against hers so lightly she wasn't sure it had happened. Then, opening her eyes, she found his gaze boring into her own, cinnamon into sage.

The next second, she was jolted back to reality as she felt the butterflies in her throat heave their way into the back of her mouth.

Tearing away from him and pushing away his hands, she was grateful for her quiet feet as she threw herself down the hallway. She gingerly closed the door in the bathroom, locked it behind her, lifted the toilet seat, and threw up.

Chapter Twelve: Good Riddance

Following the burn to get to the hill with the large stone, the darkness does not terrify me, nor the thick fog. I am sick with the horror of what will happen if we are discovered. We only have a little time to travel before my presence is missed.

Once I get to the stone and feel his strong arms around me, his calm, blue eyes will reassure me that everything is going to be fine.

"Rhea, dear, breakfast is ready," Mrs. Coffey sang into the crack of the door.

"Yes, ma'am," she said as she stretched. "I'll just freshen up."

"No rush, dear."

Mrs. Coffey hummed as she walked down the hallway and away from her door, the same tune Roarke hummed when he cooked. Rhea smiled, thinking of him cooking in his kitchen.

Roarke! She squeezed her eyes tightly, remembering what had happened the night before. *Sweet Jesus. How am I ever going to face him?*

Memories of running to the bathroom and vomiting flooded back. After Rhea had locked herself in the bathroom, Roarke had knocked on the door. She had whispered through the crack, "Could you please go away? This is embarrassing enough."

"Can I get you anything?"

"No, thank you. I have all I need here," she told him and closed the door to his continued apologies.

Sitting up in bed, she rested her head on her knees, wanting to curl up under the covers and not come out, but Roarke's mother waited for her. After opening the bedroom door and checking that the coast was clear, she headed to the bathroom.

After a large breakfast, during a walkabout the neighborhood, Mrs. Coffey gave Rhea details about the city and their area, the distillery, and the docks, and then they made their way to church.

When they stepped inside the charming beige triangular church with a tall tower to the right, service was about to begin. They sat side by side on a wooden pew near the center of the church, amongst young families, teenagers, and elders. A beautiful, elegant woman with exotic features and long straight jet-black hair sat next to a tall man in a dark suit in the front pew.

The woman reached across to brush something off her partner's shoulder, and as he turned to bend his head in her direction, Rhea was shocked to see that the handsome man was David Cojocaru. His features set in a look of attentiveness and peaceful tranquility. *What on earth is a man like that doing in church?*

After service, parishioners had tea and coffee with pastries at the back of the church, and Mrs. Coffey circulated, introducing Rhea as a family friend. Then, behind her hand, Mrs. Coffey whispered to Rhea, "Some busy-bodies always want to know what Roarke is up to."

"Can't blame them. Roarke's an interesting man," Rhea commented as Mrs. Coffey turned to greet a friend.

"I guess there is no accounting for taste," someone whispered in her ear. Rhea spun around to face David Cojocaru sporting smug self-assuredness as the night before, yet looking the picture of piety in his dark suit and pale blue shirt.

"David!" Mrs. Coffey turned toward them, and to Rhea's complete shock, she put her hands on either side of his face, kissing his cheek.

David returned her warm embrace. "Mrs. Coffey."

"You look wonderful, dear. We've missed you the past month."

"You know what a perfectionist Meredith is. The renovations to the family house in Romania are her baby these days. She's a stickler for keeping the traditional architecture,"

When David spoke to Mrs. Coffey, his accent changed to be very similar to hers.

"Is Meredith here? And the children?" Mrs. Coffey scanned the room.

"Unfortunately, Willem has been avoiding church, and the girls stayed with their nanny today. Meredith's speaking to Mrs. Glendale about a donation for the Bible Studies class's trip to Rome."

"David, you both do too much." Mrs. Coffey patted his cheek affectionately and turned back to Rhea. "Rhea, this is David Cojocaru. He's originally from this area and has made quite a name for himself."

"Yes, we met last night."

Her shock over the polite relations between David and Roarke's mother must have shown on her face, because Mrs. Coffey put her hands on her hips.

"Please tell me you two were civil to each other." Mrs. Coffey pouted at David.

"As civil as we always are."

"Rhea, the boys have never gotten along, but David's mother and I are old friends. We grew up in the same area, close to where Roarke has his cottage now, actually."

"Angus and Martin are absent today?"

Mrs. Coffey pursed her lips. "Martin had a few too many last night, and Angus had bad dreams. I found him in the kitchen this morning, asleep at his teacup."

"Funny you say that." Rhea furrowed her brow a little. "I had strange dreams as well last night."

"Maybe I shouldn't say in the church." Mrs. Coffey leaned toward them. "But from time to time, Angus swears he wakes at night to find a woman standing at the foot of his bed. He's always a bundle of nerves the day after."

"Your home is haunted?"

"I don't think so. Angus is the only one who sees her, and he's woken to her when he's been sleeping in other places."

David cleared his throat. "I don't know what ghosts are, but I believe in them."

"You, David?" Mrs. Coffey smiled up at him. "That surprises me."

"My father always told me his ancestral home in Romania was haunted. One story in particular caught my attention. One day his mother was in the sitting room when she looked up to find two shadowy figures standing in the doorway. When she screamed, they darted down the hall."

"That would be frightening." Rhea arched her eyebrow at the tall man.

"It gets even stranger, my dear." David took a step closer to the attentive women. "On the day my grandmother was buried, myself and a distant cousin were walking down the corridor toward the salon as we headed to the kitchen. We happened to glance into the sitting room, and there, in her favorite chair, sat my grandmother. She turned to look at us, and in our fright, we started and ran."

"You think she came back to see you all one more time?" Mrs. Coffey asked him.

"I don't know." He ran a hand through his blue-black hair. "But studying Physics has made me think of time differently. Is it set? Is it fixed? Einstein said the distinction between past, present, and future is just an illusion. We like to separate our lives into periods, minutes, hours, years, centuries, but how does it work, really?" He looked up at the stained-glass window depicting Christ on the road to Calvary. "Grandmother used to say angels are sent to earth to guide spirits into the afterlife, but some spirits won't go because they have something yet to do. The angel leaves a portal behind for the spirit, so they may cross over when they've completed their task. Maybe the house just has a portal."

Looking back at the two women standing hypnotized by his words, he smiled. "We'd scared her, and she'd scared us, but who were the ghosts? Us or her? There are lapses in time, and when that happens, everything we think we know about reality in the universe ceases to exist. Dark Matter is called dark because it is not visible to us, even with all our technology and because it represents our ignorance of the world and our universe."

Rhea smiled. "My mother always said running water causes strange things to happen. Water is the source of all life, and spirits are drawn to it, the life in it, and the energy."

David turned his full attention to Rhea, and a genuine smile crossed his lips. "Our ancestral home is built on underground caves fed by water from a nearby valley."

Mrs. Coffey glanced at her watch and put down her teacup and saucer before turning to Rhea. "Look at the time. Roarke wanted to leave soon after lunch."

"Meredith will be sorry to have missed you." David bent to kiss her before turning to Rhea. "Pleasure to see you again."

On the short walk back to the house, Rhea was lost in her thoughts when Mrs. Coffey halted and turned to look at Rhea. "You're wondering why I'm so friendly with a man who despises my son."

"Maybe a little."

Mrs. Coffey sat on a bench in front of a small thicket of trees and patted the seat for Rhea to sit.

"As far as I know, David and Roarke have never liked each other. I think things happened between them when they were younger. Even as a young man, David had connections around here, and I think my boy was a wee bit jealous. Roarke has asked me to stay out of it, and I have to respect his wishes."

Rhea sat and listened.

"David did some bad things when he was younger. I'm aware of that, but his father was an absolute beast. Between David's antics and his father's alcoholism, the neighbors were not overly kind to Ella, David's mother, but I stayed true to my friend."

"Roarke says you're the kindest person he's ever known."

"I felt for her, and David's always respected the way I treated his mother when others were cruel," She took a deep breath. "In truth, I understood her."

"How do you mean?"

"I know how it feels to stay with a man because you're still in love with who he once was." She fiddled with the handle of the purse on her lap. "When Roarke's father left us, I was devastated, but Ella's problem was that her husband stayed."

Rhea thought about her mother and how her love for Rhea's father had overwhelmed her. "I've never understood." She watched a crow flying overhead, "Why don't they just find a way to fly away?"

"I blame time." Mrs. Coffey closed her eyes and raised her face to face to the sky, where the sun's rays had just peaked out from behind some clouds, brightening everything they touched. "After a while, one day leads to the next. You think maybe you can wait, and it'll get better."

"My mother used to say you can have enough money and enough love, but there's never enough time."

"She sounds wise." Mrs. Coffey smiled in the sunshine, "Are your parents well?"

Something about the way they were speaking made her feel like opening up. "My father drowned a few years ago."

Mrs. Coffey's eyes flew to Rhea's face. "Drowned? Oh, dear."

Rhea coughed lightly to rid herself of the small lump in her throat. "Um, he had gone fishing with a neighbor. Unfortunately, the weather turned nasty. They never found the bodies."

"Oh, my darling." Mrs. Coffey patted Rhea's slim shoulder. "How awful."

"Yes, but at least I grew up in a happy home. My parents adored each other."

Mrs. Coffey sighed. "My first husband and I were married quite young. We struggled to make a living in those days, and as our arguing increased, my husband stopped loving me. He went with other women, and I turned a blind eye, but the kicker came when I lost our child."

Rhea caught her breath and looked with sympathy at the other woman. "I'm so sorry."

"So was I, but my husband wasn't. He'd grown so cold by then that he said *Good riddance. It would've been just another mouth to feed.*

Both women watched a young couple crest the hillock hand in hand and disappear over the ridge. Mrs. Coffey cast her eyes upward and seemed to be fighting tears. "I was mourning my baby, and her father was glad she was dead. I couldn't forgive Gordon for that. He left us the following year. Went to Edinburgh and started a new life."

They sat in silence for a moment before Mrs. Coffey turned to Rhea. "How'd your mother take it when your father died?"

Rhea took a deep breath. "She cut off all her hair and stopped talking. One day, she walked into the forest and never came out."

Mrs. Coffey turned to her with a shocked expression. "What?"

"She could be alive or dead. We don't know. No one's ever found her." She bent to pick a blade of grass and twist it in her fingers. "But my nieces say they sometimes see a woman watching them from the woods."

"How could she survive if she's still alive?"

"Trust me, she could survive."

"She didn't know how to be without your father?"

"I guess not." Rhea gave the other woman a sad smile. "Love destroys as much as it builds."

"It sure takes a toll on some of us."

"Your first husband has passed now, hasn't he?"

The other woman nodded her head.

"If you don't mind me asking, how did Roarke take it when he died?"

"He only ever said one thing about it, and then he never spoke of him again."

"What did he say?"

Mrs. Coffey sighed again. "Good riddance."

Roarke and Rhea exchanged very few words until they were out of the city. Roarke concentrated on driving, and Rhea took in the sights, asking a few mundane questions to fill the silence. After about twenty minutes, they approached a wide river surrounded by thick forest, but Roarke pulled the truck onto a small car park instead of crossing the bridge.

Turning to Rhea, he said quietly, "This river has a nice footpath next to it. I thought we could go for a wee stroll."

"Sounds good." She was out of the truck before he could say another word.

Walking in silence, they listening to the gentle lapping of the river against the shore and the light wind rustling the branches of the trees. Roarke walked a little ahead of Rhea. At one point, he stopped abruptly. She had been watching a vulture fly, and she brought up solid into his back before falling on the pebble beach.

Glaring up at him, she groused, "Watch what you're doing."

"Me?" He offered his hand, which she slapped away. "You walked into me. You're always in such a bloody hurry."

"I wasn't in a hurry that time!"

"Were you watching a bird?"

"What?" *How did he know I was watching a bird?*

"You're always looking around, watching birds, looking at the clouds or trees. You fall all the time, not because you're clumsy. You never look where you're heading."

She sighed. "There may be some truth to that. Still, you're the only one I run into."

"Then be more careful around me." His voice had an edge to it that seemed to say he meant that in more than one way.

"You're kind of hard to get around. You're the size of a Mack truck." She hopped to her feet and brushed the sand off her jeans.

Bending to pick up a few rocks, he shook them in his hand. "Rhea, look—"

"Oh, God, Roarke. Are you going to make me talk about last night?"

"I'm afraid so." He threw one of the rocks and watched it plop into the river. "I need to apologize."

She looked at him in surprise. "You? I'm the one who needs to apologize."

"What? Why?" He looked at her with a shocked expression.

"I got sick. We were having such a wonderful time, and I go and vomit and ruin everything." The words came spilling out of quickly. "The champagne, wine, vodka, beer, the food. I ate so quickly. I can't believe I did that. I am so embarrassed."

"You're embarrassed? I made you throw up!" He yelled the last sentence and shook his head so comically Rhea started laughing, and soon, Roarke joined her, his shoulders moving up and down in the manner she found so charming.

When she caught her breath, she said, "Oh, Roarke. The food and booze made me throw up, not you."

"Regardless, I was way out of line. I'd had a lot to drink. Never a good excuse, I know." It was his turn to spit out his words. "But you smell so nice and looked so pretty, not that it's your fault, and . . . and . . . it just won't happen again. You have to believe me." He crossed his hands in the air in front of his face. "It won't."

"Roarke. I believe you." She stepped forward.

Putting his hands on top of his head, he closed his eyes. "Do you still trust me?"

"I do. Neither of us should have drunk as much as we did."

"I was the one at fault, not you."

Starting back to the truck, Roarke stopped when Rhea said, "We ran into David Cojocaru at church this morning."

Roarke turned around and looked at her very seriously. "I thought you might. Did he speak to you?"

"Yes, he did. I was astonished at how well he and your mother got along."

Roarke sighed deeply. "Our mothers are chummy."

"Does she know . . . about your past together?"

"She knows he sold drugs, and I think she thinks I just disapproved."

"Isn't it strange that a woman who seems to be as strait-laced as your mother would be so friendly with him, knowing he sold drugs?"

"When I was younger, she called him bad news and told me I was never to go around him or his friends. Then, it kind of changed. She still didn't want me to be around with him, but I could also never say a bad word about him. I remember one day after I stopped working for him, I called him a wanker, and she whacked me upside the head, telling me not to speak against someone when I don't know what they have to deal with."

Rhea stopped and turned around to look up at him as the late afternoon sun hit his face at an angle that made his brown eyes almost green against the heavy forest behind him. "How can a man go from drug-pusher to philanthropist in a few short years?"

"His mother was a cook, and food always interested him. He used drug money to open his first restaurant and then another. His father, Petran, was born into a wealthy, noble Romanian family, but he'd fallen out with them. Whatever happened, I never knew, but I know Petran had vowed never to return to Romania. His anger and alcoholism prevented him from making anything of himself, so he depended on David's mother, Ella, to bring in money."

"Petran thought people were racist toward him, but it was just an excuse. The truth was Petran thought he was better than us."

"His wealthy family never helped them?"

"The grandmother would send David money, being her only grandchild, but his father would just send it back."

"He finally drank himself to death when David was in his early twenties. His uncle, Petran's brother, had died in a car accident, so when the grandmother passed, with David at her side after reconnecting with her, the old lady left everything to her grandson."

"Making him a very wealthy man." Rhea leaned on a large boulder, and Roarke came to sit against it. "Why did he wait to reconnect with his grandmother?"

"At times, when his father was alive, his father heard he'd had contact with her, and he took his anger out on David's mother. David cherishes his mother, wife, and children above all things, and so he kept his distance to protect her."

"Is he all that bad if he cherishes the women in his life?

Didn't he love Isabel?" Rhea bit her lip as she finished.

"He used to tell me love was a man's greatest weakness and to love as little as I could. His father got the better of him through his love for his mother, his weakness. There was a time when he cared for me, and he resents me for that. I think I hurt him, and he goes out of his way to hurt me back."

"It's going to be difficult."

"What is?"

"I have to write a book about you and the things that have influenced you. How can I write about who you have become when I can't share information about one of the people that, I feel, has shaped you, probably, the most?"

"David Cojocaru didn't shape me. I made something of myself despite having him in my life."

"Yet he's a constant presence, isn't he?"

Roarke looked at her with anger flashing in his eyes.

"Don't get angry with me. I'm just stating facts. I've seen him on television, the award show, in church, and you talk to him on the phone. He blackmails you, for Christ's sake." She threw up her hands. "How the hell am I meant not to say anything about him?"

Roarke wagged his finger at her. "You mention even one thing about him, and I will sue you and your publishing house, not to mention what David might do."

She sighed and waved her hands around dramatically. "Yes, yes, I know."

"Good."

"He inherited Granny's money, and . . ."

Roarke stood up and turned from the river to look into the forest. "With his successful restaurants and his grandmother's money, there was no end to his ambition. He divided his time between Romania and here. His mother has a lovely home here, and she'd never leave. He went back to school and studied Art History and Physics. Brilliant man. He educated himself so when he hob-knobbed with society, he could fit in. He began dabbling in art and artifacts. He's made another small fortune being an art broker. Excellent instincts. He donates money to museums and helps both Scottish and Romanian artists gain recognition. Oh, and he became a Venture Capitalist. The money he must have, I can't even imagine. People in our old neighborhood have forgotten his shady past. They now see a local boy who made a name for himself and gives back to the community. The place is cleaner and more respectable. Kids aren't looking for trouble."

"People change, I guess."

Roarke glared at her again. "He hasn't changed. He just puts on a good show."

"Are you jealous?"

"Jealous? Of what?" His hands flew to his hips.

"Forget I said anything." Rhea pushed herself off the rock, smiling at him, hoping to change his humor. "Now there's the fight for the castle."

"Yes, the castle. Davey wants that resort and golf club badly. The cherry on top will be taking it from me."

"As a philanthropist, doesn't he see how the castle will help the kids?"

"He doesn't give a shit about the kids. He does these things to be seen doing those things. It's a show. He's a heartless, selfish bastard." Reaching into his pocket, Roarke took out his keys. "He tells everyone that the resort will provide jobs for the locals, but by using the castle in the way I would like, the locals would still get jobs. The street kids need it desperately. They're in a fight for their lives."

"Why don't the twins just sell it to him if they need the money?"

"They're friends of mine and believe in what I am doing. They're waiting for me. I'm certain I can get the money."

"Hence the movie and the book."

"Exactly." He cast his eyes upward. "Also, they don't want the place just to be another spot that caters to the rich. The castle's been in their family for long generations. They want to keep it as a heritage site everyone can access. Something they and their children can be proud of."

"Funny how some simple things get so bloody complicated."

"People wonder why I live like a hermit. The truth is it's just easier that way."

Rhea knew Roarke enough to understand that a pensive mood was coming on, so she slapped him as hard as she dared on the knee. "Come on, hermit. If we don't get back soon, Ian'll be greeting us with a shotgun."

"Now you're slapping me?" He drew to his full height and peered down at her, trying to look imposing, even as he grinned.

Rhea stepped forward and craned her neck to look up at him. "I'm not scared of you, you big refrigerator. Yeah, I think sometimes a tap might do you good."

Laughing again, he reached down to pinch her cheek. The intimate gesture shocked her a little, and when he released her cheek, her hand caressed the spot where he had pinched her. Her face must have shown surprise, because he immediately reached for her elbow. "Did I pinch you too hard? I'm sorry."

"No, no." She smiled, still with her hand on her face. "My father used to do the same thing. I'd forgotten, but it's nice to remember."

"You had a good father?"

"Yeah. Papa made his mistakes, but yes, he was a great man."

"He cherished you?"

Rhea nodded.

"My sister always said that was what she missed the most

about not having a father around, the feeling of being cherished by her father."

"Her husband certainly cherishes her," Rhea commented. "At dinner, she said something, and he ran his hand across her shoulders and brushed her bangs away from her face. It was so tender."

He cocked his head to one side. "You know, my dear, you seem to be getting a wee more, dare I say, romantic as the days go on."

Glancing around, she took in the lazy river and the wind stirring the changing late summer leaves. "I can't argue with that. This place is getting to me."

Roarke's eyes crept over her face. "You're under Scotland's spell."

"Yes." She dropped her gaze to her hands to avoid making eye contact and risk him seeing something she didn't want him to see. "Under Scotland's spell."

Roarke cleared his throat and spun his keys around his finger. "Yes, all that to say, Yans is a gem. A good man who treats my sister like gold."

"Good God, he'd better. You're a hell of a big brother to piss off."

Roarke laughed—he looked like he was about to pinch her cheek again, but didn't, and they both turned toward the truck. Roarke stepped ahead of her on the way, and as Rhea watched him striding away, she tripped over a rock and fell to her knee.

Roarke turned and made a step toward her, chuckling as she pushed herself up. "Jesus, woman, could you stay on your feet today?"

"I've a bit of a hangover, you know. It makes me wobbly."

As she stood and dusted off her jeans, something caught her eye in front of the large stone. Bending and picking it up, she looked at Roarke. "Never guess what I found?"

Walking toward him, she dropped her find into his open palm. "It's another one of those nails like we found on the beach."

Turning the long square-sided piece of metal in his strong fingers, Roarke shook his head and looked at her in surprise, "I'll be damned."

They took a few minutes to see if they could find anything else but found nothing. Then, getting in the truck, Roarke commented, "You're one of those people who find things easily. I never find what I'm looking for. Maybe I need to stop looking."

Chapter Thirteen: Splinter and Mouse

I watched the pair of them fight the attraction growing between them. Gone was any pretense of denying their fascination with each other, yet they both tried to fight it in their own ways.

Rhea kept up with her notes and her recordings, and Roarke worked, both watching the other in secret, in a covetous manner.

The next afternoon, Roarke had gone outside to do his chores and chop some wood. Rhea had stayed inside to transcribe some of the recordings when she heard Roarke's angry yell from outside and then heard metal on metal and a heavy thud. Rhea and ran out the front door, thinking maybe Willem and his crew had returned. Instead, she rounded the corner to find Roarke sitting on the ground, with his back against the large piece of tree trunk he used to chop his wood. He was barefoot and looking down at his foot. "Bloody splinters!"

"Get inside, and I'll look at it."

Without putting down his injured foot, they limped their way to the house. By the time she dropped Roarke onto the sofa, Rhea was winded from the exertion of having help support the big man, but she was also a little flushed from being so close to him. As she'd led him into the house, she could feel his muscles tightening and contracting under her hand, which had lain on his chest.

She hurried into her bedroom and bathroom, gathering the

things she needed, and came back into the sitting room. Placing everything on the table, she straddled the table with Roarke's foot between her knees. "Okay. I'm going to get out the splinters and then apply a bread poultice to the wounds to clean them."

"What the Devil is a bread poultice?"

"It's an old remedy. Just trust me and sit still."

Peering down at the splinters through her reading glasses, she found five in total. She grabbed the large one and pulled it out without warning, causing him to jump and swear loud enough to wake the dead. She yanked out the others and pressed the soapy rag against the wounds as he grimaced and swore.

Smirking, she looked up at him over the rim of her glasses, smiling. "You're ticklish."

"Oh, shut up about it!"

When she finished, she told him to wipe his foot clean, and she rose and went into the kitchen. "I need to get the poultice. I'll be right back."

She went into the kitchen and put milk on the stove. As soon as it came to a boil, she placed two pieces of bread in a shallow pasta bowl, covered the bread in milk, and mushed it to create a kind of paste and carried it to the coffee table. Before she went to work, she poured Roarke two fingers of whisky.

"You're starting to read my mind," he told her, taking the offering gratefully.

She straddled the table and took up his foot again. "I'm going to apply the poultice, and it's really hot, but it has to be. It won't burn you, but it will be hot for a while. Stay still and don't pull your foot away."

Rhea loaded one side of a rag with the paste and pressed the paste side against Roarke's skin. "Shit!" He banged his free hand on the arm of the chair and tossed his head back against the back of the chair while she wound the gauze around his foot. "That's bloody hot!"

"The hot bread and the milk work together to pull out germs and infections, and if there's a splinter I missed, it will probably get it and clean the wound."

"Where'd you learn to do this?"

"When I was growing up, people still used old remedies to take care of things, as the doctor wasn't around every day."

After she had put everything away, she walked back into the sitting area. "Keep that on until you go to bed, and then, if we need to, we can apply another, but I think you'll be fine. To be honest, I'm kind of glad you got those splinters."

"Why is that, sadist?"

"Other than finding out the big man is ticklish?"

He glared at her.

"I'll finally get to cook. I've been going through the fridge and spice rack, and I think I have all I need to make a nice Chinese dinner."

They sat in silence for a moment until Roarke said, "Did you ever think you were born at the wrong time? That you would have been better suited to some time in the past?"

"Of course, and so do you, I know. Yet when I think of our modern dental hygiene, I am very, very happy with some aspects of modern life."

He laughed. "That's true, I suppose."

"My father told me about a time when he was young, and he had a bad back tooth that became infected. He went to the nurse. Our village had the only nurse for miles around, and she had taken a trip and wouldn't be back for a few days, but there was a girl there that the nurse was training. When she saw how much pain my grandfather was in, she thought to remove the tooth herself. However, it was a harsh winter, and the pack ice had prevented the supply ship from bringing in the supplies. They had no novocaine, no cocaine, nothing to dull the pain. My father got drunk as a skunk and returned with his brothers. They held him down as the girl tried to extract the tooth."

As she spoke, Roarke's face paled, and his mouth turned into a grimace.

"The girl ended up cracking the tooth off at the base, and there was nothing more she could do. The nurse returned the next day, and my grandfather was delirious with pain and fever. Still, with no pain killers, only alcohol, his brothers held him down again as the nurse set to work, pulling out first all of the little fragments of teeth that had cracked off, and then finally, cutting into his gums to pull out the roots of the tooth."

"My God." His hand went to his mouth.

"Yup. Modern times has its pluses. Besides, we can't wish to be a part of a time we never knew."

"Okay. Hypocrite. You're obsessed with the past."

"You can learn a lot from the past, and I like to learn."

"I think you're looking for something."

His comment, for some reason, shook her to the very core. "What could I be looking for?"

"You tell me." He fiddled with the tassel at the corner of a throw pillow. "Did your fascination with ghosts and everything begin after you lost your sister and father?"

"I want to know that each of us makes a mark on the world. All of those people who came before, are they forgotten? People should never be forgotten if we can help it. That's why we should share stories and discuss the past. The people in those stories existed, and they deserve to be remembered."

Roarke looked pensive. "What if ghosts are just people who don't want to be forgotten? They don't want their memory to pass away in time, all memory of who they were, snuffed out. What if a part of them stays behind to say *I'm still here?*"

After he uttered those words, a strong gust of wind hit the house and so startled Rhea that she jumped to her feet. An icy torrent of air sent unmitigated terror through her, and Rhea inched closer to Roarke. They both gazed in the direction of the hallway, where the door to the second floor had banged hard against its moldings once, twice, and three times.

Rhea's head spun around to look at Roarke as he looked back at her in slight shock. "Roarke, I'd very much like to get some fresh air."

He hopped to his feet and grabbed the walking stick he had earlier asked Rhea to get from the mudroom. "I was thinking the same thing."

With that, he hobbled to the door as fast as he could, but not faster than Rhea, who flew.

Not wanting to go too far from the house, Rhea spent a little time taking pictures of the cottage and the farm, not trusting the details to memory, and Roarke went into the woods to check on the hole he had dug in the woods to support a new sewer tank.

Rhea heard yelling, realized it was Roarke's voice, and ran into the forest. She called his name and located the sound of his voice coming out of a deep pit in the ground. Getting on her knees and peering down, she saw Roarke covered in mud and looking up at her from the bottom of a hole about three feet wide and eight or nine feet deep.

"What . . . the . . . heck?" She smirked down at him.

"Don't start with me! I'm in no bloody mood!" He shook his finger up at her. "I'm stuck down here. Go and get the tall ladder on the back of the house, will you?"

"How did you get in there? Did you fall and hurt your bad foot?"

"My foot's fine!" he yelled up at her. "And go into the

mudroom and bring an old toque."

"Why do you need a toque?"

He sighed. "There's a wee mouse down here, and I need the toque to scoop him up without him biting me."

"A mouse?"

"Aye. He scurries around me, and I'm afraid I'm going to step on him."

At that moment, something dawned on her. "Roarke McCallum. Did you fall into this hole trying to save a mouse?"

"Don't be daft! I came into the hole to inspect it and found the mouse."

"You got in there to save the mouse."

"Shut it, Rhea! Go and get the bloody ladder!"

"You jumped in to save the mouse. Say it, and I'll go and get the ladder." She stood and folded her arms in front of her.

"Oh, for pity's sake!" He was yelling now. "I hate you sometimes, you know that? Yes, I got in to get the mouse. Go and get the bloody ladder!"

She left and returned huffing and puffing, dragging the long wooden ladder, the toque on her head.

"Took you long enough," Roarke said as she peeked over the edge of the hole.

"I'm not big and burly like you. I had to drag the freaking thing."

"Throw down the hat."

She threw the hat down, and after a few desperate attempts to collect the mouse, Roarke looked up at her. "You're going to come down here and get him. I'm too big and can't bend down enough to get him."

"I'm not getting in there."

"The sides are too steep for him to get up. So he'll stay down here and starve to death, poor thing."

"Shit." She muttered as she started lowering the ladder down to Roarke with a great deal of effort. Finally, Roarke managed to climb from the hole, and Rhea descended. When she got to the bottom, she located the small, brown mouse quivering against the earth wall, looking at her with inky black eyes, and her heart melted. After her second attempt at dropping the toque over him, she scooped him up.

"Got him."

Roarke was on his belly with his arms in the hole. "Great. Give him to me."

She went up the first few rungs of the ladder and handed the hat up to Roarke. "Got him. I think I dropped my keys. Could you take a look for me?"

Hopping off the ladder, she looked for something shiny in the trampled mud at her feet. Roarke gripped both sides of the ladder, and before she could react, he had hoisted the ladder halfway out of the hole, being careful of the hand holding the hat at its base.

"Hey!" she squealed up at him as she tried to grab at the ladder without success. "What are you doing?"

He grinned down at her. "I'm going a little further into the woods to release him. No sense in letting him go so he can fall into the hole again. I'll be right back."

"*Tabarnak! Reviens ici, imbécile!*"

"Don't know what you're saying!" he yelled. "I'll be back shortly."

She could hear him laughing as he walked away.

"*Je te tuerai quand je sortirai d'ici!*" she screamed after him. *I'll kill him when I get out!*

Roarke's footsteps and laughter disappeared. Soon afterward, Rhea heard footsteps in the space above her. "Lower that bloody ladder right now. Roarke?"

After demanding and then pleading for him to lower the ladder, she received no reply, but she could hear the footsteps creeping around the hole. Rhea then realized whoever was circling the hole had lighter footsteps than Roarke. It was a much gentler tread, and she was struck with acute panic. Any second, and someone might poke their head over the side of the hole, and she was unprepared for what she might see.

Pressed herself against the wall of the hole, she crouched down as far away from the surface as possible until she heard Roarke's heavy footsteps coming toward her. At that moment, the light tread above her head stopped as Roarke's head peered over the edge.

"Hey, Rhea."

"Did you see anyone else in the woods or around the hole?"

"No, there's no one here but us. Look, I'm sorry. That was a rotten trick to pull." Roarke lowered the ladder, and Rhea guided it to the bottom. As she did so, she glimpsed something shiny in the mud, and thinking it was Roarke's key, she scooped up the handful of earth and climbed to the top, heaving herself over the ladder and collapsing onto the grass.

"I hurried back as soon as I could." Roarke had his hands in the air in front of him. "Don't start. I'm so sorry for doing that. You know how I have a short temper, and you had laughed at me, and I had to get even, but it was cruel and mean, and I'm a bastard, and I will never leave you stuck at the bottom of a hole again. I promise."

Roarke had closed his eyes as he spoke, and when finished, he opened one eye, but Rhea was not angry. Instead, she told him of her strange experience down in the hole, and even now, she could tell they were not alone.

"The mouse is fine, by the way."

"I'm glad." She had crawled a little closer to him, and he jumped when she whacked him in the arm.

"Ouch!" He laughed and rubbed at the spot, even though she knew she hadn't hurt him at all. "Okay. I guess I deserved that."

Then, without warning, she thrust her head toward his and kissed him on the cheek. He blushed again and backed off a little. "What was that for?"

"For the mouse." She smiled at him. "With all your faults, you are a wonderful man."

"Thank you." He shook his head and blushed. "You're a roller-coaster. I never know when you're going to hit me or kiss me."

"That's not a nice thing to say to your knight-in-shining-armor."

"My what?" He looked at her in shock.

"If I were counting, this is the second time today I've saved you from disaster."

He laughed outright. "How's that?"

"Besides Splinter-gate, I've also saved you from being attacked by a field mouse."

"I wouldn't say that I was under attack."

"Whatever you say, Princess."

That made him laugh, and she chuckled with him until his laughter subsided. "Oh, and I found your key, but it's covered in mud."

"I didn't really lose my key. I was just trying to get you in the hole."

Rhea removed some of the mud from the object. It was another nail similar to what they'd found at the castle.

Roarke looked down at it and back at Rhea. "You and the nails. Now it's just plain weird."

When Roarke woke up, it was eight o'clock. He stretched and felt rested, but it was late for him to rouse, and the animals needed tending. He realized he hadn't felt rested for a long time. The usual worries popped back, unbidden, into his head. His anger and frustration built as he thought about the long-overdue conversation he would have in a few days. It would change his life forever, probably for the worse, but it was unavoidable.

The next minute, some of that fear and anxiety left him, as for some strange reason, the image of Rhea looking up at him from her pillow entered his mind, and he found himself smiling as he threw his long legs over the side of the bed and reached for the t-shirt on the foot of the bed. As he put his hands on his mattress to push himself off the bed, he froze for a second. *Roarke, old man, this isn't good. You feel a little too warm about that woman, and it won't do either of you any good. That's a woman you can't have, not now, not ever.*

On his way, as he was passing the open door of the guest room, he turned and looked inside. Finding it empty, he went over to inspect the window and stopped to look at the framed picture of Liam that Rhea had on her dresser. He picked up the silver frame and looked down at the young boy's smiling, freckled face. His hair was shiny, jet black, and his eyes were a soft brown. Roarke smiled down at him, noting the lip prints where Rhea had kissed the picture.

Pausing to listen for the sounds of movement from the living room, he breathed in her perfume, with notes of orange, sandalwood, rose, and musk. Then her coconut-orchid body lotion, and before he left, he picked up the thin silver chain with its silver cross, native symbol, and the Alaskan black diamond that usually hung around her slim throat.

He tiptoed out of the room, as little shame-faced at having poked around in her things. He headed toward the bathroom but glanced at the sofa.

She was sleeping on her side, facing outwards, one arm over the edge of the white duvet, and in the course of her sleep, the neck of her sleeping gown had slipped down over one shoulder, showing the curving line of her square shoulder and the prominent clavicle he loved.

Walking over to the sofa and lifting the edge of the duvet, he looked down on her sleeping form, the loose material of the gown falling across the swell of her breasts, the flat area of her stomach, and he could make out the shape of her slim, rounded hips. The gown had risen over her knees, and both legs were bent, exposing sinuous thighs. He lowered himself over her, using his arms to keep most of his weight off her body.

She didn't open her eyes, but her head tossed on the pillow as her body arched up against him, encouraging him to press more of his weight upon her until a soft moan escaped her lips. When he kissed her, she responded by grabbing the back of his head and crushing her mouth to his. Bracing himself on an elbow, his fingertips traced her clavicle and the front of her breast, pausing when she shivered.

A sound outside the window woke him from his reverie, and he looked to see a small robin sitting on a swaying branch outside. He realized he had been standing there, watching her sleep, a fantasy playing out in his head. Embarrassed, he turned away from the sitting room and shuffled toward the bathroom, banging his toe on the island as he did so.

Outside the window, a little robin burst into song, and Rhea awoke from her sleep, vaguely aware of Roarke swearing and the ghost of a beautiful dream slipping away from her.

The following evening, Rhea had just hung up the phone from talking to Liam when Roarke went over to the window and peeked outside. "Hey, Midas is down by the edge of the forest. Poor guy, he's not getting as much attention now that the puppies are here. Fancy going for a walk?"

A few minutes later, in the deepening twilight, Rhea and Roarke were walking Midas home to Ian's, edging the forest, and she had asked him about the sword in the upstairs room.

"That sword has thirteen stones down its length." Roarke grasped Rhea's elbow as they walked on the small, stony path. "Maybe that's why I don't like it."

"People are so superstitious about the number thirteen." Rhea shook her head. "Especially Friday the thirteenth."

"The Thursday before Jesus was crucified, there were thirteen people at the table, and he was crucified on a Friday," Roarke was throwing a stick ahead of them, which Midas would return, dancing around until he threw it again. "There's also the fear of the female side of things. Some say fear of thirteen stems from male fears of the female body, as women menstruate thirteen times a year, and menstruation is something men can't do. The moon also has the same cycle as a woman, twenty-eight days, and controls the tides and the seasons. The origin of all life. It's about men wanting to control what cannot be controlled."

Midas returned with the stick, which Rhea threw, and it flew into the forest instead of ahead of them. Midas dove into the undergrowth and thrashed about looking for it.

"Plus," Rhea continued. "Witches believe there are thirteen stages to life. The first twelve are here on Earth, and the thirteenth is for the afterlife. Hence, thirteen equals death, the unknown, and the supernatural to those who don't understand the beliefs."

Midas continued to rummage for his stick as twigs, and low branches broke and snapped under his weight.

"Those being men, of course," Roarke commented with a snort.

"Of course." Rhea laughed, stepping in front of Roarke just as Midas's stick landed at her feet.

Bending down, her hand froze as Midas leaped from the woods. Roarke threw the stick and smiled at Rhea, who hadn't moved from her spot, a strange look on her face.

"What is it?"

"The stick landed at my feet."

"So?"

"Midas came out of the woods after the stick. He wasn't

bringing it to me. He was retrieving it."

Realization dawned on Roarke's face as his head turned in the direction of the woods. "So, who . . ."

A chill crept over them just as the wind stirred the branches of the trees nearby, causing them to dance around in the dim light and giving a glimpse of the dark shadows inside the forest.

Roarke cleared his throat. "Anyone there? You're on private property." He received no reply save the rustling of the leaves. "Stay here."

Grabbing at his elbow, she tried to keep him at her side. "I don't think you should go in there."

"The trees look thick from out here, but once you're in there, they thin out. I'll be able to see if anyone's there."

Still, his face looked very nervous as he stepped off the path and into the woods. Rhea could hear him calling out, and a few minutes later, the big man tumbled out of the woods, grabbed her by the wrist, and dragged her through the field and away from the woods.

Rhea ran to keep up with the pace he set. "Roarke? Is someone in there?"

"Worse." He turned to give her a nervous grin. "No one at all."

The following day, Rhea looked out the small window next to the fire. The tree swayed in the wind as rain dripped off the needles.

The description of Roarke at the beginning of the book was proving challenging, as it was going to be very important to give the reader a clear image of him in his natural state. Rhea turned when Roarke burst through the front door wearing straight-cut blue jeans and a long-sleeved, white cotton shirt. He shook the rain out of his hair and held out a letter to her.

What made Roarke McCallum so attractive and exciting,

despite his impressive physique and strong, masculine looks, was the energy that exuded from him. There was something electric in his aura, a force making him larger than life.

"A magnetar," she half-mumbled to herself.

"What?" The hand holding the letter dropped to his side, and he looked confused.

"A magnetar," Rhea looked at him, but her eyes were a little out of focus. "It's a neutron star with a powerful magnetic pull. It's more powerful than a supernova, and the energy from its gamma rays is unbelievably strong. Magnetars are captivating, compelling, and terrifying."

"Okay," He blinked hard a few times, shook his head, and held out the letter again. "This was in my letterbox."

"For me?" she questioned, stepping forward to take the small, blue envelope. As she took the note out, a small sprig of white flowers fell to the floor.

"White heather, it's for good luck."

Roarke picked up the small sprig and held it under Rhea's nose. Light and floral, it was also earthy and musky.

Inside the envelope was a handwritten letter,

Dear Rhea,

We'd like to extend a dinner invitation to you — seven-thirty, tonight, at our family home. We'll be hosting Burns Night in autumn. Ian told us Roarke is helping you research Scottish customs and legends, so we thought you'd enjoy it.

You can bring Roarke too if you'd like.

Agnes and Senga

Smiling, she handed it out to Roarke. "It's a dinner invitation."

Roarke's eyes scanned the note. "Nice of them to let me tag along. That'll be fun, and you can see inside the castle and manor."

Walking to the kitchen, he poured tea for them both. "We'll

be staying in for the majority of the day."

"Why?" She glanced out the window. "It's just a little rain. *Je ne suis pas fait du chocolat.* I'm not made of chocolate, as they say in Québec. I won't melt."

Roarke laughed. "I know you won't melt. I just need to stay close to home today."

"That's good." She sat across from him and put a little milk in her tea. "You're my captive, then. I can pick your brain all day."

"Guess so."

Glancing to her right, Rhea looked at the large painting hung over the dining room table. "I've wanted to ask you about that painting. Where did you get it?"

"My sister, Tessa, painted that."

The large painting was a big blotch in an odd butterfly shape with corners and edges of various shades of crimson and burgundy on a blue and white almost cloudy background. Over the red blotch was another medley of colors, beige, tans, and browns in the shape of an elongated, malformed rectangle with blurred edges. "It's amazing."

Roarke drew a little closer to his sister's painting. "What do you see?"

Rhea was hesitant. "I don't want to tell you. You'll think me dark."

"I already think you're dark."

"Well." She drew a deep breath. "I see an armless, headless, legless torso."

Roarke turned to look at her, his brows pulled together as he regarded her from under heavy lids.

Hopping down from the stool, she went over to the painting. "In the center is the torso, and the crimson is the blood in various stages of drying, and it's pooled down here at the bottom where it's very burgundy. Then, at the top, the light red blotches seem to create the image of a man, looking down at a book wearing a soldier's hat."

She took a step backward and turned on her heel to look at him as he sucked on his bottom lip and peered at her strangely. A few seconds passed until finally, she threw her hands up. "What?"

"Most people see a butterfly."

"Oh." She pressed her lips together, looking abashed.

He nodded his head. "A pretty, red butterfly."

"I see."

"It's called The Butterfly."

"I get it!" She came back over to her stool. "I knew you'd think me morbid."

His lips twitched.

"What do you see?"

"Not a headless, legless corpse."

"Another fragment of my diseased imagination."

"I see the sea." He looked at the painting in a misty way. "The blue and white is the land, and the rest is a wine-dark open sea."

Rhea spoke quietly, "I knew a man who hated the sea. He couldn't even look at it. He told me he hated the sea because it reminded him of his sins."

"What?"

"The sea reminds him of his sins."

"Why?"

"Not sure." She stretched. "Maybe the sublimity of it. I assume being near the ocean makes him feel small, reminds him of death."

"Was he a bad man?"

She glanced again at the painting. "Yes, he was."

Turning, she walked to the side window to watch the rain.

Roarke walked over to stand behind her. "I was eleven, playing down by the wharf in a fishing village on the West Coast. I got too close to the edge and fell in. A huge undertow pulled me under. A few men were bringing in their boat and managed to pull me out."

"An old man sat on the wharf, fixing a net, and he whispered something to the other men, *The sea maun hae it's nummer.* I found out later what he meant. In some areas, it's considered bad luck to save a drowning man. The sea takes the saver of life instead of the saved."

Rhea shivered, thinking of her father.

"The sea god'll come back and claim his *nummer* someday."

"Then why do you sail?"

"Because I love it."

"You like tempting fate."

"I'm not afraid to die. The sea god can claim me. It's just the vastness of the sea that's scary and not knowing what's underneath you. Especially since my buddy told me about globigerina ooze."

"What?"

"When certain planktonic species die, their shells settle on the bottom of the ocean floor. The shell deposits are very thick and just sort of shift around with the movement of the water. I imagine sea creatures, giant squid, goblin sharks, all hanging out in there." He plucked at a piece of lint on her shoulder, causing her to shudder. "I know. Scary to think of."

As eerie as the thought of globigerina ooze was, it was not what made her shudder.

Chapter Fourteen: The Cairn

The occurrence at the cairn shook them to their very core.

On the bumpy road to the castle, Rhea kept fussing with her form-fitting purple dress and trying not to overthink how Roarke had blushed when he saw her. She was also willing herself not to glance over at him, so handsome in his kilt, black shirt, and matching vest.

As they passed the pink boulder, Rhea asked Roarke if they could stop. A few minutes later, they were standing at the top of the hill.

"It's funny." Roarke leaned on the boulder. "This place feels strange. It's like time doesn't move the same up here. Tamara told me her mother believes in thin places, where the spirit world and our world meet. Maybe this is one. It's hard to believe what happened on this stone. It makes you feel like time isn't what we think it is."

"Time is affected by the events in our lives. My father once told me he looked in the mirror one day, and an old man was looking back. The day before, he had gone to hop the fence to tend a sheep, and he fell over because his body wouldn't let him do it. It was so shocking to him. Maybe that's why he went out in the boat the day he died. Mother had forbidden him to go fishing, and he had started doing a safe job. Maybe that day, he wanted to feel young again."

"He died fishing?" Roarke watched two goldeneye ducks fly from the nearby forest and land in the small loch on the other side of the hill.

"He did."

"Did you know the word soul means sea in Germanic languages? It stems from the early Germanic belief that souls originate in and return to the sea."

Before long, they were lost in their thoughts until Roarke stretched. "I guess we should get going. Excuse me for a second. I hear the call of nature."

Roarke stepped toward the forest. Just as he finished relieving himself, he heard a woman softly weeping. When he looked over his shoulder, Rhea stood at the boulder with her face in her hands.

Hurrying back, he stood in front of her and placed his hands on her elbows. "Rhea, what's wrong? Why are you crying?"

Taking her hands away from her face, he saw her face and eyes were dry. "I'm not crying. There was one of those nasty clegs flying around. I was protecting my face."

"Oh." He looked abashed. "Sorry, I could have sworn I heard a woman crying."

"To be honest, I thought I heard a woman crying, too."

Roarke dropped his hands from her elbows, and they both looked over their shoulders, suddenly chilled to the bone.

"Come on." Roarke grabbed her hand. "Let's head to the party, or they'll start without us."

In the truck, neither of them said another word until they reached the castle.

The party was at the manor and not the castle itself, and as soon as they pulled up, Senga and Agnes met them at the door. While Roarke went to get a drink, the women showed Rhea around the beautiful mansion before joining the others in the drawing room.

All the men wore kilts, some going whole hog with sporran, stockings, and all, and the women wore plaid of some sort. In addition to Agnes, Senga, and their husbands, Ian, Ellie, Jack, Mike, Trace, Tamara, Miriam, and her husband were there.

When everyone had arrived, Agnes ushered them all into the large dining room to sit at the huge oak table set for fourteen, with Agnes and Senga at either end. The general chatter died down when Agnes rose to speak.

"Lads and lassies, my sister and I are very pleased you all could make our impromptu dinner. As you all know, Burn's Night is held on January twenty-fifth, but since our spouses couldn't make it home this year, Senga and I didn't hold our party until now that we all can be together. Raise your glasses in a toast to Rabbie Burns."

After the recitation of the Selkirk Grace, dinner began. Two teenaged girls and a boy were helping Agnes and Senga serve.

The first dish was a leek and chicken soup, called cock-a-leekie, and a variety of bread.

To the delight of the guests, as drinks were topped up, the skirling of bagpipes could be heard coming down the hall, and Paul, dressed in traditional highland wear, strode into the room playing the pipes. Behind him was a young server holding a tray. They were piping in the haggis.

The haggis was served with neeps and tatties and a whisky gravy, followed by a dessert of Tipsy Laird Trifle. A variety of traditional toasts accompanied the meal, and guests read snatches of Burns' poetry.

After dessert, everyone chatted and sipped whisky and coffee. Agnes and Senga came to sit by Roarke and Rhea.

Senga began, "Roarke, we hate to tell you this, but David Cojocaru has contacted us. He's found a second location that would serve for the golf resort."

"He doesn't want the castle?" Roarke asked happily.

"No." Agnes fixed her grey eyes on her whisky. "He still

wants this property, but he'll take the other in a pinch."

Senga reached out and touched Roarke's hand. "The owner of the second property has given him a deadline for his final decision. He has two weeks to decide."

"You have two weeks to decide," Roarke finished.

"A bit less." Senga tapped his hand. "You know we want you to have it, but we're getting desperate to sell. If he pulls his offer and then you can't get the financing, what will we do?"

"I understand." Roarke smiled mirthlessly at his two friends. "You'll still give me two weeks to work some magic?"

"Under two weeks, I'm afraid." Senga rose as her husband called her name.

"I'm sorry, Roarke." Agnes's eyes filled with tears. "Our families have plans for our future, and we can't turn down an offer when you're unsure if you'll get the money or not."

"My dear friend." He reached into his vest to hand her his handkerchief. "You make your decision for your family. Just give me a little time."

After both women had left to talk to their guests, Rhea turned to Roarke. "Are you okay?"

"Bastard." Roarke snarled. "I should have known he'd never let me have it."

"Can anything be done?"

"I'll talk to a few friends, but it doesn't look good. The studio has already done everything they can."

"I think this is the only time in my life I wish I were rich. Then you'd get the money."

Roarke reached over to caress her cheek with the back of his knuckles. "What a sweet thing to say."

Across the table, Ian watched them, and Rhea heard him mutter, "Keeping their distance, my arse."

Rhea collapsed in a chair after dancing with Ian. Music

filled the large dining hall, and everyone was dancing and laughing.

Paul sat down next to Rhea. "You look like someone who's having a good time."

"I'm having a grand time."

His blond hair was shorter than the last time she had seen him, and he looked dashing in a navy sweater and navy and green kilt. Rhea noticed Roarke glance in their direction while he sang an old song with Senga.

Paul leaned toward her. "I've brought something for you and Roarke."

"Really?"

"I've heard you're staying with him and researching myths of the area. It makes sense that you would want to stay at Roarke's cottage, considering where it's located. So much history."

Rhea looked at him in surprise. "What kind of history do you mean?"

"The old village used to be right around there, and the . . ."

Roarke strolled over to them, holding a small plate of Scottish tablet. "Hope I'm not interrupting."

"Not at all," Paul replied, shaking hands and smiling at his friend. "I was just talking to Rhea about your land and its historical significance."

"Aye, Paul." Roarke shook his head. "Don't go filling her head with nonsense."

"Nonsense?" Paul laughed. "How many times have you told me of something weird happening at White Heather? Everyone just assumes Rhea's staying with you because of the events in that area. Unless . . ." He eyed them both with suspicion and humor.

Rhea interrupted him, "Nothing like that is happening."

"Paul." Roarke looked behind him and back at them. "The truth is, Rhea's the ghost-writer I told you about, but we didn't tell people because we want everyone to be natural around her."

"God, how stupid am I?" He shook his head. "That makes sense."

"Wait." Rhea sat up a little straighter. "You said you had something to show us, something about Roarke's land and its history."

"I do." Paul held up a hand between himself and Roarke. "But mate, don't be upset that I haven't shown you before. We keep it in the family. However, if Rhea were writing about our area and its legends, she would want to know about it. It's a story that needs to be told."

"Okay." Roarke rubbed his hands together. "Now, I need to know."

Paul stood up. "If you two would like to step into the sitting room."

A few moments after excusing themselves from the others, Roarke and Rhea sat on the couch in the hunting-themed drawing room, and Paul sat on the coffee table in front of them, some photocopied pages in his hands.

Paul scratched his head and cleared his throat, and turned the paper so they could see it, "This is a part of the story of Islean and Thomas not everyone knows about."

"What?" Rhea reached for the page, and Paul handed it to her. Roarke looked over her shoulder.

Paul touched her knee to get her attention. "Before you read, let me give the context."

Rhea put the paper down, and both she and Roarke gave Paul their utmost attention.

"My family is from Thomas's clan, and I believe you know how our women were Howdies and medicine women."

Rhea nodded. "I get the feeling some of the women around here continue in the old ways. Herbalists and such?"

Paul sucked in his lips hesitantly. "Aye, that's not for me

to say." Then he looked up at them and winked. "Do you know Steaphan's part in the tale?"

"Roarke filled me in a little."

"He had spied on Islean for her father and told the women of her burial place, but Steaphan shared more of the tale with his wife and daughters after he wed. This story got spread orally through the family until my grandmother wrote it down."

Rhea handed the paper to him. "Could you read it to us? It's your family's story."

Paul took the paper and settled himself in an armchair next to the sofa. He cleared his throat and glanced at the closed door behind them before he began.

"The laird ran Thomas through and left him to die on the rock, but Islean had freed herself with her hidden dirk and cursed them all before opening her own throat. The last thing the men saw before the heavy fog hid the lovers was Islean lying over Thomas. The other men were too scared to go into the strange, eerie mist, but what no one knew was, driven by his love for her, Steaphan had gone into the fog.

"He held Islean's head as she bled out, and before she died, though she couldn't speak, she pressed Thomas's dirk into Steaphan's hand and gestured to the brooch on her shoulder. Steaphan removed it, and Islean died with her hand on both.

"The others never knew Steaphan had been with Islean when she had passed or that he had pledged to keep their love tokens together.

"Thomas was buried in the old graveyard, but as she had taken her own life, Islean could not be buried in consecrated ground. Her spiteful father buried her in an unmarked grave, the location known only to him and a few of his men. He even refused to tell his wife where he had buried her child.

"The lovers' deaths further fueled the already hostile feud between the two clans, and in the years that followed, they set out to destroy each other.

"But it had been Steaphan who had laid Islean's body in the ground. Being unable to endure her mother's grief, Stephan told her where the grave was, and she and her sisters began to visit her burial spot.

"The mothers of Thomas and Islean made their peace with each other behind the men's back. Out of respect for the lovers or out of grief, for whatever reason, eventually, the howdies accompanied Islean's mother and sisters to the burial spot, paying their respects as well. The area is a very magical, powerful place, and considered sacred to women.

"For Steaphan, his grief would continue, as he could not give Islean her dying wish. He had lost her brooch that night, and though he searched to find it, he searched in vain. He buried the dirk in a place he knew was very special to the lovers. However, until the day he died, he believed their spirits would never rest in peace because of the violence of their deaths and because he had failed to do the one thing that might have given them some peace. Their tokens that he had sworn would be together were separated, just like them."

Paul finished reading, and Rhea looked meaningfully at Roarke, thinking of the brooch she had found by the rock. "Paul, why do you think she wanted the brooch and dirk buried together?"

"Maybe since the objects were important to them, a part of them would stay together."

"There's something else I've wanted to ask you — why does the cookbook have the name *The Trees?* I noticed the cover has a large tree on it."

"Honestly, I don't know."

Rhea turned over the pages and tapped the symbols on every right-hand page of the book, three horizontal lines, each broken by a slanted vertical line, like three overturned Z's or lightning bolts. "What are those?"

Paul leaned forward to look at them. "I've wondered about them, too. They look to me like Viking rune symbols, maybe

Sowilu. It's the rune for wholeness, nourishment, and knowledge."

Roarke stared at Paul and blinked hard. "You know rune symbols?"

"Just something I studied in college." He turned his attention back to the symbols. "*Eihwaz* looks a lot like this, too. The rune for defense and yew trees." His gaze darted to Roarke. "Say, have you shown Rhea your yew tree?"

Rhea looked up to address Roarke. "Your what?"

Roarke cleared his throat and shot an angry scowl at Paul. "There's a yew tree on the hill near the cottage."

"That big thatch of trees?"

Paul came around to stand next to Roarke. "That's not a thatch of trees. It's one tree. A yew tree."

"Yes, well." He peeked at Rhea. "I haven't shown you yet because I was gauging how you felt at White Heather."

"Aye." Paul clapped a hand down on Roarke's shoulder. "I get the willies the minute I go in there, and one day, I could have sworn I saw—"

"Enough now," Roarke interrupted. "Rhea doesn't get the same feelings as the sensitive lot around here."

"Roarke, why wouldn't you want me to see a tree?"

Paul laughed. "The tree itself is lovely. It's the graveyard you might not like."

The papers slid from her hand and onto the table. "G-graveyard?"

"Not a graveyard. Just a few headstones. I'll show you when we get back. It's nothing, really." Roarke said evasively. "Now, back to the, um, Viking things."

Rhea smirked and picked up the pages again, "I've seen something like those symbols around here. Paul, can I have these?"

"Aye, I brought them for you." Turning toward the main

door, he stuck out his chest in a stretch. "I'm going to get going. I should be home in my bed."

"I feel the same way." Roarke puckered his lips and looked at Rhea, who nodded her silent agreement to hit the road.

Rhea kept her eye out for something she had noticed on the hillside on the way home. After a few moments, she half-yelled for Roarke to pull over. The castle was behind them, and they were in a glen on the edge of a thick forest. The moon was rising, and stars were beginning to add their glimmer to the blue-black sky.

Roarke came around to the truck's passenger side, where Rhea had already gotten out and looked up at a hilltop. "What are we looking at? The crooked trees?"

Three trees in the shape of lightning bolts were standing like sentinels keeping guard over the glen. Rhea had stepped down into the small ditch and headed up the sloping hill toward the trees. "Ghost, where are you going?" In a few strides, he had caught up with her.

"Do you know why they're shaped like that?" She pointed but kept walking.

"No, I mean, I've noticed them, but I never thought about their shape."

Reaching the top, Rhea walked over and placed her hands on the flat part of the middle tree, closing her eyes and lifting her chin to tilt her face in the direction of the leaves.

"In North America, we have trees just like these, trail trees, or trail markers. Native Americans would bend the trees. The "bend" points in the direction of a trail, or water source, or some important area."

"Bend the tree?" Roarke stood behind her and played with the leaves on a low branch.

"Take a hardwood sapling and plant it where you want the bend to direct. Secure the top end to the ground with straps and stakes. The tree continues to grow unharmed, and new branches grow upward. When it's is older and can keep its shape, it's unbound, and the part staked to the ground is cut off, creating the elbow. Rhea caressed the hard bump in the oak before turning toward Roarke.

"I don't know where these came from. There are no Native Americans here."

"No." She paused to brush a few loose hairs away from her forehead. "There are women who know nature. Women who study trees and would know how this could be done."

"Women would want to send a message to other people with similar knowledge."

"The bend shows the way." She set out along the top of the hill, in the direction pointed out by the tree's elbows, with Roarke right behind her.

Wandering through the thick forest, they followed an over-grown trail, where roots tripped them and branches pulled at their hair and clothing. They found another trail marker in a small clearing, pointing them in another direction, deeper into the woods. The trees were spaced wider the deeper they walked, giving them more light from the moon. Another clearing displayed another tree and a new direction until they arrived at a large clearing where the trail narrowed.

"Something tells me this is what we were supposed to find," Roarke said in an awed voice.

In front of them were three large rings of moss-covered stones, one inside the other, surrounding a small cairn. A narrow path in the stones, plants, and flowers led to the center.

"Is this a cairn?" Rhea asked as she ran a hand down its rough surface.

"Aye. Strange." Roarke squatted in front of the stones. "Cairns were used as trail markers too. Or, to mark water lines, or for astronomy . . ."

" . . . burial mounds?"

"In the past, yes."

In the distance, the southern wind had picked up. Rhea could hear the tops of the trees stirring and swaying as the wind headed straight for them. At that moment, she experienced a rush of sensation, too powerful to be imagined, too timeless for words. She lifted her head, waiting for the rush of wind to hit, but just before it did, she spun around as Roarke cried out.

Turning, she saw him sitting on his behind in the dirt, a look of horror on his face, as he looked around him.

"Roarke!" She knelt beside him. "What is it?"

"Someone . . . someone was beside me!" He grabbed for Rhea's hand and jumped to his feet, holding her against him. "And that smell. Can you smell that?"

"The flowers?" She was alarmed by his behavior.

"Rhea." Roarke stepped to get away from the cairn, pulling Rhea with him. "I'd very much like to get out of here."

"Okay." Rhea led him out of the clearing and back the way they'd come. They never stopped nor spoke until they were walking back along the hilltop.

On the other side of the hill, Rhea saw a large pile of rocks on either side of the river and made a mental note to ask Roarke about them when he calmed down, as it reminded her of something she had dreamt about a few nights before.

Back in the truck, Roarke put his hands on the wheel in front of him and started laughing. "You must think I'm ridiculous, but it feels so good to be back in the truck."

"What happened?"

"When we walked inside the circle, I immediately felt dizzy and could smell that vile odor. I had to squat down because I thought I was going to faint. Then it felt like someone else was near me. I turned my head, and there was a black shadow, and it bent down like it was staring me in the face."

"It was so dark. How could you see a shadow?"

"It was darker than the darkness around us, and it kind of vibrated."

"Ok, now you're scaring me."

"No, no." He reached out to grasp her hand and surprised her when he pulled it up to his cold lips and kissed it. "I'm just tired, and tonight was long. The woods just got to me. Honestly, over the past while, a lot of weird things have been happening to me."

When they got home, Roarke excused himself to check the animals while Rhea readied for bed. She put on her white shift and settled down under the blanket on the sofa to wait for his return, hoping to be able to understand what had occurred. During their visit to the cairn, even though the dark shadow had terrified Roarke and drained him of energy, Rhea had had a very different experience.

It was as if something had come over her and heightened her senses. She had felt ancient spirits clinging to the trees, and in her mind's eye, she saw them project something toward her, into her. She heard insects stomping on leaves and figures and forms danced before her eyes where there had only been darkness a second before. She could identify the individual scent of each flower as well as the rich, coppery scent of a dead fox's blood mingled with petrichor.

In just a few seconds, she had become drunk with sacred pleasures that children of nature could only gift, and she knew she was never going to be the same.

CHAPTER FIFTEEN: THE YEW

I do not feel peace. I do not see the souls of the dearly departed. There is no one else in this blackness, no light carrying me home.

I am just falling as one solid emotion. Pain, anguish, anger, hatred, violence, longing, sadness, and vengeance, in one big, black, swirling orb that rests where once was my heart.

I tumble through time, gathering the darkness around me, and when I have enough energy, I can find my roots.

I climb up and out. Each time, I search, but he's where The Good go. I watch from the tops of trees, swaying with the wind and crying with the wolves. Finally, I crawl from under their beds and begin my whispers. There is no happiness after they let me in.

I live where the wind begins . . .

The phone ringing brought Rhea running back into the house, as she had been waiting for a call from Liam for two days. "Hello?" she answered breathlessly.

"Hey, sis." came her brother Sal's cheery reply.

"Sal?" She flopped down into the armchair by the fireplace. "This is an unexpected pleasure."

"Yeah, I know you're working on that important project, but it can't wait."

"Is something wrong?"

"No one's sick or anything, but we're going to have to tear down the house."

"Mom and Dad's house?"

"It's falling down, love."

"What if Mom comes . . ."

"She's not coming back, Rhea." He sighed. "The roof's falling. When a house goes unlived-in, it falls apart quickly."

"Why didn't you tell me about this sooner?"

"Why? Could you have helped?"

She opened her mouth to speak but found no words.

"Today's Poppy's birthday," he added sadly

"Yeah." she said, picking at the ends of the quilt on the arm of the chair.

"She would have been twenty-nine today."

"Yeah. *Pâté Chinoise.*"

"What?"

"You remember how Papa always let us pick what we wanted for supper on our birthdays. Poppy always wanted *Paté Chinoise*, as we have in Québec."

"That's right." She could hear him smiling. "Bit surprised you remembered the name."

"Why's that?"

"Last time I spoke to Liam, he told me you never speak French to him."

"Patrice speaks to him in French. I speak to him in English, so he can develop both languages."

"He said you didn't like for him to speak French to you."

"That's not true."

"Funny. I believe the kid. In your personal life, I bet the last person you spoke French with was Papa."

"Mom never spoke much French either."

"She wasn't raised with it." He coughed. "Dad always spoke a lot of French with us. If you remember."

"Don't talk at me as if I don't remember him!"

"You never speak about him. You never speak about Mom, and you close up when someone does. Do you speak to Liam about his people?"

"Liam knows his family."

"Not his family, Rhea." Sal sighed. "His people. The ways of his people. The old beliefs and traditions. The words we still use. Anything?"

"Why?"

"Because I'm sure when people ask about your beautiful face, you're quick to tell them where your blood comes from, but you've never fully embraced who you are, every part of you. It seems like you just chose certain aspects of your background and forgot the rest."

"Sal, Jesus!" She stood and stormed into the kitchen. "What are you trying to do to me?"

"I just find it interesting that you go to Scotland to research Scottish traditions, you went to Asia to research their history, and you have no interest in writing about your own. You don't even remember your own."

"I remember everything." She spoke the three words in a tone filled with longing and mournfulness.

"I'll put flowers on Poppy's grave for you and Raven, and I'll take the things out of the house and get it ready. Take care. *Tabarnak!*" The line clicked as he hung up.

A tear ran down Rhea's cheek as she sat in the silence of the cottage before her phone rang again. "Hello?"

"Rhea?" It was her brother Raven. "How are you doing, love?"

"I've been better." She coughed. "Our brother's an asshole."

Raven laughed with his unmistakable throaty chuckle. "You said it!"

She sniffed and wiped at her nose.

"Stop crying."

"I'm not crying."

"You upset about the house?"

"Of course." She pulled a tissue out of a box and dabbed at her eyes. "Is there any way I can help?"

"Probably not. Getting the roof done is expensive. The walls are solid, but the rest will give way without a proper roof."

Rhea would have loved to feel Raven's strong arms around her. His face, so like their mother's, his mouth quick to smile.

"How much will it cost? I've some money put away."

"That's sweet of you to offer, but we know how expensive life is. We have kids, too."

"No, I want you guys to have it." She looked outside and saw Roarke coming around the corner of the shed, dragging something weighty on a rough blanket, his muscles straining with the effort. "For the past little while, I've been saving money for a solo trip to Tibet, but it doesn't seem very important now. I'll send the money to you guys."

"Rhea."

"Listen, if it were enough for Tibet, it'd be enough for the roof."

"God, love. Are you sure?"

"One hundred percent." Her eyes welled up again. "We can't tear down that house. It's no castle, but it's ours. It's theirs. The roof is why I was really saving the money. I just didn't know it until now."

"You still being witchy?"

"I should be ashamed of myself." She sniffed again. "Whenever things happen, I just leave you guys to handle the rough stuff. I know that's what Sal was getting at."

"Don't you dare ever say that again!" Raven's voice became loud and heavy. "You're taking care of the most important thing." Finally, his voice cracked. "Poppy's son and doing a damn fine job of it."

They both started crying and laughing at the same time.

"How are Patrice and Liam?"

"They're great. Liam's with Pierre-Luc's family now, but it always makes Pat nervous because he thinks the family'll try and keep Liam."

Raven sighed. "Then why not just let him adopt Li? I know he's asked you enough."

"It's not the right time."

"I love you, but you're tough on Patrice. You know how controlling you can be and unforgiving."

"What does that have to do with anything?"

"What do you think he thinks you would do if he made you angry in any way?"

"Couldn't guess."

"You'd keep Liam away from him."

"Oh, bullshit!"

"You would. You and Pat are raising him, but you've had no formal adoption. If you guys had a falling out, you would get Li, and Pat would have no claim to him."

"I'm astonished at how highly my brothers think of me." She felt exhausted under the weight of the truth.

"You don't leave him because you're afraid of raising the kid alone."

It was the last nugget of truth, and the last of her heart's secrets flying out of its box.

Raven's voice softened. "Stop trying to control everything and let Pat adopt Li and open his guitar shop. He's still at the accounting firm, just because you want him there. You know Sal and I are close to Pat. I love you, but you need to start being fair with him."

"Let me talk to her." Rhea could hear the phone changing hands.

Hearing her brother breathing but saying nothing, she spoke softly, "Sal?"

Rhea jumped as his voice came over the line very loudly. "Love, I was out of line. I'm just so mad today. Poppy should be with us and not in the grave. The house. Mom. It all just builds up sometimes."

"I know."

"I took it out on you. I'm sorry."

"I'm not. It hurt, I won't say it didn't, but I needed to hear those things, and Raven and I figured out something for the house. He'll tell you."

"Wait. What?" She could hear the excitement in his voice as she watched Roarke walk down the path toward the cliff, Midas at his heels.

Rhea giggled. "Rave'll tell you."

"Actually, I have something I forgot to mention to you. I was going through some of Dad's old papers. Did you know we have a little Scottish blood on his side?"

"Really?"

Sal told Rhea about an ancestor who fought for the Jacobites and in the Battle of Culloden. He went into exile in Québec City and then led the Scottish regiment to victory in the Battle of Québec.

"I'll look into finding out more about that while I'm here, and thanks, brother."

"Thanks for being a bastard to you on Poppy's birthday?"

"For trying to open my eyes. Poppy's in her grave, but we're not. I'm going to try to make things better, Salmon. For everyone. I promise."

Roarke jumped a little when Rhea soundlessly appeared at his side and sat next to him at the bench overlooking the ocean. The wind tasted of salt, and grey waves scoured the shore.

He tilted his head in her direction and cocked his eyebrow, waiting for her to speak.

Rhea squinted her eyes at him. "You think you know me so well?"

Then, pulling down the corners of his mouth and shrugging his shoulders, he turned back to the waves until she spoke again.

"My brothers called."

Silence spread between them as he waited for Rhea to continue, the only sound being the pebbles of the beach crashing against each other as they tumbled in the waves.

"They were going to tear down our parents' home, but I have a little money saved that I'm going to send them to fix the roof. It's okay now."

"Your face doesn't say it's okay now."

"It's just . . ." She paused and licked her lips. "From as early as I could remember, my parents were at me to make sure I got my education, and as soon as I had the chance to leave, I did. That's what happens when you leave, isn't it? You don't go back?"

"Not true." He laughed. "I came back."

"Not the same." She glanced over at him. "You're an anomaly."

Silence again as Roarke turned his face to the sky, and Rhea watched the waves. "I've been a shitty sister. When our sister died, our father, when our mother disappeared, I left each time. Leaving the guys to deal with it all. I see now why I did that, and I'll make it up to them."

Roarke opened his eyes and turned to her, watching wisps of her hair caress her face, her eyes becoming iridescent as she looked toward the bright spot in the grey sky as the sun tried to break through the cloud cover.

"They don't think I miss home, but I miss everything. The people, the food, the sea, the hills, the beach. I always dream of home. Until I came here, and now, I always dream of, well, here."

The sadness on her face made Roarke ache to touch her, to help her. "Please don't be sad." Unable to resist, he tucked a strand of hair behind her ear.

"My brother told me that I've forgotten where we came

from. Forgotten about our blood, our traditions, and our history. Everything our parents wanted us to know and keep alive."

"If you think that's true, and you want to change that, you can. It's never too late. The possibility of change lives in every moment, every second. The sadness on your face is wrecking me."

Raising her hand to the ear he had just touched, she smiled. "I'm okay. There's just a lot of people I miss."

"Rhea, if you carry someone in your heart, how can you ever be separated?"

Rhea stared at him unblinking for a moment, and then without thinking, threw her arms around him as tears streamed down her face and wet the shoulder of his plaid shirt. "Roarke." She sniffed. "For someone so unromantic, you sure can put together some tender words."

After lunch, they walked along the cliff's ridge toward the hill that Rhea had never explored, and Midas ambled down from Ian's to visit them.

What Rhea had thought was small thatch of trees was poised on top of the hill like a bad toupee. "Is this the yew tree you mentioned last night?"

"Aye, it is."

There was a small opening in the side of the trees facing them, where a path led into the thatch's center. Despite her trepidation, Rhea headed toward the opening that split the low leaves.

Roarke touched her elbow. "I don't want you to be afraid."

At the entranceway, Midas started barking bloody murder, and Rhea glanced at the dark area inside and then back at the barking dog. "Dogs are gifts from The Maker and can see or sense what we cannot."

Roarke just smiled down at the dog and reached to pat his

head, but Midas stepped away from Roarke's touch and sat on his haunches. Then, shaking his head at Midas and crouching as low as possible, Roarke crawling into the opening, stopping to wave Rhea in behind him. Her hair and sweater snagged on branches, so she kept her head bowed until she got inside, and her mouth dropped open when she looked up.

In the center was a giant tree trunk, about eight feet circumference, and the tree spread out over their heads. A tangle of knobby, gnarled, twisted limbs created the open space by arching and touching the ground. The limbs seemed to be separate trees on their own.

Around the yew's trunk were twenty or so moss-covered grey headstones in various shapes and sizes. Giant green ferns grew amongst the headstones, and twisted bends of the branches spread out from the main trunk.

Roarke toward the trunk, his head bent. "The yew. Oldest of all trees." He pointed to a branch embedded in the ground. "The drooping branches can root and form new trunks."

"Really?"

"Aye, and there's no telling how old it is. The trunks become hollow over time, so they leave no tree rings like other trees. No way to show the passage of time."

"Roarke." She pointed to a large headstone nearly split in two by a branch. "This is amazing."

"Due to being ageless, they are associated with death, transcendence, reincarnation, the underworld, and the supernatural. That's why people put cemeteries around yew trees. They connect the living with the spirits of those who've gone on. Gateways to the spirit world. The bark being poisonous adds to the mystery."

Rhea had reached out to stroke the tree but stopped as Roarke continued.

"There's a link between these trees and doomed lovers. A legendary maiden named Deirdre hung herself from a yew after she'd been forced to marry the lord who had murdered her husband. This small cemetery is all that remains of a village that existed here long years ago. A neighboring clan drove out the villagers after a dispute. The yew tree protects the souls of those buried here."

"Thomas's clan, driven out by Islean's,"

Rhea knelt in the grass in front of the tree, and Roarke settled down next to her. "I'll tell you something else, but it's a bit strange."

"Excellent." Rhea leaned back, staring up at the branches.

"In the past, people were just buried in a burial sheet, a shroud. A few years ago, a yew tree in a cemetery on the East Coast was uprooted by violent weather, and among the roots were skeletons. They seemed to be clinging to the roots."

"Really?"

"Aye. Scientists even investigated."

Rhea sat up and crawled over to a headstone, touching the symbol in the middle. It looked like the letter "S" with three vertical lines running through it, like a money sign. "Do you know what this symbol means? It's on almost every stone. Why would a money sign be on ancient headstones?"

Roarke smiled and crawled toward her. "That, my dear, is a symbol which means Jesus Christ. The first three letters of his name in Greek, "I" *Iota*, "H" *Eta*, and "S" *Sigma*, are superimposed over each other. In The Middle Ages, Jesus was written *IHESUS*. Ian told me his clan used this symbol on their headstones and other things to show that that clan owned them."

"Thomas's clan," Rhea muttered just as a strange sort of vertigo came over her. Roarke's voice sounded far away, and her vision blurred. A magnetic force pulled her to the ground, and she would have fallen over had Roarke not grabbed her arm.

"Good God! You're white as a sheet!" He put his hands on

either side of her face.

"Sorry. I'm the teensiest bit dizzy."

"We should get you out of here. Sensitive people can have strong reactions being near a yew tree."

She looked at him with a furrowed brow. "Sensitive?"

Waving his hand in front of his face, he made to shake off the comment. "I just mean spiritual. Those who strongly feel the world around them. You can't say you don't."

Roarke got Rhea up, away from the tree, and they started down the path toward the cottage. It was then that Roarke cheekily added. "Of course, the power of suggestion works wonders, too."

The wind howled and whipped around the house when Roarke awoke to a strange, steady, rhythmic banging. He soon realized it came from the door to the second floor, which he had not re-sealed since he had shown Rhea the artifacts. Peeking around the corner at the door, he could see it hitting against the doorframe.

Creeping into the hallway and hoping to find a way to remedy the situation before it woke Rhea, he paused when the banging abruptly stopped. A cold chill crept up his back. A slight creak turned his attention toward Rhea's door, which was ajar, so he hastened to close it.

To his surprise, the bed was empty, and Rhea nowhere to be seen. He did a quick search of the house with a panicky feeling stealing over him and found nothing.

Finding the front door unlocked, he jumped into his boots, glanced out the side window, and saw Rhea walking up the hill toward the yew tree. The wind whipped at her hair and white shift, yet she seemed oblivious to the cold. He thought she might be sleepwalking, but a second later, he recoiled as he saw, to his horror, that she was not alone.

On the hill, just in front of the yew tree, Rhea stepped in slow, dreamy movements, and in the soft glow of pale moonlight, treading a few feet ahead of her, Roarke could just make out the dark silhouette of another, taller woman in flowing robes.

By the time he got outside and ran up the slope, Rhea had disappeared, but Roarke caught the slightest glimpse of white under the outermost branches of the yew. He threw himself under the low-lying branches. As his eyes adjusted to the light, he saw one of the strangest things he had ever seen.

To the left of the yew tree's curling branches and thick, tangled trunk, Rhea was asleep on an old grave, curled around a root branch sticking out of the earth. The headstone had toppled over, and her head rested on it. She looked like a baby in vitro, grasping its umbilical cord.

Where the other woman had gone was a mystery, and a foul smell was in the air, but his only concern was Rhea as he bent to wake her. "Rhea? Rhea, wake up."

After a few gentle shakes, her eyes snapped open, and she stretched catlike, perfectly comfortable on top of an old, cold grave.

Roarke brushed her hair off her forehead and smiled down at her. "Sweetheart, I think you've been sleepwalking."

Rolling onto her back and looking up at the spreading branches of the tree above her head, she whispered, "Am I dreaming?"

"Not anymore. I think you're awake now."

"Are you sure?" She turned to look at him, a strange light in her eyes and a seductive smile on her lips that he had never seen before. She caressed the curves of her body, looking into his eyes the whole time. His eyes followed her hands, noticing how the thin, damp shift clung to her skin.

"You're awake now." He sat back on his heels. "You're going to catch your death out here. You're not cold at all?"

"Yes, Roarke, I'm cold. Could you hold me?" Pushing off the grave, Rhea pressed her body against his, and Roarke put his arms around her.

"That's better," she murmured against his chest.

Before he had time to react, she moved her head from his chest and kissed him with a force that shocked him. Her hands held both sides of his face, and she pressed against him as her jaw and lips worked to open his mouth. At first, he was too shocked to react, but then his nature took over. His hands roamed her body, and he returned her kiss hard and deep.

Then the foul, rotting smell intensified and took his attention away from the woman in his arms. He pulled away from Rhea, but she held his shoulders with remarkable strength.

Suddenly, the clouds parted, and a beam of moonlight worked its way through the branches. In the dim light, there seemed to be another beautiful woman in his arms, one he did not know. It scared him to his very core, especially when she started laughing.

As he pushed her away from him, she fell back onto the earth. Delight, humor, and malice lit her countenance, which for a second still looked very different than Rhea's. Suddenly, her hands flew to her face, and when he worked up his courage to pull the hands away, it was once again Rhea's uncommon face and cat-like eyes which peered up at him in fright.

Rhea sat on her backside, shaking and looking at him in alarm. "Roarke, is that you?"

"Aye, Rhea, It's me."

"Why are we here? I'm so cold. Why are we outside?"

Realizing she had woken, he sighed. "You were sleepwalking, and I followed you up here. Let's get you back to the house, and I'll explain everything."

Roarke carried her down to the cottage as she shivered and

clutched at the neck of her shift.

As they approached the door, Rhea looked at him. "Roarke?"

"Aye." He threw open the door to the house.

"I've never sleepwalked in my life."

Chapter Sixteen: Mermaid

At the foot of her bed, I watch her sleep. She opens her eyes. I do not know what is happening, but she draws me into her, and I have no control.

Once outside, I do not know if I am inside or outside her, but we go to the tree. I revel in every sensation, so different with a body. The cold earth above his bones is sacred, and I am as close to him as I have been in many lifetimes. I am so overcome that I can't help but kiss the other when he arrives. I laugh because he knows but will not allow himself to feel the truth.

That is when she pushes me out of her body. I did not like it anyway. I feel afraid.

Roarke could hear her teeth chattering when he rested his chin against the top of her head. He went straight down the hallway to his bedroom, flicked on the light and sat her down on the edge of the bed. "Rhea, you have to get out of that damp nightdress while I start the fire. You don't have a stove in your room."

She had slid to the floor, her knees pulled up to her head, and shook so violently she was hitting her forehead against her knees.

"Rhea!"

He knelt next to her and tried to look at her face, but she was so rigid he had to use both hands to lift her head. Then, he gasped to find her face very pale, her lips a slight blue purple. She groaned but didn't reply when he spoke to her.

"Rhea, I need to get you under the blankets."

Weakly nodding, she shakily got to her feet, clutching the duvet, pulling it toward her.

"Rhea, I won't look at you." Roarke averted his eyes and lifted the bottom of her gown, wet with moisture from outside. She tumbled back onto the bed, and he pushed her legs under the duvet and covered her as he slid the gown from her head.

Starting the fire in the small black stove in his room first, he went into her room and rifled through her drawers until he found another shift. Pouring two large tumblers of whisky, he carried them back to his bedroom. He helped her pull the gown over her head, and she pulled it down over her body under the blankets, but he was dismayed to see that she was still cold and pale, wracked with violent shivers and shudders.

Sliding his long limbs out of his damp pajama pants, he pulled on another pair and t-shirt, pulled back the covers, and climbed into bed with her. "You're freezing, and until the room heats up, I'll try to get you warm. Trust me."

Rhea neither commented nor hesitated as he put his arm under her head. He put his leg across both of hers and shifted so she didn't take the burden of his weight. She placed her cheek against his chest, moving her head back and forth as if she were wiping her mouth on his white tank top.

Roarke rested his cheek on top of her head as her shivers started to dissipate and her body slightly relaxed. He kissed her temple as his hand smoothed her hair from her face.

Sighing to himself, he stayed awake long enough to enjoy being so close to her, and the room had just started to warm up as he fell into an exhausted sleep.

It was still dark when Rhea woke in Roarke's arms, warmth creeping along the middle of her body. She pulled her head back to look at his face in the dim light from the hallway.

The huge, muscular man looked so sweet and peaceful, a man she was becoming desperate to kiss and to run her hands over his hard body, to feel him moving against her and inside her. He stirred and pulled her closer, a slight moan escaping his lips.

She shivered

His eyes opened. "You all right?"

She nodded and looked up at his dark, beautiful face. He gazed at her for a moment, and she was glad he couldn't read her thoughts.

When she turned her eyes away, he let her go, and sitting up, reached for the glasses of whisky on the nightstand. "Sit up and drink this. It'll fend off the rest of your chill."

Arranging the sheet around her, she took the offered glass and drank more than she had intended, coughing as she swallowed. "Ack, I'll never get used to this stuff."

"You're not supposed to chug it." He leaned back against the headboard and smiled.

Rhea looked down at her glass. "Roarke, I remember coming down the hill, but why don't I remember going up?"

"My darling, I have no idea."

Roarke flicked her under the chin with his finger. "Just go back to sleep, love. We can figure things out tomorrow." Putting both glasses on the nightstand, he settled back down in bed. "Stay here tonight. I don't want you to get cold again."

Opening one eye, he was surprised to find her looking at him. "I can go to your room."

Stilling him by touching his arm, she shook her head. "You don't have to, Roarke. I'm just so surprised at how comfortable I am around you."

"Aye, I feel the same. Is this how it feels to be true friends with a woman?"

"Guess so. I mean, there's no attraction at all." Rhea turned her back and smiled. "It's a good thing you're so damn ugly."

Sitting up slightly, he looked down at her in shock and found her grinning. Flicking her earlobe with this middle finger and settling back down, he muttered, "Aye, it's a good thing you're so bloody ugly too."

"Roarke?"

"Yes?"

"I think you're wonderful."

"I'm not sure what to say to that." He paused for a second. "Thank you, Rhea."

"I feel strange not knowing how I got up there. I guess I was sleepwalking, but I've never done that before."

"I thought we'd take the boat out tomorrow for a few days. There's a very wealthy lady from an ancient clan on one of the islands, a distant relative of mine. She told me a while back she would help me with funding for the castle, and I may need to hit her up for more than she bargained for. I've been trying to contact her, but the estate isn't taking calls. I think I'll have to go there in person. Moreover, I think you need to be closer to the water for a while, Island Girl. Would you like that?"

"Immensely."

"Good—if you sleepwalk on the boat, at least I'll hear a splash."

In the morning, Roarke informed Rhea that he had spoken to Ian, finished his work, and she had about five minutes to get ready for the trip. Flipping her half-full suitcase onto the bed and grabbing her backpack, she threw together some clothes and essentials.

Rhea bolted to the door when Roarke yelled for the second time. "Come on, we're wasting the day." Hearing a small thump behind her, she turned and saw the brooch she had found on her first day in Scotland now lay on the floor. When she picked it up, it felt warm. A little shocked by the sensation, she flicked it into the open suitcase and turned again for the door.

The second thump froze her on the spot. She turned and felt a knot of fear in her throat as the brooch was again on the floor. Her eyes flew around the room, seeing nothing.

On impulse, Rhea stuffed it into her backpack. As she exited the room and turned back to flick off the light, the door to the second floor behind her gave a sudden bang. Focus glued to the door, she took a sidestep closer to the front of the house as the doorknob began to rattle. A strange feeling swept over her, as if someone stood on the other side of the door, someone who knew she was just outside and was waiting. She pivoted her body and ran for the kitchen.

Roarke was stuffing a few things into a small duffle bag as she ran around the corner and straight up to the island where he stood, then flung her backpack onto the counter. When he looked at her in surprise, she smiled. "Just so excited to get going."

"Right. Just lock up and we'll be off." Roarke slid his baseball cap off the countertop, and in doing so, knocked Rhea's small bag to the floor. Stooping, he rose with the backpack in one hand and the plastic bag in the other. "Is this the brooch?"

"Um, yes." Not wanting to explain what had happened, she took it from his hand and put it back in her bag. "I just want to keep it with me."

On the way to the marina in town, Roarke explained that the sail to the island would take almost the whole day, as he planned to sail slowly across a narrow firth, passing various islands before entering the sound and maybe berthing for the night in a small harbor.

In town, after a short trip to the grocery store or getting the messages, Roarke led Rhea down to the small pier and stopped by a blue and white wooden-masted sailing yacht docked in the first row of the marina.

"Here she is." He put his foot on the edge of the boat. "I had Doug run down and get her ready for us."

As he showed her where everything was and which items he had renovated, everything he touched, he caressed. Down the companionway stairs and into the ship's belly, the aft starboard side had the galley. There was a sink to one side, the stove on the other, and a deep refrigerator in the corner. The aft port side had a deep quarter berth with a table, radio, and GPS. Forward on the starboard side were bookshelves and a settee berth, which converted into a double bed when attached to the foldable table.

A swivel-mounted screen made up the entertainment area, where he also had a few devices to help with communications and information. The mast ran through the room and beyond toward the V-berth, which was in shades of white and blue like most things in Roarke's home and ship.

There was an enclosed closet, and on the other side the head, or bathroom, with sink, toilet, and handheld shower. The grated floor collected the water, and a suck-pump got the water out. He spent a lot of time explaining how his new compost toilet worked, and she listened until he started getting a tad too descriptive.

Sitting at the table, she noted all he had told her about the ship and peppered him with questions while he put together their meal.

Lunch was Finnan Haddie Salad—smoked Finnan haddock, cold potatoes, green vegetables, and boiled egg in a light vinaigrette, with bread.

Sailing into the open sea after leaving the small marina, Roarke became silent as soon as he touched the steering wheel. Rhea sat in the rubber-coated seat on the starboard side of the deck, watching the grey-green water break along the side of the boat and looking at the majestic mountains as the shoreline slipped farther away.

Eventually, she went to the bathroom, and Roarke yelled out that he was anchoring for a while as a friend had radioed telling him dolphins were in the area. When she came back on deck, she was alone. She looked all around, but Roarke wasn't there. Panic swept over her, and she ran from one side of the ship to the other, screaming his name. "Roarke!"

The only answer she received was from the seagulls until she heard Roarke yell her name. She spun around and found him in the water, smiling and waving at her.

Leaning over the side, she screamed, "You scared the shit out of me! What are you doing?"

"What does it look like? I'm swimming."

"In this water? It must be freezing!"

"Go on. It's invigorating. Jump in."

"You're crazy." She rolled her eyes at him, watching him tread water.

"You said you loved to swim."

Gazing down, she leaned over the side and plunged her hand in, pulling it right back as the cold water assaulted her senses.

Rhea's thoughts went back to calm days in her childhood when the village's women would take their children down to the sandy cove to let them splash around in the waves.

One bright, clear day, Rhea had swum farther out than she ever had before.

Though some of the other mothers were yelling for her to come closer to shore, her mother did not comment. Standing, Margot removed her dress and took down her straight blue-black hair, tendrils falling across her face in the gentle breeze as she walked into the sea.

When the water became deeper, she swam the rest of the way to her daughter, and Rhea threw her arms around her mother's neck, wrapping her legs around her waist. Margot's strong legs kept them afloat.

"Rhea." Margot pressed her nose to her daughter's. "You look so beautiful. Like the mermaid in our storybook. I wanted to be a mermaid too."

Rhea giggled. "Mom, you're prettier than any mermaid."

Roarke's voice broke her from her reverie. "Are you coming in or not?"

Without comment, she shed her gym pants, walked to the back of the boat, and dove into the water, shooting back to the surface with a scream of shock.

Sticking her head back into the water, swam toward Roarke as he approached her.

"I can't believe you did it!" He laughed. "How does it feel?"

Before she could answer, a wave caught her on the side of the head, and she dipped below the water. Surfacing again, she sputtered and reached out instinctively to Roarke. He caught her arm, and she leaned her weight on him, laughing and wiping water out of her eyes.

"Cold, Roarke," she replied, as every nerve in her body tingled. "It feels cold and wonderful!"

Another wave caught them, throwing them closer still. Suddenly uncomfortable with the closeness, Rhea pulled away. "Okay, then try and keep up."

Instead of swimming with him, she headed in the opposite direction, turning to find him some distance away, watching her.

"You're a beautiful swimmer, Rhea."

Plunging his head into the sea, he headed toward her at great speed, his long body cutting a V on the surface, so streamlined he barely splashed. Pausing just before he reached her, he dove beneath the water. Unable to see where he was, Rhea looked for him when something grabbed her ankle. She screamed, kicking out, and made contact with something hard and wet.

Breaching the surface in a bubble of air, he was laughing and holding the side of his head. "Hey, watch where you're kicking."

"Not funny," she yelled, "I thought Nessie had me."

"Nessie's landlocked."

"Her cousin then," she mumbled through chattering teeth.

He looked at her face. "You're turning blue. Let's get you back on the boat."

They swam back to the boat, and after mounting the small ladder, Roarke turned and helped her up, wrapping her in his discarded plaid shirt, rubbing life back into her arms, and tousling her hair until she stepped back giggling.

"I'm good. I'm good."

"I didn't think you'd get in."

"I used to swim in the ocean when I was young. My mother loved to swim."

"You looked like a mermaid out there."

Roarke turned her toward the companionway stairs, saying, "I'll be right down. I just need to turn on the propane."

She shivered her way down the small flight of steps. He came scrambling down after her.

"I'll start the fire."

"You . . . you have a fireplace on the boat?"

"A propane wall furnace. It makes everything nice and toasty."

Rummaging through her bag, she watched Roarke go to a small silver box connected to a pipe that extended up through the ceiling. His wet shorts clung to his body, and water from his hair ran down his back. He opened the small door to the furnace, lit the gas, and left his finger on the button for a few seconds before closing the door.

"I'll just turn on these two small AC heaters, and you'll be warm as freshly baked bread before you know it."

She still shivered, looking into her bag in dismay. "You going to change?"

Putting the bag on the table, she pulled his shirt closer to her. "In my haste to pack, I only ma-managed to pack some underwear and sundresses, my shift, and the t-shirt I'm wearing. Nothing warm."

"And your pants got wet on deck." Turning on a heater near his sleeping space, Roarke crouched over a trunk on the bulwark side. He took out a white t-shirt and opened a fresh pack of white boxer briefs, handing both to her. "Get out of your wet things. These might be a tad roomy but should suffice."

"Thanks." She headed to the bathroom. "I'm s-so scatter-brained sometimes."

"Just a second." He stepped around her to lift out the showerhead and mount it on the stand above her head. "There. Have a hot shower. Towels are in the cabinet below." He stepped out and closed the door behind him.

With shaking fingers, Rhea undressed, placed her wet clothes in the sink, and turned on the shower. She shrieked as the cold water hit her already-cold body, "*Roarke!* This is colder than the ocean!"

"Give it a minute."

Even as he spoke, a warm flood of water came streaming over her head and body. She used his shampoo to lather her head and body. Reluctantly, she shut off the water, toweled, and dressed. However, when she stepped out into the hold, she shivered again.

Roarke, dressed in dry clothes, stopped rummaging through a cupboard to stare at her.

"W-what?" She still shivered.

"N-nothing. No sense standing there and shaking, love. Get in bed and warm up."

She stopped shivering long enough to stand a little straighter and scowl at him.

Rolling his eyes at her, he turned back to his search. "Go on. It still needs to warm up in here."

Stepping around, she looked at the triangular bed, the open area at the tip stuffed with cylindrical rolls of extra blankets, and muttered, "Less than twenty-four hours, and I'm shivering in his bed again." Hopping up, she squirreled under the thick white duvet and pale blue top sheet, sinking into the enveloping, fluffy softness that smelled of flowery detergent and bleach. "Smells heavenly."

The sheets and pillowcases were silky soft as she made snow angels between the covers. "Seriously." She stretched. "This is the most comfortable bed I've ever been in."

He chuckled as she covered her head with the duvet and pulled her knees toward her chin, her body heat warming her little cocoon as she listened to Roarke tinkering with the small stove and humming to himself.

The boat's motion had a rocking-chair effect, and before she knew what was happening, the swaying motion had rendered her incapable of conscious thought. Within five minutes, Rhea was sound asleep and was still asleep four hours later.

Rhea woke to the sounds of the hockey game coming from the living room. Her feather bed was warm, and the lighthouse beam illuminated the little lump in the crib at the foot of her bed.

Through the crack in her bedroom door, she saw her father sitting at the kitchen table, his handsome face lit with the smile he reserved only for her mother, who sat on his lap in her long, white shift. Gabriel had one hand around her waist, and with the other, he ran his fingers through the curtain of long, blue-black hair that fell like a silky waterfall down her back and shoulders. Margot ran her delicate fingers down his straight nose and under his strong jaw.

Gabriel spoke in his deep, rumbling voice, "After I came home, I was sitting at the kitchen window having a cup of tea and watching you on the little hill, hanging our children's clothing on the line. Some of your hair whipped across your face, mixing in with the fur around the collar. I thought there's no woman more beautiful than you on the face of the planet. God never made a more beautiful human being."

"Me in my old blue cassock made you think that? Really?"

"Oui, mon amour." He wrapped a tendril of her hair around his index finger and kissed it. "And my next thought was, how did that woman ever get stuck with the likes of me?"

Margot bent her forehead to his. "How dare you say such a thing about my husband. There's no finer man in the world."

Rhea smiled and settled back down in bed, hearing the soft crinkling sound of her sister's diaper as she adjusted the position of her chubby little legs.

The last thing she heard was the sound of the chair scraping along the wooden floor and her mother laughing. "Stop looking at me like that. That's how we got the last one."

Roarke had three choices—make up one of the two smaller berths, which were much too small for him, or wake Rhea and put her in one of the berths, disturbing her much-needed sleep, or slip into bed with her and suffer her admonishments when they woke up.

Reminding himself that they had slept together the night before, he crawled up onto the platform, lifted the corner of the duvet, and slipped underneath, lying on the top sheet. *Mother would say to leave space for the Holy Ghost.*

To his surprise, she didn't stir when he stretched out and sighed as the soft mattress relieved the pressure on his tired body. Even though he was exhausted, he lay there, his mind wandering to thoughts of the sweet woman breathing beside him. Since she had fallen asleep, he had missed her. *How can you miss someone when they're in the same room?*

Now, lying next to her, he felt content. Unwilling to delve deeper into his feelings, he focused on letting his mind go blank and was almost asleep when Rhea rolled closer to him. Both hands curled under her chin in fists, she pressed her forehead against his shoulder and rubbed it back and forth before lying still again.

Lifting his arm, she slid down to rest her head against his chest, her soft body pressed to his side. His other hand rested against the back of her head, his fingers splayed in the silky, red-brown tendrils.

Nuzzling her head with his nose, he felt a change in his body. *Damn it to Hell!* To keep his mind and hands from wandering, he thought of the least sexy thing could think of, his brother clipping his toenails. Sleep came over him almost immediately.

Rhea fluttered her eyes open at daybreak and found herself, once again, in bed with Roarke. His long limbs were curled against her frame, spooning her, an arm over her torso. His forehead rested against the back of her head, and his gentle breath caressed her neck.

As if he could sense she was awake, Roarke pulled his arm across her body and rolled onto his back, stretching his arms above his head. Turning to look at her, he smiled. "Good morning."

"Morning." She smiled back.

"Now, I know you're wondering why I'm here, but—"

"Stop. You needn't explain. I've learned not to question your judgment. Besides, I just had the most comfortable sleep of my entire life."

"I slept well myself."

"How do you ever get out of this bed?"

"Aye, I made it a bit too comfortable. You'll get up soon

enough." Roarke smirked. "When you have to pee."

Rhea glanced at the clock, six-fifteen. "Wait!" She exclaimed as her hands flew to either side of her head. "Have I been asleep ever since I crawled in here?"

"Aye."

"What time did I get in here?"

"Around four o'clock last evening."

Jerked herself up into a sitting position, she clutched the duvet to her chest and exclaimed incredulously, "I've been asleep for fourteen hours?"

His deep laugher filled the small space. "Aye."

"How is that possible?"

"Jetlag."

"Impossible. I've been here too long."

"Aye, and you've been staying up late and waking up early on account of being nosey."

She ignored the jab. "I've never slept fourteen hours straight in my life."

"I always sleep like the dead out here too, with the fresh air and the motion of the boat."

"I slept so good last night."

"You slept so *well* last night, Miss Writer. Not so good."

"I had such vivid dreams. About home, my parents. They were telling each other secrets. God, they loved each other so much." She paused and looked at her hands. "Too much."

Roarke turned to her, propping himself up on one elbow. "That's a strange thing to say."

She ran a hand across her forehead. "It's just that my mother couldn't live without him."

He stayed quiet for a few seconds, his brow furrowed. "When did she die?"

"I don't know."

"What do you mean?"

"I don't know if she's alive or dead."

The furrows of her brow deepened as she played with her nails. "My father wasn't supposed to go fishing that day. He hadn't fished for nearly ten years, not since he had hurt his back and began working at the motel in the next village, but one of the men needed an extra hand, and my father had gone along to help him. Said he wanted to feel the spray on his face again.

"My mother begged him not to go because she'd dreamt of a white fox and the little man in the forest. They were warning her. She had also dreamed of them before Poppy's death." She ran her hand across her forehead. "They never found his body. Eventually, they called off the search, and mother cut off her beautiful hair, so close in some places that she cut her scalp. After I left for college, the boys said she would spend more and more time in the woods or along the shoreline. One day, she walked into the woods, and no one's seen her since."

"She could still be alive?"

"Could be. Sal thinks she went to the woods to die. Raven thinks she's alive but doesn't want to live in society anymore."

"Wouldn't a search party have found a shelter or signs of her?"

"Not if she wanted to stay hidden."

"Do you think she's still alive?"

"I don't know." She squirmed around, trying to scratch an itch in the middle of her back.

"I don't mean to . . ."

Rhea stopped squirming and looked over at him. "Look, what I know is that my father's death drove her crazy, and whether she's alive or dead, I'm never going to see her again."

"Wouldn't you like to see her again?"

"Not really, not if Mom could have been with us all these years and chose not to be." A solitary tear rolled down the side of her face. "My father was an amazing man, but I've never understood how you can love someone so much that you can't go on without them or how you could leave your family."

Roarke picked up her tear with the tip of his finger. "Do you think he would've done the same if she'd gone first?"

"Don't know. Mom and Papa were strong together, but separately, they weren't. Mom was growing withdrawn after Poppy's death. Dad's passing shortly after just put her over the edge."

"I think their love was beautiful."

"Yeah, I'd forgotten how beautiful they were. I forgot the way they looked at each other. I was with them last night. I can feel the ghost of my dream this morning."

A soft, almost mystic radiance clung to the air in the small hold, and a solemn hush spread between them until Rhea whispered, "You're right."

"About what?"

She started to wiggle out from under the covers. "I need to pee so badly my back teeth are floating."

Laughing loudly, Roarke stretched again. "You go pee, and I'll get the kettle on."

Rhea sat, still eating her eggs, sausage, black pudding, tomato, and toast as Roarke sat across the table from her sipping tea. "Why'd she cut off her hair?"

"What?"

"Why did your mother cut off her hair?"

Dipping the edge of her toast in her teacup, Rhea nibbled at it. "First Nations have certain beliefs when it comes to hair. There's power in hair, and it connects you to the infinite because it can reach out like an octopus's tentacles and draw power and knowledge from the world. Braided hair means unity with the infinite, and loose flowing hair means the freedom of nature. It's symbolic of Mother Earth, whose hair is the flowing grasses."

"You told me your mother loved to lie in the tall grass to recharge."

Smiling, she sat back. "Cutting hair is symbolic of loss. A new time without a loved one."

"That's beautiful, really."

"Mom was so vain over her hair. It was so black it had a blue cast when the sun shone on it. I'm the only one who didn't get her blue-black hair."

Roarke rested his chin in his hand and looked at her in the morning sunlight. "Your hair's insane. Dark and rich, like coffee or chocolate, but in the sun, by the sea, when it rains, there's a fire to it. Sometimes even a subtle violet hue." He ran his fingers through its length. "It feels like running water."

A shiver flew up her spine. Rhea was terrified to look up at him, as he would surely see the fire he sparked in her eyes, and she changed the subject. "Tell me now that we're not traveling, swimming, or sleeping, how did I get up on that hill the night before last? You've done a most excellent job of dodging having to explain it to me."

"Aye, I've been dodging your questions because I don't have any answers."

"Did you hear me when I left the house?"

"I heard a noise, got up, found you were not in bed and saw you climbing the hill."

"You saw me walking up there?"

"Aye, Rhea, don't be scared by this, and I know I was probably mistaken, but I thought I saw a woman with you."

Finished her tea, she put down her mug. "I've been dreaming of a woman I've never met ever since I got here, and I feel her sometimes when I'm alone. It's not an accident. Something similar used to happen to me when I was a child. My great-aunt frequently visited me, and I would sometimes hear the voice of a girl my age who had died, but I was never afraid of them. As I got older, I closed my third eye."

"Well, then." He swallowed another swig of tea. "Here's the other creepy thing, when I found you, you were asleep on one of the graves."

Rhea stared at him, unblinking for several seconds before exclaiming. "I was asleep on a grave!"

Roarke nodded. "What do you remember?"

"Not a God damn thing. I fell asleep and woke up sitting on the ground. I know I was smiling at you, but I don't know how I got there."

He looked uncomfortable and flashed her a shy smile.

"What? Is it bad? Worse than asleep on a grave?"

Roarke sighed apologetically. "You kissed me."

A look of utter astonishment passed over her face, and she put her hands on her head. "I what? It's not true! Why would you say that?"

"Maybe I shouldn't have told you."

"It's not possible. I would surely remember that."

"I panicked when I found you and tried to wake you. It took a few seconds, but you woke and looked very strange. You didn't look like yourself. Then you kissed me, but you were somewhere else. You could have been dreaming you were the Queen of Sheba. I'll give you more details later."

"Strange to have shared the first kiss with someone and not even remember it."

"Really?" he scoffed as he made to stand. "I spent half my youth being told about kisses I didn't remember."

CHAPTER SEVENTEEN: GHOST BRIDE

Marriage portends a lifelong commitment and a partner through time unless it is ended after a year and a day.

The lovely jagged shoreline of Mull came into sight. As they wound their way around the island, turquoise waves lapped at dazzling white sandy beaches. On one side, they saw the tip of the Munro that was the mountainous core of the island itself.

"We're coming up to the town." Roarke turned the steering wheel and leaned toward the windshield.

Coming into the sound, they passed a small white lighthouse positioned on its private island and then into the busy port of call. A light fog drifted into the different layers of glens, slopes, and mountains. A small castle came into view to the right, and a stretch of mountains rimmed the shoreline.

When the town itself came closer, Rhea was awed by the charm of the hamlet. The houses and shops were all different colors all along the waterfront, like a box of crayons. With not a cloud in the sky and maybe influenced by the color around her, Rhea had changed into a pale yellow sundress under a deep green cardigan.

After getting the boat settled at the small marina, Roarke grabbed Rhea's hand and hauled her along the wooden pier toward the shops.

"Let me guess, Roarke." She laughed as she struggled to keep up. "You're hungry?"

In a small blue restaurant, they dined on what was, according to Roarke, the best fish stew in the world and crab cakes. After lunch, wandering along the waterfront and into various galleries and gift shops, Rhea purchased souvenirs for Liam and Patrice. Next, they spent an hour in a museum housing a library and artifacts that absorbed Roarke's attention. Later in the day, drawn to the sound of wind chimes, Rhea led Roarke over to a small shop.

Inside, the scent transported her back to the floor of her small apartment — sage, sandalwood, lavender, and a host of other fragrances. The walls were all in various shades of green. Even the wainscoting was a soft grassy green.

In the center of the room, a large glass case displayed crystals, rocks, jewelry, gems, candles, soap, daggers, mysterious liquids, and figurines of mystical entities. Chalices, flatware, mortar and pestles, and utensils cluttered a huge bookshelf along with books dealing with witchcraft and general well-being.

Homemade woolen clothes, from mittens to Guernseys, covered a sizeable wooden cabinet and ladder. Roarke pointed out that the most complex stitching was found in Scottish fishing villages, and Rhea commented that in the Canadian Maritimes, people also wore Guernseys.

A large velvet pallet displayed an assortment of silver jewelry. Roarke leaned against the glass case to get a better look. "I've always loved silver. It always reminded me of fish scales." Turning his head, he looked at her chain. "That's why I look at your chain so much. The silver against your bronze skin is so beautiful. Gold shouts, but silver whispers."

His index finger touched the hollow of her throat, just above the silver charms of her chain, and it felt as if the air between them was suddenly full of a charged, palpable energy as thick as smoke.

Rhea bent toward him. "That was no whisper." She cleared

her throat and turned in the opposite direction. Just then, a small, older woman with a long silver braid falling over one shoulder came from a dark corridor at the side of the room, holding a small plant in a clay pot. As she went around the corner, she nodded her head once in greeting. Setting the pot on the glass counter in front of a wall of drawers, she started filling a small cloth drawstring bag, ignoring them.

Rhea had been looking down at a large amber crystal but looked up to cast a curious gaze at the back of the woman's head. As she did so, the old woman stopped what she was doing, lifted her chin, and turned toward Rhea.

This lady's for real. She felt the energy from the woman's gaze piercing her as if it were a blade. The penetrating green eyes seeming to seek whatever good or bad lurked in Rhea's heart. She dropped her gaze to the floor.

"Lift your head." The woman's voice tinkled like water falling on tin, yet there was a rasp to it, like a female version of Roarke's.

Rhea looked up to find the woman standing against the edge of the counter. Her thin lips parted as she whispered, "As above."

Rhea projected her energy into the other woman's eyes. "So below." Even after all the years, the power of the words filled her with happiness. The older woman's mouth split in a wide grin as she came around the counter and held Rhea by the shoulders.

She abruptly released her hold on Rhea, staring at something over her shoulder. Rhea looked behind her but saw nothing. When she turned back, the woman had moved toward the door, her hand dragging across the glass top of the counter.

"Granny?" Roarke asked, his voice tense. "Is everything okay?"

Several seconds later, she cleared her throat and looked

him in the face. "You've got a ghost attached to you."

Roarke looked at her in amused shock. "I've got a what?"

After blinking her eyes several times, her face changed expression. "She's gone now." She walked back around the counter. "You've an intelligent ghost. Most ghosts can travel, but they don't think they can as they're often connected to a certain spot. This one is very sharp. She figured out long ago that she can move around as she sees fit."

"I don't understand."

"There's a ghost connected to you. However, the ghost's not with you all the time because she needs energy to visit this realm and to make her presence known."

"You saw a woman?" Roarke looked concerned. "Attached to me?"

"To one of you."

Rhea leaned against the counter. "Ma'am? Just out of curiosity, what did she look like?"

"Long hair. Beautiful, sad eyes. A long-sleeved dress or coat. I could only see her from the waist up." She picked up a stack of papers and shuffled them. "She wanted you to know she's with you."

"Why would she want that?"

"Maybe she has something to tell one of you or something she wants you to do."

"Can you tell us anything else?"

The older woman smiled at Rhea. "She was trying to get her name to come through, but all I could pick up was the letter "I.""

Roarke opened the door and stepped outside without looking back. "Come, Rhea."

Rhea apologized to the woman and ran after him down the cobblestone sidewalk. Eventually, he stopped and turned to look her full in the face. "I don't believe a word of what that old hag told us. These people prey on others to scam money."

Rhea opened her mouth to speak, but Roarke raised his hand to silence her as a sad looked passed over his face, and he plunked down on a nearby bench. "I know strange things sometimes happen at the house, hell, everywhere we go, but I don't believe Isabel is haunting me."

"Roarke, I never said anything about Isabel, but if that's where your mind went, then maybe that's something you should think about." Sitting beside him on the bench, she took his big hand in hers. "I haven't known you for long, but other than the fiasco when we first met, all I've seen in you is a caring man who'd never deliberately hurt anyone."

Roarke scoffed and leaned back, saying nothing.

Rhea hopped up on the bench and put her hands on his chest. "Hey! The things you do for kids, the ways you are with your friends, me, even your animals."

"I don't know about that."

Rhea slapped her hands on his chest. "You're a good man who needs to put the past behind you." Then, leaning back, Rhea sat cross-legged on the bench and looked up at Roarke's profile. "Maybe that's good advice for both of us."

They watched a sailboat glide across the sound before Roarke spoke again, "You feel guilty about what, exactly?"

"Talking to Sal the other day brought it back to me. I stayed away from home and never saw my father much the year before he died. After that, I felt I had enough responsibility with Liam. Maybe Mom might not have left if I'd stayed closer." Sighing, she played with the charms of her necklace. "I left everything for my brothers. I hauled ass and never looked back. Now, I think I resent not being able to haul ass again."

"I left my family, too. Only after I returned did I realize how much they needed me."

Rhea's head dropped to rest on Roarke's large shoulder, and he reached up to put his arm around the back of the bench, resting his head on the top of hers. The intimate gesture felt very natural, very safe and reassuring.

"Now, I've been rude to an old lady," Roarke murmured against the top of her head.

Smiling, she stood and tried to pull him to his feet as he laughed at her attempts. They returned to the shop, where the older woman seemed to be waiting for them. However, she didn't look up when they entered, despite the bells ringing on the doorframe. Instead, she was carrying a stack of books, and as they entered, the top book fell to the floor.

Rhea and Roarke both bent to retrieve it, and in the process, they soundly knocked the sides of their heads together. Roarke rubbed his head as he put the book on the counter.

The woman thanked him through her laughter. "Do either of you know what that means?"

Both shook their heads, still rubbing them and smiling.

"It means you're soul-mates." She put the books on the counter and turned to hold out her hand to Roarke. "My name's Moira. I think we got off on the wrong foot."

"I'm Roarke, and this is Rhea."

"What's your family name?"

"McCallum."

"Oh, I've just the thing to show you."

Moira walked into the dark corridor and came out a minute later with a strip of dark blue and green tartan cloth. "This is your family's tartan from the early nineteenth century."

"No way." He handled it carefully. "Extraordinary. How much is it?"

"Nothing. It's a peace offering."

As not many people were around, Moira offered them a cup of tea, and went to put on the kettle, giving Roarke and Rhea time to explore the shop. Finally, they all settled on benches at the counter as Moira brought them tea in lovely china cups and saucers with delicate pink roses and gold edging.

"You have to let me give you something for the piece of tartan." Roarke reached for his cup, taking it from Moira's small, heavily veined hand.

Moira shook her head and grinned. "Look around, maybe something else will strike your fancy, and you'll buy that."

Roarke pointed down at the silver jewelry. "I do like your silver."

"Aye. There's just something magical about silver. It's healing properties and connection to the moon, psychic abilities, dreams."

Reaching below the counter, she drew up the silver charm and chain Roarke had been pointing at. "Is this what you like?"

"Aye."

Attached to a delicate silver chain was a beautiful pale iridescent stone, silvery and mirror-like within a frame of Celtic entrelacs encircled by tiny diamonds. Suspended from it was another smaller stone with entrelacs on either side. The stone glowed with an almost ethereal light.

Roarke's head flew up to look at Moira in delight. "Is this from Knox? Moonstones?"

"Aye." The older woman played with the end of her braid and regarded him with surprise and a touch of admiration.

"Is it for sale?"

"Aye." Moira edged back to her stool and cup of tea. "I'll not give it up to just anyone."

Roarke sighed. "Probably too rich for my blood anyway." Regardless, he sat it on the glass next to him and kept gazing at it as they sipped their tea.

"Are you two married then?" Moira asked when there was a lull in the conversation.

Rhea almost choked on her tea. "No, I work for him."

"Really?" Disbelief was evident in Moira's tinkling voice. "There's no way I believe that."

Roarke laughed. "My Lady, it's very much true. She's writing my book."

"La-dee-da," Moira laughed. "You carry yourselves like you're much closer."

Wanting to change the subject, Rhea asked, "Moira, speaking of marriage, what's hand-fasting? I was reading about it in one of your books."

"Hand-fasting?" Moira picked up the strip of tartan Roarke had laid on the countertop next to his teacup.

Blue eyes twinkling, and with a mischievous smile, the older woman took Roarke's right hand. "Young lady, come and give me your right hand." Rhea did as she was bid. Moira took Roarke's hand, palm down, and placed Rhea's on top of it. Then, taking the strip of cloth, she used it to bind their wrists together. They both looked down at their hands and then at each other, confused yet intrigued, as Moira tied a small knot at each frayed end.

Her leathery hands sandwiched theirs as she closed her eyes and began muttering in Gaelic. Rhea closed her eyes as well, and all she was aware of was Roarke's strong, rough hand and the cold, feathery touch of the older woman. Moira's words wove a magical spell around them, and she didn't know what was happening until she heard her name.

"What was that all about?" Rhea inquired when she came to her senses.

The older woman smiled as she unwound the tartan. "I hand-fasted you." Moira reached under the counter for a pair of scissors and sliced the strip through the middle, tying one half on Roarke's wrist and the other on Rhea's. "You're married for a year and a day. After that time, if you decide to stay together, you have a formal ceremony, but if you decide to split, you can."

Roarke laughed and threw his head back. "Good God, are you serious?"

"Sweet Jesus." Rhea didn't share the humor of it. "It's not legal or anything, is it?"

"Of course not." Moira laughed. "You didn't say any vows, but the spirits were watching, so don't take it entirely as a joke."

Rhea looked at Moira straight in the eye. "I take marriage very seriously."

"As do I, my dear. Handfasting was a temporary trial marriage and an ancient ceremony. Forbidden in the sixteenth century, when all people had to be married by the clergy."

"Why do it?" Rhea glanced at Roarke to find him listening with interest.

"It's like taking marriage for a test run. These types of ceremonies are coming back, even if they aren't legal. People are fixing them into their legal ceremonies to respect the old traditions."

"I don't mean any disrespect, but I . . ."

"Oh, just have fun with it, girl," Moira smirked at them and winked.

Roarke leaned forward to whisper to Moira, "She's a bit of a prude."

"I can tell," Moira whispered back.

Rhea stuck her chin out. "I'm not a prude."

"Then, if you're not a prude, don't forget to consummate the marriage. As I said, the old spirits might take offense if you don't."

Rhea's jaw dropped in shock and indignation as the old woman turned to Roarke and smiled, "Is that doing you a favor, young man?"

Bending down to kiss the older woman's hand, Roarke winked. "Oh, aye."

Moira and Roarke continued to chuckle as Rhea turned

away and walked back toward the bookshelf. "You two are making fun of me."

"Oh, girl." Moira lifted her teacup to her lips but didn't drink. "There're things inside us that, like in the depths of the oceans, can't and won't stay hidden forever."

"I don't know what you mean," Rhea murmured while playing with the end of an orange scarf.

"Yes, you do," Moira said with confidence.

Luckily for Rhea, Roarke changed the subject. "Moira? I'm just curious, do you actually see spirits?"

Sliding a tea biscuit off the plate of cookies, she was still watching Rhea. "If I blindfolded you and brought you into a room where two other people were sitting in complete silence, would you know they were there?"

"I believe I would."

"That's exactly how it is. I feel ghosts and spirits, and I know where they are. Some I see with my eyes, others are shadows, and others are in my mind's eye. We all can see or feel them, but we've been taught that such feelings are creations of an over-active imagination. We're just smart monkeys, and instinct is behind every drive and reaction we have. All animals react to their environment."

Rhea walked back over to where they were sitting.

"They're in their own dimension." Moira looked at Roark, and he stopped chewing. "The spirit world can sometimes overlap with ours."

"Why is it that sometimes you say ghost and sometimes spirit?"

"Spirits have crossed over into the light and just come to visit people, usually in our dreams. They make you feel calm and comforted. Unfortunately, the ghost has not crossed over, and they're earthbound. Business here is unfinished. Ghosts give an eerie, uncomfortable feeling. Most ghosts like to make people feel skittish because they are more open to suggestions by the ghost. That's why they like to lure them to quiet places, like attics or basements."

Rhea looked meaningfully at Roarke, "Or the unused top section of a cottage."

Roarke sighed and shook his head. "I can't believe in things I don't see."

"I bet you've felt them. Ghosts gather energy to appear, and it takes practice and enormous effort on their part. If they can sense someone is keen to their presence, they might be excited enough to try. Imagine if you were invisible and someone noticed you. They like to listen to our conversations. They think we're interesting."

Rhea spoke up, "I read about something called The Psychic Staring Effect. It's a sensation of knowing you're being stared at, which protected our ancestors from predators and enemies. Could communicating with spirits be like that? A survival tool?"

"Aye, and we have so much to learn from them." Moira touched Rhea's hand, her soft skin warm and comforting. "The young woman with you is full of emotions, anger, sadness, happiness."

"Seeing spirits has taught you things?"

"Aye, but the most important gift I've received from them is living in the moment. When we die, we don't regret the shoes we didn't buy, but we regret what we didn't say or do." Then, grabbing the last chocolate biscuit out of Roarke's hand, she passed it over to Rhea, who took it with a giggle. "I know not to take the last biscuit without offering first."

Patting their hands, she stood. "Take what you've been given and run with it for now."

They glanced at each other, and a shiver went up Rhea's spine as Moira continued, "There are threads that connect certain people like thin, silver chains. They stretch but never break. So, take time to understand your connection. Take time just to be."

Even before leaving the shop, Rhea's mind had begun to spin, and they were both quiet as they left and walked uphill into the quieter braes and onto a wide, tree-lined street.

Rhea asked Roarke if she could have a few minutes to herself and suggested meeting in an hour at the small café on the waterfront.

Walking down by the water and along the jetty that protected the small harbor, she watched the seals playing in the sea and basking on rocks in the fading sunshine, content in their world. Finally, Rhea realized why her brain felt addled, and her emotions were in a whirlwind. For once, she was not going to let life pass her by.

A little while later, at the small café with yellow umbrellas, Roarke sat with a pot of tea and a tray of scones, cream, and jam. He made small talk, but she gave him glib responses.

Finally, Roarke reached over and placed his hand over hers. "Rhea? Don't overthink—"

Rhea interrupted him with a flurry of words, "For a reason, I can't explain. I feel I've known you forever. I trust you, and I don't think you'd ever deliberately hurt me."

"Aye, that's all true."

"Moira's right." She played with the strip of cloth on her wrist. "Could we take a day off?"

"A day off?"

She looked at him shyly, "From the book, from everything. Just take a day and just be us. Rhea and Roarke. Two people who enjoy each other, maybe even care for each other."

He looked up at her and nodded. "Aye, two people who care."

"Look, Roarke, in a few short days, I'll leave, and both of us will continue with our lives, but I feel we're in each other's lives for a reason, beyond the book. I'm changing while I'm getting to know you. My friend, who's a twin, told me she feels more like herself when she's with her sister, and I feel more like myself when I'm with you. I don't know what it is, but I know it's real, and we should see what it's about while we can, because soon, you'll be here, and I'll be there."

Giving her a perplexed look, he sat back with his teacup. "We would continue our day as two people just hand-fasted by an old witch in a trinket shop?"

"Roarke." Rhea reached up and took down her ponytail, shaking out her hair. "We've a connection, and we deserve to explore it. So let's be."

"We take this day. This one day." He regarded her somewhat suspiciously. "This doesn't sound like you."

"I know." She picked up her teacup but didn't drink. "But it sounds like someone I used to be."

"You could stay longer."

"I could, but not for much longer." Rhea put her teacup down. "I have to go back. I miss Liam, but Roarke, I'll never forget my time here with you."

His chocolate eyes took on a misty look as he gazed at her. "Honestly, I feel too many things I can never put into words. I'm not sure what you have in mind for these twenty-four hours, but we won't be able to go back to the way things are now."

"I know. It's because things are simple between us that I want to give us this time. Something has shifted for me." Rhea brushed a finger across his knuckles. "We don't need to discuss our feelings or make plans because we already know what the future holds."

"Aye." Roarke picked up his cup and looked out toward the sound. "That's why I've been keeping my distance. I don't want us to get hurt."

"What can it hurt to have just one day where we don't need to be guarded? We both know what's coming. I finish my job, go home, write your book, raise Liam, and pick up my life. You go to The States, make your films, and come home with the money to start Project Castle. I'm needed there, and you're needed here. Considering what must be, can't we take just one day and have what is?"

Leaning toward her and looked deep into her eyes, seeming to search for hesitation, "Twenty-four hours. I think we deserve that."

Grinning broadly, Rhea settled back in her chair as Roarke put his cup to his lips to take a sip. "And I want to sleep with you, Roarke."

CHAPTER EIGHTEEN: FIRST NIGHT

We never had a proper ceremony, nor wedding night, just a fleeting moment of bliss in a barley field. I always give them their wedding night before I begin my whispers.

R oarke choked on his tea and slammed the cup back into its saucer, tears welling in his eyes as he coughed.

"Roarke!" She slapped him on the back as a waiter came running over with a glass of water.

"All right," he managed as he coughed, and Rhea sat down just as the waiter recognized Roarke.

"Niall Shaw?" The young blond man stared at Roarke with bug eyes and an open mouth. "Oh, my God! I just gave Niall Shaw a glass of water."

Roarke's coughs subsided, but he still sputtered a little when he spoke and dabbed his napkin on his wet shirt. "Whist. I don't need a score of people knowing."

The young man nodded. "Of course, mum's the word." He started to back away from the table. "Can I get you anything else?"

"No, thank you. Tea went down the wrong pipe."

After the boy walked away, Roarke leaned toward Rhea and looked at her as if she were insane. "What did you say?"

Rhea leaned toward him until their noses were only a few inches apart. "I want to sleep with you. In the same bed."

"We have done. Two nights in a row. And—"

Rhea silenced him with a finger. "Since we're taking twenty-four hours off, I don't see why we shouldn't explore every possibility."

Still eying her warily, he didn't say anything.

"We don't have to do anything, and I'm not saying we will do anything, but I'd like to say goodnight to you and not have to leave your side. I dread it when we're not in the same room."

Roarke's eyes softened into a warm amber as Rhea continued.

"Patrice and I haven't lived together for years, and I haven't dated anyone since, but there's this pull with you as I've never known. What this lure is, I'm not sure, but it's more than just the way you look."

"Aye," he murmured as he tucked a lock of her hair behind her ear. "There's something there, all right."

"Tonight, we sleep in the same room. I'm not saying we will *do* anything, but if we did . . ."

Eyebrows raised, he seemed to be holding his breath. The hand holding the teacup to his mouth seemed frozen.

"I haven't been with a man in many years."

She stopped speaking as he started sputtering and choking on his tea again. Waving away the young waiter coming to their table and looking down on his tea-covered shirt, Roarke grinned.

"You have to stop doing that. We don't have to do anything at all, but if we do, it'll be as you want it to be." Reaching into the inside jacket of his pocket, he pulled out a small box. "While you were gone, I got you something."

Rhea opened the lid to find the silver moonstone reflecting the light of the setting sun. "The moonstone?"

"Aye. Maybe you could keep it with you in Canada until you can come and visit my castle."

"I love it, but you should be saving your money for the castle. Was it expensive?"

"Not so much. I had to have it, but I'd look silly wearing it.

It belongs on your neck." Roarke's eyes were full of meaning. "Just promise you'll bring it back to Scotland one day."

Rhea's eyes turned deep green as they filled with tears. "I promise." She slipped the pendant over her head. The silver was similar to the chain she already wore, the moonstone and diamonds lying about an inch lower on her chest. Resting her hand on her pendants, she beamed at Roarke.

"How does it look?" Rhea tilted her head to give him a better look at the necklace.

"It makes your skin glow. It's a very lucky necklace," he answered in a heavy voice. "If it's around your neck."

Rhea tapped a tattoo on the back of Roarke's hand, "Now, husband. What do we do?"

Putting a hand on either side of her face, he murmured, "I'd like to celebrate our marriage."

She closed her eyes and smiled at his touch. "Fine by me."

Pulling her forehead toward him, he kissed her brow. "This is the best suggestion I've ever been given."

"I'm glad."

"This is so weird." Roarke chuckled and shook his head. "I always said I'd never marry. Oh, I know it's all in fun, but I guess it counts as far as a marriage for me."

"Me, too."

"But I have a few things I'd like to do, ghost." He grazed his index finger along her shoulder. "Will you excuse me for a while?"

"Um, sure." Before she had even gotten the words out, he had already stood. "I'll stay here and get some writing done."

"Perfect." Stepping forward to kiss the top of her head, he turned to walk away, saying over his shoulder. "First, I need to change my shirt."

"Okay," she called after him, "but this doesn't count for the twenty-four hours."

He gave her a thumbs-up, turned a corner, and disappeared.

After Roarke turned the corner, Rhea's hands flew to either side of her head, and she hissed to herself. "Oh, my God! What have I done?" Only when she saw the young waiter staring at her in concern did she smile and compose herself.

About an hour later, Rhea closed her notebook after finishing a description of the island. When she saw a tall broad man walking toward the restaurant, Rhea's stomach did summersaults.

Roarke wore a green and blue kilt and a white collared shirt under a grey Guernsey. He waved when we saw her, his confident stride enhanced by the sway of the kilt about his knees.

Rhea was aware of a presence at her elbow. "Would you like more tea, or are you waiting for Mr. Shaw to return?"

Without taking her eyes off Roarke, she pointed in his direction to indicate that he was returning, and the young waiter exclaimed, "Good God! I wish I looked that good in my kilt. I'd be beating people off with a stick."

Smiling at his remark. "I'm sure you do fine."

"Do better if I was seven feet tall with hair like that." He sighed.

"It's all confidence, which he has in spades."

"If you're not confident, you've no business wearing a kilt."

"Something wild about a man wearing a kilt. Teases a woman with her own wildness."

"Plus, it makes our weapons look better." He chuckled and stepped away.

A few seconds later, Roarke stood before her, his arms open wide. "What do you think? I went back to Moira's shop and got a kilt."

"You look like you stepped out of a woman's imagination," she answered honestly.

"A man doesn't get married every day. Gotta break out a kilt."

"On behalf of everyone who sees you, thank you."

Tucking a few bills under the tray, he held out his hand to her. "Come, my dear. Let's take a walk on this most lovely of evenings."

They waved to the young waiter and chuckled when he almost spilled the dish of seafood on an elderly couple in his haste to wave back.

Hand in hand, they walked along the waterfront and up through the small alleyways between the attractive brightly colored buildings. Roarke had inquired about the woman he had come to see and learned she was very sick in hospital, and the family was taking neither calls nor visitors.

He sighed. "That was the last person on my list to contact to get help with the castle. I hate to say it, but I think David has officially won."

"Oh, Roarke. I'm so sorry you came here for nothing."

"Not for nothing." He turned and smiled at her, albeit a little sadly. "I'm still going to enjoy my visit here. You don't get hand-fasted every day."

Rhea didn't know if the kilt was drawing attention to him or because he wasn't wearing his usual ball cap, but many people recognized him, stopping to speak, shaking his hand, or asking for his autograph.

Even though he smiled and stayed polite, he eventually whispered, "Now you know why I grew out my hair and always wear a hat."

Nodding, she let him lead her onto the woodland walk where they stopped on a small humpback bridge to chat and watch ducks.

Rhea stepped up to the tower viewer in the bridge's center

and looked at the distant Munro. She was so caught up in the scenery she didn't notice Roarke come up behind her until he cleared his throat.

"Ahem! Stop hogging the viewer. I'd like to have a look."

Laughing, she spun around to find Roarke right behind her. She was on the step, and even though he was still a little taller, they were almost at eye level. As she gazed back at him, his eyes grew softer than she'd ever imagined they could be, and he closed the gap between them as his eyes dropped to her lips.

Rhea felt none of the awkwardness she usually felt around men. On the contrary, being this close to Roarke and knowing what was about to happen only made her feel giddy and eager, and she could hear the blood in her veins rush toward her chest in a deafening roar.

Roarke's hands cradled Rhea's face, and he caressed her cheekbones with his thumbs as his gaze roamed over her face, stopping again at her mouth. When she licked her lips, Roarke tilted his head and moved toward her, pausing just as their lips were about to meet and leaning back to look at her face in the fading sunlight. She closed her eyes as he pressed his firm mouth against her pursed lips, then pulled back to look at her again and smile.

Releasing her face, he gripped her shoulders and pulled her to him, kissing her with an intensity that made her light-headed. His lips moved over hers with deftness, his mouth closing first over her top lip, then the bottom. When the tip of her tongue pressed against his, he moaned into her mouth and pulled her even closer. His kiss was deep, rolling thunder enveloping her senses, waves crashing into her body.

When they finally broke the kiss, Roarke leaned his forehead and nose against hers and blinked hard as the world spun around her. "Now that . . ." He breathed against her mouth. " . . . was a first kiss to beat them all."

Looking into his chocolate eyes, she began, "You said I kissed you under the yew and—"

"No," he interrupted, placing a finger on her lips which she then kissed. "This was our first kiss, when I kissed my bride."

Upon returning to town, Roarke took her to dinner at a beautiful two-story whitewashed building with black trim around the windows and doors. A small patio on the sidewalk overflowed with happy patrons enjoying the fine evening.

"What a beautiful building." Rhea sniffed at the fragrant air almost dripping with tantalized odors seeping out from the fans of the building's kitchen. "Are we eating here?"

"Aye, and we're staying here, too."

"Staying here?"

Roarke smiled in a very self-satisfied fashion. "The rooms here are charming. Quaint and old-fashioned. I wanted you to have a nice room for your wedding night."

"I love it, but I love the boat, too."

"I know, but a room is more fitting for tonight." Roarke ran a hand down the side of Rhea's face.

Rhea sighed and closed her eyes.

Roarke continued, "This used to be the town library, and as you're such a nerd, I thought you'd like to sleep in a library."

She narrowed her eyes at him. "Smartass. We'll have to go to the boat and get some stuff."

"Already done." He stopped just in front of the door. "After I booked the room, I bought a few things and went to the boat. Dropped our bags in the room, changed, and came to meet you."

"All planned out, eh?"

"Yup." He pulled open the door to the restaurant and gestured for her to enter. Lanterns in the center of each wooden table lit the small space, and the walls were dark green, the décor being splashes of gold and brown.

Behind her, Roarke closed the door and yelled out, "Hello everyone!"

All chatter stopped, and every head turned in their direction with curious gazes until Roarke grasped Rhea's hand and raised it with his own. "We got married today!"

The air filled with cheers, especially when Roarke yelled, "Drinks are on me!"

Sitting at a small table in the corner, they had champagne and dined on halibut, venison with red currant and red wine reduction, and sticky toffee pudding. Rhea and Roarke had only a little time to chat throughout the evening as most guests came to wish them well. A young woman gave Rhea a penny to put in her shoe for luck.

The restaurant owners brought out a traditional Quaich, a two-handled drinking bowl, and they sipped whisky from it. An older woman brought Rhea a sprig of white heather, evergreen with tiny, bell-shaped white blossoms, and explained how important it was to bring good fortune to the couple. Her husband had noticed some growing on the rocky terrain behind the restaurant.

Rhea asked Roarke if he was worried about the news getting out of his marriage. "Never really thought of it, but it could garner more attention for the films."

Later, they walked up the narrow flight of stairs to their room. At the door, Rhea squealed as Roarke lifted her, cradling her in his arms as he turned the key to the door and crossed the threshold. The room was cozy, with ornate red-brown wooden moldings. Candles flickered, and the fireplace was lit, casting light on a small bookshelf laden with books, a dresser, and a large, four-poster bed, with a wine-colored duvet, white linens, and fluffy pillows. An open bottle of wine and plate of fruit and cheese rested on a small table covered in white lace. Excusing herself as soon as he put her down, she flew into the bathroom, mumbling about wanting to freshen up. The truth was that she wished to gather her thoughts. When he bent his head toward her face, she bolted for the bag on the bed and dodged him as he stood with a confused yet amused look on his face.

After washing and putting on her white shift, Rhea stood with her back pressed against the door, palms flat against the strong oak. When she opened her eyes, she stared at her terrified face in the large gold-edged oval mirror above the sink.

Taking another deep breath, she turned the doorknob and stepped out of the bathroom, sliding around to the other side of the door, quietly closing it behind her. She found Roarke sitting on the wooden red cushioned bench along the stone wall, resting his head on the stone with his eyes closed. He had removed his Guernsey and sat in his dress shirt. Then, kicking off his shoes, he sighed.

When her gaze returned to Roarke, she found him looking at her. "I didn't hear you come out, ghost."

Rhea smiled but never moved from her spot.

"What's wrong? Cat got your tongue?"

She looked down, her hands leaving the door to straighten her white shift against her thighs.

"You looked beautiful today in that yellow dress, but you look even lovelier now." Roarke's gaze ran over her body. "I've always found this shift of yours, as you call it, very fetching."

She still didn't speak, just kept looking down, shifting her weight from one foot to the other.

"Can I get you some wine?"

Rhea nodded, and in one quick movement, she headed toward the table, pouring two glasses of claret red wine. Lifting a glass to her lips, she drank and glided toward him, still drinking.

Roarke chuckled. "Rhea, I asked if I could get a glass for you."

That made her titter, causing a bubble of laughter to form on the surface of her too-full wine glass, and drops of deep-red wine splattered on the front of her white shift. "Oh, look at me."

Hurrying over to him, she handed him the two goblets, almost spilling them on him in the process.

"Looks like blood on snow."

"It'll stain." Rhea ran to the bathroom and dabbed at the wine stains with a wet washcloth, then re-emerged, still dabbing at the gown.

"You can always put on one of my t-shirts, like after our swim. I enjoyed seeing you in my clothes."

Taking her goblet of wine, she peered down into its contents. "I've heard my brother say something similar about his wife."

"It's intimate. You wouldn't wear just any man's clothes."

"I liked it, too. The shirt smelled like you." Rhea finally looked at him. "And it'd been on your body."

His gaze bore into hers until she looked away and down at his hands caressing the wood. "You like the bench?"

"You can feel time on the wood, rooms it sat in, conversations had on it. Long before all that, it had stood strong and tall in a forest, breathing and sharing secrets with other trees and the mushrooms."

"I love how you think about things, Roarke. I hope I can write your words the way you speak them." She felt rather than saw his smile. "I love your hands. Hands that can wield an ax, lift a car, yet pluck gentle notes on the guitar, and cradle a tiny puppy."

Roarke pulled at his collar. "Yes, my hands. Too bad these monstrous things are too clunky to undo tiny buttons. I'll have to tear myself out of this shirt."

"Let me help you." Standing in front of him, she reached for his collar, and her small hands shook.

Reaching up, he took both of her hands in his. "Rhea. We don't need to . . ."

"Roarke, I think you know I'd never do anything I didn't want to do." Pulling her hands free, she rested her hands on either side of his neck, looking into his eyes, all timidity gone. Then, with trembling hands, working from the top, aware of the smolder in his coffee-colored eyes, she unbuttoned his shirt.

As she undid one button and then the next, the back of her fingers grazed across the taut skin at his breastbone and the soft cotton of his undershirt. As she got closer to the bottom, she pulled to free it from the top of the kilt.

When his shirt hung open on either side of his torso, she lifted his right hand and turned it over to undo the two small buttons at his wrist. Then, as she tilted her head, a tress of her hair fell over her shoulder, and he twirled the silky red-brown strand in his strong fingers before brushing it off her shoulder, his hand rubbing her skin.

A tremor ran through her at his touch as she picked up his other hand. Still holding his hand, she pushed back the cuff of his sleeve, exposing the skin on the inside of his wrist, and pressed small kisses on the thin skin. His pulse jumped under her lips as she ran the tip of her tongue along the veins, feeling them swell.

Roarke's hand came around from the back of her shoulder, tracing the rounded top of her breast before dragging his fingers down along the tip. He reached under her arm and up her shoulder to pull her closer with his other hand.

Rhea placed her hands on his breastbone, sliding them under his shirt and over his shoulders, pushing the shirt until it dropped behind his back. Brushing a stray lock of hair off his forehead, with her heart pounding, she pressed her forehead to his, breathing erratically, feeling his warm, wine-scented breath on her face.

He tangled his hand in her hair and pulled her head back as his gaze ran over her face, and his breathing became shallow as she leaned in to place a hesitant, tender kiss upon his lower lip. He didn't move, and he didn't close his eyes. She pulled away and shifted her body to sit on his thigh as her hand crept around to grasp the back of his neck, pushing his head toward her own.

The moment their lips met, his hand dropped to her hip and closed around flesh and bone, the other hand holding her tight. His mouth crushed hers with such force, she thought her lips might bleed.

Within minutes, both were breathless, and Roarke pulled out of the kiss. Reaching back to remove her hands from behind his head, he pulled them together in front of his chest. For a few seconds, he just stared down at their hands, and then his eyes closed tightly. Seeing hesitation and doubt, she didn't know what to say that would tell him all she could ever want was to be there with him.

Pulling her hand out of his grip, she held his chin, forcing him to look at her. She hoped with all her might that her eyes spoke the words she could not seem to say. Relinquishing her hold on his chin, she stood, stepping out from between his legs and pivoting her body in the direction of the bed.

Roarke didn't stand, only continued to look at her until she pulled at his hands and smiled, willing him to stand. A broad smile split his mouth, and all doubt left his face. He pulled their entwined hands to his chest, causing her to take a clumsy step forward, bringing up solid against his legs.

Rhea's head tilted back as he rose to his feet, his body grazing against hers, a mountain of tanned skin and muscle. Pressing her against him, her cheek against his chest, his hand held her by the waist. He rained kisses on her head and dipped his head low to kiss her shoulder and nip her earlobe before kissing her forehead and the tip of her nose.

Rhea's hands crept up his back and shoulders, and her fingers ran along the inside of the top of his kilt. She tilted her head and kissed him deeply, running her hands up and down his body.

Roarke bent at the waist, hooking one arm behind her thighs and lifting her against his chest. Crossing the room, he lowered her onto the bed, the soft duvet pillowing around her. With a hand on either side, he bent to kiss her, his tongue skimming across her upper lip and inside her bottom lip. All while his hand ran down Rhea's body from shoulder to buttocks and her bent knee. Roarke's fingertips brushed the inside of her thigh but stopped when she inhaled and pressed her legs together.

Roarke chuckled as Rhea covered her eyes with her hands to conceal her embarrassment. He moved her hands away from her eyes and folded them on her stomach before standing. With one hand, he reached behind his shoulder and pulled at the back of his undershirt, pulling it over his head and shaking out his hair.

Rhea found the way Roarke removed his shirt intensely erotic, and she rose to kiss his tight abdomen. Pushing her back onto the bed, he lowered himself on top of her, and her knees opened for him. He brushed away a strand of hair from her face as his mouth again closed on hers.

Roarke pulled at the tiny bow that held the neck of her white cotton shift together. "I've always wanted to pull at that wee bow," he murmured against the soft, bronze skin of her chest, his lips kissing a hot trail down the tip of her breast.

When Roarke's mouth gently tugged at her breast, a surge of pleasure shot straight to her center. Anywhere his mouth touched her, her skin vibrated. When his hand crept up her thigh until his fingers lay just below the apex of her legs, Rhea quivered. The quivering turned into shaking as she pressed her thighs together again.

Roarke didn't seem surprised at her reaction, and while he didn't move his hand, he bent his mouth to her ear to whisper, "You know I won't hurt you."

Rhea smiled up at him. "My love, you're so sweet, but I think we both know you're probably going to hurt me."

"Not if we take our time and you trust me."

Rhea tentatively ran her hand down his chest down to his turgid length.

When her fingers encircled it, he moaned before speaking. "You're in charge here. I'll do anything you want. All you have to do is let me."

Running her fingers up and down his thickness, loving the firm, smooth skin under her hand, Rhea lifted her chin for a kiss, keeping her eyes open as he looked down at her, his eyes glazing over as she worked her hand up, down. When he lowered his lips to hers, she turned her head to deepen the kiss. Releasing her hold on him, she put her hands around his neck, hooked one leg around his waist, and crushed him against her. His hand cupped her most private of places, and one of his fingers slid inside her.

At that moment, her body heat increased. When he broke off their kiss to lower his head to her chest, he flicked his tongue over one nipple and then the other. The muscles of her body tensed and went rigid.

Moving his finger inside of her, he turned his hand and rubbed the spongy spot behind her belly button, sending a shock straight through her. She jumped, and he looked down at her with a mixture of desire and concern. "You okay?"

Without commenting, she nodded and angled her hips to press his finger deeper inside her. When his thumb rubbed the area above, the feeling awed her and jolted every nerve of her body.

Running the tip of his nose over her face, neck, and chest, he gasped when she gripped his hardness and guided it to where she wanted it to be. His finger left her as he nudged the sleek tip of his firmness against her sex.

As he edged into her little by little, his first thrusts caused some discomfort, but when he drove deep inside her, she felt pure, unadulterated pleasure and cried out, wrapping her legs around him, pressing him deeper inside her.

Exhaling deeply, Roarke rolled his shoulders as his body rhythmically slid in and out of Rhea as if they were dancing. The gyration of his hips brought her closer to the edge of all reason and reality. The steely contours of his body rubbed against her. His teeth nipping at the tender flesh of her neck were too much sensation. She felt as if her entire body was exploding under the thrusts of his thick member inside her body.

When he arched against her, she grabbed his upper torso as her center shattered. Behind her eyelids burst explosions of light, and her muscles rocked and pulsed against his firm erection until he begged her to stop.

Rhea didn't stop, couldn't stop. Instead, she tightened her muscles around him until she became liquid. Locking her mouth over his, she whispered his name into his mouth just as his body slammed against hers. He stiffened as he emptied himself inside her in a shattering release, leaving him twitching above her.

It was only afterward, when they lay spent in each other's arms, that they laughed when they realized she still had on her shift, and he had not removed his kilt nor his socks.

The next time they made love that night, it lasted a little longer.

CHAPTER NINETEEN: LISTEN TO THE WITCHES

I watch them, bodies locked in passion, and the usual anger and frustration coil me snakelike. I am the dark shadow in the corner, waiting to whisper.

Then it happens as the time before, and I am pulled toward her, like smoke to beauty. She draws me in, as so many draw down the moon, locked in the gravity I had forgotten existed, spiraling toward and then inside her until I'm a heartbeat, strong and healthy, pounding to an ancient rhythm.

Eyes flutter open, and the light hurts. Next to the river, our field of gold, the barley, glistens in the rays of the dying sun. The field undulates as the wind makes love to it, and Thomas's body slides over mine, becoming mine. He smells of the woods after a thunderstorm, fresh rain on soil, elemental. The fluid flowing in the veins of the gods.

The wind promises the everlasting, and I am haunted. I remember the heart, the gold, and the scent.

What has she done? I am afraid.

In the small hours of the morning, Rhea awoke and sighed contentedly, snuggling even closer against Roarke's chest, her head on his arm. The arm across her waist stirred and pulled her closer.

Opening her eyes, Rhea was shocked to realize that Roarke lay on his back. *Whose arm is across my waist? Who is cuddling against my back?*

A cold chill crept up Rhea's neck as the mattress moved as

if someone got up. Then, the weight across her waist disappeared.

Something moved like a shadow against the wall, gliding until it disappeared near the foot of the bed. Her instincts told her to be afraid, but with the shadow came the memory of cold delicate fingers running through her hair at some point the night before, and she knew whoever had come to visit meant no harm.

Settling back onto her pillow, Rhea's last thought before sleep again overtook her was of a sad girl wandering the hills near Roarke's cottage. *She just wanted to feel a part of our joy.* As she drifted off, her skin tingled in the chill morning air as she headed toward White Heather, the breeze rich with the delicate scent of heliotrope wafting from the flowing blond locks of the melancholy young woman walking ahead of her.

Hunger roused the couple from bed, and their first stop was at a lively corner restaurant for a massive lunch of bouillabaisse, and a plate of Scottish cheeses, oatcakes, and fruit chutney.

After visiting the castle on the outskirts of the village, a stronghold from the Middle Ages, they stood on the hill looking over the town, harbor, and nearby isles. Roarke turned to Rhea. "I dreamed of you last night."

"You did?"

"Aye." He turned back to the sea. "You were by the sea in a place I've never been and pointing at something near some trees, but I couldn't see what it was. You were a ways from me and jutted your chin to tell me to go in that direction. The funniest thing is that I realized before we had even met, I had dreamed of you."

"Weird, but somehow it doesn't shock me."

"Aye, weird, but I think we both know we were destined

to meet." His eyebrows knitted together slightly. "I sometimes feel energy pass between us, like a physical exchange of something. That's how I know these feelings are genuine. A similar thing happens when Brian puts me in a headlock or when after a day of hard work, Ian claps me on the shoulder and says, Well done, son. It's nothing that can ever properly be said, just felt."

Rhea took a deep breath. "How come I'm the writer, but you always seem to have the words?"

"The deepest feelings have no words." He laid a kiss on her head and took her hand to start down the hill.

After he had been silent for some time, Rhea asked, "Visiting the castle made you think of your castle, didn't it?"

"Aye." He stopped to pick a blade of tall grass. "It's always in the back of my mind anyway. I can usually find a solution to any problem, but I don't think I'm going to figure out how to make money appear in time."

"In every second lives the possibility of change. You never know what's around the corner, what's in store."

"I've always just believed in my intuition. I've always trusted my gut. Now, I think there's more than that. Since you showed up, I almost feel like we're being led somewhere."

"I know. Every step I've taken in life has led me here, to you, and this place."

"Rhea, do you have the brooch with you?"

"Strangely enough." She cocked her head to one side. "I do. For some reason, I stuck it in my bag this morning."

Stopping on the rocky path, he ran the blade of grass along her chest. "You were wearing it in my dream."

Rhea suddenly grabbed his arm. "Hey, maybe Moira can tell us something about it."

"Evil minds think alike."

Stepping into the bright shop, they found Moira at the

counter. When she saw them enter, she rolled her eyes. "Oh, great. You two again."

"Hi, Moira." Roarke tapped her withered hand with his index finger. "We were wondering if you could tell us a bit about an artifact we have."

As Roarke handed the brooch over to Moira, he asked, "Oh, any news on Mrs. MacLean?"

Moira cradled the brooch in her palm. "She's still in the hospital. I'm afraid they don't expect her to get well any time soon."

Rhea furrowed her brow a little. "Who's Mrs. MacLean?"

"She's the woman I came here to see." Roarke watched Moira study the brooch. "Did I not mention her name?"

Smiling, Rhea rested her elbows on the counter. "Remember the day I talked to my brother, and he told me we had a splash of Scottish blood?"

"Aye, I teased you because all North Americans claim to have some Scottish blood."

"That was the name he gave me. Maclean. Alec MacLean." Roarke and Moira both turned in her direction as she continued. "My father's mother was part-Scottish. Sal and Raven think since I'm here, I could look into it a little."

Roarke stood up a little straighter and looked at her with all seriousness. "MacLean?"

When Rhea nodded, he shook his head with a smile. "Thomas's family name was MacLean."

Realization dawned on Rhea in a flash. "That's interesting."

Turning back to the brooch, Moira cleared her throat. "Lovely Luckenbooth brooch. Where did you get it?"

"Out in the country. Highlands."

Moira faced the right corner of the room. "I think it belongs to her."

"Really?" Rhea looked around excitedly but saw nothing.

"I knew it! I knew she had something to do with it. Moira, could you please ask her what she wants me to do with it?"

"She wants you to bury it."

"Bury it?" Roarke asked, and as he did, the open window behind him slammed shut, and he jumped.

Moira smiled. "She doesn't seem to like you very much."

Roarke's hand was on his chest. "I've noticed."

"I see a dirk or sword."

"Great!" Roarke exclaimed, "Now the ghost is going to gut me in my sleep."

Moira laughed. "No, dafty. There's something about a dirk that she wants doing."

"Thanks be to Jesus."

"I dreamed about a dagger a few nights ago." Rhea reached for the brooch, taking it from Moira's hand.

"You did?" Roarke lodged his hand on her shoulder.

"Yes." Rhea settled in a stool by the counter, rubbing the brooch with her thumb. "Actually, I have been having the most vivid dreams since I've been here. I haven't told you much because I thought you'd think me silly."

"I'd never think you silly."

Rhea looked at Roarke and then back to Moira. "See, there's a legend in the area where Roarke lives about a boy named Thomas . . ."

" . . . and the girl, Islean?" Moira finished.

"Aye." Roarke nodded. "You know the tale?"

"Of course."

Roarke went on to tell her all they knew about Thomas and Islean.

Moira went around the counter and turned on her computer. After a few minutes of searching, Moira called them over. "You're Canadian?"

Rhea nodded, and Moira continued, "A MacLean fought in the battle of Québec. He led his regiment to battle during a vicious snowstorm, blasting their pipes."

Moira turned for Rhea and Roarke to see.

"Very cool," Rhea commented.

Roarke slipped an arm around her shoulders. "Scottish blood would account for your charm and good looks."

Moira looked over to the empty corner again. "If you have a connection to Thomas and Islean is connected to the brooch, then that is maybe why she can communicate with you so easily."

"You think she's our ghost?"

"Very well might be."

"Islean could feel you had a link to Thomas. Some believe people on Earth are connected to those like themselves in the afterlife. So she might just feel as if you are kindred spirits, and she wants you to help them."

"I don't know how."

"You said your friend, Paul, told you she had killed herself with her love's dirk and then wanted them buried together?"

"Aye." Roarke stared at Moira as if what she was saying was the most fascinating thing in the world.

"Maybe she just wants you to keep the brooch and dirk together. Bury them, I guess."

"We don't have the dirk."

"She'll find a way to show you. Just keep your mind open to her."

Moira read something on the screen and looked up at the couple with shock. "Did you say you were from the area close to Alloway Castle?"

"Aye," Roarke replied. "Why?"

"I have the news opened up here." She toyed with the end of her long braid. "I hate to tell you this, but Alloway Castle caught on fire last night."

"What?" Roarke jumped to his feet.

"Aye. The fire is out, but there's been considerable damage."

Roarke's face drained of color, and Rhea stood as she spoke to Moira. "Friends of his own the castle, and it's extraordinary. I'm afraid we'll have to be going."

Thanking Moira, they hurried to the inn. Roarke called Agnes. After hearing the fire was out and no one was hurt, he told her they would be there first thing in the morning. Although their mood had altered after hearing the news of the castle, the couple found some solace in each other's arms.

Once the ship docked, Roarke and Rhea headed for White Heather to drop off their bags and freshen up. They went upstairs to check on everything, and Rhea laid the brooch on the table with Roarke's collection.

"Just put it here for safekeeping."

Five minutes later, they headed for the castle. At first glance, they saw no damage. However, once they had parked the truck amid various police and fire vehicles, a heavy odor of smoke filled the air. Toward the top of the structure, there was charring and scorching.

"Roarke!" Senga's yell carried over the still glen as she stood at the front doors of the mansion, waving them over.

Affording the castle another glance, they got back in the truck and drove the short distance to the manor, where another bevy of vehicles littered the front drive. The door was open.

"In the kitchen," came a yell from inside.

Senga greeted them in the kitchen, where Agnes and Ellie sat at the long wooden table, drinking tea and eating poppyseed cake.

The windowsill circling the room was littered with shells, rocks, bones, feathers, wood, fruit peel, and crystals. Bunches of drying herbs and flowers dangled from the ceiling. Cluttered upon shelves were bottles of tonics and salves, preserved foods, and herbs. A large cage with an open door was on a stand, which Rhea assumed housed the large crow flying over their heads.

"Don't mind him," Agnes said as she set a teapot on the large wooden table. "He's free to come and go as he pleases."

"This is the kitchen of people who can do a hell of a lot more than cook." Rhea smiled at her host, who bowed her head in reply.

"Do they know what caused the fire?" Roarke asked as he settled in a chair.

"No idea yet, but they're still investigating. Luckily, it didn't reach the older section. It just affected the newer part we'd been renovating before we ran out of funds." Agnes wiped her hand on a dishcloth.

Senga sighed. "I guess what we did get done doesn't matter much since we can't do the rest."

Agnes shook her head. "I awoke to go to the toilet and saw flames and smoke coming from the top of the castle. There's water damage, charring, and everything inside is at least a little scorched and covered in soot. Senga called you over because we aren't supposed to go near the place until the forensic team finishes their search. Fires can release any number of hazardous materials and gases."

Senga looked over her cup at Ellie and Agnes, and Agnes cleared her throat before speaking. "Ahem, I just got off the phone with David Cojocaru. He heard the news and called to check on the castle. He told us he'd be out to see it whenever it was safe as he's staying in town for a few days."

"Bastard," Roarke mumbled under his breath.

Rhea looked at him. "You don't think he—"

"I would put nothing, nothing, passed Davey"

Agnes continued with a sigh. "He also added he didn't

think in the grand scheme of things, it would matter much. A new roof was the first thing on his agenda anyway once he owned it. He didn't take back his offer, but he reduced the bid on account of the cost of the repairs."

Rhea did not miss how both women were finding it difficult to look at Roarke. Nevertheless, they were going to take David's offer. One look at Roarke's face told her he knew it, too.

"We need to sell fast now," said Senga, reaching over to grasp Roarke's hand lightly. "The fire's pushed the need. On top of not having the money to maintain the castle or improve it, we would also need extra for repairs and fire damage, and our insurance wouldn't cover much."

Roarke cleared his throat. "Girls, I had a call earlier in the week." He looked over at Rhea, "I didn't say anything to you because it didn't matter much at the time. Unfortunately, they're having trouble with the weather at the location where we'll be filming, and it might be postponed a few weeks later than originally thought."

"Roarke, we're going to sell to David Cojocaru," Senga stated straight out.

The women looked at each other, "We have no other choice."

"I know, girls." He patted the back of Senga's hand. "Just give me another day. I have a few last calls to make. That's all I ask."

Senga looked at her sister, who smiled, so Senga lifted her hand to pat Roarke's cheek. "Okay, my old friend. We still have a bit of time."

Ellie coughed. "Roarke, I want to ask you something, but it's a bit of a sensitive question."

"Go ahead." He watched the crow hop across the countertop behind Agnes. "We've been friends for years. You can ask me anything.

"If you're a rich actor, why do you need money?"

"You think I have a couple million sitting in my bank account?"

"That's what everyone thinks."

"The way it works with a film is The Stage Actors Guild processes payroll. Actors get paid as they complete the work. For these films, I'll also get points on the back end. If the movies do well, I get a certain percentage of the final revenue or profits from the film months or years later."

"I see."

"You're what they call cash poor?" Rhea angled one of her eyebrows at him

"A wealthy person with a ton of cash in the bank is sometimes a contradiction—people like David being exceptions. I made good choices with my money, but the shelter eats up everything. It's like a house. It generates expenses but not income. My money's also in investments, but those deals may not see returns for months or years. Stocks need to be left on the market to grow, and I need money now."

"I see," Ellie repeated with a sigh.

"I want to keep myself comfortable, too. I need to keep my small emergency fund and personal homestead upkeep."

Ellie got up to get the pitcher of water by the sink and Roarke turned his head and smiled tenderly at Rhea.

When Ellie returned to the table, Rhea saw humor in her black eyes as she looked from Roarke to Rhea, then elbowed Agnes and jerked her dainty chin at the couple. Narrowing her eyes suspiciously, she asked, "What were you doing in Mull?"

Roarke turned from Rhea and looked at Ellie. "I'm sorry? Did you ask me something?"

"It's okay," Ellie smirked at him. "You were distracted."

"Last night, when you called, you were in Mull." Agnes

rested her chin on her folded fingers. "What were you all doing there?"

Rhea swallowed hard and answered. "Research for my book, and I found out I have a Scottish ancestor."

"You enjoyed the island then?"

"Very much, and we met a wonderful woman named Moira."

"At the gift shop on the corner?" Ellie smiled.

"That's her." Rhea smiled in return.

Ellie glanced over at the sisters and smiled mysteriously. "She's a very talented woman. She knows her craft very well."

Rhea tried to gauge Ellie's expression. "She told us a spirit was around us."

Ellie's smile dropped from her face. "What kind of spirit?"

"You know the big boulder between the inn and Roarke's cottage?"

"Islean's?"

"Aye, it sounds like it might be her."

"What?" All three leaned forward in their chairs.

Rhea and Roarke tried their best to explain what had happened to them, what Moira had told them about the ghost, and what they had learned about Rhea's ancestry.

"Rhea, do you actually think you're a distant relative of Thomas?" Senga asked, putting air quotes around the word *actually*.

"No. Yes. I-I just think it may be possible. A descendant of Thomas' did come to Québec. I might be way off, but it would explain why I seem to have a link with Islean. It would also explain why I find Ian and Ellie's eyes so familiar. I think my grandmother's eyes were like that."

"Or maybe she's just been trying to tell her story all along, and you were the only one who listened," Agnes offered.

"You're under the protection of the Selkie if you're kin to Thomas. That would make you our distant cousin," Senga interjected.

"The Selkie from that family legend Ian told me my first day here?"

"Aye, and the witches and wise-women elevated Islean to almost goddess status in this area." Ellie looked over at Roarke. "Once they did that, things changed for Thomas family. The crops grew better, and animals prospered, even in difficult times. A few men became merchants and military leaders, gaining great respect amongst the people and accumulating wealth. Eventually, after the Jacobite Uprising, economic change and altered royalties began to undermine the clan system, and many leaders were reduced to simple landowners."

"Such was the fate that befell Islean's family," Senga interjected. "Our family prospered, and we eventually came to own the very castle that had once belonged to Islean's family."

Rhea took a sip of tea. "She's trying to tell me something. I dream of her. I've heard voices. I've even seen her, I think."

"Where? At the cottage?"

"No." Rhea swallowed. "Here."

The two sisters exchanged glances and listened as Roarke and Rhea told them how they had both seen things when they had visited the old part of the castle.

"I wonder why, after centuries, Islean's connecting with someone?"

"It makes me jealous," confessed Senga.

"Rhea might be a distant cousin to Thomas, and through her mother, she has a Native American awareness of the world around her."

"To be honest." Rhea set down her teacup and glanced at Roarke. "I also dabbled in a bit of Wicca when I was in college."

"Really? Why did you stop?" Ellie asked as she motioned to the crow with a bit of cake. He fluttered down and hopped across the table, causing Roarke to jump back in surprise.

"I've never told anyone about it." She glanced at Roarke. "I used the few things my mother taught me and read some books. One night, I was doing a simple spell, and I neglected to do a salt circle for protection. Almost immediately, I had a strange feeling I wasn't alone. I'd called something forth."

"You opened yourself up. Did you think it would be so simple to shut it down again?"

"It was. Until now. I had connected with spirits when I was a child, but being here is the first time it's happened since I stopped practicing in college."

Roarke brushed crumbs onto the plate in front of him. "We have a brooch from Islean. We know Thomas's dirk is probably important because she used it to kill herself, and we know Islean's family buried her in an unknown location."

Roarke reached toward the piece of cake on Rhea's plate, but she slapped the back of his hand. "Is it really unknown?" Rhea asked no one in particular and held out a morsel of cake to the crow.

"Why are you asking that?" Ellie watched the crow hop over to Rhea.

"If it's none of my business, just let me know, but I noticed in Ellie's Gran's cookbook there were little symbols, and one kept drawing my attention." Rhea went on to tell the women about the cairn they had found on Burn's Night. "The walkway was positioned so that it was facing the setting sun at this time of year. Fall solstice."

"What are you getting at?" Senga smiled.

"Three bent trees, the same markings in the cookbook, led us to the cairn. Is the cairn Islean's grave?"

Senga, Agnes, and Ellie all looked at each other until Ellie spoke. "Aye, that's where she's buried."

"Ellie!" Senga admonished.

"What? She already knows."

Ellie leaned on her elbows. "Islean's mother was distraught

that she wasn't buried in consecrated ground, and she asked the women of our family to cast a spell of protection over her grave. They considered the deaths to be the actions of proud, stupid men."

They all looked at Roarke, who defensively held up his hands. "I wasn't even born yet."

Agnes continued, "They began to revere her."

"Aye, we have never forgotten Islean," Ellie added.

"What should we do?" Rhea addressed the women in front of her, "I don't know what she wants me to do."

"Moira told you to bury the brooch and dirk together to put the spirits at peace. In a few days, it'll be Mabon, on September twenty-first, the Witches' Thanksgiving. Day and Night are equal lengths, a time of balance. It finishes the year and is the best time to ask the spirits and the goddess for forgiveness. The goddess is turning into her Hag phase, and it's the time for redemption. To start fresh before Samhain, the New Year."

"Maybe you both could come with us to the cairn, and we could bury the brooch and dirk together."

"Provided we can find the dirk," Rhea added. "It could be anywhere."

"Moira said Islean would lead you to it." Senga's eyes were glittering with excitement. "Rhea, take tomorrow to connect with her." Senga rested her chin on her knuckles. "If you tried to meditate, you might get something."

Before Rhea could object to the mere thought of mediating to summon a visit from a vengeful spirit, Agnes interrupted, "Could Islean have started the fire?"

"That's absurd," Ellie blurted out

"Why? Now that we're going to sell the castle, her castle, and give it back to her kin, as Roarke and David are both distant relatives to Islean."

Roarke furrowed his brow. "David, too? Didn't know

that."

"His mother and yours are cousins as well as friends."

"Would she really try and burn it down, though?" Rhea asked.

"If she were angry or frustrated enough," Agnes added. "Or maybe she wanted to get you two back here."

"Why?"

"You're leaving soon, aren't you?" Agnes touched Rhea's hand. "She needs you, now."

"Okay." Rhea ran her hands down her ponytail. "But what is the importance of the brooch and dagger? I understand they're important to her, but what will burying them do?"

Ellie reached over to touch the pendants at Rhea's chest. "Psychometry is the belief that objects have an energy field around them, and if you tap into the field, then the object will give you knowledge of its history. Like this chain you wear. It carries a piece of you and a piece of whoever gave it to you."

"Like when psychics hold the ring of a missing woman to help police find her?"

"Exactly, and in a step further the item and its energy, its knowledge, can be passed on to people. The item can connect people and spirits. It can create like a wire, where energy, information, even emotions can pass between the living and the spirit world."

"Like a pathway which can bring a spirit forth?"

Senga smiled at her twin. "Mother said if you find something at your feet, it's a gift from a loved one. Spirits can leave things for the living, or even lead them to certain things."

"Islean and Thomas could be connected to the brooch and the dirk. Maybe those two items they gave each other kept them tethered, tied to this world, but they remained apart. Spirit forms have eternal life and aren't limited to time and space. They come and go as they please."

Rhea looked at her hands. "I feel as if their spirits are

apart."

"Of course, they are," Agnes agreed. "The clan killed him, but she took her own life."

"The forgiveness of sins." Ellie's black eyes glittered excitedly. "Roarke should ask Islean for forgiveness."

"What?" he yelled, causing the crow to fly up to rest on top of the door.

"Your family wronged her. You think it's a coincidence that the men in your family don't have good relationships?"

"It's a stupid self-fulfilling prophecy set up by a superstitious culture. Everything I've seen leads me to believe in the spirits, but I refuse to believe that the men in my family have shitty luck with women because an over-zealous ghost is stalking them!"

"I just don't understand how."

"Look, putting the onus on a vengeful spirit is cowardly. Maybe, just maybe, the men in my family are arseholes!" Shooting to his feet, he stalked to the window over the sink and turned back to the women. "It's not because of a curse. The fault lies one hundred percent with us!"

At that moment, a gust of wind came through the kitchen, extinguishing the candle burning next to the sink. The crow flew down from the top of the door and settled on the back of the chair Roarke had vacated as Roarke gripped the sink behind him.

The four women all looked from the crow to Roarke and then back at each other before bursting into raucous laughter.

"What exactly is so funny?" He moved his hands from the sink to his hips. "Because I certainly don't know."

Rhea dabbed at her eyes with the sleeve of her sweatshirt. "You're so charming."

He cocked up his eyebrow and looked around at each woman in a confused manner. "Ladies?"

"Roarke." Ellie, still smiling, interlaced her fingers and

rested her chin on her hands. "You're a big oaf, but you have your moments. An apology only counts if you *truly* feel remorse. You can't hide what's in your heart."

"You should ask for your family's forgiveness. Someone just told us that we're on the right track," Senga gestured to the crow that cawed. "She needs to forgive before she can be forgiven."

"Maybe then they can be together." Rhea smiled up at him. "What's more important than helping a spirit go into the afterlife and maybe be together with their loved one? What's more important than love, than our eternal souls?"

The crow cawed again and flew out the open window over the sink, the tip of his wing grazing Roarke's cheek. Roarke lifted his hand to where the feathers had touched his face, a strange look in his eyes. Then, sitting in the chair again, he sighed. "Why're we even discussing this? We have more pressing matters. Very shortly, I'll be in the States and the castle will belong to David."

"And Rhea will be gone," Agnes added.

"And Rhea will be gone," Roarke repeated, looking down and running his hand along the table's smooth surface.

Senga covered Rhea's hand with her own. "Are you two going to try to keep your relationship going over the distance?"

"That's something we haven't . . ." Rhea began but then stopped. "Wait . . . how do you know . . ."

"We're not—" Roarke tried to interject.

"Save it." Ellie held up her hand. "My blind grandfather could see what's happened with you two. Roarke, you're more yourself than you have been in years. Rhea makes you more, well, *you*. If that makes sense."

Senga patted Rhea's hand. "It's a beautiful thing. Your eyes change color when you look at him. The energy between you is somatic."

Feeling Roarke's gaze, Rhea turned to him with a sad smile.

Roarke sighed and twirled a lock of Rhea's hair around his finger. "So, while we're enjoying the last of our time together, all we have to do is wait for a spirit to lead us to an ancient dirk, bury it, and wait to see if the mean ghost-lady forgives me for the crimes of my ancestors. All while, the bane of my existence, David Cojocaru, steals my castle. Sounds fun."

"David." A thought had just occurred to Rhea. "When I met him in the city, he told your mother and myself something his grandmother told him. If a spirit doesn't want to go into the afterlife, the angel who'd been sent to guide him leaves a portal that the spirit can use to cross over when they've done what it is they have to do."

"That's pretty deep for David," Roarke scoffed.

"Maybe that's it. The cairn is a portal. Maybe if we bury the brooch and dirk, if she's satisfied and forgives for the mistakes of the past, she can cross over."

"That would make a good movie." Roarke shrugged his shoulders and grinned. "All right, ladies, what do we have to prepare for this Mabon ceremony?"

"We'll give you a few small preparations to make, but Rhea needs to be open to any messages sent her way." Ellie smirked slightly. "Follow any suggestion she may have, however subtle or seemingly insignificant."

Senga smiled. ""Rhea, you know to do whatever you need to do to keep your body relaxed, and your mind blank. Anything to channel that special magic."

Rhea knew what they were hinting at, one of the most ancient forms of magic, where energy got drawn from the connection between male and female and then used to fuel a magical purpose.

The three witches smirked at her, and Rhea nodded, knowing she was turning at least seven shades of red.

Chapter Twenty: Land and Sea

Ancient knowledge flooded Rhea's mind and body as her spirit freed itself from the box she had locked it in long ago.

After returning to White Heather, Roarke and Rhea walked barefoot along the white sand beach below the cliff as rock pipits and sandpipers scuttled over the shoreline and rock pools. The day was warm, even if the sky was overcast and the astern wind blew over the tall grass dancing next to the sandy shore.

"It's marram grass," Roarke told Rhea when she asked its name.

Stepped into the tufts of muted green, she turned to him. "Think lovers made promises here?" Then, dropping into the grass, she lay with one hand lifted toward him.

Smiling down at her, he dropped their shoes and lay beside her "You remind me of the woman in the novel your mother told you about."

"You remember that?"

"I remember everything you've ever said to me."

They stared up at the pewter sky on their backs, listening to the rhythmic pounding of the waves shore and the rustling whistles of the wind in the tall grass. Finally, Roarke propped himself up on one elbow and ran his finger down her nose. "Would you like to sleep here?"

"I will if you're with me." She kissed him, and her body rose to press against him, her hand moving from his neck, down his back, and along his buttocks.

With a soft moan, he dropped his hand from her face to run it along her neck, clavicle, and shoulders. Pushing aside the straps of her bra and dress, his hand ran back and forth along the smooth skin of her breastbone. "I love this part of your body," he murmured as he kissed and licked along the trail his fingers had just made.

Rhea tasted sea salt and the sweetness of Roarke's saliva in her mouth, breathing in the heavy, heady freshness of the grass. Above them, seagulls flew, their cries filling the air with music. Triggered by her surroundings and the sandalwood scent of Roarke, she crept her hands under his jacket and shirt to rub the stiff muscles of his chest. Roarke had to shift his weight and nestle his lower body between her legs. Running her hands across the corrugated angles of his tight stomach, she slid one hand down the front of his jeans, where his sex strained under the material.

Closing his mouth over hers, he lightly squeezed her sensitive breast, and the tip of his tongue slid between her parted lips. Feathery caresses deepened when she dug her heels into the earth and fumbled with the button of his jeans.

Roarke released her mouth. "Here?"

"Here." She pressed her palm against his mouth. "Not another word."

Shaking her hand away from his mouth, he kissed her savagely, a hand on either side of her head. She tugged the top of his jeans down, exposing his narrow waist and lean hips. Reaching beneath the elastic of his underwear, releasing his erection from its material bindings, she gripped it. Her other hand formed a circle at its base, pressing down, and she ran her fingernails ran along his sinewy shaft, lightly squeezing the sensitive tip with each pass.

Groaning, Roarke pressed his forehead to hers, sliding one hand to her stomach and running along the span of her hips. Turning her slightly, he skimmed his hand along the curve of her bottom.

Rhea arched her back to lift the bottom of her cotton dress, and after sliding her underwear down one leg, she positioned him at the part of her that ached for him. His breathing had become harsh and uneven. The tip of his erection rubbed up and down her opening before the smooth cap slid into her, stretching her to accommodate him. Then, gripping her hips and angling them slightly, he drove his hips forward, giving her his entire length in one swift, smooth thrust, filling her.

Roarke caught her scream in his mouth as he slowly rotated his hips, grinding against her pelvis. Whimpering, Rhea pressed her palms against his chest, lifting her hips, wanting all of him. Letting go of her mouth and lowering his face to her shoulder, he pulled almost entirely free of her body and then slammed back in. Her back arched even further, and her eyes closed tightly. Roarke pounded her body, sliding out and hammering back in at the same rhythm as the waves that beat the shore, over and over again.

Rhea felt as if the flesh were sliding off her very bones. She could feel Roarke everywhere. His hard fingertips raked at her skin as the tips of his teeth nipped the tender flesh of her neck, chest, shoulders, and breasts. She thought once again of a wolf.

His strong hand pulled one of her knees high against the side of his ribcage as he dug his fingers along the length of her buttock, thigh, and calf, his short fingernails scratching at her muscles. His breath came in irregular gasps against her skin and her hair spilled around her on the grass.

Some wild, feral version of Roarke had taken over. Rhea reveled in it with arms not embracing her lover but spread wide on the grass at either side. She had never felt more human and yet something infinitely ethereal at the same time. Beneath his slamming thrusts, her shivering body rocked. Fingers and heels dug into the sandy soil beneath them. Every time he thundered into her, she sank deeper and deeper into the earth under the weight of his massive, muscular body, feeling that the ground was opening up to swallow them both.

On and on, Roarke poured his entire, firm shaft into her body, eliciting little cries from her as he somehow seemed to get deeper with each ramming thrust. A heat was spreading inside Rhea's body as she lurched toward a jarring, pulsing climax.

Roarke lifted her other knee, again catching her cry in his mouth as she thrashed beneath him, sucking at his bottom lip. A light spray of seawater splashed against her face, and she licked at the salt on her lips. Overwhelming spasms racked her body, and in a frantic explosion of sensation, she shuddered and screamed as a wild eruption from her core threatened to rend her in two.

When Rhea's muscles rhythmically contracted around his hardness, Roarke drove harder and faster than before, plunging on and on into her flesh as the blood in his veins burned with an ancient fire. When his climax came, he clamped his teeth into the tender flesh of her neck and erupted deep inside her, spilling himself into her center with soul-shattering intensity.

The pumping of his thickness sent Rhea over the edge again in palpitating, blinding waves, and Roarke let go of her neck and threw his head back, slamming against her in a profound shudder. When his large frame fell and melted on top of her, she was a senseless, incoherent pile of skin and bones, left to the scavengers, aware of nothing except the sound of the waves slamming into the shore.

Rhea sat by the sea wrapped in Roarke's jacket, facing the setting sun

"You're every colour of autumn," Roarke said to her when

she turned to him, and then he asked in all seriousness. "Are we in love?"

Without even stopping to think, she answered shyly, "I think so."

"I've never been in love before."

"Never?"

"Not if this is what it feels like."

"Me neither." Rhea put her hands on his shoulders "We may have to be physically separated, but we'll stay connected."

"Why don't you stay?"

"It's unrealistic."

"Why?"

"You know why. I need to return to my life, to Liam."

"I need you here." He rubbed the tops of her feet with his hands. "I don't think I'll be able to breathe without you now."

Rhea felt the depth of his words in her heart but couldn't ignore the reality of their situation. "How do I make my living if I'm here?"

"Writing. The book will be a success. Just be with me and write."

"Leave Liam to be abandoned twice."

"Maybe you could be here with me part-time. Every few months or something."

"What would you have me do? Run back and forth across the globe, jumping between the two guys that I lo—" She stopped and covered her head with his jacket.

He raised his eyebrows and grinned at her, "The guys that you . . . what? Say it. You love me."

Under her covering, she nodded.

Pulling the jacket off her head, Roarke brushed her hair away from her face and kissed her. "Ghost, I love you, too. I always have."

"You have?" Rhea placed a hand on either side of his head.

"Aye."

"I can't choose between you and Liam. Liam will win, and he needs me every day."

"Aye, I know, and I love you the more for it. Ghost, no one should have to choose between their lover and their family."

"Like Thomas and Islean."

"All of my life, I've been chasing something. I was never happy where I was, never satisfied. Loving you has made me realize I now know what I adore more than anything else."

Touching her cheek, he whispered, "Us?"

"No," she answered honestly. "Liam."

Surprise gave way to solemn appreciation as Roarke nodded, and Rhea threw her arms around his neck. "I love us more than I thought I could love anything, but going back to Liam is what I need most. It's the purpose I'd been seeking my whole life."

"I understand and respect that."

"It's through you that I finally see it." She pressed her cheek to his. "Because it's the only thing that could ever have me walk away from you."

"Let's just enjoy what we have and hope for more time in the future."

Rhea closed her eyes as a deep sadness swept through her body, as powerful as physical pain. In a remote part of her where she kept things too painful for her to address, she wept.

Roarke grabbed her wrist, and her eyes flew open. He held a finger in the air. "You hear that?"

Somewhere in the distance, a high screeching wail resonated from the treetops for a few seconds before dying out, shaking them both to the core with its lonely eeriness.

Roarke turned toward the sea and hugged his knees. "I don't even want to know."

"Me neither." Shivering, she pressed his jacket closer to her body.

Letting the ocean waves hypnotize her, Rhea allowed herself a moment of wistfulness.

"Do you know what makes the waves, ghost?" he whispered.

"Wind, I suppose." She sat a little closer to him. "My father said waves are the heartbeat of the ocean."

"Storms on the ocean generate wind, and the strength of the wind creates waves. Over distance, the waves become uniform, creating a swell, like a wave train, creating energy." Putting an arm around her shoulders, he rested his head on hers. "The rhythm of the tides is created by the moon, sun, shape of the land, the Earth's rotation."

"The ocean and the entire planet need storms?"

"Aye. I guess we all need our storms."

Rhea interlaced her fingers with his. "Big man, you certainly can be poetic. I have to use that in the book."

Roarke laughed. "Please don't."

Walking hand in hand toward the cottage, Roarke and Rhea stopped walking at the same time.

Something was wrong. The energy around the house was thick and charged, like before a thunderstorm. Rhea's heart pounded, sweat broke out all over her body, and within a matter of seconds, she had lowered herself to the ground as a sense of impending doom and loss of control swept over her. Her body trembled, and her breath kept catching in her throat.

Roarke knelt beside her. "Rhea? Panic attack?"

"Not panic." She shook her head violently and spoke, not knowing where the words were coming from. "Something's changing. Everything's going to come full circle. It all starts now."

As suddenly as the feeling came upon her, the tremors

stopped, her breathing regulated. Other than a slight head-ache, Rhea felt the same as before the attack. She looked at Roarke and repeated. "It starts now."

They got to their feet and headed for the front door, where Roarke motioned for Rhea to stay behind him as he unlocked it, turned the handle, and stepped inside. For a few seconds, nothing happened, but then Roarke's breath came out in a hiss, and he stood rigid.

Peering into the house, she saw nothing, but she could feel anger. Something menacing and horrid. "Roarke?" She stood in front of him and tried to bend his head toward her.

He turned his neck, his focus still on a spot at the end of the corridor, but after a few more seconds, his gaze fluttered down to her face.

"I-I saw *her*. She's here."

"Who's here?"

"End of the corridor. When I opened the door, she stood in front of me, a dark face with even darker eyes. Just deep, dark holes."

At that moment, the door to the second floor slammed against its jam three times and stopped. Roarke ran down to stare at the entrance, and Rhea followed him. Opening the door, Roarke took a step inside the doorframe. The house shook as if wind had hit it, and he halted. Finally, he just headed up the stairs, the heavy tread of his boots on the wood upstairs floor telling her where he was.

"Rhea, it's all clear."

Mounting the stairs, she was aware of a sense of foreboding that had not been in the air the last time she was there.

"What the . . ." Roarke muttered from the small yellow bedroom where he kept his artifacts and relics. "What the hell?"

Rhea stepped into the small room to find him standing in front of the open wooden chest.

"My collection." He looked up at her, "Everything's gone."

Rhea inhaled sharply. "The brooch? The sword?"

"Everything." He slammed the lid of the chest back into place and spun around to look at her, his hands pushing back his hair.

"Who would want to take your artifacts?"

The wolfish glint came into his narrowed eyes. "David." Bounding down the stairs, he dialed a number numerous times.

Upstairs, the lightest of touches ran across the top of Rhea's shoulder, and she felt a slight push on her lower back as the light brown curtains around the window fluttered. Walking around the chest and looking outside, she saw a figure run from the edge of the woods and toward Ian's.

She turned to look behind her at the empty room. "What do you want me to see?"

The only thing she heard in reply was Roarke yelling up the stairs. "Rhea! Come down!"

Downstairs, she ran over to him, placing her hands on his chest. "Do you really think David broke into your home?"

"A friend of mine thinks the sword could be worth a small fortune, but David doesn't want Scottish artifacts to sell. It doesn't matter how much they're valued. He just wants to have Scottish history."

"I don't get it."

Roarke went into the kitchen and grabbed a glass of water. "Art advisors and dealers advise clients on what to buy and where to find various items. His clients are people with a lot of money to burn. For whatever reason, he's been after that sword since I bought it."

The sound of wheels on the driveway brought Roarke flying to the window. He turned to look at Rhea as he flung open the front door. "It's okay. It's the boys."

Rhea followed behind him as Mike, Ken, and Doug got out

of Mike's black jeep.

Roarke kept his face casual. "Hey, guys. What brings you all up here?"

Ken stepped forward. "We were up to see if Ian wanted to come with us for an overnight, but he wasn't home. We thought we'd come and see how Rhea was surviving."

"Hi, guys." She smiled at them.

"You should know that wee weasel Willem is sniffing around the area. He almost ran us over." Doug sniffed in disdain.

Roarke started. "You saw Willem up here?"

"Aye, he was coming from the road to the bothy and driving like a bat out of hell." Mike stroked his beard, shaking his head.

"He's on his way back to the city." Roarke kicked at a rock at his feet. "To David."

"David Cojocaru isn't in the city," Doug commented. "Ken and I saw him at the pub in the village this morning, eating breakfast. He told Miriam he and his wife rented the Cameron property on the hill to look over a few things in the area. Had security set up and all."

Ken chuckled. "He commented that he guessed you had taken your boat out, as it wasn't in its usual spot by the wharf."

"How the hell does he know which boat is mine?"

"It's named after your mother and sister, Clara Tessa. He's been around a lot lately, and everyone knows that's your boat."

"Son of a bitch! We hadn't landed yet from Mull, and he sent that wee prick to rob me!" Roarke ran up the steps and into the house, returning with his keys and heading for his truck. "Guys, do me a favor and stay here with Rhea, will you?"

Rhea ran to the truck. "Where're you going?"

"Stay here. I'll be back soon."

"Where are you going? To David?"

Jumping into the truck, he turned the key in the ignition. "This thing with me and David's got to end."

Revving the motor, he spun out of the driveway, deaf to Rhea's objections.

After he disappeared around the corner, Rhea quickly informed the men of what happened. "Does he expect me just to stay here?"

"Let's go in and have a cup of tea. Think about everything."

"Don't you guys get it? He's going to David, and the mood he's in, it won't end well."

"Oh, no. I'm not getting mixed up in that stuff." Ken shook his hands in front of his chest.

"We have to! Roarke's in danger."

"He's a big boy, Rhea. He can handle himself." Doug stepped up the stairs to go into the cottage.

"Fine. Then just give me a ride to that house where David is staying."

"And have a size twelve boot up me arse for doing it? No thanks." Doug turned around on the porch.

Midas came around the corner of the house, followed by Ian.

"Oh, Ian." Rhea ran to him. "I'm so glad you're here."

"What's going on?" He tilted back his bibbed grey hat.

"Roarke just ran off to find David. He thinks he had Willem steal his artifacts."

"Why would he think that? I've got his artifacts."

"You've got the artifacts?" she asked incredulously.

"Aye. Rebecca called from the inn to give me a head's up because she heard Willem and his cronies saying Roarke was away. Willem was going to get some sword to give to his father as a surprise. I went in with my key and took them for safekeeping."

"You mean to say that Roarke's going to confront David and accuse him of stealing something he doesn't have?"

The men looked from one to the other.

"We have to stop him!" Rhea's voice edged on hysterical, and she grabbed at the sleeve of Doug's coat. In response, Doug just looked at the sky and shook his head.

Ken tried to grab the keys out of Mike's hand, but he pushed him away. "Why are we waiting? Rhea's right. We've to stop Roarke before he does something stupid."

Everyone headed for the jeep, as Rhea called over her shoulder, "Ian, stay here in case Roarke comes back?"

"Aye, but you'd be better off staying here with me," Ian yelled after her.

"I can't." She jumped into the back seat with Ken. "I have to make sure Roarke is okay."

A tall wall of stone fenced in the land and a large steel gate with a sign marked Private Property No Access blocked the private road from the main road as they drove by the estate. Nearing the estate, Mike slowed down but did not stop. He jerked his head in the direction of the gate. "See the cameras? Security guards in that manse."

"That lock on the gate has a digital keypad." Ken added. "He's a stickler about security. Without the code, you need to be buzzed in."

Mike stopped the jeep out of sight of the gate. "We'll just wait here and see if Roarke arrives. I took a few shortcuts so that we might've beaten him."

"What if he's already inside?" Rhea craned her neck to look over the back seat.

"We can't do anything about that now."

"We gotta get in there." Rhea already had her hand on the

door handle.

"We can't get in there." Ken put his hand on her arm. "If he's already in there, the damage is done."

"If he's in trouble? If he needs help?" Rhea looked imploringly at Doug in the front seat, who shook his head at her.

"Lass, we don't even know if he's in there."

"If anything happens to him, and I didn't try to help him, I'll never forgive myself."

"What would you do against the likes of Cojocaru and his security?"

"Call for help." Patting at her pockets, Rhea groaned in frustration. "Damn it! I don't even have my phone."

"Well then." Ken tapped her on the arm. "We'll just wait and see."

Less than two minutes later, Rhea was sick of waiting. She pointed ahead of them on the road. "I'm just going to walk up the road a little."

"No, you're not. Anything happens to you, and Roarke'll skin the lot of us." Ken threw his arm across her chest.

Pushing Ken's arm back at him, she sighed. "Nothing's going to happen."

"Don't move out of this jeep!" Mike wagged his finger at her, and Rhea slumped back in the seat. Then, a second later, she opened the jeep door and jumped out.

"Rhea, hold on!" Ken pulled out his phone. "At least take my mobile. The code is two-zero-zero-five." He lowered his voice. "Don't do anything stupid, but I turned off the volume just in case you do."

Giving Ken a weak smile, she set off down the road, around the bend, and then turned, walking straight into the heavy woods surrounding the property. The stone wall ended around fifty feet after the gate, replaced with high weld mesh security fencing with spiked tops.

When Rhea tried to climb over the fence, the toes of her

sneakers couldn't get through the narrow rectangular slots. Kicking them off and tossing the over the fence, she managed the painful climb in her socks. Finding her sneakers, she continued through the woods.

A few moments later, she saw an opening in the trees and came out behind a large, three-story manse made of beige stone. Reflecting the meager sunlight made it appear gold against the lush green of its surroundings.

Remembering the security cameras, she edged her way along the forest line, keeping to the trees. Turning the corner of the house in the driveway, which swept its way around a central flower garden, she saw Roarke's old orange truck and debated two ideas. Sneak around and try to get in or go to the door and ask to enter.

Mustering up her courage, she stepped onto the gravel driveway, trying to appear calm and confident. She walked up to the large double doors and pushed the bell. Receiving no reply, Rhea moved the handle. Finding it locked, she decided she would have to resort to sneaking around back.

Behind the mansion, she made her way to the large covered gallery bordered by flowers but froze when she heard loud voices coming from the open door of the patio.

Suddenly, Rhea was grabbed from behind, and a large, rough hand clamped over her mouth and pulled her around the corner of the mansion.

"What do we have here?" The sneering, gravelly voice was Willem's.

After Willem directed her into the mansion at gunpoint, Rhea found herself outside an open, wooden door. Despite being terror-stricken by the gun at her ribs and the unstable young man holding it, she registered the sound of Roarke's angry voice coming from within the room.

Willem pushed her toward the entrance, and she stumbled

inside. David Cojocaru stood behind a large oak desk, and Roarke was on the other side.

David looked around Roarke to the people at the door. "What's this?"

Roarke spun around, and yelled her name, but Willem stopped him before he could step toward her. "Don't move, Big man. I've got a gun to her back."

Roarke looked up at Rhea's face, and she nodded.

David Cojocaru lowered himself into the chair behind his desk, crossed his legs, and laced his fingers across his knees. "Now, why would she be here?"

"I caught her snooping around outside."

Roarke glared at Willem. "Let her go, and I won't kill you."

David cleared his throat loudly. "Son, take your friend and sit on the couch there. Roarke, stay where you are. Don't bother arguing."

All three sat, Roarke resentfully with David peering at him over his knuckles. "Before we continue with our conversation, would you mind telling me why your friend here was snooping around outside?"

Roarke leaned forward in his chair, grinding his teeth as he spoke. "Davey, could you ask that gobshite to put down the gun? It's not necessary, and if she gets hurt, in any way, I'll hold you responsible."

"Until I get some answers, he'll stay exactly as he is."

Rhea tried and failed to pull her arm out of Willem's grasp as she spoke. "I knew why Roarke was coming here, and I wanted to tell him that I found what he was looking for."

Roarke spun around in his seat. "Really?"

"Yes." she shrugged her shoulders. "Ian did."

"Now, see there." David folded his arms. "As I said when you first got here, I had nothing to do with anything that went missing at your home."

Rhea had been wracking her brains trying to figure out

how to get the gun out of Willem's hand, but the martial arts that she had at her disposal couldn't help her in her present situation.

"Fine," Roarke muttered. "Considering everything, I think you can understand why I would think you had." He jerked his thumb at Willem. "This wee shit was near my home."

"I don't know where my son is at every minute of the day."

"If it's anyone's business," Willem piped up from behind them. "I was out for a drive and thought I'd check on our piece of land."

Roarke spun around again and pointed his finger at Willem. "My arse. You were on my property! You stay the hell away from my place."

"Temper, Roarke." David laughed coldly. "You and your wee friend are trespassing here. Something bad happens, and you always think it's me behind it."

"It's a coincidence that you're in the area and the castle we're fighting over almost burns down? Then my collection goes missing, including the sword that you covet?" Roarke ran his hands along the top of his head. "God, Davey! When will this be over between us? What did I do to you, other than stop working for you? I never sold you out. I never told anyone anything."

"You never wondered why you started working for me in the first place."

Roarke leaned forward to look David in the eye. "I never put much thought into it."

"No, nor would you," he leered. "Roarke, you should get on your hands and knees thanking God each day for being attractive, because you've never been that bright."

"Davey, why do you insist on tormenting me? You have money, power, and prestige. Everything you ever wanted. What else do you need?"

David snarled, "What do I need? How about some common bloody courtesy?"

Roarke shrugged his shoulders, a look of confusion, marring his handsome features.

David chuckled. "It's time I told you a wee story."

Chapter Twenty-one: Truth

Every morning should be approached with an air of anticipation and trepidation, as it is often the most mundane mornings that turn into monumental days, ending with a sleep that changes us forever.

"What story of yours could I possibly be interested in?" Roarke snarled.

David settled back in his chair again. "Do you remember that part of the park that was wooded? Where people would go to get high? Now it's where they start the park run on Saturdays."

"Yeah, I remember. My mother didn't want me going there."

"You went anyway."

"I used to cut through on my way to school some mornings," admitted Roarke. "Shitheads like you were still asleep."

"Mind your manners, Hollywood," snarled Willem.

"Shut *ye geggie, Bampot,*" Roarke barked from over his shoulder.

"One morning, I was in around that area of the park," David interjected. "It was early, and my father had been drinking the night before. I wanted to be out of the house before he woke up with a hangover. Mother was gone, so I didn't have to stay. I went behind a storage shed to take a piss, and as I rounded the corner, I saw something that made my blood run cold." His eyes took on a strange, haunted expression, "There was a man bent over a small unconscious child, trying to stuff the kid into a large duffle bag. When he saw me, he sprang to his feet, knowing I'd seen what he was doing."

"For a few seconds, we just stared at each other until vile images started filling my head of what that animal probably had in mind for that kid. I knew from experience how hard it is for a child to fight off a grown man."

"I flew at him, beat him to the ground, and kicked him bloody. He just curled up in a ball, begging me to stop in his little whimpering voice. That pissed me off even more. How many kids had he hurt who had curled up in a wee ball and begged him to stop? Eventually, he stopped begging. Stopped crying. I stopped and looked down at my hands. I didn't even remember taking the knife out."

Roarke took in a ragged breath.

"I checked the kid. He was alive and breathing, a thin stream of blood next to his ear. Then, I recognized him. He lived a few doors down from my mate, Colin."

David glanced up at Roarke, who sat transfixed by his tale.

"The kid wouldn't wake up, and I couldn't be seen with an unconscious kid, but I couldn't leave him where he was. I certainly couldn't go to the polis. I had a rap sheet a mile long, and I knew even if I explained, no one would believe me."

"I threw the kid over my shoulder and made my way to Colin's back garden through the back alleys. Once at Colin's place, I counted the doors until I guessed which one was the mother's. I knocked at the window, and seeing her boy, she flung open the door, grabbed him, and brought him over to the couch. She was leaving to take him to hospital, and I quickly told her what had happened, and she understood why I couldn't go to the police."

"Later, she came to the house, and when my mother went to make tea, she told me her son would be fine and didn't remember anything. I'll never forget how she grabbed me, nearly squeezing the life from me. When she let me go, we were both crying."

He paused for a moment, lost in the emotions of his memory. "On that day, your mother and I agreed to keep our secret from everyone, including you. I'd saved her son's life, and she protected mine with her silence. I suspect Martin knows everything, but he's kept silent, too."

Roarke spoke, "I don't remember any of that."

"No, nor would you." David looked at his hands with Roarke staring at him in stunned silence.

"I was never the same. I'd killed a man but never felt an ounce of regret." David leaned back in his chair. "After that day, my eyes found you everywhere. You made me feel proud. Proud that I had done something good for once."

"Something good?" Roarke questioned, "You killed a man."

David thumped his fist on the top of his desk. "I didn't kill a man. I killed a pig. You, of all people, should be grateful that I did."

"Self-righteous prick," mumbled Willem from behind them.

David spoke before Roarke could respond to Willem. "I watched your family struggle. My father had died, good riddance, and I could take care of my mother. Regardless of me selling drugs, your mother always treated me as if I deserved respect. She always invited my mother round for tea when the other ladies in the neighborhood treated her as if she were the drug seller.

"I started giving you wee jobs, running errands where you could make a bit of money. I got you a small job delivering groceries as well. That way, when you brought home money, your mother wouldn't suspect it was because of me. She certainly didn't want you working for me."

"How could she not have known?"

"Then you spit in my face the first chance you got."

"The hell are you talking about?" Roarke asked angrily. "I

left your side after a man died, and because of you, I had a hand in it."

"Not the first crooked politician to die." David leaned forward again. "You weren't so bloody noble about selling drugs, were you?"

"I was young, Davey," Roarke shot back. "I couldn't see the consequences."

"Bullocks!" Davey spat. "You loved it all until that politician died, and when the going got rough, you took off. It still weighs on your consciousness, I see."

"Nothing weighs on yours." Roarke pulled at his hair in frustration. "How is it that you could save one child's life and yet kill others with the drugs you sold them?"

"If someone is old enough to buy drugs, they take responsibility for their actions. Life gives us choices."

"That's ridiculous reasoning." Roarke laid both of his hands on the desk in front of him. "If there were no drugs to buy, kids wouldn't try them and get hooked."

"People make choices." David rose to his feet. "Just like Isabel did."

Roarke's lip curled as he spoke, "Isabel should've left here. Should've gone home."

"You were an asshole to her."

"What about the baby? What about Willem, Isabel's son?"

"He's your son!"

"How do I know that?" David whispered.

"Wh-what?" Roarke stammered.

"Wh-what?" Willem stammered after him mockingly. "Go ahead. Pretend like you didn't throw her and me away."

David's head flicked over to gawk at Willem. "Willem! How do you know any of this?"

"A few years ago, I heard you and Mother talking when you thought I was away. You were discussing my mother, Isabel, and how Roarke could be my father."

"Why didn't you ever let on you knew anything?"

"Why the hell would I want anything to do with this idiot? You'd said he threw my mother away after he knew she was pregnant. I made it my mission to torment this asshole."

"Wait a minute." Roarke held up his hand. "You two idiots think I'm his father?"

"She was also with you when she got pregnant," David snarled. "I tried to believe he was mine. I could never get a paternity test because I wanted him, and I feared a test would show he was yours. Can't say he doesn't look like your lot."

"Davey." Roarke's voice took on a soft edge. "I'm infertile. I was sick as a kid, and it caused infertility. That's how I knew the baby wasn't mine. I left Isabel because I knew the baby was yours. I knew of your affair."

"Really?" A look of joy and relief fell over David's handsome features.

"Really."

David's shoulders slumped. "I had a shitty father. You did, too. I just wanted to prove history doesn't need to repeat itself. Whether he was mine or not, I would give the baby the love and support I never had. I began to detest you because I thought you had thrown them out."

"In addition to our past, you also hated me because you thought Willem might be mine and because I'd turned Isabel out for being pregnant?"

"Aye." David looked over at his son.

"No, Davey. It was you she had wanted all along."

David dropped down in his chair, his hands over his face until he started laughing and everyone else just looked at each other in confusion. "Ah!" David took his hands away and shook his head, grinning. "Thank God! It is such a relief to get clarity on that. Son," David looked at Willem. "Now we know the truth."

"Good to know, Da." Willem grinned. "I was a bit scared

that not being my biological father might be why you haven't changed your will to give me my share."

"Why are you so fixated on that? All your life, I've treated you like a king, all the while knowing you might not be mine."

"I know you're sick, Da." Willem's face took on an even harder look. "Without the changes to the will, Mother could do anything with the fortune. You've been grooming me all my life, and I deserve more than my sisters."

"This is all about money?"

"Aye, I want what's mine."

"Now, Willem, if anything happens to me, you know your mother will be fair. She may not be your biological mother, but she always loved and took care of you."

"I don't want her to be fair." Willem's voice was louder. "The kids don't know anything! I want to be in charge of my future. You're sick anyway. Just split everything between Mother and me before it's too late. I'll take over. I'll take care of the girls, but as you always say, there can't be too many chefs in the kitchen."

"This is all about your greed." David snarled at his son.

"I learned from the best."

"You're only seventeen and haven't even begun your studies. I've spoiled you."

"No, Da. You taught me to go after what I want and never to settle." Willem pulled Rhea a little closer to him. "Now both of you are here, we can discuss everything I want."

Willem just grinned down at Rhea before looking at Roarke. "The family is going to be spending more time in Romania, and I've no interest in that, so I'm going to set myself up in the city. With the money Da is going to give me, and the money you're going to give me."

"Why the hell would I give you any money?"

"I know Da's secrets, and why he's been getting money

from you for years, about the politician. You're now going to start giving that money to me. I'll keep your secret safe, and you can have your lady back."

"I'm warning you for the last time to take that gun off her!" Roarke turned back to David. "Would you do something about this?"

"He can't do anything." Willem stood, pulling Rhea up with him. "I decide what happens in this room right now. Quite simple, really. Roarke agrees to give me money, Da, you will make arrangements in the will, and I'll keep both your secrets, and for extra incentive, I've got the sword."

David looked at him and jutted his chin at Rhea. "She said Ian has the artifacts Roarke thought were stolen."

"I don't know about the other artifacts. I left them." Willem sneered. "But I took the sword."

Roarke snarled at the young man. "You broke into my home today. I knew it! Give me what's mine, or I'll tear this place apart!"

"It's not here." Willem's hard, handsome face split with a grin. "I couldn't risk anyone seeing me with it on the security cameras, so I took it somewhere no one'd ever look."

"Willem, you know how important that sword is."

"Aye!" Willem yelled. "Which is why I'm keeping it until the will gets changed!"

David's eyes had narrowed. "Don't do anything stupid, Son."

Willem put his arm around Rhea and smiled at him. "Father, I've no interest in going to Romania, and it's about time you start letting me in on the family business. I'm going to hang onto the sword until you turn over some of the assets to me."

"I've told you before, you haven't finished school, and you don't have the knowledge to get involved. You're too young."

"Maybe the girl and I'll go for a drive while you two make

some decisions on how to get what I want."

"Don't touch her!" Roarke shifted his weight to stand but sat back down when Willem jabbed to gun into Rhea's ribs, causing her to wince in pain. "If you hurt her, you son of a bitch . . ."

"Temper, temper, Roarke." Willem angled his body toward Rhea. "We wouldn't want my finger to slip, would we?"

"You little . . ." Roarke started, but Willem spun Rhea around and pushed her ahead of him toward the open door, the gun at her back. "Let's take a wee drive."

There was a heavy thud in the hallway, and both Rhea and Willem started. Willem pulled Rhea toward him, his arm around her waist, pinning her left arm. He angled his body to look in the direction of the noise, his gun hand distractedly pointed to the ceiling.

Rhea swung up with her right hand and delivered a solid hammer punch to his nose in one swift movement. When he yelped and let go of her, she turned and brought her knee up into his crotch as hard as she could. Willem crumpled immediately, dropping the gun to bring his hands to his groin. When he fell to his knees, Rhea delivered a low roundhouse kick to the side of his head, laying him on the floor with a yell.

The forms of three men now crowded the doorframe. Doug stood to the right, holding a two-by-four. Mike and Ken stood on either side of him. Ken pointed at Roarke's gaping mouth and grinned. "Eh, Roarke. You might want to close that before someone puts something in it."

"Who the hell are you?" yelled David as he bent over his son, writhing on the floor in agony.

Roarke had run over to the gun, put on the safety, and tucked it into the back of his jeans before grabbing Rhea in a suffocating hug. "Are you all right?" he murmured into her hair.

"Are you kidding?" She pulled away to grin up at him. "That felt great! And my old Kung Fu instructor said I would never be good at self-defence!"

"You could've been hurt." Roarke cradled her face in his hands.

"No way I was getting in the car with him—Self-defence rule number one. Never let them take you to a second location. Never. It'll be isolated, and you'll be the focus of the crime. I waited until the gun was pointed away from me and took my chance."

"Who the hell are you?" David repeated to the three men standing in the doorway, who were trying to figure out the scene in front of them.

"David," Roarke said, recovering from his shock. "These men are friends of mine." David gripped his son's chin, looking at his bloody nose as he continued to squirm in pain, "How did you get in here?"

Doug gestured to Rhea. "Ken followed her and came back to tell us that he saw someone grab her and there was no guard at the station."

Ken continued. "Then I tried the gate, and it opened without the code."

"Why would there be no guard at the gate?" David's elegant brow furrowed, and he turned his head to look down at Willem. "What were you up to today?"

Roarke stepped forward. "Whatever it was, it wasn't anything good."

"Aye." David stood and stared down at his son. "My son and I have to have a long chat. I'm not happy with men who threaten women. I can't believe you did that."

"I wouldn't really have hurt her." His angry voice was muffled by the shirtsleeve he held at his nose.

"Wouldn't do you any good to try." Roarke grinned at Willem and then Rhea. "She kicked your ass." He raised his hand to Rhea, and she gave it a high five.

David put his hands in his pocket and looked at Rhea. "Will you be going to the police?"

"I don't think I can, considering I was the one trespassing here. Willem will just say he took the gun out in self-defense, not knowing why I was here."

"Thank you." David stepped toward her. "This whole thing has been such a mess, but rest assured he will not go unpunished."

"Check the gun, Da," Willem sneered. "It's not even loaded."

"Shut your hole before I really get angry."

"You raised the little shite," Roarke mumbled. "I can't believe you'd let him hold a gun to her."

"Listen." David began to roll up the sleeves of his shirt. "I didn't know why you were here or why she was here. I thought my son was looking out for my best interest."

"He's only concerned with himself."

Rhea ran into Mike's arms and hugged him tightly. "Thank you for distracting him with that noise in the hallway. It was the moment I needed."

"Lass." Mike blushed. "To be honest, it was an accident. Doug tripped on the rug and hit the table to stop from stumbling."

Roarke grinned as Rhea went back over to stand beside him, grabbing his hand. "For once, I'm glad he has two left feet."

Willem righted himself and pressed his back against the door. "That bitch broke my nose!"

Roarke took an angry step toward him. David got to Willem first and delivered a sound whack to the side of his head, sending him back to the floor with a howl of pain. "Call her a bitch one more time, and you'll spend the next two weeks in hospital."

Turning, he stepped over to Rhea and stood before her. "I'm so unbelievably sorry all of this happened to you. I assure you I'll deal with my son appropriately, as it seems we all misjudged each other today. I never raised him to be this way. I wish there were a way I could make it up to you."

Rhea looked at Roarke and then back at David. "I think you and Roarke need to start making things up to each other."

David gazed at her face curiously, and his eyebrows pulled together slightly. "I don't know what it is, but you remind me of someone I used to know. I just can't place who."

Rhea smiled and half-whispered, "Maybe it'll come to you in a dream."

David sighed. "Roarke, maybe you and I can make a new arrangement. To be honest, I respect what you're trying to do with those kids and the castle. How about I invest in your castle?"

"My castle?"

"His castle?" Willem sat up, wincing as he did.

"Aye. I've been dabbling in currency trading. I made a huge chunk, and I've been looking for a good investment. I'd give you most of the money you need for the castle and be a partner. It'd be something my family could have their name on and be proud of. Plus, a brilliant philanthropist teaming up with a movie star to buy an ancient castle would send social media into an uproar."

Rhea chimed in, grinning. "That would be more publicity for the movie and the book."

Willem glared at his father. "Why would you do that?"

David slicked back his black hair with both hands. "Son, we've hated him for no reason all these years. He did nothing, and I'm just so happy now to know you're mine after years of wondering otherwise. Despite your actions today, which you will pay for, but you're still my son."

"I hate the prick."

"Regardless, we're going to do the right thing by him."

"You're serious?" Roarke beamed from David to Rhea, who beamed up at him.

"Just one thing." David smiled at him. "I still want the sword."

"Why the hell is that sword so important to you?"

"Neither one of you is getting that sword." Willem snorted, and David clipped his son on the back of his head, making him wince.

"Do whatever you want. You won't find that sword," Willem muttered.

"I know this kid." David scratched his head. "He won't tell me where it is any time soon. He stole it today and was in your area, so it's still around there."

"I'll look for it as I'm hunting another treasure anyway, and you try and get him to tell you where he put it." Roarke sighed. "But Davey, do one thing for me." Roarke gestured to the hallway, "Will you tell me about the sword?"

The two men walked into the hallway, and Doug, Ken, and Mike formed a wall around Willem. When he opened his mouth to speak, Ken's upraised fist silenced him.

When Roarke and David returned a few minutes later, Roarke smiled down at Rhea as he approached her.

"Satisfied?" David asked, and when Roarke nodded his head, he continued, "Just go and see if you can find the sword. I'll help you with the castle and invest in it, but you'll have full control."

"It's a deal."

"Roarke," Rhea piped up. "I think I might know where Willem hid it."

"Really?"

"I think I have a good idea."

"Good luck with that," sneered Willem from the floor.

"You'll tell me where it is," David snarled.

"You're the last person I'll tell."

Roarke took a step toward the door. "Maybe we should clear out. You two gentlemen have to talk and maybe head to the hospital."

"Don't worry, Roarke," Willem remarked. "You haven't seen the last of me. You two might have made your peace, but I'll have no part in it."

Roarke stepped over to the young man. "You stay away from us."

David stepped in front of Willem, "Don't worry. I'll keep him clear."

The men and Rhea stepped out into the hallway, and Roarke followed them before looking back. "You're sick, David?"

Putting his hands on his hips, he sucked in his bottom lip and looked down at the floor. "Aye, but the doctors can't tell me too much."

"Is there . . ."

"No." David put his hand up and smiled. "I'll be fine, but I'm looking at life a tad different these days. Take advantage of the time you're given."

"Aye, I will." Roarke watched Rhea hugging each of his friends before looking back at the man who had saved his life. "Thank you, David."

For an instant, pride and sadness were in the each's eyes before David broke the gaze to look at his son. "Get outta here so I can try and talk some sense into this stubborn, spoiled boy."

"Good luck with that." Turning, Roarke walked into the hallway and joined his friends.

No one spoke until they got into the jeep outside the gates, and they all watched as a black car with tinted windows passed them and drove up the long driveway.

Rhea sighed and squeezed the bridge of her nose. "I don't know about you guys, but I'm gonna go get drunk."

After Ken called Ian and confirmed he hadn't seen the sword, Rhea and Roarke said their goodbyes to their friends and headed for White Heather.

Once on the road, they started discussing how David would be backing the castle project, and Roarke commented, "Well, if one film will be my swansong, they might drop more money —"

Rhea interrupted. "Did David tell you why he wanted the sword?"

Roarke nodded slowly, his knuckles white as he gripped the steering wheel. "You know how the sword has such a strange curve?"

"Yes. You said it was the style for the period."

"I got it from an old Italian man who had returned from his family's estate in Naples. They had to sell their ancient estate and many of their family heirlooms. He returned with a few relics in storage that he initially hadn't wanted to part with. In the end, being an old bachelor, he decided to put them up for auction, as he was moving into an old person's home."

"Retirement village, Roarke."

"Whatever." He grinned. "Do you know who Vlad Tepes is?"

"You know I do." Rhea rolled her eyes at him. "Bram Stoker's inspiration for Dracula. Vlad Tepes, the Prince of Wallachia, the Impaler."

"Some historians believe Vlad was buried in a monastery in Romania. Others say he'd been captured and later ransomed by his daughter, Maria, who had married a nobleman in Italy, and Vlad had died there."

Rhea's head spun toward him. "What?"

"The sword I have is a *kilij*, the preferred close-range weapon of Vlad Tepes."

Her jaw dropped in shock. "Are you trying to tell me that's his sword?"

"David needs to conduct several tests on it, but . . ."

"There's a chance . . ."

" . . . that it may be a sword that might have once been that of Vlad the Impaler."

"Oh-my-God."

"Historically speaking, it's insanely valuable. For a proud Romanian, it's priceless."

"You're just going to hand it over to him?"

"Small price to pay for the castle. Besides, I know him. He'd never sell it but would make it accessible for everyone. A Romania, a Wallachian, should have it."

Rhea rested her head on the back of the seat. "Unbelievable."

"His father, Petran, had been estranged from his family because, despite being the eldest, his mother decided the family home and fortune would be going to his younger brother when she died. Petran hadn't shown that he was worthy. He left Romania for spite. He used to like to dig at David that he was only half Romanian anyway."

"He sounds positively hateful."

"He was, but since his brother died and David has the estate, he has proven himself worthy of carrying the family into the future. Too bad David's wee shit of a son seems to be more like his grandfather. Unfortunately, sometimes history does repeat itself."

"Roarke," Rhea spoke with hesitation. "I don't really know where the sword is. I just said that so maybe Willem would slip up and give us a clue."

Roarke chuckled. "I figured as much."

They stopped talking for a little while before Rhea spoke again. "Soon it'll be Mabon. I know that today's been crazy, so I'll understand if you don't want to go to the ritual. Seems kind of silly now."

"No." He furrowed his brow as if seeing something on the road. "If anything, today just reaffirms why we should do it." Reaching over, he squeezed her hand. "Everything's changed since you've been here in a thousand different ways. It's like my life was a jigsaw puzzle, all deconstructed. Every day with you, it feels like more pieces come into place."

"I don't think I had much to do with it. Maybe it all would have happened whether I was here or not. Coincidence."

"You don't believe in coincidence." He smiled at her. "As Tennyson wrote, "I am a part of all that I have met." In one afternoon, I've made peace with David and got the castle. You've everything to do with it."

Rhea smiled up into his face. "Okay then, let's put this ghost of ours to rest."

The following day, Rhea's eyelids fluttered open a golden shaft of early morning sunlight spilling into the room between the crack in the curtains. Still, it only lasted a moment as a shadow crept across the pillow when a cloud covered the sun.

Turning her head, she looked at the strong, handsome man next to her smiling in his sleep. The groove of the dimple in his cheek softened his angular bone structure. His countenance carried the same warmth as the fleeting ray of sunlight. Yesterday had been monumental, as he had made peace with his demons and had some peace of mind. In the seventeen days that had passed since she had arrived, she had faced many of her demons as well.

As she stared at the wall, faces from her life seemed to drift beneath the silhouetted shadows of the leaves that caressed the smooth stone like long, slender fingers. Rhea saw Liam's grinning freckled face, cheeks stuffed with take-out poutine, and Patrice's elated expression during a guitar solo. She would go ahead with Patrice's adoption of Liam.

The astonishing depth of her love for Roarke had given her a new understanding of her parents, and while discussing the book the night before, she knew she was on her way to being the writer she had always wanted to become.

Rhea realized her puzzle pieces were coming together also, like Roarke's. Their sacred gift to each other. She also knew one other thing. Gazing at the strip of tartan around her wrist and listening to the ticking of the old alarm clock sitting on his nightstand, she choked back her sadness at the reminder of the lingering impossibility of a future with Roarke.

Wanting to stay close to home and keeping her mind open for messages she didn't believe she would get from Islean, Roarke and Rhea saw to the farm and visited Ian. That night, Roarke found Rhea staring up at the bothy on the hill. "What're you looking at?"

"Thinking of my mother." She sighed. "One night, we were at our cabin, and I was looking at a full moon over the hills. It was so quiet, and the moon made me feel so alone but in a good way. Like it was all mine and I was the only person in the whole world. The following day, I went back to the beach very early, and my mother was sitting in the same spot, watching the sun come up over the same hills. I sat next to her, and she said, "Baby, the afterlife might consist of a lot more than just Heaven and Hell." She pointed to the dark hills turning purple and the pink and orange sky reflecting on the still pond below them, "Could anything in Heaven be as beautiful as that?"

"She said nothing more?" Roarke put his arms around her and kissed the top of her head.

Rhea shook her head. "She did that all the time. She would just say something glib and go on about her day."

"Maybe to give you something to think about but leaving you to develop your own ideas."

"I just remembered something else. One of the first nights I was here, I woke up and stood here looking up at the hill. I was thinking of that same memory, and I saw a light in the bothy. It was just for a second, but I saw it."

Nodding, Roarke seemed deep in thought. "Why would someone come in the middle of the night to a condemned building? Especially when there are several well-known bothies in the area which are in much better shape."

"Exactly. I've a strange feeling about it."

"Oh shit! The bothy is on David's plot of land, and David's household would have the keys to it." Roarke got to his feet. "Fancy going for a wee walk on this fine evening?"

CHAPTER TWENTY-TWO: SACRED SYMBOL

When nature calls your name, you have no choice but answer.

Armed with flashlights and the key and in a light sprinkling of rain, Roarke and Rhea walked up the small, worn path toward the bothy. Roarke led the way. "Nobody's torn this place down yet, and I have no idea of David's plans, but it's a part of the landscape."

The single-story thatched-roof cottage sat lonely and eerie in the little patch of woods, and there were spaces between the horizontal slabs of wood boarding the windows. If there had been a light inside, as on the night she had seen it, it could be visible from White Heather.

Roarke pushed down the hood of his dark raincoat and inspected the slats while Rhea shone a light inside the window. "Doesn't look like the wood has been moved or repositioned at all."

A low, ominous rumbling of thunder sounded in the distance, and a rustle of movement from the woods made Roarke jump and spin around, only to see a small animal scurry off.

"Damn mouse," Roarke muttered as he turned back at a grinning Rhea. "Shut it."

"It frightened me, too." She chuckled. "I'm sorry."

"Aye. You look like a sympathy card."

Roarke picked up the padlock on the iron hinge and inserted the key. It turned with a grinding sound, and he pushed open the door. Rhea moved around him as he shone his light back and forth around the small cottage.

All was silent, except for a steady drip as rain came in through a hole in the ceiling, creating a small pool of water on the floor. There was nothing inside except the brick fireplace against the wall.

"Look!" Rhea shouted as she shone her flashlight on the dusty, dirty floor. A small path led from the fireplace to the door as if someone had been walking there.

"Aye. There even seems to be a few footprints over there." Roarke took a few hesitant steps on the left of the path, as Rhea did the same on the right.

A deep quiet settled over the small dwelling as if all sounds from outside had stilled.

Rhea knelt in front of the fireplace and looked around. There was something shiny beneath a floorboard, and when she touched the piece of wood, it moved. "This floorboard is loose."

Roarke seemed to be sniffing the air. "What's that stench? Like something foul and rotting, like the smell I get back at the house. I always thought it was the sewer or some patch of earth with sulfur releases, but maybe it comes from here."

She gave him a strange look. "What are you talking about? I was going to ask you what the lovely smell is. I've smelt it at your house too. It's flowery but almost smells of pastry and fruit. Heliotrope."

"Are you daft? I almost can't stand to stay here."

"Regardless of what you smell or don't smell, there's a loose floorboard here, and I'm pulling it up.

"Wait!" He knelt beside her, "Let me do it. Any wild animal might be under there."

"Big talk from a man scared of a field mouse."

Roarke glared at her and made to speak, but she shushed him as her eyes slid to a dark corner a few feet away. There was a form there, greyish and small, a little lighter than the coal-blackness around them. As she watched, it vibrated for a second and then sank into the floor.

In the dark cabin, Roarke bent toward the loose floorboard, and as his fingers touched it, what felt like a small, cold hand clutched his wrist, and the putrid, acrid smell returned as if something rotten was in front of him.

Falling backward, he scurried on his backside until he reached the wall. He couldn't breathe the air — it smelled thick and polluted. He watched Rhea kneel in the same spot he had just bolted from, unfazed by the fact that he had left in haste.

"Get away from there! Something grabbed my hand!"

"Roarke, be quiet." Her eyes closed, "She smells amazing."

Her comment shocked Roarke. "She? Who are you talking about?"

Rhea smiled as a firm yet gentle pressure led her hand to the loose floorboard. She pulled it up, put her hand into the small opening, and touched something covered in plastic. Pulling up her hand, she gapped at a large stack of one-hundred-pound banknotes in a clear, plastic bag. She was so dumbstruck she didn't even hear the thud behind her as Roarke fell to the floor.

A few moments later, Roarke felt feathery touches on his cheek and nose. Opening his eyes, he inhaled as he watched the chubby behind of a small brown mouse creep along the wall next to him. The mouse turned to look at him and then continued on his path. Drained of energy, too exhausted even to call to Rhea, it was all he could do to keep his eyes open and watch her pull things from under the floorboard near the fireplace.

After a few minutes, she glanced over at him and then came hurrying over to him in shock. "Roarke, what happened?" Kissing his forehead, she felt it with the palm of her hand.

Roarke tried to rise from the floor, only to slump back down with another small thud. "Weak," was all he managed to say.

"Roarke, I've found thousands of pounds." She shook his shoulder lightly. "It must belong to Willem."

Nodding, Roarke peeked over Rhea's shoulder, where the tiny mouse stood on its hind legs sniffing where the inside row of horizontal boards was missing.

Rhea sat down next to Roarke and ran her hands along the top of her head before looking at him apologetically. "The sword isn't there. I scanned under the floor with the light, at least what I could access."

Roarke still watched the mouse, the beam from his flashlight almost directly on it. The critter leaped into the air and disappeared into the hole created by the walls beneath the window. A second later, it leaped out again and sat on its haunches. Its beady, black eyes stared at Roarke, who tapped Rhea on the knee. Then, overcome by some a sixth sense, Roarke mustered enough energy to point to it.

"Look there."

Standing, she edged over to where it sat, and the little creature bolted for the open door.

Looking down into the hole, Rhea inhaled sharply as she looked back at Roarke before reaching into the gap between the boards. When she raised her hand, she gripped the hilt of the elegant, elaborate, missing sword.

Later, at White Heather, Rhea was working on her notes

when Roarke staggered into the kitchen. She jumped up to help him to a chair. "Honey, you shouldn't be out of bed. It's only three o'clock, and you're still weak."

"I'm powerfully thirsty. Could you get me some water?"

After she brought him a glass of water, they started discussing events of the night before.

"I think she drained your energy and used it to manifest."

"She?"

"Yeah." Rhea closed her laptop, pushing it aside. "Spirits need energy to manifest, and I think she used yours."

"Great." He drained his glass and held it up for Rhea to refill. "Maybe I've just been tired, and it's catching up with me."

"Maybe, maybe not. I've been researching, and I'm quite certain our ghost drained you. It's called energy shifting. The Conservation of Energy. Like how some people drain you of energy and others make you feel energized. She wanted to get our attention."

Roarke sighed and sat back in his chair. "Whatever. I'm too tired to care."

Rhea glanced at the cash in front of them and grinned. "Want to know how much there is?"

"Aye." He smiled back.

Rhea took a breath before she answered. "There are forty thousand pounds here."

Roarke's tired smile turned into a grin. "Excellent."

"Am I right to assume this is probably Willem's money?"

"I'd say you're correct."

"Criminals need to launder their money so that people don't ask questions, right?"

"Aye." Roarke stifled a yawn. "It takes time to launder money. I remember David talking about it. If you own a restaurant and sell ten lasagnas, you report that you sold twenty-five. In the meantime, you need to stash the money. It would make sense that Willem would hide his extra money so he wouldn't need to answer David's questions."

"What're we going to do with it?"

"Keep it." Roarke stifled another yawn. "Put it back into the community."

Reaching out, he pulled the sword toward him. "I can't believe we found it."

Rhea placed a hand on the sword. "Look at it tomorrow. We need to get to bed."

Roarke reached out for her. "When I woke and you weren't beside me, I didn't like it. I missed you."

She rose up on her tiptoes and kissed him. "I'll miss you, too."

As they looked into each other's eyes, a sadness passed between them, a feeling as deep and clear as the sun's rays lighting up the bottom of a stream.

In bed, the nearly full moon flooded the bedroom with soft light, and Roarke ran a finger down Rhea's profile. "I love your nose. Your entire face. If we had time, I would tell you every tiny detail about your face that I love, like that slightly crooked tooth." He made to touch it, and she nipped at him playfully.

Nuzzling her neck with his nose, he crept his hand around her belly to rub the curve of her hip. "There's no one in the entire world like you, ghost."

He trailed his hand higher to run his thumb across the sensitive tip of her breast, causing it to pucker, as he followed his caress by lightly blowing on it. "What were the girls talking about when we were at the castle? What special magic did they tell you to invoke?"

"Nothing too important."

Continuing to breathe on her breasts as he spoke. "What was it about?"

Rhea sighed. "It's just a type of energy that gets created when two partners are intimate. That energy can be projected into other things, willed into a specific outcome."

He kissed the engorged peak of her breast, licking it to make it shimmery in the pale moonlight, causing her to inhale sharply. Heat spread from his lips, under her skin, and down to the meeting of her thighs.

"Maybe we should try it, if it helps us get messages from Islean."

Rhea smiled at him, her eyes half-closed. "We already did."

Taking the glass of water on the night table, he took a sip and then dipped a finger into the water. Letting droplets fall onto her flesh and into her belly button, he bent his head and sucked the water out. His hand slid down her belly and stopped at the junction of her thighs.

Roarke smiled down at her as he brushed his hand around the curve of her inner thigh, then brought his index finger up and between her folds and further into her receptive body.

His voice dropped to a husky whisper. "I've always thought the female body itself is a magical place."

"That's just it. It is," Rhea choked out the words as Roarke's finger slid out and then back in before stopping altogether, leaving her muscles throbbing around his finger.

Strange orbs of light flittered across the ceiling as he slid another finger into Rhea's body. His thumb stroked the center of her most sensitive flesh, plunging her into a frenzy as simultaneous explosions lit up the backs of her closed eyelids.

Outside, the air was suddenly filled with the screams of foxes in the distance as females asserted their territory. Roarke shivered, but Rhea smiled, closing her eyes and panting slightly, when he pressed his palm against her sensitive flesh as she moved her hips. When her body exploded from the inside out, she clawed at the rumpled sheets.

Roarke lowered himself to kiss her neck, and over his

shoulder, Rhea watched orbs of light shoot across the ceiling and out the window. Then, as the cries of the foxes stilled, she smiled to herself and curled her arm around her lover's neck.

September twenty-first, Mabon

Mabon arrived damp and dreary, and once again, Rhea found herself awake in bed, staring down into Roarke's face trying to memorize every line, every detail. Finally, Roarke opened his eyes and smiled sadly at her, and she knew they were thinking the same thing. In four days, she'd be leaving.

Roarke still seemed a little weak, and Rhea was tired. They'd been having moments of realization of what their lives were going to be like without each other, making them both unbelievably melancholy.

Luckily, many chores needed to be done, and Rhea had to write. They worked and tried to clear their minds. By dinner, a gulf had grown between them. Though they were still physically together, each had begun shutting down and putting up the walls they both had always used to protect their hearts.

Sitting at the island, Roarke munched on berries and made plans for the castle, and Rhea sipped tea and worked on the book. The silence strained and stretched in the small cottage. Every time someone sniffed or cleared their throats, the sound seemed to echo in every room, a reminder of the emptiness growing inside each of them.

Finally, Rhea had enough. "This house is too quiet."

"Aye." Roarke twirled the basil leaf he held between his fingers. "The quietest it's been in a long time."

"Honestly, I'm in physical pain today, and it's almost too much to bear."

As if he knew exactly how she felt, he came around to her side of the island, putting a hand around her waist, drawing her to him, and burying his other hand in her hair. "I feel the same."

Rhea smiled up at him. "I gathered as much. You didn't even have seconds of your macaroni and cheese."

Next to Rhea a brandy snifter housed the nails from the beach, the bridge outside the city, and the hole on Roarke's property. She tilted the glass to look at them. "Something Senga said the other day's been running through my mind."

"What's that."

"She said when you find things at your feet, they're gifts from a loved one who has passed, and since I've been here, I've found things at my feet."

"Those nails." Roarke jutted his chin at the glass.

"These nails," she agreed. "What if Islean is putting them in my path?"

"Moira said our ghost would find a way to communicate her wants to us."

"What's so important about these nails?"

"How on earth did she . . ."

Rhea put up her hand. "Do you really want to waste time thinking of *how* right now? We should be thinking *why*."

"If we talked to someone who knows about old things, they might be able to give us more information." Roarke walked over to the couch to pick up Rhea's sweater and hand it to her. "I know just who to ask. How would you like to grab a pint?"

A short ride later, Roarke and Rhea sat at the corner table of Miriam's pub. She brought over two pints of Guinness and sat them down. "You keep looking at me funny, McCallum. What's up?"

Roarke started laughing. "I was just wondering if Chris is around. We found something we'd like to ask him about."

A few minutes later, his red hair disheveled, Chris came bounding down the stairs to the pub and came to sit with them. "Hey, Roarke."

"Hi, Chris. This is my friend Rhea, and she found a few old nails. We were wondering if you could tell us anything about them."

"No problem." He grinned. "I hope I can."

Rhea produced the small container that held the nails and handed it to him. The young man took off the lid and placed the nails on it. He held one up and studied it. "It's from the eighteenth century. The cross-section is square. It's from a time when nails were all hand-made at a forge. From the nineteenth century, the cross-sections were rectangular, and modern nails are round."

Rhea picked one up and studied it herself.

Chris's sky-blue eyes glittered. "Without a vast supply of nails, the Industrial Revolution couldn't have taken place. Nails started being mass-produced in factories."

"I see. Is there anything special about them?"

"Not really. They're pretty typical to find when metal-detecting because they were used to connect wooden beams." Chris looked over at Roarke. "Did you find them on your land? Down by the river?"

"No, we didn't. Not anywhere near there."

Chris got up and walked into the museum, returned with several nails in his hand. "They're identical to some nails I found while detecting by the river on your land."

All three picked up the nails for comparison. "Yes, they are the same, but how much variety would there be with nails?"

"Not much. Other than that, I can't tell you much more."

Miriam came over and put her hand on her son's shoulder. "How's the tête-a-tête going?"

"Oh, grand." Roarke put down his glass. "We just wanted some info about these nails."

"Those are just like the ones from the pile of rocks at Roarke's."

"A pile of rocks?" Roarke asked.

"Aye, by the river."

"Oh." Roarke glanced at Rhea. "There are two piles of rocks on either side of the river where an old bridge used to stand."

"A bridge?" Rhea sat up straight and furrowed her brow.

"Aye, but that bridge was hundreds of years old, and it fell so long ago no one even remembers it standing."

"I've been dreaming about a bridge." Rhea put a hand to her head. "The night you found me at the Yew tree, I had a very vivid dream about a young man and woman walking on opposite sides of the river. They put their hands in the water, walked onto the bridge, and held hands."

Miriam smiled. "Some ancient marriages or betrothals were done in that manner. A lovely tradition."

"If that had been them . . ." Roarke started.

"Steaphan had been watching Islean, and he might have seen them do it," Rhea finished.

"He buried the dirk in a place he knew had special significance for the couple."

"He might have buried it at the bridge." Roarke jumped to his feet and leaned toward Rhea to whisper. "The nails were to lead us there."

"You're looking for a dirk?" Chris said as Rhea placed bills on the table.

"Yes." Sliding her wallet back into her small backpack, Rhea readied to leave, as she assumed they were about to go and poke around near the remains of the bridge. "It's very important to a friend of ours."

"It's valuable?" The young man chewed at the corner of his lip and rubbed his palms on his thighs.

Rhea placed a hand on Roarke's forearm, the change in Chris's behavior alerting something in her. "It's priceless to my friend."

Chris stood and started backing toward the staircase, his hands in front of him. "Listen, Roarke, don't be angry with me, okay? You always said I could keep anything I found."

"What are you talking about, Chris?"

"Wait here." He turned and sped up over the stairs.

Rhea turned to Miriam. "Do you know what that's about?"

The older woman shrugged. "He's sixteen. They're always lunatics at sixteen. Pick your battles and don't ask questions unless you're prepared for the answers."

"I'll keep that in mind when my son turns sixteen."

Chris came back down, placed an object wrapped in a tea towel on the table, and motioned for everyone to sit. "I wasn't going to sell it or anything. I just wanted to investigate it myself before handing it in. I know what I'm doing. I knew I wouldn't damage it."

"What is it?" Roarke asked as he tentatively reached for the tea towel.

"You'll see." Chris sighed as he thudded down in a chair. "To be honest, I'm a bit afraid of it. I've had bad dreams ever since I've found it."

"Aye," agreed his mother. "You were on the couch the other night and half-scared me to death when I went to the kitchen."

"You'd been on the couch, too, if you'd woke up with a spooky woman crouched on the foot of your bed."

Roarke and Rhea exchanged glances, and Roarke's hands shook as he unwrapped the object in the tea towel.

Miriam inhaled when she saw the small dirk. Set in metal, it had various designs running the length of the grip.

Roarke picked it up and studied it as Chris talked animatedly. "It was corroded when I found it, but I've been restoring it. I knew it was special. I just wanted to work on it myself. Thirteen inches, the blade is backed, and it is so well-preserved."

"It's beautiful." Roarke handed it over to Rhea. "I just wish we could be sure this is the one we're after."

Rhea looked at the hilt, and her gaze flew back to Roarke's face. "It is."

Roarke looked at the side of the handle which Rhea had turned toward him and squinted his eyes in confusion. Rhea pointed to something carved on the top of the hilt, a money sign with three lines. "The symbol. For the first three letters of Jesus's name. The symbol used by Thomas's family."

"Like on the headstones near the yew tree." Rhea ran a finger across the dull blade. "I guess she found a way to get it to us, after all."

Touching the hilt, Roarke smiled. "Now we just need to figure out exactly what she wants us to do."

Chapter Twenty-three: The Ceremony

He taught me to hope, but they ripped my future out of my hands. Dare I hope? If I lose my faith again, where is there left to go?

That evening, all participants met in the small carport near where Roarke and Rhea had parked the evening they had found the cairn. They carried a small sack with their memory jar, candles, and sheets of paper with their blessings. Roarke had the dirk tucked into his belt, and Rhea carried the brooch in her breast pocket.

The sky was dark and cloudy, and energy coursed in the cool autumn air, almost giving it a pulse. The north wind came galloping lustily down the hills and jostling the black robes that all the women, save Rhea, were wearing, pressing them against their bodies.

Without ceremony, Ellie, the leader, turned toward the bent trees extending out of the hill line on the horizon like three broken fingers. The small procession followed. Rhea saw the twins, but there were also about ten other women.

The wind howled around them, like a dog trying to get attention. They walked in silence. Flame-gold and fire-red leaves blew up and around their heads until they were safely within the shelter of the woods. By the time they approached the cairn, the playful wind was just a light breeze, ruffling their hair.

The procession stopped on the path a little away from the

cairn, and Ellie turned. "Roarke and Rhea, wait here until we've done our traditional ceremony, and then we'll ask you to join us."

The women slid eerily like bats into the woods. Roarke and Rhea sat with their backs against the trucks of ancient trees as chanting filled the midnight blue night air. Rhea whispered to Roarke how they were calling on the goddesses and powers of North, South, East, West, earth, wind, fire, water, the salt circle for protection, and the Mabon Incantation.

Eventually, a black form floated toward them and guided them to the cairn, where the gifts Roarke and Rhea had brought were in various places on the stones, and the four candles sat at each compass point. The women were evenly spaced with a small gap for Roarke and Rhea.

A roll of distant thunder accompanied a sense of foreboding filling the air. Rhea caught several of the women looking up at the sky, checking for changes in the weather. Then, when swirls of light fog billowed out from the forest and danced around them, Roarke grabbed at Rhea's hand.

Ellie again blessed the area as everyone moved toward the cairn and held hands. Once the space was blessed, she circled it three more times, giving an Incantation for Mabon and holding a black-handled *athame* above her head,

"The harvest is ending.
We have the earth's blessings, and we give thanks.
The grapes are harvested, and it is the time to make merry.
To Dionysus and Bacchus, we give thanks.
Day turns to night, and light becomes darkness,
Life turns to death, and we dance with the Dark Mother.
Hecate, Demeter, and Kali
Nemesis, Morrighan, and Tiamet,
You who embody the crone, bringers of destruction
We honor you.

We celebrate the balance of Mabon,
Equal hours of light and darkness,
We bring gifts and ask for blessings.
Blessed are we on this day."

The participants stood in silence for a few moments until Ellie spoke again, "Tonight, we have a special request for Islean, the guardian of these woods. Your descendent has come to speak with you, and those present beseech you to hear him."

Roarke stepped haltingly forward into the light of the small fire at the front of the cairn.

Shaking his head a little, he took the dirk out of his belt and held it in the air. "Islean, I ask you for forgiveness for our ancestors. We have the dirk and the brooch, and we will bury them here. Forgive us, and you will also be forgiven. There is no set punishment. We just pay the price. I know you've forgiven Thomas's family, and I ask you to do the same for ours. I'll be responsible for my actions, I swear it. I'll find balance, I swear it. As long as life and breath persist, there is hope."

The air seemed to grow denser and heavy with the scent of flowers, though Roarke wrinkled up his nose. The rumble of thunder sounded nearer, and the light fog swirled around their feet, giving Rhea the impression that those around her were floating.

Rhea suddenly was aware that the space Roarke had just vacated was no longer empty. Instead, a shadowy figure stood beside her, directly behind Roarke, saturating the air with her presence.

Roarke felt a prickly static moving up his arm and down his spine, even to his toes. There seemed to be an energy transfer and a rush of both heat and intense emotion ran through his body. Before he had the chance to do anything, he was swooning, and all before him grew hazy. He fell to his knees, and the dirk flew from his hand. A black shadow figure next to him leaned in toward his face. He opened his mouth just as he felt an intense force hit his body, and the air left his chest with a *doof.*

Roarke doubled in the middle and gripped his stomach. The shocked women looked on as, in the next second, his head then flew back, as if he had been stuck below the chin, and he fell backward onto the ground.

"Roarke!" Rhea stepped toward him.

"Rhea, no!" Senga held out her arm to her. "I think he's an inductor. His body's acting as a vessel, bringing energy forward."

Roarke rolled around on the rocky path around the cairn, holding his stomach and trying to catch his breath.

Rhea reached toward him, "Last night, we were in the bothy on the hill, and we felt her presence. She was trying to materialize, and Roarke became very weak. He even passed out."

A spot of light had appeared and hovered above Roarke, who stopped thrashing and took a deep breath. The light waxed, waned, and grew larger. One of the women pointed a shaky finger at the willowy shadow beside Rhea.

The light above Roarke grew brighter, but as he struggled, it fizzled out completely, disappearing in the thick night air.

An unearthly scream exploded through the night and surrounded them. It moved through the trees, rising higher until a loud crack of thunder silenced it.

The silence that followed was more terrifying than the scream. A silence full of malice that seemed to be breathing.

Roarke had regained the ability to speak and now stared at

the darkness beside Rhea, where the willowy shape had disappeared. "I don't think I'm forgiven."

"What does she want?" Agnes had backed up and leaned her hands against the small rock wall behind her. "Is this the wrong place?

Rhea turned to face the women gathered. "I think we should close the circle. There's only one other place I can think of where she might want her things buried. Roarke and I can take them there."

"Rhea, I'm not sure I can even walk." His head was back in his hands. "It's not as bad as last night, but it's still bad."

"Just rest a bit as I close the circle." Ellie released the powers and closed the circle. When finished, she knelt beside Roarke and placed both palms on either side of his head. Rhea assumed she was giving him an energy boost, and each woman came and put a hand on either Ellie or the women in front of them.

Roarke still sat on the ground, trying to gather his wits, and Ellie turned to Rhea. "I don't think it was Islean trying to materialize. I mean, I could see a shadow beside you. Do you think it could've been another spirit? I sensed male energy."

"So did I, but I thought it was coming from Roarke."

"No, there was someone else." Agnes stood beside Ellie. "Maybe Islean was trying to summon Thomas here, and it failed."

Senga came to stand with her sister. "If two spirits are trying to manifest, they will need a great deal of energy. I'm feeling quite weak myself. If I were a spirit, this would be the perfect place to gather a great deal of energy from willing participants. Maybe they needed our energy, but this isn't the place where their things should be buried."

"Aye. That makes sense."

Rhea rubbed the back of her hand across her eyes. "I know of only one other place to put these ghosts to rest. Provided I can get this big guy out of the woods."

A short time later, a red candle burned at the pink boulder as Roarke and Rhea stood like two sentinels. The brooch and dirk sat next to the candle. The wind had died down, and the threat of rain had passed, leaving the air clean and clear. Thin, wispy clouds ran across the face of the full moon.

Rhea hadn't said anything to Roarke, but she could feel the ghost as soon as they got out of the truck. She was aware of every sound and movement from nature, insects buzzing, rodents scurrying in the grass, leaves whispering. Everything was alive, and it was as if Rhea were feeling the night for the first time.

When Roarke's shovel made the first crack in the rich earth, a mist poured from the nearby forest. When Rhea inhaled sharply, Roarke looked up at her.

"Nothing." She smiled nervously.

"Nothing, my arse." He hit the earth with his shovel again. "I've had the willies since we got out of the truck."

Roarke's strong back made short work of the shoveling, and over his shoulders, Rhea watched. The fog seeped from the dark forest like long fingers reaching out to her. Roarke didn't even notice until it began swirling around him.

By the time they felt the hole was sufficient, the mist had entirely covered the boulder and the two lovers. They both knelt, and Rhea took out the brooch, placing it gently in the black earth, and Roarke laid the dirk on top of it.

Both began filling in the hole with their hands, and Roarke replaced the small patch of green grass. The candle sputtered in a sudden draft of wind came from the other side, and all light was gone.

Not seeing a hand in front of her face, Rhea stood and groped for Roarke, saying his name but receiving no reply. She backed up until she felt the cold of the stone behind her and stood, reached out for him again. She sighed in relief when she touched the softness of cloth.

"Thank God." She exhaled, "Why didn't you answer me?"

When her hand moved down, the flesh she touched was cold and smooth, like a marble statue, and as the fog cleared slightly to let in some of the moon's light, she could make out the figure of a young woman standing in front of her.

Islean was young and lovely, with wide eyes and a delicate face. Her curling blond hair gathered around her head with a strip of cloth. She wore a flowy white petticoat with thin blue stripes, an apron, a short brown jacket, and a neckerchief fastened with a round brooch.

The living and the dead regarded each other with curiosity and intimacy, as if meeting an old lover.

"I know you." Rhea smiled at Islean, who smiled back, yet as her haunted eyes looked around her, they became sad. A sadness, so profound, it seemed chilled the very air around them. A sadness Rhea had last seen in her mother's eyes.

"You're looking for him," she asked her ghost. "For Thomas."

Islean didn't reply, just bent her neck and buried her face in her hands, just as Rhea began to feel weak as if her energy were bleeding from her body. She slid down the stone until she felt the cool earth beneath her. Dizziness and nausea overcame her, and her eyelids fluttered as she sank to the ground, her head resting on her arm.

From somewhere in the distance, she was aware of the sweet song of a night bird, and the fog began to part as a young man in old highland garb walked up behind Islean and placed his hand on her shoulder.

Turning, Islean looked at Thomas, her hand reaching to cup his cheek, and he placed his hand on hers, beaming down at her, his smile so bright the moon above seemed dulled by its radiance.

She flew into his arms, and he lifted her, spinning her around and around, their laughter filling the night with heavenly music. The last thing Rhea saw before she passed out was the lovers standing, their foreheads together, tilting their heads for a kiss they had waited an eternity for. Just before their lips met, fog enveloped everything, and Rhea slipped into unconsciousness.

When she awoke, Roarke was shaking her shoulder. She opened her eyes, and he gathered her into his arms, rocking her slightly until she pulled away from him. The fog was gone, and the night was clear again.

"Where were you?" She reached up to touch his cheek. "I couldn't find you."

"Answer this first." He sighed. "Was Islean here?"

Rhea nodded.

"I figured." He shook his head. "I passed out. She took my energy again. I really wish she'd stop doing that. I woke up on the ground."

"I fainted, too."

"Why?"

"Thomas came."

Roarke's eyes grew large. "You saw him?"

Rhea nodded again. "They're together."

"Was she . . . was she happy?"

"Deliriously."

"Tell me what happened."

"I'll tell you in the truck." She placed a hand on the cold earth to push herself upright. "I'm freezing. You never told me that having a ghost suck the life out of you makes you so cold."

"Aye." He stood and pulled her to her feet. "It's fun stuff."

"I don't feel anything different, though." Roarke looked at Rhea's profile silhouetted against the night sky as they slowly made their way down the hill to the truck.

"Me neither. I thought I'd feel some change."

A small creature scurried out from behind a rock in front of them. "Mouse again. Does it —" Roarke began, but Rhea cut him off.

"Shhh! Do you hear that?"

Gently breaking the silence of the night, tinkling laughter drifted to them on the wind, a mix of a babbling brook and silver bells, and a young man's voice floating strong and clear in the night.

Rhea beamed up at Roarke, and he laughed, his shoulders bouncing the way she loved. Feeling like intruders, they held hands and hobbled down the hill.

Rhea sat beside Roarke in the truck, his arm around her, her head on his shoulder, and she told him what she had seen. Moonlight flooded the night sky as they drove on the purple road ribboning the hills and lochs.

Once in the driveway of White Heather, Rhea yawned as she walked to the cottage door. A strong wind came up from the north with a sudden blast. Rhea stumbled a little, but Roarke caught her against his muscular body. As he looked down, an incredulous grin split his handsome face.

"I'll be damned." He bent to pick something up at Rhea's feet and held it out to her. "I believe this is for you."

Between his thumb and forefinger, he held a small sprig of white heather.

CHAPTER TWENTY-FOUR: KEEP YOU

The only thing that keeps the wound from reopening is the strength of the stitches.

Images from the night before swam in Rhea's mind as she awoke from a deep sleep. She had slept like the dead.

Roarke spooned her, his breath soft against her ear, his hard, muscular body warm and comforting. She smiled and turned her head to look at him, a little taken aback by what she saw. His face was more relaxed than she had ever seen it, and there were no longer shadows beneath his eyes. He had the look of one who had found peace of mind.

Turning back, she tried, unsuccessfully, to untangle herself from him. Instead, he tightened his grip on her waist. "Don't leave," he murmured into her hair.

She laughed. "I'm bursting."

Reaching toward the bottom of the bed, she picked up his t-shirt and pulled it on as Roarke stretched and yawned.

Returning from the bathroom, she passed him in the hallway, and he placed a little kiss on her shoulder. "Go on back to bed. I'll make you some tea. We only slept a couple of hours, and I'd like another snooze."

"Bring me a piece of toast to go with my tea?"

"Your wish is my command, my lady."

Before she turned back into the bedroom, she looked out the small window at the end of the hall and pulled back the white lace curtain. The sky was cloudless and blue. A light breeze stirred the tops of the long grass near the forest, where the deciduous trees were changing into fiery reds, sunset oranges, and golden yellows. A day alive with unknown promises.

Turning, she looked in the bedroom at the rumpled, white duvet, the room bright with the sun's rays on cream-colored walls. Shadows from the tree outside danced across the painting of a lighthouse, the waves coming to life.

Her obsession with neat beds always amused him. Knowing it would make Roarke laugh, she made the bed. Then, pulling on a tank top and underwear from her bag, she sat on the edge of the bed, conflicting emotions plaguing her spirit.

Flopping back and turning over onto her stomach, she cleared her mind, and faster than she could have imagined, her eyelids felt heavy. Still seeing the leaves silhouetted by the bright sun on the inside of her eyelids, she peacefully dozed.

Twenty minutes later, Roarke came into the room, carrying a tray of tea, buttered toast, jam, and cheese, which he set quietly on the bureau, just as the towel wrapped around his waist began to slip. He had taken a quick shower while waiting for the kettle to boil.

Grabbing at the ends of the towel to prevent it from falling and looking up at himself in the mirror, he noticed that he looked younger. Then, turning his head this way and that, he leaned forward to look at the whites of his eyes, which were so white they looked bluish, and the circles under his eyes were gone.

Alone in the kitchen and bathroom, Roarke had noticed that shadows that once lurked in the house's corners were also gone. All negative energy had disappeared, and what remained was the true essence of the cottage, a place that was once full of love and children's laughter.

Behind him, a little sigh escaped Rhea's lips. Then, as he

turned to look at her, the room was flooded with dazzling sunlight, and his wife lay sleeping on the bed. Even though he knew their union was not legal, he felt she was his wife in his heart of hearts.

Rhea lay on her stomach widthwise across the bed on the white duvet, one foot dangling off the edge, the other bent at the knee. Her silky red-brown hair spilled around her tawny feline face. Shadows of the leaves outside the window flitted and twirled on her body. One arm arched above her head, and she had wrapped a lock of hair around two fingers. The white tank top deepened the color of her tanned arms and shoulders, and her bubble gum pink underwear made his heart skip a beat.

One hand still gripping the towel, he leaned against the bureau, watching her sleep, and whispered sadly, "Why can't I keep you?"

Three things flooded through him at that moment—extreme happiness, deep sadness, and the most intense need to touch her, to be inside her, and to stay that way.

His hand relaxed, dropping the towel.

Looking down on her as she lay sleeping, one hand gently rubbed the curves of her foot. Roarke watched the corners of her mouth raise in a smile. Then, before she could open her eyes, he leaned forward and whispered huskily, "Don't open your eyes. Don't move."

The bed creaked as he rested his knees against the edge and lowered himself near her, running his hands down her back and kissing a line across her shoulders. "Just stay exactly as you are. This is a dream, and you needn't do a thing."

As he kissed her, drops of water fell from his wet hair onto her body, and though the room was warm, she shivered as cool droplets landed on her skin. He softly licked at them. His firm calloused hands rubbed and massaged the muscles in her back, arms, buttocks, legs, and feet, taking his time before moving to another part of her body.

Giggling gently, she moved as his fingertips tickled behind her knee, but he stopped and whispered again, "I just want to make you feel good, okay?"

Rhea nodded, and her smile grew.

"Do you want this? Like this?"

Nodding again, she sighed and licked her lips, waiting.

Roarke's fingers inched up the length of her thigh and crept toward the middle of her spread legs. He ran the tip of his index finger along the crevice under her panties, just barely touching her. She inhaled sharply as a jolt of electricity shot through her, and his finger hovered just above her opening.

Moving his hands to brace her by her hips, he pulled her toward him on the edge of the bed and bent her straight leg back. With one hand around himself, he pushed aside the bright pink material that covered her most sensitive places, sliding her underwear to one side but not removing it. With exquisite slowness, he gently pushed his smooth tip into her welcoming body. Rhea held her breath as her body stretched to take him.

Roarke pushed a little deeper and then withdrew, pausing again. Then he went deeper still, withdrew, and paused again. Her mind went blank as he eased into her, the bed creaking under their weight.

It took every inch of her self-control not to move. Taking one of her hands, Roarke pushed it under her pelvis, and with his other hand, pushed down on the small of her back. Multiple sensations thrilled her already nerve-wracked body. His sex inside her and the pressure of her hand sent tiny tingles through her entire body. Roarke's strong hand pressing down on the small of her back caused the strangest, most euphoric titillations to emanate from just behind her belly button.

Her muscles began a type of involuntary squeezing and releasing, and Roarke groaned in pleasure. Thrusting again, keeping one hand on the small of her back, with the other he gripped her shoulder, and when he pushed into her, she sheathed his entire fullness. His thrusts were slow, withdrawing until just the tip remained inside. He stilled, causing her inner muscles to clench until he plunged back into her with his full length.

First he began to vary the depth and angle until she no longer knew where or how she would be receiving him next. Then his thrusts became faster and faster, and the pressure inside of her grew until her back arched, and she threw herself back against his body as he began to gyrate in slow circles. Her body exploded, clenching and shuddering all around him.

As his climax came upon him, he emptied his body inside her in a convulsing moment of release, their cries filling the cottage.

Later that day, Roarke received a call and told Rhea he would be gone for a few hours. She took the time alone for a long walk around the property to gather her thoughts. She went to the cliff, the gym, the yew tree, thinking of all the things that had happened since she'd arrived.

In three days, she would return to her regular life, and this adventure, where she had learned so many things about herself, would be over. However, Rhea was adamant that she would fill each day with as much love as possible, because soon enough, Roarke would go one way and she another.

Stepping out of his truck and slamming the door, Roarke gingerly picked up the sword wrapped in an old towel and walked toward David Cojocaru's elegantly clad back, facing the bothy on the hill.

Turning to face him, David told Roarke, "I do wish you'd get a mobile. You're so hard to track down."

"I like being unavailable, and people got along just fine without mobiles not so long ago." Roarke handed the sword over to him, and David just stared down at it. "You don't want to look at it?"

"I'd rather be alone when I do." He looked back to Roarke. "Is your friend staying here, or will she be one of the people who can never find you?"

"Rhea's returning home in a few days. We'll part ways."

"If that's going to hurt you, I'm sorry, but maybe that's a good thing."

"Why's that?"

"Willem's disappeared." David licked his lips and wiped at the corners of his mouth with the back of his index finger.

"Shit, David!" Roarke whipped his hat off his head and balled it up in his hand.

"We know he took a train to London. After that, the trail's cold."

"What should I . . ."

"Listen, Roarke." David gripped him by the upper arms. "Willem had an overseas buyer for the sword, someone offering an exorbitant sum for it. He's furious that he doesn't have the sword anymore. I have no intentions of selling it, but I can't promise he won't bother you, or her, again."

Roarke repositioned his cap on his head. "Maybe it's good Rhea's getting out of here. Myself as well."

"I'll find him. It just might take a little time, and I've got most of the funding for the castle. We can meet the twins in a few days to start the paperwork before you go to the States."

"David." Roarke stuck out his hand, and David shook it. "I can't thank you enough."

"Don't worry about it. I owe you." David turned to walk

toward his black luxury car.

"No, Davey." Roarke stepped toward him again. "You never owe me anything."

David slapped his hand gently on Roarke's face, then turned and got in his car. "Roarke, be careful when it comes to Willem."

"I'm sorry your son's gone."

"He's big enough to take care of himself, but he's still my son." With those words, he turned his car on the patch of grass and sped off.

In his truck once more and heading home, Roarke decided to go into town and do a few errands before returning. He needed time to think. Hearing Willem was on the loose made him anxious for Rhea's safety.

She will be leaving and will be safe. Safe and away from me. There'll always be things from my past coming back to haunt me. I'm best on my own.

An hour later, Roarke pulled into his driveway as Rhea burst out the front door with her bags and a furious look on her face. Before he could even get out of the truck, she had flung her bags in the back and wrenched open the passenger door, screaming at him. "The airport! Drive! I've got to go!"

Turning to her, he reached out to touch her hand, but she pulled it away. "Rhea, what is it?"

"Drive!"

The wheels spun out and sprayed gravel around the drive as they headed toward the road.

Rhea rummaged in her small backpack, pulling out her wallet, passport, and checking that she had everything, while Roarke remained silent and confused. Finally, she put her bag down and pulled her hair out of her ponytail, only to smooth it and put it up again. "Patrice called. It's Liam. He's okay, but he took a baseball to the face. It knocked out three of his teeth, and he has a ton of stitches."

"Oh, my God!"

"He's been asking for me. I managed to get a flight leaving in a few hours." Tears began streaming down Rhea's face. "I had no way to reach you. Why the hell can't you carry a phone?"

"I'm sorry. I couldn't have known."

"Jesus!" She wiped the tears from her cheeks. "I get it. It's your lifestyle. You don't need one, but I needed you, and I couldn't get you."

Rhea turned, looking out the window on her side of the truck. Roarke glanced over at her. The distance between them could have been a mile. She seemed to be as far away from him as she could get. "I'm sorry, Rhea."

Saying nothing, she buried her face in her hands, and he helplessly watched her shoulders as they moved with silent sobs.

Maybe this is for the best. If Rhea leaves angry with me, or at least if there's tension between us, it will be easier. If she feels she can't rely on me, that's a good thing. It will help her get over it all.

"Should never have left him. Should never have been so selfish." Rhea's voice softened a little. "Say goodbye to every-one for me."

"I will."

"And rub Laz."

Roarke swerved to avoid a pothole, and Rhea bounced around in her seat.

"We're keeping Laz."

"You're not giving him away or selling him?"

"How could I? He's your dog."

Tears welled up in her eyes and spilled down on her cheeks. "Oh, Roarke. I'm sorry our time's been cut short."

"Me, too. Very sorry, but Liam will always win. As it should be."

"Roarke." She leaned across to bury her face into his shoulder, and the warm dampness of her tears soaked through his t-shirt.

"My love, we don't have anything to say. We regret nothing."

"Not a thing."

"One day, when your son needs you less, and I can settle down, we'll find each other again."

Rhea took a deep breath. "One day . . ."

"There's nothing more to say. Nothing more for me to do than walk away from the greatest thing that ever happened to me. No big deal."

Rhea looked into his deeply into his eyes, and he recognized the first time she ever lied to him. "Everything's going to be okay."

At the airport, ticket in hand, Rhea took the cup of coffee Roarke handed her and watched as he sat and grunted, stretching his long legs in front of him and squirming in the too-small seat as they waited for her to go through security.

Rhea leaned over and kissed first his cheek and then his lips. "I'm so *very* glad to have met you."

"I'm fifty pounds lighter." Roarke touched his forehead to hers and moved his head back and forth. "And ten tons happier."

"Me too." She buried her face into the flannel of his chest. "Twenty." Her voice was muffled as she spoke against his chest.

Smiling, he ran his hand down the entire length of her ponytail. "I love you," he whispered into the top of her head. "I just can't believe you're leaving."

"I'm not. Not really."

"What do you mean?"

"I left my heart at the cottage."

"It's great, though, isn't it?" He squeezed her. "We know somewhere in the world, someone loves us completely and for exactly who we are."

"Yeah." She smiled. "When you're alone, sailing or walking by the sea, you'll know someone wishes they were with you."

"When you're walking in the woods, or sipping tea, or sitting through a boring meeting, you'll know the same."

"If I could just call you . . ."

"I can't let you go over and over again. I can't . . . I can't . . ." Roarke ran his hand along his forehead as a tear rolled down his face.

"I know. You need to be able to go. You need to focus on the castle. You need to be free, and I need to focus on our book and my son."

"Hearing your voice would make me ache with loneliness."

"To be honest," she confessed. "If we held on but then changed our minds, I'd break apart. It's easier this way."

"You know, in my entire life, you're the only thing I've ever truly wanted. You're all I've ever wanted." He kissed the top of her head and breathed in her scent. "Your sacred hair."

A very perky-sounding young woman came over the intercom and announced that her flight was boarding. They stood up and stretched before Rhea grabbed her small backpack.

"Don't stay after I go in. I want to think of you driving home through the hills on your way back to the place we both love. Go home, have some tea, and then visit my dog."

"Your dog will be very safe until you can come and get him." His voice broke on the last word.

Rhea flung herself into his arms. "You have to go. I'm going to fall apart if you don't."

The final call came over the intercom.

"Now you have to go."

When their lips met, they didn't close their eyes, and when they pulled away, he winked at her and dropped her hands. Then, spinning around, she headed for the security gate without looking back.

Roarke watched her through the glass of the security gate as she went through. When she picked up her backpack and started to move toward the departure hall, she looked at him through the glass and put her hand to her chain, fingering the silver charm he had given her the day they were married, and brought it to her lips for a kiss.

Roarke stood up and held up his hand in parting, exposing the strip of tartan Moira had bound to his wrist when they were wed, and he drew it to his lips in a kiss.

Rhea turned to walk down the narrow corridor but couldn't resist turning back to glance at him one more time, but he was gone.

The next few days were the hardest of his life, even though his family visited. When they went to the beach, he told Maren the birds were show-offs, and she agreed. When Maren asked her what happened to the window in the guest room, Rhea's room, he told her about the tree branch. He hadn't had the heart to replace the glass, as when he saw the boarded-up window, he remembered that night in detail.

Rhea was everywhere he turned, and it filled him with both never-ending joy and relentless misery. After his family left, Roarke made arrangements with Ian, and even though he had over a week to go, he left White Heather, heading off in his boat before going to the States.

Rhea finally arrived home and went directly to Liam and Patrice. He was sleeping when she arrived, but when she went in and kissed his forehead, his eyes fluttered open. "You're back!"

"Of course, I'm back, Baby." She hugged him close to her until he coughed. She inspected his still-swollen mouth and stitches, carefully kissing every inch of his face. "Go back to sleep, and we'll visit in the morning."

"You're not leaving again, are you?"

"No, baby."

"I was dreaming about my Mommy."

"You were?" She brushed some of his black hair off his forehead.

"At least, I think I was dreaming." His light eyebrows furrowed. "She was sitting right where you are."

A chill ran up Rhea's back, and the ends of her hair seemed to stir though there was not a draft in the house. "She was?"

"Yeah. Her hair's so black and long. Her braid wraps around her shoulder."

"Yes, her hair was gorgeous." Kissing his forehead, she rubbed her cheek against his.

Turning over on his side, he tucked one of his hands under his cheek, and his eyes closed voluntarily. "Thank you for my dog."

Rhea shivered. "Your dog?"

"Mommy said you got me a black dog in Scotland, but you had to leave it there for now."

She slowly straightened up on the bed and looked around. "A black dog?"

"Yeah. A man's taking care of it for me for now. I can't wait to see my dog." He smiled, and his head drooped further down on his pillow. He rolled over and was breathing deeply within ten seconds.

"Holy shit." Rhea's eyes wandered around the room.

Patrice came in and placed a hand on her shoulder. "What is it?"

"How did Poppy know about that?"

"Know about what?"

"Tell you over some tea?"

Patrice and Rhea sat in the kitchen most of the night, sipping tea and eating the Scottish shortbread she had brought home. Rhea told Pat all about Roarke, and he told her all about Marie-Claire and Benjamin, the young mother with the little boy who had captivated him in Florida.

"Rhea. Why did you let Roarke go?"

"Liam needed me." Rhea rubbed at her eyes with the backs of her hands. "I couldn't stay there forever. My life's here."

"It was easy to let him go?"

"Of course not."

"Maybe you let him go because you didn't feel like it was the end."

"What do you mean?"

"Do you feel like you'll never see him again? That was all the time that you'll have?"

She thought about it only for a second and shook her head. "No, I don't feel that way at all. It feels like he's just in the next room. I'll turn a corner, and he'll be there."

"If your instincts are telling you you'll be together again, then you will."

"Is that how you feel about Marie-Claire?"

"Yes. Especially since she's from here." Patrice glanced up at her under his eyelashes. "Does that bother you?"

"No," she answered truthfully. "Does it bother you that it doesn't bother me?"

He laughed and closed his blue eyes for a moment. "Not in the slightest. It was weird meeting Marie-Claire. I felt the same way as when I met you. Like I was meeting someone I was meant to meet."

"Really?"

"Yeah, Rhea. You changed my life and brought Liam to me. I feel like Marie-Claire is going to be special, too. Ben and Liam are close in age, and he just dotes on Li."

"I'm glad you're happy, Pat."

Patrice sighed, and his handsome face turned pensive. "You've got a lot of work to do in the next few weeks, I guess?"

"Yeah, but I don't know how I'll muster the courage to do it. How can I look at my notes, my pictures, when I know I'll just miss Roarke?"

"Not meaning to be hard-hearted, but you've waited for this opportunity for a long time. You've got to do it. This is your shot."

"I know I've got to do it. The problem is *how* to do it."

"Let me know if you need any help." He shook his light brown shoulder-length hair, as was his habit.

Rhea buried her head in her hands. "Oh, Pat. I heard what you said, but it's hard to believe that I'll see him again. I don't even know where he is right now. He could be anywhere."

"Even after what happened with you both, he still refuses to carry a phone?" Patrice leaned against the sink.

"Said he didn't want to be tempted to call me. We had to sever the ties cleanly, or we'd just torture ourselves for a while. I can't imagine having to say goodbye again. Once almost killed me. Twice would end me."

"I still think it's stupid not to have a cell phone in this day and age." He wiped his hands on a dishtowel.

"Would I need a cell if it weren't for calling the handful of people that I love?"

Patrice shook his head.

"He's like that. Only he takes it to the tenth degree." Rhea walked to the sink and put her mug into it. "Enough about that. Let's talk about your shop." She had called him from her layover in Toronto and told him she would fully support him leaving the firm and opening his music shop. Patrice was pragmatic at first, but when he realized she was serious, he'd been delighted by her change of heart.

"Rhea, we have time for that."

"We need to start making plans. You need to be ready with the shop before you completely leave work, and . . ." Rhea shot up straighter. "Oh, I forgot to tell you. The lawyer called. We can meet with him early next week."

Pat looked at her in confusion.

"For the adoption."

Patrice jumped and grabbed at her shoulders. "Are you serious? You're *actually* going to let me adopt Liam?"

Rhea giggled as Patrice jostled her back and forth. "Yes. Yes. Stop!"

Patrice's long, elegant fingers covered his mouth, and he looked like a small child who had been told he was going to Disneyland.

"You're his father, and soon you'll have the paperwork to prove it."

Twenty minutes later, Rhea walked past Liam's door to find Patrice sitting on the floor, his upper torso stretched out, and his head rested on Liam's arm. They were both fast asleep.

She walked into the living room, lying down on the couch with a blanket. She fell asleep in Patrice's apartment, thinking he was right, except for one thing. In as many happy scenarios her wistful brain could put together, with everything they both had happening in their lives, she could not imagine how or when she could ever see Roarke any time soon.

Rhea eventually went back to her apartment after crashing on Patrice's couch. She sat down at her desk overlooking the street. It had been her favorite place to sit, but now she almost felt like a stranger in her own home.

Trying to work, Rhea looked at the two notebooks she had filled up in her time in Scotland but couldn't make herself open them. Instead, she got a glass of wine. Halfway through her drink, when she opened the first notebook, his name was the first thing on the page. The tears began as memory upon memory flooded her mind, and she decided to give herself over to her longing and melancholy.

The next night, after looking at the pictures she had taken, she cried so much she hyperventilated and had to breathe into a paper bag, staring at her blank computer screen.

The following day, she had a panic attack as she realized in despair that she couldn't write the book because she was afraid of delving too deeply into her memories. That night, as she tucked Liam into bed, he was strangely quiet.

"Bud? Is there something wrong?" She took the empty water glass out of his hand and placed it on his nightstand. "You're kind of quiet tonight."

"I'm okay," he replied quietly. "Are you okay?"

"Me?" Rhea was a little surprised at his question.

"You seem sad."

Rhea pulled him toward her and into a bear hug. "Oh, bud. I'm fine. I'm just a little worried because I have to finish my project, and I'm having some problems getting started."

"It's about your book?" He pulled away from her and settled himself back onto the pillow that Rhea had propped against his headboard.

Rhea could see there was something else on his mind. "Yes, my book, but what are you thinking about?"

"Well." He looked down at the stuffed blue jay he always

slept with. "I don't want to forget my Mommy and Daddy."

"You won't, baby." She rubbed his smooth arm.

"I think I will."

"You won't because I'll tell you something about them every day."

"You will?"

"I will." She poked at the blue jay. "Do you remember why your Daddy got you the blue jay?"

"We were at a garage sale, and I wanted it because one day, my Mommy and I were watching blue jays, and my Mommy said birds were show-offs."

Rhea got a flash of walking up the beach and saying those exact words to Roarke.

"Mommy always said birds know they can fly, and we can't."

That's where I got that!

"Unbelievable." She giggled at him.

"Tell me something about Mommy."

"She loved your hair. She cried when your friend Alex cut it when you were playing."

"Did I have long hair?"

"Yes. To our people, hair, especially children's hair, is sacred. She wanted your hair to stay long. She was so proud of our ancestry."

"I'm part native too?"

"Yes, and I need to talk to you more about it. Your mother knew so much more than I do. I guess I didn't listen as well when our parents were telling us things, but I promise to remember more and learn more, okay?"

"Okay." Liam settled down in his bed, and Rhea pulled the covers up around him. "Mom, do you think I could grow my hair out long again?"

"I think your Mommy would like that very much." She kissed his head again and stood.

"Mom, sometimes, I think I don't want to talk about them

because it hurts too much."

"Yeah, I understand that." She sniffed.

"But when I *do* talk to you or Dad about them, I feel better. Being apart hurts, but talking about them and thinking about them makes them feel closer. It feels good to remember."

From the mouths of babes.

"You know, Li." She leaned against the doorframe. "You're a brilliant young man."

Giggling, he pulled his blue jay closer to him and turned over. "Good night, Mom."

"Night, Baby." Turning off the light, she left the door open a crack and walked out to the kitchen, where she prepared a cup of herbal tea and took it over to her desk.

Taking a few deep breaths, she turned on her computer and opened the document she had started in Scotland. Opening the first notebook, she swallowed the lump in her throat and began to read. She didn't cry, because Liam was right. Remembering didn't have to make you sad. It could make the moments come alive again, and she needed that.

Rhea worked relentlessly, and soon she had a first draft to send her editors, which they ended up loving.

Later that week, she had a surprise for Patrice. They were watching Liam play baseball for the first time since his accident, the only kid playing with a mouth guard.

"Pat," she asked through a mouthful of hotdog. "Do you think you could get a few days off?"

"Why?"

"I have to go to Toronto for the book, and I booked myself into that wilderness retreat in Nova Scotia for a few days. They're located near the reserve, and the record keeper for my grandmother's band has information for us."

"Good for you." He sipped his energy drink. "Why do you need me to get time off?"

"I was talking to Sal and Raven, and they wanted us to

come home for a few days to celebrate the baby's birthday and my book, but also to celebrate you adopting Liam."

"What?" He shook back his hair from his face, "That's nice, but not necessary."

"It was their idea. The family wants you to know they are one hundred percent behind us."

It was Liam's turn at bat, and Patrice turned to watch him as Rhea continued. "I'm pulling Li from school for two weeks regardless. You might as well go with him."

Rhea could see the ghost of a smile forming on Patrice's lips, his handsome face coloring a little, and she knew he was secretly pleased. "Will Sal take me fishing?"

"You can bet on it. It's just too bad you're such a shitty fisherman."

Patrice pushed her lightly on the shoulder. "Li'll be stoked."

A few days later, Liam and Patrice headed to the island, while Rhea spent two days in Toronto meeting with her editor, leaving with a list of adjustments to be made.

At the retreat, she had time to be alone and collect her thoughts. The changes to the book were easy to make, and though she had a deadline, she knew she could relax a little.

Cooking over an open fire and sleeping under the stars, Rhea felt like herself. She thought of Roarke every second, but writing had proven to be therapeutic. Though her longing and loneliness never lessened, she knew if he was still in Scotland, he was five hours ahead of her, and if he was in California, she was four hours ahead of him. She spent much of her time trying to deduce what he was doing.

Reaching into her breast pocket, she took out a small piece of paper and held it to her nose, breathing deeply.

While packing for her trip to Toronto, Rhea had received a

small package from Federal Express, and inside was a cashier's cheque for ten thousand dollars and a note from Roarke with no return address.

Ghost,

I thought I saw you in the woods yesterday, but it turned out to be a red squirrel sitting on a pile of leaves. I mistook you for a squirrel. That's how desperate I've become. You know that tingle you feel in your feet when you've jumped from a height? I get that feeling all the time when I see a woman with hair similar to yours or smell your perfume, which you were kind enough to forget. I feel like I'm falling . . .

David said to use Willem's money for the castle, but I thought you should have this, considering the role you played. Put it to use on your parent's house or Patrice's shop. Just use it, please.

I promise to try my best not to feel alone. I'll know wherever you are, I'm not far from your thoughts, even if you're not in my arms.

I'll carry you everywhere with me. I have no choice. You're half my soul.

Oceans,

Roarke

Lying on her back and looking at the stars reminded her of nights spent with him, and she didn't feel alone. Rhea knew she was not far from his thoughts, but she wished, with all her might, that she was also in his arms.

CHAPTER TWENTY-FIVE: HOME

Returning home comes with baggage, but the weight of the heart is the hardest to carry

R hea stepped off the plane at the small airport a few towns over from her own, breathed in the sweet, salty air, and felt the electricity surge through her. Coming home felt like being plugged into an electrical socket, the only place on earth that could do that.

Two cars full of people met her in the luggage terminal, Raven, his tiny, sandy-haired wife, Charlotte, their daughter, Ruby, Sal, and his tall, athletic wife, Veronica with Rain and Baby Robin, Liam, and Patrice.

On the drive to the village with Raven and Charlotte, Ruby and her mother filled Rhea in on the party plans. Raven was quiet but told her that the house was quickly rented out to a retired American politician named Karen Crossman after they repaired the roof. Rhea would stay with them, and Patrice was crashing Sal's.

Disappointed at not being able to stay at the house, Rhea turned to her brother. "I've heard a lot of Americans come to the island, renting or buying houses."

Turned onto the smaller road leading to their village, Raven smiled. "Yeah, people just travel through and decide to stay. Karen showed up the other day, and Donna at the store told her we had a house she could rent."

Their quiet fishing village lay sheltered in the harbor and surrounded by forest with a long mountain range dotted with lakes and ponds, bogs, and rivers. The first thing Rhea did after she dropped her bags was to go down to the ocean and wash her face. When she looked up, Liam was doing the same thing, his jet-black hair dripping with salty brine.

Back at the house, Raven held out one of Charlotte's famous crumb cakes. "Sis, bring this cake down to the lady at the house. Charlotte thought it'd be good for her to have with her tea."

"I just got here." Rhea smiled and tried to back away from the cake. "Can no one else go?"

"No. We're getting supper together." Pushing the cake into Rhea's hands and turning her around, Raven gave her a slight push out the door. "She's a very nice woman, but come back quickly. I've made rabbit stew."

Rhea sucked in her breath and grinned at the mention of her favorite meal. "You have not."

"Oh, but I have, my dear." He cupped his hands around his mouth and looked around conspiratorially. "Mine's even better than Mom's."

Taking the cake, Rhea stepped out into the bright late-October sunshine. Taking a deep breath, she walked up the familiar lane to the front of her mother's round house. Knocking on the door a few times, she received no reply but could hear the sound of someone chopping wood in the back. Coming around to the back, Rhea stopped midway as a strange feeling overtook her. Every hair stood on end as she felt a tingle in her feet and a sudden apprehension made her hesitate.

As Rhea stepped to the back of the house, the cake fell to the ground when she screamed.

In that second, which could have been an hour or a day, Rhea felt a bliss only gifted to people a few times in their lives, a feeling as profound and timeless as the sea.

"Hey, ghost." Roarke stood before her, in her family's back

yard, the ax now at his feet, his white t-shirt clinging to him with sweat. The look on his face conveyed the depth of his own emotions. "You're early."

Hearing the deep rumble of his voice and his Scottish brogue sent vibrations running through her. Standing just a few feet away, he put up his hands in front of him. "Listen. Please don't be angry with me. Just give me one minute to explain."

A solemn silence spread between them, and the only sound was the wind stirring the tops of the tall grass. "I was motivated by fear, letting you go. David told me Willem had run off somewhere, and I was so afraid for you, but now he's been arrested for theft. David will get him out, but I know you and me together. We can protect each other. I've decided to let go of my fear."

Still too shocked to react, she just stood in the grass, staring at him.

"I know you said you only had the strength to leave me once, and our lives will always be pulling us apart, but that's not necessarily true. I only had the strength to leave you once, like that. Thinking I could never be with you again, but I realized I can leave you if I know I'm coming back to you. If you need to spend the winter in Canada, because of Liam and his hockey, which I've started watching, by the way, and I need to be in Scotland or filming somewhere, big deal. We need to spend a few days, or weeks, or months apart, okay. People do it all the time. I've even got a mobile now."

The only movement from Rhea was the wind blowing her hair across her face.

Roarke clapped his hands. "I've got Ian for the farm and my staff from the shelter. Pearl can fly with me or stay with Ian. I've got a good team, and Rhea, you've got a good team, too. Pat and Liam just want you to be happy."

Lifting her hand, she used her index finger to brush her

hair across her forehead but still said nothing.

"Oh, God." Roarke was looking more nervous by the minute. "Okay, look, what it comes down to is there's always going to be us. This connection will never happen to me again because it can only happen with you. I know it. You know it. We'll be apart at times until we're back together. Didn't Islean and Thomas teach you anything? What we have is profound. This unexplainable, all-consuming feeling is too deep to be anything other than sacred."

Tears filled her eyes, and she cupped her hands over her mouth and nose.

"Rhea." He took a hesitant step toward her. "You told me on the day we met that love was the most destructive force on earth." He fell to his knees in front of her. "If that's the case, destroy me, love. Rip me to shreds, but don't tell me to go."

Unable to control herself any longer, Rhea ran at him, flying into his arms, wrapping her legs around his waist as she kissed him hard on the mouth, her hands gripping the hair at the back of his head.

Laughing as she covered his face with kisses, Roarke struggled to speak, "Rhea, um, Rhea? Aren't you going to ask me . . ."

"Don't care. Don't care." Rhea pulled back to look deep into Roarke's eyes. "You're here. Don't care about anything else."

"God." He sighed, his voice taking on a deeper tone. "How do you do that?"

"Do what?"

"You're in my arms for less than a minute, and every fiber of me wants you."

"Then take me inside."

Still with her legs wrapped around his waist, he took the ten steps to the open backdoor and tripped on the bottom of the doorframe, he caught himself, but Rhea let herself fall to the floor and pulled him with her. She grabbed at either side of his face and kissed him. Together they slid up the hall until Roarke could kick the door closed with his foot.

His strong hands ripped open her thin, blue plaid shirt, and buttons flew as she unzipped his shorts until she could pull them down. Roarke kicked them off over his sneakers as he tried unsuccessfully to undo her bra, resorting to caressing her breasts roughly on top of her bra.

His hands pushed down her shorts and underwear at the same time, and she managed to get one leg out before his hand found her center. Being confident she was ready, he thrust himself into her, driving her back on the hardwood floor as her moans and sighs filled his mouth.

Roarke stopped to grab a towel next to the washing machine and lifted Rhea to put it under her bottom, tilting her hips so he could drive even deeper inside of her. Over and over, he thrust into her body.

Rhea writhed under his weight and groaned in pleasure as she gripped the doorframes on either side of the narrow hallway. Her orgasm came on her suddenly, and as her body exploded, she was unaware of anything else, as fireworks popped off behind her eyelids. Then his body tensed, he stilled, and when he shuddered and fall against her, she wrapped her arms and legs even tighter around him.

"I love you, Roarke."

"I love you, Rhea." His lips tickled her collarbone as he spoke.

"I don't want to be without you."

"I can't be without you. That's why I'm here." Roarke leaned up to look in her eyes again in all seriousness. "Rhea?"

"Yes?" She looked back at him adoringly.

His brow furrowed in concern. "That cake you dropped, it wasn't one of Charlotte's, by any chance?"

Rhea paused for a second and then burst out laughing,

squeezing his head between her hands. "Don't worry, my love. It only fell in the grass. We can salvage it."

"Wasn't Rave making some rabbit stew?"

Sometime later, after going back outside to get the cake, Rhea saw Liam and Patrice strolling down the path between Raven and Sal's houses. She put the cake on the step and pulled at Roarke's arm. "Roarke. There are some guys I want you to meet."

"Those guys?" Pointing at the two approaching figures, Roarke smiled warmly.

"Yes," Rhea announced proudly. "That's Li and Pat. Don't be nervous. They're awesome."

"I'm not nervous."

They were still a stone's throw away when Liam ran toward them. He ran first into Rhea's open arms, and then to her shock, he slammed into Roarke, who got down on his knees and put him in a headlock. Patrice walked toward them, watching them wrestle. When Roarke stood up, the two tall men reached for each other, grinning as they fist-pumped.

"Hey, big-man," Patrice greeted Roarke warmly. "Don't forget you owe me money."

"Morning, Pat."

Rhea stood in the midst of the three, looking at each in turn. "What the . . ."

Patrice held up his hands and grinned at Rhea. "When Li and I got here, Sal informed me Roarke had taken up residence at the house and you were not expected for a few days, so I planned a camping trip for the three of us."

"But then Uncle Sal and the girls ended up coming, too," added Liam, always excited to be able to share adult secrets.

"What? Together?"

"Yup. We went camping for two nights." Patrice cupped his hand around his mouth and leaned toward her. "Big-man didn't catch a thing."

"Neither did you!" Roarke jabbed a finger playfully in Patrice's chest.

"True. Liam and Rain were the only two to catch anything."

Liam looked up at his mother. "They gave up too easily. They spent most of the time talking, cooking, and eating."

"Doing what we do best." Roarke patted his stomach.

Patrice took Rhea's hand. "I wanted Roarke and Liam to get to know each other. With me around, so Liam understood that Roarke's going to be in our lives, and even though he tends to burn cheese-on-toast, he's a good guy."

"Roarke told Dad he wants to marry you." Liam giggled as he threw his hand over his mouth, as all three adults looked down at him in shock.

"Liam!" Patrice pulled his son into his arms before looking up at Rhea with a greasy grin. "I don't know what he's talking about."

Rhea looked at Roarke, who stood frozen, looking back and forth from Liam to Patrice.

Liam wrestled away from his father's grasp. "It's true, Mom, I heard them talking. Roarke wants to marry you in Granny's garden before the film starts shooting in Montréal. He asked me for permission to ask you, and I said it was okay."

Rhea was too stunned to speak. Instead, she just stared at Roarke with her hands on her hips.

"Liam," Patrice began. "I think you kind of stole Roarke's thunder. I think he wanted to ask your Mom himself."

Liam turned sheepish eyes up to Roarke. "I'm sorry."

Roarke reached down to ruffle his hair. "No worries, big man, but I guess the cat's out of the bag now."

Patrice cupped his ear in the direction of Sal's house. "What's that?"

"I don't hear anything," Liam said.

"Coming, Veronica!" Patrice turned and started running toward the house. "Come, Liam. Aunt Ronnie wants us."

Liam took off after his father as Rhea and Roarke again found themselves across from each other in fighting positions.

Roarke lowered himself to the ground and pulled Rhea with him. "Let me explain."

She settled cross-legged across from him and waited.

After a moment, Roarke pointed his finger at Patrice as he ran back to the house with Liam close behind him. "This is all his fault."

"His fault?"

"Yes. If you're not happy, blame him." Roarke ran his fingers through his hair. "In the States, filming was postponed due to weather troubles, and they had to find a new location. Then Willem was arrested, and that obstacle was gone. I thought it might be okay to call you, but I couldn't reach you. You had called Patrice from my landline, so I called him to see if you were okay. He told me the retreat doesn't allow guests to have their mobiles, only for emergencies. We talked for quite a while and he invited me here, knowing you'd be coming when you finished in Toronto and Nova Scotia. Sal said I could stay in your parent's house and wait for you."

Reaching out, he took both of her hands in one of his. "Get this! The movie is now being filmed in Montreal."

"No!" Rhea straightened her back, and her jaw dropped in shock.

"Aye. I'll be near you, and in the future, we could split time between Scotland and Canada. I know you need to stay here for Liam, but I would jump back and forth. You could come with me sometimes but stay here the majority of the time."

"But what about . . ."

"Listen, Rhea. If anyone could make this work, it'd be us."

Rhea threw herself at him, and with arms wrapped around

his head, she breathed into his ear, "I love that idea."

"Do you really?"

Pulling away from him so she could look in his eyes, she said her favorite word, "Aye."

"God, we have to work on that atrocious Scottish accent."

"When does filming start in Montreal?"

"Next week, so get some closet space ready. When we leave here, I'm coming to Québec with you. I'm already taking online lessons in French. Bloody hard language, but at the same time, what makes it difficult is also what makes it beautiful. Kind of like you."

"Watch it," she grinned.

"And how's it going with the book?"

"They love it! They think it's going to sell well."

Roarke made a jackpot cha-ching sound.

"They may have two other projects to offer me, too. Which goes along with the plans you've made. I can research and write from anywhere."

"Is that so?" Roarke picked a tiny bluebell from the grass and spun the stem between his fingertips. "I hope you can write on the waves. We might need to take a sail when we get back to Scotland. Liam says that's the first thing he wants to do."

"That's wonderful." She threw her arms around his neck. "But don't be fooled. He just can't wait to see his dog."

"That dog?" Roarke pointed at Sal's house, and Rhea turned just in time to see Liam walking down the road being pulled by a small black shaggy Newfoundland.

Rhea spun around to look back at Roarke. "Is that Lazarus?"

"I couldn't come without him, could I? He was just old enough to fly, and he did great." He watched Liam and the dog for a second before adding, "I wanted Li to like me. I figured the dog might win me some points."

"It worked like a charm, I'm certain."

"McCallum charm, my dear. Works every time." He looked down at the tiny delicate flower in his hands. "Most of the time, but you still haven't addressed the most important thing that your son said."

"I know what my son said, but you haven't asked me anything."

Roarke cleared his throat. "I want to marry you. I want to have a life with you, and I don't want to wait." He held out the flower. "Will you please be my wife?"

Rhea's eyes glittered with tears as she took the blossom. "I'm already your wife."

"Aye." Roarke caught a teardrop making its way down her cheek. "Liam's adoption party has turned into a wedding party also."

Rhea looked both delighted and shocked. "What?"

"The family has everything ready." He stood up, grinning, and pulled her with him. "We need to eat well and get a good night's sleep. We're getting married tomorrow."

"Tomorrow?"

"Aye." Roarke walked toward the circular house again, pulling Rhea with him. "They're going to put you to work the minute they see you, so before they come after you, you might need to freshen up."

A thought suddenly crossed Rhea's mind. "Your mother's going to kill you for not being able to have your family here."

"My mother's okay. We've agreed to have another small ceremony in Scotland when we go back. No choice really, she threatened to kill both of us if we didn't."

Rhea stepped closer to the house but then spun around to look up at his grinning face. "Wait a minute! Were you so sure I'd say yes?"

"I-I-I . . ." he stammered. "I took a chance, but Rhea, would I even be here if I doubted how you felt about me? Do you doubt how I feel about you?"

Shaking her head, she laughed at him, "No, but shit, a little air of mystery would be nice."

Back inside her parents' home, which looked as it had the last time she was there, Rhea was both elated and sad, empty and full. The décor was the same, wooden furniture made by her father, out-of-date white appliances, and splashes of blue and green. The only thing missing in the kitchen was her mother standing at the counter, her long black braid hanging down her back. Rhea dissolved into tears for the third or fourth time since arriving.

Roarke came around and hugged her shoulders. "Poor sweetheart."

"Don't pay her any mind." Sal's voice came from the open kitchen door behind them, and they turned to see his handsome face, deeply tanned from the sun. "She doesn't get emotional often enough."

Rhea left Roarke's arms and curled up against her brother's broad chest, inhaling deeply. "You smell like Dad."

"Shit, if I come home smelling like tobacco, Ronnie will kill me." He went into the bathroom and re-emerged, gargling a mouth full of toothpaste and mouthwash.

Roarke wandered into the living room, where pictures of her parents and the family they had made together hung on every wall. He stopped in front of one photo and pointed at the lovely face in the frame. "That's Poppy, yes? I dreamed of her before I came here."

"Of Poppy?"

"Aye. I thought it was you, but it was her."

Sal slapped a hand on Roarke's shoulder. "Mom always said they communicate with us when we sleep. I guess she was reaching out to you."

Chapter Twenty-Six: The Visitor

All of the ghosts visited, and were at peace.

The following morning, Rhea stepped out of the bedroom feeling the happiest she had ever felt in her life. Her sisters-in-law had helped with her dress, a cream-colored, loose, satin gown which Charlotte had altered from one of her mother's old gowns. It hugged Rhea's body perfectly. Li and Pat had stopped in to give her a wreath of periwinkle forget-me-nots and bluish-purple bluebells to wear in her unbound, loosely curled hair. Charlotte and Veronica had wrapped tresses of her hair around the wreath.

"I don't know why you girls made me get dressed so early," she'd admonished her sisters-in-law. "You know I'm going to spill something on my dress."

"You spill anything, and Charlotte will be performing a funeral ceremony instead of a wedding," said Veronica as she set a plate of scrambled eggs and toast on the table with tea. "Don't say a word. You need to eat."

As Rhea made her way toward the kitchen table, she glanced over Veronica's shoulder. The window behind her overlooked the field of long grass that rested on the forest's edge leading to the Eastern Hills. A movement and flash of black and blue in the grass had caught her attention. Brushing past Veronica, she slowly walked to the window. A flush crept over her face as a dawning realization hit her like a clap of thunder.

Charlotte put her hand on Rhea's shoulder and gazed out

the window as a figure made its way to the house.

"Oh, my God! I've gotta get Raven and Sal!" Veronica bolted for the door.

"Stop!" Rhea halted her sister-in-law mid-step and turned from the window to the door. She stepped out onto the porch, crossed the path, and walked out into the tall grass barefoot, the lace overlay of her dress catching on the grasses and her hair blowing in the light, late October breeze.

Raven, Sal, Pat, and Roarke had just stepped outside onto the porch in time to see Rhea walking in the grass. Roarke stepped off the porch, but Raven stopped him, "Stay here, Roarke."

Rhea stopped about ten feet away from her visitor, and the two just stood for several long moments before Rhea spoke, "Hi, Mom."

Margot Walsh was wearing a flowing blue dress, her long, black hair draped around her like a cloak, dancing in the breeze. She gazed at her daughter with absolute adoration. "You're so beautiful."

Rhea smiled and reached out to touch her mother's hair. "Your hair grew out again."

"Time will do that."

"There's a bit of silver in the front."

"Time will do that too."

Rhea dropped the silky lock of hair. "How did you know?"

"Raven. Don't be angry with him, but he thought I'd want to be here."

"How did he know where you were?"

"He's always known how to contact me in a pinch."

"What?" Rhea's brow furrowed in confusion.

"Raven understood why I had to go. He's good at keeping secrets."

"Yeah, I guess so." Rhea ran her hand over the top of the grass.

"I had to go, baby." She took a step toward her daughter. "I had to step away from it all before I drowned in my grief. It was bad enough to lose Poppy, but then your father. I always knew what you all were doing and what your lives were like. You were all adults when I left. I knew you'd be okay."

Rhea nodded, not knowing what to say.

Her mother took another step toward her. "Rhea, if you don't want me here, I'll . . ."

She was cut off as Rhea flung herself at her mother and knocked her off balance as they both tumbled into the grass. They gripped each other tightly, laughing and crying at the same time.

Rhea buried her face into her mother's silky, sweet-smelling hair. "I don't care where you've been or why. I'm just so thrilled you're here." Rhea swept a lock of her mother's hair off her face, reveling in the feeling of her soft skin. "A few months ago, I would have been very, very mad, I've changed. I've no time to be stubborn, selfish, and unforgiving anymore. I'm happy in a way I've never been before."

"Rhea!" Charlotte screamed from the porch. "Rhea, get out of that grass this instant! If there is as much as a spot on that dress, I'll skin both you and Margot alive!"

Margot laughed as she got to her feet and pulled her daughter up with her. "Oh, Charlotte, she's a spitfire."

"Why do you think Momma's-boy Raven loves her so much?" Rhea brushed bits of greenery off her dress. "She reminds him of you."

Margot caressed her daughter's chin and gazed into her eyes. "I'd forgotten how much of your father you have on your face."

"I'm writing a book about you and Dad, and your lives."

Margot picked a piece of grass out of Rhea's hair and took her hand. "You're happy, baby?"

Rhea nodded and walked toward the house, her arm

linked around her mother's. "His name's Roarke."

The family had decorated the garden gazebo in blue, red, and yellow, Roarke's tartan colors. A long green carpet split the yard in two, with a small spattering of guests seated in white chairs in rows of five on either side.

Margot led the way, followed by Veronica and Charlotte, then Ruby and Rain, each with a hand on Robin's stroller. Patrice sat near the front of the gazebo, softly playing a Beatles song on his guitar.

Rhea was happy to see that Sal, Raven, and Liam wore top suits and kilts in Roarke's tartan in the gazebo. Roarke stood straight and proud, looking at her as if she were the only person in the world, dabbing at his eyes with his knuckle.

Liam came down the carpet and met Rhea halfway, and they walked down the aisle together.

Reaching the step to the gazebo, Liam reached under the wood to pull out the six-inch heels that he had hidden there for his mother. Rhea looked up at Roarke's handsome face and winked at him as Liam grinned and balanced Rhea so she could slide them on. Everyone chuckled as she stepped unsteadily up onto the gazebo.

Roarke grinned, and from behind his back, he pulled out a small bouquet of wildflowers he had picked from the garden in front of the house, tied with a small piece of ribbon. Without breaking eye contact with him, Rhea handed over the bouquet of white roses to Rain, who happily took them from her hand. Rhea held the small bouquet to her nose and placed it in front of her.

"Ready?" Roarke whispered.

Rhea wobbled on her heels, and Roarke steadied her by holding her elbow. The well-wishers giggled again as Rhea whispered back, "Oh, I'm ready. Gotta get married so I can get these heels off."

Margot Sioui watched the ceremony with pride from her seat in the front row, gazing lovingly at the children she and Gabriel had created. As Rhea said, "I do," Margot felt fingers in her hair and heard her name on the breeze.

"Hello, Gabriel," she whispered just as she noticed two translucent orbs of light floating behind Liam. "I knew Poppy and Pierre-Luc would make an appearance today."

The party was in full swing when Rhea managed to get a moment alone. Excusing herself to go to the bathroom, she instead walked out the backdoor and down to the beach. Staring out at the rolling grey-green sea, she let her mind drift away.

"Penny for your thoughts?" Roarke wrapped his arms around her and kissed the top of her head.

"Just thinking about life and possibility."

"Possibility?"

"Yeah." She took a deep breath of sea air. "When things happen that you don't like, or never wanted, you need to have faith in tomorrow. You never know what's out there, in that great big world, just waiting for you to find it."

"Speaking of finding things." He dropped something from his hand into hers. "This belongs to you."

Rhea opened her hand to find a brooch, a heart wearing a crown, run through with a thistle and a small garnet stone. "It's a Luckenbooth brooch!"

"Thought you should have one for your wedding day."

Holding it up to the sun, she watched the light play inside the garnet, and Islean's face appeared in her mind's eye. "She has her brooch, and now I have mine."

Reaching into his pocket again, Roarke pulled out a strip of tartan and flicked it out of its folds, letting it catch in the wind. "And I had this made for you when I had the guy's kilts quickly made in Scotland. I couldn't give it to you before because there was too much happening."

Draping the strip across her shoulder, he pulled the ends together on her opposite hip, pinning it with the brooch. "I had the nails you found melted down for it. I added the garnet because my friend told me it symbolized a lover's constancy and friendship."

As she looked down at her brooch and then up into her husband's eyes, tears flowed down her cheeks.

"Rhea, pull yourself together." He kidded, dabbing at her tears with his sleeves. "You've cried enough in the past few days to fill a boat."

"Crying purifies the soul, my love. Brings salt back to the earth."

Rhea turned around and wrapped Roarke's arms around her as they stood and watched the waves.

"Think we'll ever get tired of watching waves, ghost?"

"Probably not." She looked down at the matching strips of cloth on her and Roarke's wrists. "As long as there are storms on the seas, we'll have waves. *V'la l'bon vent.* Here's the good wind."

Roarke nuzzled her neck with his nose. "So sexy when you speak French. Sal did half of the toasts in French."

"Our father was French."

"Say something else."

Rhea thought for a moment and turned her head to look at her husband. "*Je t'aime comme la mer aime le vent.*"

He closed his eyes and nodded in appreciation. "That's the stuff. So what's it mean?"

"Where's the fun in that, husband?" Then, turning back to watch the sea beat out its ancient rhythm, Rhea took a deep breath and smiled. "Translate it for me when your French is better."

The End

About the Author

Originally from Newfoundland and Labrador, Aurela Lee lives in Québec City, where she teaches English Literature and Film Studies, and is tolerated by her family. In addition to dancing (anywhere), reading and obsessing over reality television, she daydreams and writes.